Serial Killer Eyes

Happy Reading

Verla Gayle

&

Nicki Lynn

Gayle Lynn

PAGE PUBLISHING
Conneaut Lake, PA

First originally published by Page Publishing 2022

ISBN 978-1-6624-6734-9 (pbk)
ISBN 978-1-6624-6735-6 (digital)

Printed in the United States of America

Chapter 1

The hallway roiled with a smog-like miasma of fear, sweat, and power-driven testosterone. Her tall slender body parted it like a dull knife through refrigerator-chilled butter.

The clank of unnecessary chains accompanied the scuffing of shoes on the hard floor...as if she'd do anything that would screw this up.

"Movin' kinda slow there, Smith."

"Give ya six months 'fore your lovely ass is back inside and ours again."

"Six months? Hell, I've got a hundred bucks that says she'll be back in less 'n a month."

"After last night's goin' 'way party, I'm in at less 'n two weeks 'fore she'll be cravin' a welcome-back party."

Ribald laughter accompanied her slow progress down the hall.

It all deflected off her as if she were surrounded by a protective forcefield. Her pale eyes remained locked on the prize...freedom.

The gate remained closed forcing her to wait. She stood arrogantly tall despite the bodily discomfort. In her hand was a Walmart bag with all her earthly belongings—an eight-year-old's clothes so outgrown that she was forced to remain clad in prison duds and a few toiletries. That was all she had to show for the last ten-plus years.

She felt the guards invading her space. Their stench from last night's party still clung to her skin. Two of them, one man and one equally sadistic woman, pressed in on her, just daring her to protest their continued right to be tight to her side.

The clang of releasing locks rattled the portals, groaning as if agonized by having to release one who'd been expected to be there forever.

The removed chains were held to her ears and rattled, like a rattlesnake's warning. The guard's chuckle fell on deaf ears, and his salacious grin slowly ebbed at the lack of reaction.

The sun jabbed at her naked eyes. Lilacs perfumed the air. Taken-for-granted things she never thought she'd be free to savor again.

One step out. Heart awakening into a terrified pace at the thought that the guards would haul her backward laughing that it had all been just another cruel joke.

Could she survive it again?

Would she even want to try?

No! And NO!

Halitosis flooded her nostrils—cigarettes and garlic. "You'll be back, and we'll be awaitin'." Behind him a half dozen lascivious chuckles egged him on.

She didn't remember what had happened last night. She had gone away, as she had learned to do at a very young age, and came back to a bruised and bleeding body. Raped. Beaten. But not broken. Unable to fight back for fear of losing her unexpected "get out of jail free" card, she'd endured. She'd awakened with no memories. She couldn't be sure, when she heard them snickering, if that was good or not, but she had enough older memories to ruin her sleep for the rest of her life without adding this latest episode to the queue.

"Over my dead body," she said then turned to stare into his eyes. He jerked back a step into the safety of walls and locks and abused power. She almost smiled as the color drained from his ruddy jowls and his eyes widened much like a rabbit facing a starving wolf. Last night she'd been powerless against him, against them. But now...out here. Freedom was gorging her veins. She didn't have to take that ever again.

Her lips lifted in a rictus-like baring of teeth. Again he backed another step. But she leaned close so only he could hear her soft words. "You'd better hope you don't see me again. Some dark stormy night. In your house. With only the thunder to hear your screams."

Then she stepped out into the fresh April air.

4

A huge black limo swooshed past her toes and skidded to a stop. The rear door shot open without the chauffeur's help.

A well-coifed woman, in a tan silk dress revealing shapely calves and thighs, a cashmere sweater, pearls, a hog-choking diamond on the third finger of her left hand, got out. She glared down her nose as if her eyes could kill. But when not even a whiff of smoke arose, she yanked a stuffed backpack out of the backseat, shoving a blonde girl back inside. "Stay there."

Two steps brought them face-to-face—something that hadn't happened in over ten years. Blue eyes glared into pale gray as the older blonde tried to intimidate the younger raven-haired woman. But others with more power had attempted such bullying tactics and had failed, and so did she. The blonde growled, baring her brilliantly white capped teeth in a snarl, only to entice a lazy quirk of the other's unlacquered lips.

With a frustrated growl, the blonde whipped her body around. The backpack arced full swing toward the younger woman, but she easily deflected it, letting it land at her feet.

"There's your filthy lucre," the older woman snarled. She leaned in, teeth bared as if to rip the slender throat from the young woman. "If you ever try to hit me up again…"

"You'll what, Mommy dearest? Fuck another judge and whisper more lies in his ears? Marry him? Of course you'd have to off the current hubby/judge, but that's not that much of an impediment to someone like you."

"Why you—" The mother swung a roundhouse blow that was easily caught. Squealing, she launched her blood-red talons, but her pilates/yoga muscles were no match against hour-after-hour of bore-dom-induced sit-ups, planks, shadow boxing, pushups, and running in place.

The wrists that the daughter held in her fists were almost deli-cate. A little tightening of her fingers surrounded the bones enough to make her mother wince.

"Careful, Mommy dearest, your age is beginning to show." She almost laughed aloud, if she could still laugh. The woman had flinched—her Botox-lifted face had just enough movement left in it.

"You little bitch." She twisted to be free.

The daughter held on long enough to prove she was releasing her of her own record, not losing her grip.

"It's the shits, isn't it, Mommy dearest, when the cub grows up and lo and behold they learned their lessons well and are just like their parents."

For a long moment, time stood still; pale silvery eyes clashed with bright azure blue ones.

The with a flip of her perfectly coiffed blond head, she pivoted like a ballerina. At the limo's door, she shoved the wide-eyed preteen blonde sprite back. "I told you, Cheyenne, stay in the fucking car!" To her older daughter, she jerked her head at the backpack. "That's it. Don't come whining for more and keep your lying mouth shut."

"Afraid people might believe the words of an adult whereas they ignored an almost catatonic child?"

An ugly snarl pulled at her stiff face. "Everyone would see you're a liar."

"Really? Then why don't we just test that out." Not that she ever would. She'd buried that so deep it'd take a deep-sea drudge to get it up.

"Don't you dare." But there was just a hint of a crack in her veneer. "Cheyenne! Get back."

She looked across the trunk where another young blonde stood. "Dakota! Get in the fucking car. I mean it!"

Dakota took a moment after her mother slammed the limo door, looked at her older sister, and smiled. A seemingly heartfelt warmth rocketed through the older sister, surprising her with a nibble of a...feeling.

"Dakota!"

With an impish, almost conspiratorial grin, Dakota leaped back into the limo a second before it sped off.

She watched it go. *Was Dakota the one?*

Didn't matter. Over and done with. Water under the bridge.

And then there was the hiker's backpack revealed by the exit of the limo. It looked stuffed with goodies and even had a bedroll tied to the bottom.

Goodies?

Maybe.

Stuffed with newspapers? A definite possibility. Just something to get her hopes up.

Or it could be a bomb—set to go off the minute she picked it up.

Most likely door number 3.

The way her older sisters had felt about her, could the younger ones be any different?

She paused a moment before shrugging. Wasn't she planning on looking for a way out anyway?

She grabbed the smaller backpack before heading for the big one.

"Come on, bag. Do me a solid."

She grabbed up the overstuffed pack and hauled it to her chest to maximize the effect.

Nothing.

"Well, hell."

How sweet it would have been.

"Oh, well."

She swung the huge pack to her back and grabbed the smaller one. There were always other ways of ending things that didn't involve suicide.

Texas sounded like a wild and wooly, bullets-flying, no-holds-barred kind of place. Just the kind of action she required.

Chapter 2

The roof resounded like a snare drum in a Sousa march. The wipers could barely clear the windshield long enough for the driver to see the glistening street.

"Come on, Pete. Pull into the Quickie Mart. I'm hungry."

The big white man looked into the rearview mirror at his charge. "We're almost at the hotel."

"Sure." The former GQ-cover gracer flashed his devilish grin. "But wouldn't a dog taste good? And give this"—he swept his hand at the streaming windows—"a chance to clear."

The black man in the passenger seat grunted. "Been pouring like a sumbitch for hours. Don't seem like a couple minutes'd do much good."

"But, Joe, doesn't a good old roller dog on a stale bun sound good?" The notorious woman's heart-melting smile blazed. "You know you won't get anything like that from room service."

"No," Joe admitted, "but I bet we could get us a couple a T-bones about yay big." He spread his ham-like hands about a foot apart.

Pete, the other bodyguard nodded, expertly pulling the car out of a wind-driven skid. The rental was having some hydroplaning issues, forcing him to all but crunch the steering wheel to prevent a passing truck from slipstreaming it into the guardrail. Muttering some not very nice comments about the rain, the traffic, the wind, and even Minnesota in general, he flipped on the blinker.

Ruarke Sinclair leaned back, shaking his head. Two rainouts in a row. Two more makeup days for his Yankees. And the season was just in its third week.

Pete guided the car through the gas islands to a spot in front. The convenience store's lights tried their best to fight off the rainy night's gloom.

"Wait here." The back door opened.

"No, Ruarke! Damn it!"

But Ruarke Sinclair stepped out, fancy leather shoes skidding slightly on the greasy concrete, and stepped into the limited protection beneath the eave. Huddled there, under the overhang, a trash bag-covered person arose in front of him looking like a hunchback. Part of a huge backpack peaked from under the black shroud.

"Don't go in."

Ruarke paused, his hand frozen as it slipped into his pocket for some panhandler change. "What?"

But the figure turned away and shoved into the store.

Through the huge windows, he could see the clerk hassling the newcomer, gesticulating at the bags the homeless person was hauling.

Aware that given half an excuse his bodyguards would be joining him, Ruarke pulled the heavy glass door open, jangling the overhead bells, and stepped into the eye-squinting brightness. Much as he liked the two men, and God knew he needed their protection from that crazy woman, he sometimes felt smothered by their constant presence.

The backpacked kid had hiked up the dripping plastic and was divesting the huge pack per the shrieking attendant's commands. The kid gave Ruarke an unwavering stare, pale icy eyes glaring from beneath heavy black brows. Thick raven lashes gave the pale eyes even more impact. The kid, Ruarke doubted he was even old enough to shave, gave a short "no" jerk of his purple-and-gold capped head.

The Vietnamese clerk got in the kid's face again, diverting that penetrating stare. Spell broken, Ruarke followed his nose to the ready and waiting food.

There were six tube steaks rolling on the machine. Ruarke took them all, stuck each into a surprisingly fresh bun, doctored each up with the works, and nabbed a box from the donut area to put them in. On the way back up front, he nabbed some chips, stuffing them under his pit, then detoured to the coolers for three Cokes. Long arms totally laden, he finally neared the checkout counter just as loud voices erupted.

Two masked men waved pistols around. The two women who'd been waiting for the clerk to quit hassling the kid and check them out began shrieking.

"SHUT UP! SHUT THE FUCK UP!"

The one in the checked flannel shirt turned the automatic sideways gangsta style at them. The Somali woman dropped her basket, disgorging its contents. She covered her head with her long fingered hands as she dropped to her knees, a gun to her head.

"Hey!"

The two turned on Ruarke as he rounded the end of the rack.

Both guns spurted fire. A blow to the chest took his breath, and his leg buckled under him. The Yankee's first baseman went down as neatly as a quarterback blindsided by a blitzing linebacker. The chips crunched beneath his long, lean body. His ribs popped the cans, spewing carbonated sugar water as he landed. His brain seemed as frozen as his lungs. He looked up at the pale-eyed kid atop him.

"Stay down," the kid hissed.

Not a problem for a man who couldn't breathe or think.

More cracks of gunfire. The air stank of gunpowder.

For a moment there was silence. Then came the ululation of wailing cries filling that void.

Each panted breath brought a deepening stab of pain. The floor had twin streams of red oozing across the tiles.

"Ruarke!"

He looked up at Pete's horrified face. For just a moment, the highly trained bodyguard seemed to not have a clue about what to do, then he was digging out a handkerchief and pressing it to Ruarke's chest. Joe dropped to his knees, digging his sausage-like fingers into Ruarke's thigh making him arch back and scream.

"Just lie still. Help's on the way."

A hand on his shoulder as the other pressed at his chest tried to keep Ruarke still.

"Wha—?"

Pete leaned closer, squashing their snacks with his knee. "Quiet, man. It'll be all right."

Ruarke tried to speak, twisting around to see past the two mini giants. "The kid!"

Alerted, Pete reached to his left armpit and the holster there. But Ruarke flailed with scary weakness at Pete's arm.

"Saved m-m-me."

Pete relaxed a tiny bit. He looked around but failed to see the kid his boss was muttering about. For having been "saved," the man was in bad shape. Pete knew the sounds of a sucking chest wound when he heard it. Over his shoulder, he saw Joe working to staunch the gushing blood from a bone-shattered thigh.

Pete looked down at his friend's shocky face. The wheezed breathing made his own chest hurt. Pete's fingers shook slightly as he brushed a strand of dark blond hair from Ruarke's clammy forehead.

"We'll find him,"

"S-saved m-m-me."

Pete squeezed Ruarke's shoulders, fighting back tears, knowing that the saving wasn't a done deal. Yet. Not by a long shot.

"We'll find him."

He only hoped it wasn't a promise made to a dying man.

Chapter 3

If Texas was the destination, why the heck was she heading straight west? But then that was the direction the trucker had been heading. Beggars can't be choosers. Not on a frog-drowning night like this.

The trucker offering her a ride was pretty much a cliché of a trucker: bearded, hefty, flannel shirt, and jeans that could stand a run through a washer.

He'd been happy enough to pick her up even though he couldn't possibly discern her gender under the rain gear. Boy? Girl? Didn't seem to matter as he reached across the wide cab and shoved open the door.

The interior light had been enough to let her discern that he did not intend this to be a "free" ride. But Santee had had enough of "putting out" or having it taken to last her the rest of what would hopefully be a very short life.

She looked up full force at him. Rain dripped from the bill of her cap into her eyes and like ice cubes coursed down her back. "Ain't happening," she said softly.

He'd already started drawing back from her glacial stare. The ride offer was already being rethunk. But then he stopped. Without looking at her, he eased back but left the door open.

She stood a moment, the rain plinking off the cheap plastic rainshroud.

"Goin' far as Worthington." The load of hogs voiced their complaints, their stench eye-watering even in the rain.

Didn't matter as long as it was west or south. Santee shrugged the big pack off and heaved it up into the truck. The smaller knapsack easily flew onto the seat.

They rode in silence, her watching him and shivering while he warily watched her. She would have smiled if her mind could have made her face work that way. His being leery of her at least kept him on his own side of the cab. Meanwhile her hand remained in the pocket of the knapsack, fingers caressing the knife's haft.

He suddenly broke the silence, causing an infinitesimal twitch of her shoulders. "You got lice or what?"

She raised her brows questioningly. He flicked his eyes to her left hand, digging at the back of her neck. She forced her hand away nails stained red. "No."

He gave a huffy grunt. "Don't want bedbugs neither in here."

"I can tell you're a real cleanliness freak."

He shot her an angry look. "You got no right complainin'. I picked you out of the rain like a drowned rat."

Santee noted the gold band on his left hand. "A real good Samaritan."

He nodded smugly.

"Does your wife know you give rides to young hitchhikers? Because I'm doubting I'm the first. And we both know it wasn't out of the goodness of the bottom of your heart. More like wanting some goodness for something a might further south."

He cast her a glare. "Ride oughtta be worth somethin'. Wouldn't a hurt you none to give me some thanks."

She nodded. "It sure isn't going to hurt me at all."

Their eyes locked for a moment. He broke it with a huffy breath.

The back of her neck was demanding relief, but she clenched her left hand into a fist and fought it down.

Not long later a blue sign passed by.

"Rest area ahead?"

He grunted affirmatively.

"Dump me off there?"

"Think an ugly twit like you'll git yerself a better ride, think again." He hacked up a wad of phlegm and spit on the floor. "Lucky to even get a ride, looking like you do. Next one's not likely to be as easy goin' as me."

"Not your concern."

13

He hauled on the steering wheel and activated the brakes. "You got that right, missy."

The rig squealed to a stop in a well-lit and well-filled parking lot. A fine mist drifted through the overhead lights.

Santee opened the door, watching him carefully lest he make a grab for her now that he could take his hands off the wheel, but he just sat staring out the windshield. Still, she tossed her bags out first before moving to get out.

"Thanks."

"I wouldn't a hurt you none, you know."

"Nothing but my self-respect."

She easily swung to the ground. The engine roared almost before she touched down. A backwash of diesel exhaust and hog manure gagged her.

Her hand rubbed at the nape of her neck as she surveilled the lot.

*****

Makayla Evans was five years old, and she desperately wanted her mommy and daddy. Her thumb was in her mouth, something she hadn't done since she became a big girl. Her tongue probed two gaps where teeth used to be.

And she had to pee. She wiggled to hold it in, but that made everything down there blaze like fire again. She knew better than to call out to him. Her achy face and almost swollen shut-eye were the results of the first time she'd done that. The smelly spot in the closet's corner was a last resort. When she'd done it there before, he'd gotten really mad.

The heavy chain around her neck pinched her skin between its links. It made her think of the neighbor's dog, chained up in the backyard and mostly forgotten.

Tears dripped from her chin. She prayed that God wouldn't let her mommy and daddy forget poor Skippy. Her thin bruised arms wrapped around her knees. She and her daddy had taken water to poor Skippy when the bowl got turned over on hot days. They even had a bag of dog food that Daddy fed the dog late at night when the neighbors wouldn't see.

Daddy said that they had to look out for the poor helpless animals. Though she wasn't an animal, she sure hoped her daddy was looking for her and would come soon before... She shuddered, eyeing the thin light line seeping under the door.

Shadow feet breaking the light sent her tight to the wall. But there was no hidey-hole there. She'd searched and searched.

Muttering sounded outside, growing louder, sounding more upset. Makayla huddled as small as she could. She knew that soon he'd come for her.

She buried her face against her thighs. "Hurry, Daddy. Please hurry."

Then a different sound brought her head up. Bad, bad words were being shouted. Smacking sounded like when the man whomped her across the face. A table or chairs scraped as they skidded across the wooden floor and fell over.

He shouted bad, bad words, words her mommy'd wash her mouth out with soap for saying, but no other voice sounded, almost as if he were fighting a ghost. She had seen *Ghostbusters* with her mommy, daddy, and Tony. Maybe it was a good ghost like Casper, who'd come to save her.

Heavy treads shook the floorboards.

The bad man's voice changed from bear to bunny. It sounded like when they all went to church on Sunday and spoke to God. Had God sent her an angel?

Hesitantly she leaned to the door, angling her head so her good eye was in the light. But she still couldn't see anything.

"Puh-please d-don't. I be g-g-good. Never d-d-do it again. Never ever. P-p-promise." He sounded like he was crying.

Makayla touched her swollen lips, the split burning like fire. She talked funny too, now, but the bad man didn't like her to talk, so she had stopped.

Suddenly two shoe toes appeared in the thin band of light beneath the door. With a gasp Makayla scooched backward, slamming up against the wall. Her down-below parts screamed at the movement. A jingle of keys and the door eased open. Makayla raised her arm against the sudden flare of light, sore ribs making her wince.

The person in the doorway was tall and thin. It stood there, just looking and letting Makayla look and smell the clean scent of rain and wet grass, not stinky sweat and barfy breath.

The person held out their hand. Makayla looked and looked but couldn't see anything to be scared of. Carefully she oh so slowly eased toward the hand. The chain clanked and rattled; it tried to hold her back, but Makayla knew, just knew, that now she was safe.

Squatting down, the person took Makayla gently in their arms. Their body was so warm and almost glowy. Just like an angel. She felt so safe, her aches receding.

A second later, the chain clattered to the floor. And Makayla scrunched into their neck, feeling warm and safe for the first time since Daddy come'd in when she had a bad dream and rocked her in his arms. A hand cupped the back of her head, keeping her from looking around, even when the grunting-like-Porky-Pig sounds grew louder and then softer as they went through the stinky house and out into the fresh rain that dripped so delightfully cool on her matted hair and down her neck.

"I sorry."

Angel paused at the opened rattle-trap pickup that the man had dragged her into that day after school.

"You've got nothing to be sorry for." The voice sounded like the person had a cold, all froggy and rough. "None of this was your fault."

Makayla shook her head, but before she could say anything, she was gently placed on the cracked seat. An old smelly blanket settled around her shoulders. Then Angel squatted down to her eye level. Angel's eyes were like trying to look through an ice cube. But she wasn't afraid. Angel's long-fingered hands cupped the sides of Makayla's face. It was so warm she felt the heat going deep inside, making her boo-boos feel so much better. Even down there.

"Remember." Makayla was drifting into sleep. "This was not your fault."

"Not my fault," she mumbled. "Not my fault."

Makayla awoke to hands lifting her out into the rain. She knew by the cigarette stink that this wasn't her angel, but gentle words rumbled in her ears. She leaned into his chest feeling nearly as safe and protected as when her angel had carried her.

She looked around at the faces around her. Women were crying, hands covering their mouths. Even the big men had tears running down their faces. "Angel?" she cried, craning to see past the crowd. "Where are you, Angel?"

"Don't you worry," her carrier said, the words catchy and growly. "No one's going to hurt you ever again. Not while I'm around."

Makayla eased back; her injuries still pulled at her but not so bad as before. "Angel!" She searched the crowd squinting into the bright lights. "ANGEL!" She wiggled as if to get down, but he held on.

Desperately she looked up at the cop-hardened, teary-eyed man. "I gotta find her!"

"Honey—"

"I gots tuh say thank you!" Tears started to flow down her bruised and swollen face. "I dinn't say thank you!"

The cop awkwardly patted her back, not wanting to hurt her as the bloody shirt and stained panties indicated she'd been. "He knows, honey. He knows." The cop took a moment to eyeball the crowd before hauling the little girl into the hospital. Was her angel out there, or was he part of all this? And who the hell had called in to report a kid that looked an awful lot like their missing little girl sleeping in a ratty pickup in the hospital parking lot?

Brakes squealed as Makayla's parents rushed up. The big cop eased the little girl into her mother's arms, shaking her father's hand and accepting his thanks, knowing that he and the rest of his men had done squat to get this little girl back into her family's arms.

His steely eyes searched but missed the shadowy hint of movement. A blink against a raindrop caused him to miss it.

Chapter 4

Ruarke Sinclair was awake, but he wished he was still in a drugged-out never-never land. Not that he hurt...at least not too much. But it was just everything and everybody was so damn gloom and doom. Maybe it hadn't completely sunk in through his thick skull that life as he'd so enjoyed it could be a thing of the past. He was just realizing how much he was defined by his homer-hitting prowess, his off-season modeling gigs, the oh-so-adoring rabid Yankees fans, though a few had gotten carried away by their zeal, hence the need for Pete and Joe.

Now a guy who seldom got a cold or the flu was looking at the very real possibility of losing his leg or being stuck with more operations and a ton of rehab in order to limp around with a brace and cane the rest of his life. He was thirty years old, for heaven's sake! Still in his prime both on and off the field, or so the ladies assured him. And now this!

Voices in the hall caused the big black bodyguard, Joe, to go on high alert. Ruarke's parents jerked up from their exhaustion-induced snoozes.

Pete showed in the doorway giving Joe the okay nod, which let everyone draw a deep breath and relax. Ruarke frowned as his heart rate slowed down. He hadn't always been so jumpy.

Ruarke vaguely remembered seeing the man and woman before—detectives who'd tried to interview him. But he'd been so out of it that they'd finally given up.

The lead detective, fiftyish, black, slender, in a new suit, moved to the bed after nodding at the others. "Sergeant Jim McCann." His sharp gaze roaming over Ruarke's tractioned leg and body-wrapped chest. "Maybe you remember me and my partner?"

Ruarke held up his hand that still had tubes stuck into the back of it. "Sir." The sergeant carefully took Ruarke's fingers.

McCann motioned to his partner. "Detective Janice Beyer."

The well-endowed blonde was about Ruarke's age, but she had old eyes, eyes that had seen a lot of very bad stuff. She was fit and dressed in a navy-blue suit cut to show off her assets, probably to get men to underestimate her keen mind and skills.

Before the shooting, it might have worked on Ruarke too. He had a thing for busty blondes, as his two ex-wives were testimony to. But now his body parts didn't even twitch. A nonreaction he'd noted earlier when a very lovely nurse had given him a bath. At least he hadn't embarrassed himself, but the continued lack of any action down there was getting worrisome. Had some major muscle been ruptured? God! He shuddered to even think it.

Ruarke indicated to the others in the room. "My parents, Robert and Regina Sinclair. And my friends, Joe Johnson and Pete Jackson."

The detective went to shake hands, saying that they'd already met. The female detective moved closer to the bed, her sexy muskiness enveloping him. Her ocean-blue eyes cataloged his almost nudity. Still nothing stirred down south. What the hell was going on?

Sergeant McCann was convincing his parents and Joe to take a break. Ruarke's mom had to kiss him, smooth back a lock of his dark blond hair, and assure him that they'd be right back.

"Why don't you and Dad go to the hotel and take a nap?" he said, but she looked horrified at the idea. "Pete and Joe will be here." She started to say something snarkily uncharacteristic. She and his dad loved the two men but seemed to feel they'd dropped the protection ball.

"Mom." Ruarke tightened his left fingers over hers. "Take a break. Joe and Pete have this."

Reggie sniffed and nodded. On the way out, she patted Joe's hunched shoulder and kissed his cheek. She whispered something, and the big black man's back straightened.

Ruarke raised his hand to his dad, Rob, as they left.

Joe said, "I'll be right outside." Then he pulled the door shut behind him.

Ruarke gestured the cops to the vacated chairs, knowing they were not going to be happy with his lack of any new info.

They each took out small notebooks and pens.

"So what happened that night?"

Ruarke described getting Pete to stop so he could get snacks.

"Alone?" McCann said.

"Yes."

"Was that normal?" Beyer asked in a sexy, husky voice. "I mean you had bodyguards for a reason. So why weren't they guarding your body?"

"Because I told them to wait in the car." Their silent skepticism made him add, "They're great guys. We're good friends. But sometimes…sometimes I just need a couple of minutes to myself. Like a normal guy."

McCann nodded. "So you went in and…?"

"And nothing out of the…" He frowned at the blip of a memory.

"What?" McCann urged.

"Someone bumped into me outside."

"What did they look like?" McCann said.

"What did they say?" Beyer said.

Ruarke remembered the rain lashing his eyes. The kid's bump hadn't been much, just enough to break his stride. As for looks? The kid'd been covered in black plastic with something covering his head. All Ruarke remembered was the humpback effect of what must have been a huge hiker's pack on his back.

"So it was a guy," Beyer said.

Ruarke made a shrug, but the stab in his ribs told him that was a bad idea. "I can't swear to anything."

She gave a soft disgusted snort.

"Don't the security cameras answer any of these questions?" Ruarke said. He hated that his memories were so vague.

"Well," McCann said slowly, "seems the cameras got zapped by lightning in that bad storm we had last fall, and they just hadn't gotten around to getting them fixed."

"So," McCann continued. "You went in alone. You were bumped by some guy."

"More like a kid. Teenager, maybe."

"Okay. And the kid did what?"

"Went inside ahead of me. The clerk was hassling him about the pack, so he was taking it off by the counter. I went around them to get the food. When I came back, I heard loud voices. A woman screamed. I knew something was up."

McCann leaned forward. "But you didn't take cover?"

Ruarke shook his head, knowing now that it had been pretty foolhardy. "I came around the shelf, and two guys were there with guns."

"What kind of guns?"

Ruarke had grown up on a ranch. Guns had been a part of his childhood, but there had never been a need on the ranch for those kinds of weapons. "Looked kind of like an UZI that you see in the movies." His inability to name the make and model seemed to lessen him in the lady detective's eyes. But Ruarke found he didn't really care.

"Then the shooting started, and someone slammed into me, driving me sideways to the floor." He motioned to his chest. "I knew I'd been hit here, but not—" He motioned weakly at his right leg. The sight of it made him sick and depressed. So much for leading what others deemed a charmed life. How fast things could change.

"And the person who knocked you out of the way?"

Ruarke thought back to the kid who'd covered him with his own body. Even as bullets zinged overhead, the pale-eyed kid had looked him in the eyes and began plugging the spurting hole in his leg with his finger. Agony had shot white-hot through him, his scream challenging the *rat-a-tat-tat* of the UZIs. Chips bags sprayed them with greasy salty bits. But the kid had stayed with him. Probably kept him from bleeding to death. Though he knew it could have been… probably was the same kid, Ruarke shrugged, earning another jab through his chest.

Beyer leaned closer, minty breath overcoming the room's disinfectant tang. "Was it the same kid who accosted you going in? Was he one of them?"

Ruarke looked into her large hungry eyes and lied. "I don't think so."

McCann eyed him with an "I'm not buying this" coolness. "Are you sure? What did he look like? Could you describe him to an artist?"

Ruarke shook his head. "I was pretty much out of it. What did Pete or Joe say?"

McCann eased back, eyes still probing. "They admitted to seeing the kid, but neither could provide much of a description. Claimed to be too busy with you. The kid seems to have taken off as soon as your men took over."

Good for him, but Ruarke didn't express that out loud. "And security cameras in the area?"

Beyer growled and moved as if to kick at the bed leg before stopping herself. "So far nothing helpful."

Ruarke fought down a grin at the kid's slyness. His phone on the bedside table rang the tone of his best friend since kindergarten. "That's all I can remember, so do you mind—"

With ill grace and the admonition to call if he remembered anything more, they left their cards and walked out.

Ruarke picked up the phone, eyes getting misty. "Hey, Miri."

"Oh, Ruarke—"

———————————

Chapter 5

May was turning out to be a much nicer month, drier and warmer. Birds trilled their mating calls. Frogs in the creek croaked for the girls. A squirrel danced and chittered in the old oaks.

The campground was still pretty desolate. Too early, even this far south, wherever this was, for there to be very many campers. Santee didn't know or care where she was. The quiet aloneness after so much forced togetherness was glorious. Her yellow tent, so bright it almost made her squint, was only one of three in a capacity of about twenty. The other two were scattered far enough away, as if they also felt a driving need for peace and quiet.

On the picnic table before her was a large buff-colored envelope that she'd found hidden deep in the backpack. It contained a wallet with a South Dakota driver's license in the name of Santee Smith. A VISA credit card in that name and $50,000 in one-hundred-dollar bills. Plus, there was a fair-sized sheaf of papers that her addled brain couldn't decipher, though she'd been working on it for several days.

She knew she had a supposed home address as shown on her license. There appeared to be bank statements that showed her worth to be about half a million dollars. No wonder Mommy dearest didn't want to see her ever again. She'd already forked out at a rate of over $50,000 a year in "hush up and never come back" money.

How her sisters, Dakota and Cheyenne, for they were the only ones who could or would have done this, had managed she had no idea. She just knew for certain that her older sisters wouldn't have lifted a finger to help her out as they'd shown ten years ago when all they'd have had to do was tell the truth and corroborated her testimony to keep her out of juvie prison.

She also figured Dakota and Cheyenne were behind the eager-beaver young lawyer who'd suddenly taken an interest in her case, found the injustices, and got her freed. Santee rubbed her hands over the bristly stubble on her scalp. Heck, she hadn't even known she had a second little sister. Dakota had been two; Cheyenne had not even been born yet. And who was her mother? Mommy dearest hadn't looked pregnant during the trial as far as she could remember.

She winced and fought down the nightmare that all too glee-fully tried to burst free. No way was she going back there in her memories.

So why they'd do it? How they'd do it? What did they expect to get out of it? All a complete mystery to her. Santee gathered up the papers, tapped them into alignment, and restuffed the envelope.

The ramifications of this were for another day.

The pack at her side hid a whole other conundrum.

How had two little girls managed to acquire two automatic pistols, a sawed-off shotgun, and a black AR automatic rifle?

Was she glad to have them? Certainly. But for criminy sakes! They were twelve or fourteen at the oldest. Just what kind of "little girls" was she dealing with here? And what was their agenda?

Santee knew this was going to come back and bite her in the ass as sure as her name now wasn't what she'd been called her whole childhood.

Oh, well, if things worked out as planned, she wouldn't be stuck with it for long. She just had to come up with a better plan. The last couple "end of days" situations had fizzled out on her.

Meandering south again, as the rides took her, felt good. Surely Texas would be the answer.

The interstate traffic was unbelievable. Zip, zoom, and zigzag. So many people with seemingly so little time to enjoy the ocean-tanged air. Though she couldn't see it, she knew it was there. But should it be off to her right? Going south, with her in the passenger seat of the semi, shouldn't the Gulf be on the left?

She looked at the big-boned woman easily handling the big rig. Her permed red hair was a wiry Medusa cap, and the leather vest showed off a multitude of tats on her arms and chest and a gecko creeping around her neck. She'd said her name was Maizie, and that about covered their conversation, which was just fine with Santee.

"Um, Maizie?"

The woman glanced at her for a second. "Yuh?"

"Where are we?"

She grumbled an uncomplimentary diatribe about the driver of the minivan full of kids that had just weaved into her lane, a tragedy in the making. "Florida."

"What!" Granted it hadn't looked like what she'd expected Texas to look like, but Texas was a big state and very diverse.

"You said you were looking for a ride south."

"Um, yuh. Texas."

Maizie shook her head. "Florida."

"I told you I was headed for Florida?"

Rusty hair flailed at her sharp nod. "Yup."

Santee took off the purple-and-gold ball cap and ran her hands over her hair. Approaching an inch in length, it was feeling shaggy. "Shit."

"You wasn't headed to Florida?"

Santee just shook her head. Her right hand went to her nape and began digging at the short hairs.

"Then why'd you say you was looking to get to Florida?"

A very good question indeed.

*****

Riordan and Remington, though not twins, looked enough alike to be twins. Just thirteen months apart, Rio was a bit taller than Remmy, but they were both slender, towheaded, blue-eyed typical boys. Both had been sent home from school ill. Remmy had thrown up all over his lunch. Rio had thrown up all over his math book and down the back of Sara Miles's neck.

Sick as they were, they still cringed at their mother's strident screech. She slapped at their stepdad, making him jerk the steering wheel.

"You're a doctor, for God's sake." She flailed again. "You've always got time for other sick kids but not your own."

Technically Rio and Remmy weren't his, but he wasn't about to say that. "At least Jamie, Trey, and Trev aren't sick."

"There you go again! Jamie this and Jamie that. It's always Jamie first!"

"Now, Rachel," he said, so tired of this old worn-out fight. Jamie was his by his first wife, Mary, who died of cervical cancer six months before Rachel got her claws into him. He realized now that she'd decided a doctor was a better deal than a minor league baseball player. This was way before Ruarke Sinclair had become a household icon.

She slapped at him, making the van swerve again. "Don't you 'now Rachel' me, John Coulter. I've had about all I'm going to take of this shit. You're constantly putting Jamie over your other kids. And I won't have it!"

John sighed. She didn't seem to realize that she was including her two kids with Sinclair as his. And he was fine with that. They were great kids. He was proud to be their daddy. Rachel would be happy as a lark if he'd take her hints that Jamie should be sent away to school, leaving them with Rio, Remmy, and their two-year-old twins Trey and Trev. And sad to say she was eroding his resistance away. He didn't want to, but it might be the best for everyone, including Jamie, if the boy went to boarding school. But the pamphlets she left scattered around were either about schools in New England or places like Switzerland. He'd never see the boy.

"John!" Rachel screeched in his ear, making him jerk yet again. She slapped at his face. "I won't be ignored!"

Ahead taillights flashed, but John didn't see as he blocked the claws headed for his cheek. "Rach—"

"Daddy! Look out!" Rio screamed.

But it was too late. Their van rammed an Impala, skidding it to the left while the van ducked right, sideswiping a concrete truck, its big drum rolling and rolling. The heavier vehicle held its ground, ricocheting the van back into its lane smack in front of a semi. Brakes screeched. Metal shrieked.

The van was lifted off its wheels and catapulted forward. It began flipping over once, twice, three times, actually clearing three vehicles before settling into the middle of pandemonium.

Cussing, Maizie fought to avoid the inevitable. But superior mass won. The truck plowed into the crumpled pile, brakes squealing as the trailer skidded sideways, jackknifing into the next lane, tossing smaller vehicles aside like Tinker Toys.

For just a moment Maizie looked at Santee. Behind them, vehicles were still playing bumper cars. The radiator hissed and spat steam up from under the hood.

"You okay?"

Santee nodded. The seatbelt had cut in but kept her from shooting through the windshield.

Maizie reached for her phone. Waylon Jennings still wailed from the speakers.

Santee tried her door, but a box truck was punched into the side. The side window had shattered glass into the cab, but surprisingly Santee hadn't been cut. Bruised ribs seemed to be her only complaint.

From the window, Santee could see the box truck's driver holding his hand to his bloody face, but otherwise he seemed unhurt.

Grabbing her bags, Santee shoved them out the busted windshield. They landed on the crumpled hood and slid down to the road. Feet first, Santee followed, sliding down the hot metal, landing awkwardly on the biggest pack. Nabbing both, she headed forward into the chaos.

Ruptured gas tanks disgorged their contents near hot mufflers and tailpipes. Stunned people were being dragged from the crumpled messes. Cries for help were being heeded by other normally insular drivers.

Santee zigzagged between and over until the van was in view. Tossing her packs to the concrete barrier, she paused to help an older man out of his car window, nabbing him under the arms, his back to her chest, and easing him backward. His legs slipped out a moment before she noticed the odd angle of the one. He cried out as his feet hit the road, barely conscious as the leg bent even further in the shin where no joint was meant to be. Santee eased him backward to the road barrier and set him carefully down. The leg showed jagged bone but wasn't gushing, so it didn't seem life-threatening, but what did she know.

A woman who did seem to know something shoved past Santee, a towel in her hand. She knelt at the old man's side and put pressure on the injury, her touch making him cry out again, but his cry was just one in a cacophony of screams and sobs.

The need to find that van dug in its talons again, blocking out all the others in need. Dodging around the old man's crumpled sedan, she saw it, upside down and skidded under the rear of a tractor trailer. Its wheels were still spinning, as if the driver thought he could still get them out of this situation.

She slid to her knees, dampness soaking her jeans. The windows were popped, glass bits scattered into a mix of gas and antifreeze. The roof was collapsed to mere inches. Nose almost to the ground, gagging on the combined fluid stenches, Santee called, "Anybody in there?" It was a stupid question, she realized, since obviously there had to have been people in there. The correct question would have been "Anyone alive in there?" But it was a question she, for some reason, dreaded to ask, especially if the answer she received was "no."

"Help!"

Stinking air rushed into her starving lungs.

"Help us!" a boy called.

"I'm coming." But how? She slammed her palm against the door panel, which did nothing but sting her hand. There just wasn't enough clearance for her to wriggle inside.

"Fire!" a distant cry resounded. A wail of sirens whooped in the unnatural silence.

Santee jerked around, but there was no sign of flames…at least not yet. "I'm coming!"

The van seemed to be canted slightly, so she hustled around to the other side where there was indeed all eight to ten inches of window showing.

From the scabbard hooked inside her jeans, Santee grabbed the knife and slithered inside. Immediately her head bumped another head. Terrified wide blue eyes met hers.

"Hi," she said as if this were the most normal of circumstances. "I'll get you out of here."

"Get my little brother first," he said. "He's really scared."

It barely registered that she was lying in a pile of vomit as she visually assessed the upside-down kid. "I will, but you have to go first before I can reach him."

Sounds of crying came from beyond the boy. "It's okay," he called. "This lady's going to help us both. Aren't you?"

"Yes, definitely." Santee slithered around under the boy's head, cushioning him as she reached up with the knife to the belt holding him up. "My name's Santee. What's yours?"

"Rio-Riordan." He sniffed. "Sorry about the mess."

"No worries." Getting her arm up around the boy so she could reach him was a problem.

In the distance came more shouts of "Fire!"

Santee said loudly, "So what's your brother's name?"

"I'm Remmy," the other boy said, voice clogged with tears. "Short for Remington."

"Nice to meet you both." The razor-honed knife touched what she could only hope was nylon webbing. "Here we go, Rio."

She hoped he didn't have any deeper injuries than the scrapes, nicks, and bruises she could see on his face and arms. Her gut twisted at the thought of the damage she could be doing. But it was this or let him burn. And that wasn't happening if she could help it.

He plunked down onto her chest and stomach. Santee eased backward from under him, edging out and pulling him with her. Dazed, he gawked at the mayhem and began to shake.

"Rio!" Santee grabbed him. "Are you okay? Remmy needs you to be okay!"

He swallowed hard and nodded. He was only a little boy, seven or eight, and Santee felt guilty being so tough on him, but time wasn't on their side.

"Good." She patted him awkwardly. "Now"—she pointed back the way she had come—"back that way, by the edge of the road, you'll find two backpacks. One's a great big thing and a smaller one, like you'd haul your school stuff in."

Rio watched her as closely as he could with one eye swelling shut. He followed her pointing arm and nodded.

"I need you to go find them and—" She held her hand up to stop his protest. "I need you to guard them for me and be there when I send Remmy your way."

"Okay, but—"

"No buts, Rio. I need to know I can count on you."

He drew a deep breath, which didn't seem to cause him any pain, and nodded.

"And, Rio." She looked him square in the eyes. His one and a half eye widened at the hard look. "If a fire starts, I need you to take Remmy and run. Don't wait for me. Don't look back. You run away as fast as you can."

"But—" Tears were starting to glisten.

"No buts, Rio. Can you do that for me and for your brother?"

He swallowed hard then straightened his shoulders and nodded. "I can do it."

"Okay. good." She released him and waggled her hands in a "get going" motion.

With a sob, Rio flung his arms around her neck then squeezed to the point of choking her before turning to run away.

From within the van came a plaintive "Santee?"

It jerked her out of a shocked moment. She couldn't remember the last time anyone had touched her like that.

"I'm coming, Remmy!"

She slithered back inside to the exact same situation, though Remmy was scrunched more awkwardly, leaving no room for her to get under him.

"How you doing, Remmy? You hurt very badly?"

He snorted up mucus before he could waver. "I don't th-think so. But Mommy and Daddy aren't fighting anymore."

There was blood seeping from the front onto the inverted roof. A lot of blood.

"I'll see what I can do after I get you out." She didn't think there was a hope in hell that she'd be able to do anything for the parents. The front of the van was just too pancaked.

Slapping shoes and screams of fire hastened the rescue. In moments, Santee had Remmy cut free and hauled backward out.

The air was flaring up with heat and smoke. Popping sounds filled the air, as did cries of agony and death.

Santee grabbed Remmy's hand as a wave of flames shot over the trailer that imprisoned the van. Ducking, they ran dodging through the vehicle maze and other terrified runners.

Rio had found her packs. She barely broke stride, grabbing both in one hand, and ran on with Rio hanging on to Remmy's other hand. They pounded past Maisie's truck, where there was no sign of the older woman.

It wasn't more than a few hundred yards farther that they ran out of mayhem. Cars who'd been able to get stopped without crashing were stacked up bumper to bumper. The drivers stood outside staring at the pileup and the soaring flames. With a whooping of sirens and a swoosh of displaced air, help raced past on the shoulders, only to be stopped by crumpled mess. Firemen and EMTs hopped out and raced into the fray.

The boys hugged close, making Santee both claustrophobic and warm fuzzy. Her hands kind of patted at the air above their honey-blond heads, not quite daring to actually touch them.

"So," she said, "is there anyone older at home, any older brother or sister maybe?"

"We was sick," Remmy explained. They all stunk of vomit, so Santee had kind of figured that out. "We were sent home when… when…" He buried his face against Santee's thigh and sobbed. Still her hand couldn't bring itself to comfort the heaving shoulders.

"There's Mrs. Wilson," Rio said.

"Mrs. Wilson?"

His head nodded up and down on the other thigh. "She takes care of us when Daddy's at work and Mommy…can't."

Which meant what exactly? Santee wondered. Not that it was any of her business.

"You know your address?"

Both heads tipped back to look at her like she was nuts.

"Of course y'all do. Y'all're not babies. So what say we go to your house until this is all over?"

"But Mommy and Daddy?" Remmy said.

Rio patted his slightly younger brother's shoulder. "They won't be coming." He looked up at Santee. "Right, Santee?"

Tear-filled eyes looked up at her pleadingly, making her feel surprisingly teary also. "I'm really sorry, but I don't think they'll be coming home again."

Sobbing, they clamped to her legs like leeches. Awkwardly her palms gave each back two abrupt pats before falling to her sides.

This really sucked.

Chapter 6

"He's not coming, is he?" Jamie said.

"He'll come."

Santee sat on the edge of the swimming pool, feet dangling in the water. Jamie, about the nicest preteen on the planet, sat on her left; his dog, Buddy, panted on her right. The four younger boys splashed in the shallows.

"But it's been days!"

Jamie was right. It had been days—a nightmare of explaining to cops (never a good situation if past association were any indication) who she was and why she'd left the scene. Mrs. Wilson had contacted the Coulters' attorney, who'd contacted the next of kin. But they'd been in limbo for days with no word from the lawyer.

"It's me," Jamie said. "They don't want me."

"Jamie—"

He swiveled toward her. "It's true. Rachel didn't want me. She was trying to get Dad to send me away." Tears sounded in his voice, and he swiped at his eyes. "I know he didn't want to, but I think he was going to cave, just to shut her up."

His sigh wavered and caught. "And now this! Who would want to be stuck with a gawky eleven-year-old anyway. Sure he'd want Remmy and Rio. They're his after all. And the twins 'cause they're little and cute. But me, I'm just—"

"You're just the glue that's holding this all together. They'll see that and know what a great kid you are and how lucky they are to have you and your help with this major change."

"And if they don't..." He banged his head against Santee's shoulder. "I've still got you."

Panic clenched her gut, but before Santee could burst the kid's bubble, Mrs. Wilson appeared with a whole bunch of people. In the forefront was a tall blue-eyed man with dark blond hair a little on the shaggy side. He was on crutches, levering himself around in a hip-to-toes leg brace.

Oh, shit! Santee adjusted her mirrored sunglasses, desperately wishing she'd had the brains God gave a slug with and had gotten out of here last night after the kids had been put to bed. The urge had been there, but she hadn't realized that it meant the Sinclair's arrival was imminent.

"Boys," she called to the little ones. They came out of the pool without argument. The six of them, seven counting Buddy, faced the newcomers.

Mrs. Wilson pulled out a chair from the umbrella-shaded table. "Perhaps you'd like to sit down."

Ruarke Sinclair sank gratefully onto the chair, his throbbing leg stuck straight out. They had brought a wheelchair, but he'd been too stubborn to use it. "Hi, guys," he said. "I'm Ruarke Sinclair. Your mommy and daddy wanted me to take care of you kids if something happened to them."

The little ones pressed tight to Santee. If she wobbled backward so much as an inch she'd be in the pool.

"Come on, boys," Mrs. Wilson urged. "Come meet your new family."

Heads shook emphatically. "Guys," Santee said softly, "remember, we talked about this. It's okay to be scared, but these nice people are your family, and they're going to take good care of all of you."

Trey and Trev hugged the Lab's sturdy neck. "Buddy too?" Their high-pitched two-year-old voices asked.

"Of course," Santee stated, her gaze daring them to deny that the dog was also welcome. "Buddy is a big part of this family."

The older man and woman stepped forward. In their mid to late fifties, they were trim and dressed in Western-inspired clothes, he a suit and she a longish dress. "Of course your dog comes too," the man said.

They looked up to Santee, and she nodded. "Go tell them your names just like we practiced."

Trev and Trey, with Buddy, moved forward, but Rio and Remmy refused to release their hold on her legs. They'd been through a lot. Jamie took their hands and pulled them away from her and over to the grandparents.

That left Santee to face Sinclair without any buffer except the darkest sunglasses she'd been able to find at a dollar store. With a graceful motion, Sinclair indicated the chair beside him, asking her to join him. Hidden behind the glasses, her eyes flicked to that traitor Mrs. Wilson, who could have warned her that the Sinclair who was coming was Ruarke Sinclair so Santee could have escaped, or maybe she should have made the connection. But really, what were the chances that they were one and the same?

With no way to avoid it, Santee eased forward but took the chair opposite, farther from the hulking bodyguards and further from him. She forced herself to not perch on the edge of the seat even if she wanted to give herself that couple-seconds advantage in case she had to take off. Beneath the table was her pack. As she sat, she nabbed a strap and pulled it beside her.

Her positioning forced Ruarke to turn so he could face the lovely raven-haired woman whose wariness fairly crackled in the humid air. Thankfully his bullet-cracked ribs were healed, but the leg still raised all kinds of havoc when he moved. His appreciative gaze noted her long lean greyhound gracefulness. For some inexplicable reason, she seemed vaguely familiar to him. But he was pretty sure he'd have remembered her. Her energy even brought a little twitch from down south, something that hadn't happened in so long he'd begun to despair. And she wasn't even remotely his type.

"I owe you a huge debt of gratitude."

She shook her head emphatically. "Right place, right time. That's all."

"Still—"

Her long legs straightened, raising her to loom over him. He squinted up at her, a sense of déjà vu nagged at him. Maybe not this tall woman, but someone similar had recently leaned over him like that.

"You don't owe me squat." At his raised brows, she knew she'd overreacted. "Excuse me."

Grabbing the pack, she headed toward the mini mansion.

"Santee!" Remmy's cry made her stop. The still-insecure boy ran up to her. Rio wasn't far behind. "Where you going?"

She wanted to tell them it was time for her to blow this place. But she just couldn't. Not yet. They weren't secure enough with these people to let her go.

"Just to the little girls' room, guys."

"Can we come?"

"We'd wait outside," Remmy said.

"And we could hold the bag for you," Rio said. "Keep it safe."

Santee wasn't good at reading between the lines, so it took her a moment to realize what wasn't being said. "Guys." She pushed the sunglasses to the top of her head so they could see the truth in her eyes. Leaning down closer to their level, she said, "I'm not going to just up and disappear on you without telling you."

"Mommy and Daddy did," Rio whispered. Remmy nodded in agreement.

"We talked about this. They didn't go because they wanted to."

They nodded and leaned into her legs. "But we didn't want them to leave."

Santee wasn't equipped for this whiny neediness. She wasn't an empathetic person; her genes didn't have that mothering instinct. The bag was tugged from her hand by Jamie, who seemed to have materialized from nothingness. She let it go and allowed him to grab her wrists and place her hands on Rio and Remmy's sun-warmed backs. The feel of their bare skin made her cringe, but Jamie moved her hands up and down the soft skin until she caught on and continued the caress herself. No matter how uncomfortable it made her, the boys seemed to crave the contact and hugged her tight.

"I know you didn't want them to leave, but sometimes bad things happen."

Remmy tipped his head back. "But why?"

Santee replaced the sunglasses over her aching eyes. She glanced at Mrs. Wilson, but the woman wasn't making any move to help her out. As a former teacher, she had a lot more experience at this. Though it wouldn't take much since Santee's experience was nonexistent.

"I don't know why, Remmy. It just does."

The twins were on Santee's lap. Rio and Remmy sat on the chair arms, their arms around her neck. Ruarke could tell she wasn't very comfortable with it, but the kids' adoration was obvious.

Now they were reluctant to give in to bedtime, or was there a magical phrase that got them into bed too?

When Mrs. Wilson called for the twins, there was a small mewling protest. Santee whispered to them, which got them moving. Together they went to each person, including "Uncle" Joe and "Uncle" Pete. They carefully negotiated his stretched-out leg to hug his neck. "Night, night, um…" They looked to Santee for help. She gave them an encouraging nod. Unable to say Ruarke and way too soon to call him Daddy, it came out "Wookie."

That one word was like a punch to the solar plexus. It had been so long since another little one, his little sister, had called him that. It almost made him throw up.

Remmy and Rio were whispering with Santee. Behind the yellow-lensed glasses she wore indoors, Santee's eyes shifted from boy to boy. Tears rolled down their cheeks, at which point Jamie left his book to put Santee's arms around the boys. She looked startled, as if it had never occurred to her that was what the boys needed.

What kind of person, man or woman, could be that clueless? Ruarke doubted she'd been born that way. So what had happened to make her almost afraid to touch a child?

Before long, Mrs. Wilson returned smelling of Ivory soap. "Boys in bed?" Regina—Mrs. Reggie to Santee—Sinclair asked.

Mrs. Wilson nodded and sat.

Mrs. Reggie shook her head in wonderment. "I only had the one, but I can remember the fights we had with him over bedtime."

"Mo-om." Ruarke could feel his cheeks heating at the other's grins. He even got what seemed like an amused glance from the young woman.

Reggie leaned over and patted her son's good knee. "It's okay. We still loved you." After two miscarriages, it wouldn't have mattered what he put them through. They were just so very grateful.

"You should have been here a week ago," Mrs. Wilson said. Though she'd retired as a teacher she'd soon discovered that her new budget allowed for a fraction of the traveling that she'd anticipated doing. And with her husband's death after a long bout of cancer, she had medical bills to pay, so she'd hired on with the Coulters to look after the kids after school. The job, however, had turned out to be more of a full-time nanny-cum-housekeeper-cum-cook-overseer-cum-gardener-overseer-cum-maid overseer. "The little boys fought bedtime for hours just like every other two-year-old the world over."

"So," Robert "Rob"—Sir Rob to Santee—Sinclair said. "What happened?"

Mrs. Wilson inclined her head toward where Santee and the two middle boys snuggled. "She happened."

They all looked from Santee to Mrs. Wilson.

She shrugged. "Don't ask me how, but she walked in the front door and chaos went out the backdoor. Just like magic."

"Like this afternoon's nap time?" Reggie said.

"Exactly."

Around two o'clock, the boys had started yawning and were cranky. Reggie had made the comment that it must be nap time.

Both twins were quick to say, "No, Gramma Weggie. Only babies take naps. Big boys have snoozy-poozy time."

And off all four boys went to get pillows and blankies out of the closet. They spread out away from one another and were soon asleep.

Mrs. Wilson chuckled. "Isn't that just the cutest? And the maids tell me that the bathroom problems have cleared up too."

"Bathroom problems?"

"Yes, it seems that the boys were having peeing contests, aiming from a distance for the toilet and other things in the bathroom. There were also incidents of fecal smearing on the floor and walls."

"But not anymore?" Reggie said.

"Not anymore."

"But how…"

Mrs. Wilson shrugged her still trim shoulders. "I don't know. She never raises her voice, but when she's really upset, she pulls off those glasses and looks at them with those strange silvery eyes of hers and they heed."

The alarm on Mrs. Wilson's watch went off again. She got up, and Remmy and Rio slid off Santee's lap. While the good nights were exchanged and some awkward hugs, Jamie approached Santee. She got up, grabbed her pack, and together they went to the dining room table.

"You sure you want to do this now? Because it can wait."

Jamie shook his head. Unlike the other boys' neatly shorn hair, his was longish and dangling into his eyes, as if he'd missed a trip or two to the barber. "Now's good."

Santee dug the envelope out of her hiker's pack. She'd deciphered the titles and knew that she owned a truck of some kind and a trailer. There was a fistful of investment sheets, and by the differing letterhead designs, she knew they were from a variety of sources. But the handwritten letter had stymied her.

"Can you read this?"

Jamie opened the sheet and pushed his unloved black-rimmed glasses back into place. Clearing his throat he read:

Dear beloved sister,

We owe you so much for saving us. This seems like a pittance in comparison. But we did what we could to get you out and recompense for what She put you through.

We couldn't buy you a home because we didn't know where you'd want to live, so we got a home on wheels. It is parked in a storage facility in Egan, South Dakota. The paperwork for the rental is included, as is the passkey for the gate and padlock.

Your address is a mail-forwarding company out of Egan. All perfectly legal in South Dakota. That's your driver's license address also. You have a checking account at the Egan State Bank. We forged your signature. Sorry. Checks are in the envelope. Your VISA is paid in full from that account every month. We get the statements and shift money in as needed from other investments.

As for the "other" investments? We got as much as we could out of *Her.* Of course we had to make Her believe it was you making the demands and threatening to reopen the case if She didn't fork over.

Don't worry. The judge is extremely wealthy and probably didn't even notice anything amiss. He's also getting a bit forgetful, which made it even easier for Her.

So money won't be a problem. Anything short of a huge mansion in Malibu or a sixty-foot yacht or a Lear jet we ought to be able to cover. Give us a few years of good investments and we may even be able to get you one of those too.

We have an attorney on retainer if you ever, God forbid, need him again and an accountant that'll take care of all the tax stuff. We watch over both very closely, so no worries there.

Please let us know when you are settled. We would love to visit, if you'll have us.

The phone is just a simple flip phone. If you want a smart phone, that's easily affordable. We'd love to hear from you. Our number is pro-grammed into the phone already.

We know nothing can possibly make things right, but we hope this makes things a little easier for you.

A mere thank-you cannot tell you the depth of our gratitude. You deserve so much more.

We love you soooo much. Hope you can love us after everything you went through in that awful place.

Your loving sisters,
#7 Dakota and #8 Cheyenne

Santee felt frozen in place and gutted like a trout. Her hands were shaking even though they were pressed tight to the oaken table.

"Santee? Are you okay?"

Jamie's worried voice barely penetrated. His touch shocked her lungs into sucking in a breath.

Suddenly she was on her feet listening. Though she hadn't heard anything, she knew. She took off, attracting everyone's attention as her long legs took the gracefully curving staircase two steps at a time. She was halfway up when the first cries sounded.

Midnight. In mountain time zone, it was ten o'clock, still twilight outside. Ruarke's girls were still up and under Pete's wife's, Rosarita's, watch. He was their last allowed phone call of the night.

"I wish you had come," he said.

On speaker, Shaynee and Shawnee groaned. "She wasn't nice, Dad," Shaynee stated.

"Come on, girls."

"No, Dad. You come on."

Shawnee, the quiet one, said. "You were never around, so you don't know."

"And when you were, she was all lovey-dovey butter wouldn't melt in her mouth. But ask Grandma. Rachel was not a nice person."

Ruarke stiffened. "Rachel and your grandma didn't get along?" That was news to him.

"Come on, Dad," Shaynee said. "Rachel wanted them out."

"No!"

"Yes. She said it was her house now and they should get lost."

Damn it. They'd been divorced for over five years, and this was the first he'd heard it.

"And," Shawnee said, "she was really not nice to the house staff."

"Rosarita?"

"Oh, she really hated Rosarita."

Damn it all to hell. Rosarita was a saint. Probably the sweetest, deep-down-inside nicest woman God ever made. Ruarke felt so very lucky to have her and Pete in his employ and as friends. He felt confident leaving his teenage girls in her care.

"We just couldn't celebrate her life or mourn her death," Shawnee said.

"Yuh, Dad," Shaynee said. "More like the other way around. Mourn her life and celebrate her death."

"Girls!"

"We're sorry," Shawnee said, "but we couldn't be that hypocritical."

He rubbed his bristly jaw. "I wish you had told me."

"We tried, Dad," Shawnee said.

"Yuh. You wouldn't listen. You said we were jealous."

Damn, he didn't remember any of that. "I'm so sorry."

"It's okay, Dad."

Ruarke frowned into the darkness, alleviated only by some solar lights scattered about. "What about the boys?"

They gave their "Duh" sound. "It's not their fault their mother was a bitch."

There was a rustle and what sounded like a soft snort from the dark recess of a nearby lounger. A shadowy form was barely visible.

"Okay, girls, sleep tight."

"Don't let the bedbugs bite," they echoed.

He glared at the shadowy figure. "That was a private conversation."

"I was here first," Santee said lazily, unperturbed. "So, technically you horned in on me."

The riot of blooming tropical flowers perfumed the air, but none must have been lavender because he wasn't feeling very calm. The conversation made him all too aware that baseball had been his "be all end all" and everything else took second or third place in his life. No doubt it had played a role in Rachel's infidelity with the kids' pediatrician and subsequent absconding with his baby boys to Florida, effectively cutting off his access to them.

"Do you want to stretch out on a lounger? I'll help you down and back up."

Ruarke's first impulse was to decline, not wanting to look helpless in her eyes, but it sounded so good to straighten out. "Thanks. I'd appreciate that."

Her tall lean shadow separated from the low chair and seemed to glide across the terrace to him. Standing beside her made him aware of just how tall she was. He was six feet, four inches and always found himself looking way down at the women he dated. She had to be at least six feet or even a smidge taller.

Her shoulder bucked up into his pit, and she easily handled his awkward lurching. That was when he noticed that for the first time she didn't have any colored glasses on. The moonlight seemed to glitter in the glacial-ice eyes. And danged if she didn't smell really nice too. She eased him down and carefully lifted his legs up onto the chaise. With a sigh, Ruarke leaned back. It felt so good to be outside, on his own without bodyguards dogging his every move. And surprisingly, he felt just as safe with only this young woman watching over him.

Chapter 7

Santee stared at Jamie, trying to read between the lines of what he was saying to what he actually meant. It wasn't a natural skill, and she didn't have the knack.

Jamie stood before her, her knapsack wrapped in his arms. His chin was set, and his lips trembled as if on the verge of tears.

"Jamie." She felt as if she ought to touch him or (shudder) hug him, but that wasn't really appropriate behavior. "Why do you want to take my bag with you when you go to spread your dad's ashes?"

His big brown eyes shimmered as his arms squeezed even tighter. The other boys didn't know what was going on. And seemingly the adults didn't either. "I'll take real good care of it," he muttered.

"I don't doubt that." Santee tried to keep her tone reasonable when her instinct was to yell at him and grab the bag away. "But why?"

Twin tracks started down his cheeks. "You could come with us. We'd all be together."

She shook her head; her "growing out" hair swayed against her neck, bugging her. No way was she going out in the Gulf on a little boat (which was actually a large tour boat) with a crowd of people who would probably all need to be rescued when the dinghy-sized vessel sank.

Santee gently placed her hands on the bag that Jamie was squeezing the life out of. She was very aware of the adults who had tons more experience dealing with kids eyeballing her, just waiting for her to screw up. "I told you I'd be here when you got home. Didn't I?"

Jamie nodded miserably, tears dripping off his jaw.

"So, Jamie, you either believe me or you think I'm a liar. Which is it?"

His head jerked up, eyes shimmering behind the thick lenses.

"You can take my bag with you. I'm not going to fight you for it, but that tells me that my promise—my word—means nothing to you."

Violently he shook his head, eyes pleading. But when she didn't say more, Jamie looked down at the bag and ever so slowly eased it out into her hand.

The bag was very heavy, a two-hander for a kid, but Jamie had to get used to the fact that she wasn't going to be with him after they left Florida. Santee was not going with on that itty-bitty puddle-jumper they'd be flying in. She was heading off on her own again, which she'd made plain. Mrs. Wilson was going with them, so they'd have someone they knew, someone who knew them and their routine. But it wouldn't be her.

Santee set the bag at her feet. "If you think Buddy shouldn't go along in case his love of water would prove too much for him to resist, he could stay here and keep me company." She dug out a red bandanna from her pocket and offered it to Jamie.

He took it with a watery smile. "I think that would be good. Thank you." He flung himself at her, squeezing her ribs so tightly.

Her hand wanted to pat his head, but was it appropriate or not? Instead she kind of wriggled herself free, her T-shirt stained with his secretions.

"Fine, now y'all need to get ready to go." She could feel the adults judging her actions and felt they'd judged her less than human. So true.

A wicked week passed as the house was turned upside down. Items to be shipped north were marked. Everything else was donated, picked up, and gone, leaving an echoing hulk of a house that was no longer a home.

A ton of children's tears had sent Santee fleeing to the patio.

Seemingly overnight, the kids' bags were packed and stacked by the van. The lawyer would see to getting the rest sent north.

Santee managed to get through the kids' hugs, the tears, and the begging still stoic, at least on the outside.

Mrs. Reggie had given a brief fierce hug, as had Mrs. Wilson. Ruarke stood a moment as if unsure of what to do and settled on a nod and a "thank you." Pete and Joe gave her a wave and a "bye," leaving Sir Rob standing by the van.

"Santee, hon, we'd love to have you come with us to South Dakota."

She looked at the packed airless van and knew the plane would be even worse. At least with the van, if it got to be too much, she could scream at Pete to pull over. But what could he do if she went apeshit while they were ten thousand feet in the air? Pull over to the nearest cloud and let her walk around for a few minutes? Didn't think so.

"I can't, sir."

He grinned, blue eyes, like his son's, misting. "Rob."

"Sir Rob, I just can't.

He held out an envelope that Santee tried to wave off.

"I don't need your money."

"Just take it." He bent down, unzipped her pack, shoved it in, and rezipped it. He rested his hands on her shoulders, sadly aware of but ignoring her stiffness. "Any time. Come to South Dakota, or if you need us, just call. Ruarke programmed our number into your phone."

"Oh, he did, did he?" Santee glared at the way-too-handsome-for-his-own-good man and got a nonrepentive answering smile.

Jamie and Remmy slipped out of their seatbelts to press against the window. Their cries resounded. Joe sat beside the door, keeping them from escaping. As the van pulled away, the kids tried to get to the back but didn't make it before the van turned onto the street.

The sun was a lot less bright, the air a lot less perfumed. Instead the air hummed with faint cries, her name reverberating in her eardrums.

The packs weighed at least a ton more than they had when she'd been in Florida. She shifted her shoulders to settle the big one on her back and grabbed the other.

Santee tramped out the driveway, again in search of the elusive Texas.

Chapter 8

Ruarke Sinclair wearily stood outside the workout room in the former machine shed. His life was like a bad soap opera.

Buzzing saws filled the shimmery August heat with the sweet scent of cut lumber while destroying the ranch's rural solitude. Carpenter crews worked on the two major additions to the ranch house. The hope was that more room would cut the tension before someone went nuts and started offing their brothers or sisters. The four-car garage was being converted into a huge family room with a second story of bedrooms and baths. His parents' bedroom wing off the dining room was now enclosed and ready for interior work. A plumbing crew was split between his parents' en suite bath and the second-story bathrooms, one with an industrial-sized laundry room. Electricians tried to make sure there was enough power for the huge expansion and pull new wiring throughout.

And then there was the beautiful blond buxom physical therapist. He watched as Danielle shimmied her shapely ass across to her Corvette. She gave him a huge smile with her full ruby-red lips and a "tah-tah" with her ruby-red tipped nails. She said his leg was getting so much better. And it was. The leg was stronger and less painful. So why was he still not getting any sexual response to her overt invitations? It had been five months. His body should have gotten over the trauma by now. It was getting more and more difficult to hide the fact that her blatant sexual offers were not creating their intended response or any response at all. And if it ever got out that he couldn't...

A squealing dust cloud resulted from the quick 180 the Corvette spun threw a hazy blanket over the minivan pulling in. The arriving van had to swerve to avoid the fishtailing sports car while trying to negotiate the trucks, trailers, and vans of the construction companies.

Ruarke wanted to duck back inside, but too late. His neighbor leaned up closer into the windshield when she noticed him. His girls hopped out, yelling thanks and goodbyes before trudging toward the house. The van pulled toward him just as a hand landed on his shoulder. Pete gave a brief commiserating smile before moving off to let Ruarke handle the nosey neighbor.

Brenda pulled in front of him; air-conditioned coolness drifted through the window to his sweaty body. She was older by at least ten years, and those years hadn't been kind. Too much time in the sun and cigarette smoke had ruined her complexion. Plus worry over the vagaries of ranch survival and raising five kids had manufactured strands of white throughout her dark-brown hair.

"Hey, Ruarke." She had shoved her sunglasses to the top of her head so she could eyeball him better.

"Hello, Brenda. Thanks for taking the girls."

"No problem. It's just a little out of my way, and I've got to take my youngest in, anyway." The daughter barely glanced at him. His star had fallen so far since the shooting. Prior to it, the girl, whose name he couldn't recall, would have been all over him, coquettishly batting her eyes at the famous baseball player. Now she couldn't waste precious time from texting to more than nod.

"Bet you'll be happy when this is all done," Brenda commented with a nod to the construction. "Must be costing a fortune."

It was, but he wasn't about to tell her that.

"But then it's probably just a spit in the bucket for you." Her tone was sharp with envy. Ruarke knew that her husband's ranch had suffered some setbacks in this economy. Nor was he going to tell her that with the sale of the Florida house and John and Rachel's double indemnity life insurance, not only was his house's addition covered, but the kids' colleges were completely funded, with money left over.

"With five more kids, the old farmhouse was not nearly large enough, only having three bedrooms and the one bath upstairs."

"Oh, sure," she said quickly. "I can see that." Though her family had survived with just three bedrooms for herself, her hubby, and their five kids, they hadn't had the luxury of just saying, "Oh, this won't work. We'll just have to build on." She looked enviously at the construction.

If only she knew, Ruarke thought sourly. She'd realize that the extra money and more space didn't necessarily mean they'd be any happier.

"Well," she sighed, settling her dark glasses onto her nose. "See you next week."

"Why don't you let us take next week's run?"

"Oh, no." She gave a bitter little laugh. "It's obvious you're much too busy for that." She waggled her fingers at him before enveloping him in her dust.

Well, crap, he thought as he started reluctantly for the house.

As he rounded the phalanx of vehicles, the house's front door slammed open. Shaynee stood there, hands on hips, blue eyes blazing.

"Da-ad!" she screeched.

Double crap.

"They're doing it again."

Pete, who was at his side, chuckled.

Ruarke glared at him. "Don't laugh too hard, buddy. I'm betting one of those naked little boys running around with their what have yous dangling in full view just happens to be yours."

From inside, they could hear Pete's wife's, Rosarita's, frazzled shriek. Pete said, "But Petey didn't do this until Trev and Trey showed up."

Simon either, Ruarke knew. His best friend, Miri, and her football player husband, Sam, left their two kids with Ruarke's parents during the season so the kids didn't have to switch schools twice or more depending on trades. Miri had grown up nearby, but the minute she married a black man, her parents had disowned their only child, wanting nothing to do with the half-black grandchildren. But this area was still home to Miri, and they returned every off-season, often living in a vacant house on Ruarke's family's ranch. And Ruarke's parents, who'd always wanted a big family, welcomed Miri, Sam, Madison, and Simon with open arms.

The household was in chaos. Mrs. Wilson, Ruarke's mom, and Pete's wife tried to corral the streaking naked boys with little success. Their flushed faces told of their fraying tempers.

"Da-aad! Eee uuu!" his girls cried as four little boy parts went flashing by.

"Guys!" Ruarke called as he waded in, but the boys easily evaded him, laughing hysterically as they danced around and past him. Behind him came a snort as Trey slipped through his grasp. Ruarke looked suspiciously around, but Pete looked pointedly away, his cheek muscles twitching. "If you can do better—" But Pete held up his hands and stepped back, even though he was better able, physically, to track down the little miscreants, one of whom was his. "Thanks a lot," Ruarke said.

The giggling boys raced around the butted-together dining tables, heading for the back door. High-pitched laughter resounded as they dodged through the kitchen and let the back door slam behind them.

Shawnee, his other twin, edged up to him "Oh, by the way, Dad. There was someone in the pasture when we came home."

A stab of concern hit him. The last stalker problem had been a while ago, but it always lurked in his mind. "Who was it?"

Shawnee shrugged as she bit into a crisp red apple.

"She was just standing there by that hunk of stone. You know, that one that marks that dog's grave."

Oh, he knew all right. He'd inadvertently caused the dog's death. Burying him and putting a marker had been the least he could do.

Jamie appeared. "She! And you're just telling us now?"

Shawnee stared after Jamie as he raced out the front door. She'd never seen him so deliriously alive.

Jamie leaped off the porch steps and tried to click his heels together but failed, landing hard on his knees. Immediately, he was up and racing off, yelling, "It's her! I know it's her!"

Ruarke and Pete looked at each other. "Can't be. Can it?"

Together they hurried after Jamie as Pete called Joe about a possible intruder. Pete hopped into the Polaris Ranger, leaving Ruarke to struggle into the back seat and get his bum leg across the seat. Joe came running, a shotgun in his hands. The Ranger paused barely long enough for Joe to fall in before tearing off after the awkwardly running preteen.

They hadn't even left the yard and already Jamie was starting to struggle. When Pete pulled up, Jamie was gasping for breath in the ninety-five-degree air. Grabbing at his side, he glared challengingly at them. "It's her. I know it is."

"Fine," Joe said as the barely rolling Ranger kept pace. "But get in. We'll get there that much sooner."

Joe slid out so Jamie could slide in. Again the lurching Ranger almost left Joe on his butt in the dirt.

The Ranger fishtailed, jarring a groan from Ruarke as he grabbed his leg and almost landed on the floor. "Pete," he groaned through clenched teeth. "For God's sake." He had to hang on and couldn't support the leg both.

Pete slowed the Ranger so fast Ruarke was almost dumped again. "Sorry," he said, but Ruarke didn't think he looked all that contrite.

At the gate, they could see the person—a man or maybe it was a woman—heading for the fence, where a vehicle, dually truck with a good-sized pickup camper on the back, was parked. What looked like a four-horse trailer was hooked to the bumper.

"Let me out!" Jamie slapped at Joe's leg. "Let me out! Santee!" He darted to the fence, tried to dive through the barbed wire, but snagged his pants and probably part of his leg. Jerking through and free, he was up and limping across the pasture. "Santee! Wait!"

Was that Santee? If so, how did she go from homeless and destitute to owning a home on wheels and what looked like a couple of dogs?

"Is that her?" Joe asked.

Ruarke could only shrug. "Jamie seems to think so."

His broken cries resounded through the hills. The tall figure stopped, then shoulders dropped as if resigned, turned, and dropped the pack in the dust. Mirrored sunglasses reflected the light as she braced for Jamie's launch. Still, it staggered her as the boy tried to climb her like a tree. Mewling cries resounded, slowly becoming less and less strident.

"Guess that's her," Pete said. He grinned at Joe, and they high-fived.

Pete and Joe had managed to get past her "Keep away" barrier while in Florida. She'd even allowed them to josh her, bumping shoulders even. Ruarke wouldn't have dared lest she handed him his head or hands back on a platter.

Pete drove the Ranger out the gate onto the gravel road and parked nose to nose with the big at-least-ten-year-old Chevy diesel.

"Hey, little sister," he called, lifting his hand to her. "Long time no see."

"About damn time," Joe muttered.

Ruarke watched as she tried to disengage the limpet mine attached to her chest. "How did she find us?"

Joe lodged the shotgun against the steering column. His dark eyes met Ruarke's blue across the seat back. "Who the hell cares if she can straighten out those little hellions."

"Did you give her directions?" Ruarke pressed.

Joe paused from getting out and turned back. "Wasn't my or Pete's place, neither one of us, to tell her how to get to your home. If you didn't, maybe Sir Rob."

Ruarke knew he hadn't, and his dad would have told him if he had. Wouldn't he? But Ruarke had seen his dad shove something into Santee's pack at the last minute before they left her behind in Florida. So maybe he had.

Santee tried to loosen Jamie's stranglehold, but he only clutched tighter as if to weld himself permanently to her.

Poor Rufus was whining as he sniffed at the boy's legs, which smelled of a strange dog. Rufus didn't know if he was supposed to protect his mistress or if this new human was going to be a member of their pack. Sunny merely sat wagging her big bushy golden tail. All were welcome in her world.

Shock rocked Santee to her toenails, and it took a lot to shock her. Jaime? What the heck? What was he doing in Texas?

Beyond the keening boy, a bright red sporty machine sat by the fence. Santee was rocked back on her heels by the sight of the three men. Pete and Joe stood beside the UTE staring at her. And unless she was terribly mistaken, Ruarke Sinclair was levering himself out.

What the heck? How had they managed to track her down? And more importantly…why?

Jamie kept saying her name over and over. "You're here! You're here!" He leaned back far enough to squint through tear-clouded glasses. "Thank you! Thank you! Thank you!" Then he crushed himself against her.

She was so flummoxed that she couldn't tell him that this meeting was a total surprise to her. In fact, two minutes later she and the dogs would have been long gone.

What was she doing standing in this pasture of pine trees and brittle stalky grass? For some reason, she had driven down this dusty backcountry road, parked on the shoulder, got the dogs and herself through a barbed wire fence, and now stood here by what looked like a small grave with a pitiful clutch of fake purple flowers stuck in the dry ground. Her fingers had deciphered the letters carved into the tennis ball-shaped granite—J-A-C-K. Someone had loved this animal an awful lot to go to the trouble and expense of burying him and buying a headstone. So much easier to have just let the coyotes take care of the carcass.

"Jamie." She awkwardly patted his back. What an awful situation. Just when he'd probably been adjusting to his new home and family, she had to show up and screw him up all over again. "Get down, Jamie."

He whined but eased his grip on her neck and loosened his legs from around her trunk. On his own feet, he swiped his arm across his snotty lip, tears still streaming down his cheeks. As if afraid she'd vanish if he didn't maintain contact, Jamie wrapped her in his skinny white arms, crushing her ribs with surprising strength. "I prayed you'd come."

Well, that was a first for her, being the answer to a prayer. Her family thought of her more like their worst nightmare.

"Hey, Santee!" Pete called, waving his hands over his head like a flight deck controller. He and Joe each had big silly grins on their faces, as if they were actually happy to see her.

Ruarke…not so much. Still on arm-cuffed crutches, he moved around the front of the vehicle, no smile to be seen. His leg was still braced in black from thigh to ankle. He stood hipshot, staring at her. She kind of doubted he considered her an answer to his prayers.

Oh, well.

Santee reached for her pack, but Jamie beat her to it. He hugged it to his skinny chest like it was the best prize given in a carny contest. "Jamie—" She reached for the pack then noticed the blood oozing down his leg. "What did you do?"

"Nothing." He dodged away from her hand. "I'm fine."

Santee caught him up into her arms, grateful that he was a skinny kid. "Barbed-wire cuts are not something to fool around with." She took a moment to make sure Sunny was up on her three feet before heading toward the men. Small stalks half-hidden in the ground grabbed at her tennies.

"I'm okay," Jamie said warmly against her neck. "I can walk." But he didn't wiggle to be let down.

Joe swung open a six-foot pole gate, his big broad brown face wreathed in a wide grin. He gave a quick one-arm-around-the-shoulders hug as she passed. "Good to see you, girl."

Pete plucked Jamie from her arms. When she reached for the backpack, Jamie managed to twist away and keep it, which made Pete chuckle. "Guess he figures as long as he has that, you can't be far away." He jostled Jamie and said with a laugh, "And he'd be right. Now let's see what you did to that leg. It's a good thing you've had your tetanus shot. Joe, get the first aid kit."

Those three went to the rear of the small off-road vehicle, leaving Santee with Ruarke. Their sunglasses-covered eyes kept each other at bay.

Ruarke made the first move, joining her in the shade of the pines. The gentle breeze whispered through the needles. He swung into position beside her, leaning against the gate.

"Sooo," he drawled.

Her chin came up. "So?"

He looked down at the two mutts trying to sit on her toes. "I see your family has grown."

The purple western shirt lifted with her shrug. "For now."

His light-brown brows lifted above the aviator-style rims. "For now?"

"Until I can find them a good home."

One look at the way they clung to her long bare nicely tanned legs made him doubt they were ever going to go along with that. And the badly scarred three-legged Golden would require just the right person who'd want to take that on.

He was also a prime example of a cripple needing just the right person. He fervently hoped there was someone, some beautiful kind-hearted woman, who'd be willing to take on a broken-down ball-player with seven, sometimes nine—counting Miri's two—kids. Put like that, he kind of feared it was hopeless for him also.

"I'll finish paying off the vet bills and even give them some money to cover her pain pills. Someone will want them."

"And the pit bull?"

She stiffened immediately. "Rufus is not a pit bull. His legs are way too long. The vet thinks some kind of boxer mix."

Ruarke shrugged laconically. "Pretty much the same difference."

Santee swung on him. With her forefinger she jerked the glasses down her nose so those silvery eyes could nail him. "It is not."

He straightened so his extra four inches of height would allow him to look down on her. "Is so."

"Is not!"

"Is so!"

A slight quirk of her lips and Santee pushed the glasses back into place. "Bet if I kicked you in just the right place, it would really hurt."

He winced, which the twitch of her lips showed she'd noticed. "You wouldn't do that to a poor cripple."

"Not to a 'poor' cripple, no. You look pretty uncripple-like to me."

"Don't I wish," he said. With a sigh, he leaned back against the gate. The damn leg was barking at him pretty good again. Three operations and it was still iffy.

Joe came up to them. "We've got Jamie patched up for now, till Mrs. Reggie"—he winked at Santee, who initiated the form of address that others were now using—"can work her magic."

He reached down to juggle Rufus's ear before holding out his hand. "Why don't you give me your keys? I'll drive your truck in so you can sit with Jamie."

Santee flinched, just slightly, but Ruarke and Joe noticed.

"Hate to move the boy now," he said gently. "Just when we got the bleeding stopped. And you know he's going to want to ride with you and you with him, since he's got your bag and don't seem too inclined to let go of it."

Santee looked past them, squinting into the brilliant sunlight. "I wasn't exactly planning on staying."

Ruarke's heart sank. It no longer mattered how or why she was here. His family desperately needed her to work her magic before they all imploded. Everything had sure gone to hell in a handbasket fast enough when they left her behind. "It's too late for you to head out now."

Her raven brows lifted. She tilted her head back at the brilliant orb almost directly overhead.

"That's right," Joe said with a big sappy grin. "It's way too late for you to head on out. All the good campsites'll be scooped up." He waggled his fingers for the keys.

"And besides," Pete said as he joined them, "we were about ready to eat. Seems to me you were a real good eater."

Santee stiffened as if insulted. "Are you saying I'm a pig?"

Pete held out both hands placatingly. "Not at all." When she relaxed a smidge, he added, "Unless the shoe fits, of course." His teeth flashed a huge smile.

Again, Ruarke was surprised at how easily Pete and Joe interacted with the frigid Santee. So different from how she reacted to him.

Pete bopped his hip into hers as she eyeballed him sharply, as if trying to decide how to exact her revenge. "Come on, girl. Let's go eat. I'm starving."

She looked at Ruarke questioningly. "I don't think that's too wise. It'll just confuse the kids."

Ruarke pictured the chaos he'd just left. How much worse could it get? "I don't think it'll be a problem," Ruarke lied.

Reluctantly, Santee dug the keys out of her pocket. Her gut was clenching out warnings. How had this happened?

Joe had his hand on the keys, but she didn't release them to him. He could see her mind working over the situation. "Do you have a horse in that trailer?"

She blinked at him, stymied for a moment by the abrupt topic change. She could feel the warm blood draining from her face, leaving her chilled and nauseous. She rocked slightly as if a strong gust of wind broadsided her. "No," she said. She eyed the trailer with a mixture of sadness and relief. "No horses."

Joe eased the keys from her. "I won't have to park in the shade of a tree then."

Still, Santee hesitated. She felt doomed by the navigational error she'd somehow made. "Where the heck are they hiding Texas?"

Pete snorted, making Santee's cheeks heat with the realization that she'd spoken aloud. She lifted her chin. "I can't figure out how they can keep moving a huge state like Texas around."

She knew she sounded like a lunatic, which wasn't far from the truth. But dang it, this was not the first time for this nonsense. She felt Ruarke's stare. Maybe now, knowing that she was a few bricks short of a full load, he'd be ready to rescind his invitation.

The jackass's eyes were twinkling, and his lips twitched a smile— not the reaction she was looking for.

"Texas's loss is our gain," he said.

"I hope you still feel that way tomorrow." Santee had a premonition that her presence, even if only for a day or two, was going to throw a major wrench in everything.

With the dogs squashed in and Jamie pressed tight to Santee's side, the Ranger led the way back to the ranch house. The cacophony of construction was earsplitting. Ruarke led the way through the lumber, scattered tools, saw horses, and foot-grabbing coils of extension cords. Santee followed slowly, her sharp gaze taking in the major renovations.

War whoops echoed from within as Ruarke opened the door. Santee stepped inside just as four naked boys raced around the dining room table, the girls shrieking their disgust. Joyful devilment showed on each little face until Trev, the leader, spotted Santee.

He stopped, causing a chain reaction to pile up. His hand fell away from his mouth, which was a perfect "O" of shock.

For a long moment, they were all frozen in a tableau of stunned silence. Then Santee spun, dodging past Joe and out into the sunlight.

———————————————————

Chapter 9

"Noooo!" Jamie called as Santee strode out. "Wait."

Pete blocked the door. "Give her a minute."

Jamie spun on his younger brothers. "I hate you! You ruin everything!"

"Now, Jamie," Mrs. Reggie said soothingly. She approached her new grandson and reached to touch his shoulder, but he angrily shrugged her off.

"It's true!" Jamie yelled. "She won't stay now. Not with them like that," he wailed as his head tipped toward their nakedness, lips drawing back in sneering hate. "It's all their fault she's leaving!"

"Jamie," Ruarke said calmly. "Santee's not going anywhere right now."

"You don't know that!"

"I do know that because you have her bag."

Jamie looked at the big pack clenched tight to his chest. "And Joe still has her keys."

Joe dangled the ring from his finger for Jamie to see.

"She's not going anywhere. Which," Ruarke said, "gives us time to get ready."

Two little tearstained, snot-nosed miserable faces looked up at him. The other two boys, who'd never met Santee, looked confused at the instigators of their deviltry.

"She gone," Trey sniffled.

"No, she's not," Rob said. "Come see." He held his hands out to them and led them to the front windows. All the kids as well as the adults huddled around the big picture window. Through the mass of vehicles, they could see Santee leaning against the corral fence, rocking back and forth as if in pain. The boxer mix was stretched as

59

high as he could up the fence rails on one side while the three-legged Golden pressed against her other leg.

In the corral, the three horses' heads perked up. Even from a distance, it was easy to see their nostrils flaring with whickers, though their welcome was drowned out by the screech of a table saw. One of the horses trotted to the fence, jostling for prime position by the woman. She tried to shoo them off, but they persisted. Finally, Santee rubbed the noses shoved at her. Her stiff posture eased.

"See there," Rob said to his grandchildren. "We still have time to make a good impression."

"*Sí, sí,*" Rosarita said, clapping her hands to get their attention. "We will get our pants on and wash our faces and hands and show Ms. Santee what big boys we are." Like a mother hen, she herded her chicks off to find their clothes.

Remmy and Rio looked up at their grandfather. "What about us?"

"The rest of you start putting away all these toys then go get cleaned up."

Maddie, Miri's eldest, strode up, hands on hips. "Why should we? She's not the boss!" Poor Sophie, Pete and Rosarita's daughter, stood uncomfortably beside her friend.

Rob leaned down to eye level with Maddie. "Because I said so, Madison Adams. And I'm one of the bosses in this house."

Her café-au-lait skin darkened in rebellion. "My mommy says I don't have to do anything I don't want to do."

"Your mommy isn't here," Rob said. "Which makes me top dog, and I say put away this mess and get cleaned up." He leaned into the petulant little face. "Now!"

Maddie turned to Sophie, but the quieter, more amiable girl was already heading off to find her mother. Maddie's lip poofed out in a stubborn pout, and she stamped her little feet. She looked to the others, both kids and adults, but found no one backing her rebellion. "I'm telling my mommy!" she warned as she spun around and marched off stiff as a wooden nutcracker from a Christmas movie.

Reggie let out a sigh. "And she's only five."

Ruarke patted his mother's shoulders. "Once Sam retires and they're together as a family, she'll change."

Reggie cupped her son's face and gave his cheeks a little pat. "If it's not too late by then."

Ruarke was shocked. His mother never criticized.

Had Maddie just turned into a brat since he brought the boys home? Or had Maddie always been such a prima donna, and he just hadn't known because he was off playing baseball, leaving Miri's children, as he had his own daughters', rearing to his parents?

Was his mother too stressed by five more kids in the house? Granted, space was way too tight right now. They'd even farmed all the girls out to Pete and Rosarita's house until more bedrooms were available.

Ruarke became aware of Mrs. Wilson at his side. The retired teacher had been a Godsend, helping out with all the kids. She had the kindest brown eyes and was pretty much unflappable no matter what the kids threw at her.

"It's nothing you did or didn't do," she said kindly. "The twins were a handful before their parents died. And um, Mrs. Coulter was very…um, easygoing with them."

"Except with Jamie," Ruarke said.

Mrs. Wilson's salt-and-pepper head nodded. "Except with Jamie…when Dr. Coulter wasn't home."

"So Jamie was right when he said she wasn't nice to him."

Mrs. Wilson's smile was enigmatic. She'd spilled all the dirt on her former employers that she was going to. "I'd better see how the kids are shaping up."

Meanwhile Joe and Rob had decided where to park Santee's camper. Luckily they had a spot formerly occupied by a double-wide mobile home. It had all the hookups necessary, so Joe had gone off to get it parked and ready. Pete had gone to help his wife with the kids. That left Ruarke and his dad to look out at Santee still being fussed over by the three horses.

"It'll only be for a couple of days," Ruarke said. "Maybe through the weekend."

"That's what she said, huh?"

"Pretty much."

"Well, son." Rob slapped his hand onto Ruarke's shoulder. "That's not good enough."

It surprised Ruarke that his dad wanted to get rid of Santee so quickly. She was different, standoffish, and prickly, but still… "I suppose I could suggest she pull out tomorrow."

"Tomorrow?" Rob said. "Hell, boy. I'm racking my brain trying to figure out how we can get her to stay for good."

"For good! You mean forever?"

"Of course forever. It's pretty obvious that this family needs Santee. And I think Santee needs this family. But convincing her of that…" Rob sighed. "That may be next to impossible." He continued, "I sure would like to know who abused her like that. I'd find the son of a bitch and give him a taste of his own damn medicine."

Ruarke gaped at his mild-tempered, nonswearing father.

Rob's face lit with an idea.

"What?" Ruarke asked.

But Rob just smiled and shook his head. "I've got some calls to make."

Santee sat on the hot, hard, dusty ground. Her breath had been taken away when Joe got into her truck and drove off, but she could see him from where she sat, backing the trailer into a spot some distance from the main house, out where a little village of employee housing had been set up.

Scattered on nice-sized pine-tree-shrouded picket-fenced lots were two one-story houses, a two-story square house, a large two-story building with probably apartments, and a longish single-story of what could be a bunkhouse. The buildings were painted a variety of shades of brown that fit in the rural setting. The apartment building and bunkhouse had graveled parking lots that contained a variety of pickups…from rusty and faded to almost showroom shiny. A nice playground was constructed near the apartments, with a swing set, slide, teeter-totter, pipe jungle gym, and a playhouse.

Near where she sat, a huge gambrel-roofed red barn perfumed the air with scents of fresh hay in the humongous haymow and horse smells of manure and urine. She closed her eyes, breathing in the delicious, almost forgotten odors.

Beside the barn was an open area; fire-blackened concrete footings attested to the fact that, at one time, there had been a huge structure here. Horse training arena? she wondered.

She could also smell cows coming from a much smaller red barn. A white chicken coop with a large fenced enclosure protected at least thirty clucking hens in a variety of colors and sizes. Plus there were three red metal buildings with white roofs…machine sheds. Lastly, far out into the pasture, well away from the barns and its animals, was what looked like a long narrow building with three doors facing out this side. Two of the doors were open, one showed a horse dozing inside while two glossy but bone-protruding animals lazily pulled at the dry grass in the other corral.

Santee sensed Ruarke's approach. Both dogs sat up, alert. She had no doubt that both, even the gentle tripod, would defend her as best as they could if necessary.

Ruarke laid his arms across the top wooden rail and leaned against the fence with a sigh. He inclined his head toward the horses in the far-off pens. "We found those two tied to our fence—one day last week, the other the week before."

"Someone just dumped them out here." She could hardly believe that anyone could be so cruel. What did they think the Sinclairs would do with them?

"They were both pretty skinny, wormy, needed their teeth floated and hooves trimmed. Luckily Sol knows what to do. He handles most of our vet work."

"What about a humane society?"

"Oh, sure, the county has one, but it's small. Doesn't have the budget or place to handle big animals. And they'd try to hit the owners up for a donation when they drop them off."

"Which the cheap SOBs don't want to do."

Ruarke nodded. "The thought of owning a horse is a lot more rosy than the reality of how expensive feed is and vet bills, etc., etc., etc."

"So the horses get dumped."

"Oh, it's not only horses."

She sensed a sad resignation in him.

"Last month we found three goats tied by the gate. One of the wives is trying her hand at goat stuff: milk, cheese, lotions." He shrugged. "We'll see. This spring it was an old milk cow. We got her back on her feet and milking again. And there are the chickens from the backyard chicken coops, when the work gets tedious and smelly. But worst is the cats and dogs. We've got a lot of buildings, so the cats can earn their keep mousing, and they adjust pretty quickly. It's the dogs who break your heart. They come, bellies in the dirt, ribs showing, eyes with that 'what did I do wrong?' look. A lot of ranchers just shoot them. We haul them in to the humane society, give a donation, and hope they can find them a home. Those are the people I'd really like to get my hands on."

So the big, strong man had a soft spot. For dogs anyway. But he wasn't entirely God's gift, or he wouldn't have gone through two wives. The man was young enough and good-looking enough and wealthy enough he could go through a couple more before he was done.

He turned his beautiful blue-blue eyes to her. A smile made them sparkle, no doubt having melted many a female's knees. "I think they're probably ready for you now." He shook his head, slightly too long golden hair just begging to be brushed aside by rapt feminine fingers.

Santee had to fight the roll of her eyes, sure that that move of his had accomplished many things for him in the past. But she was a coldhearted bitch, immune to male posturing.

"The look on Trey and Trev's faces when they saw you standing there was priceless," he said.

"Don't think that my being here for two days is going to solve all your problems."

His smile died as his eyes followed her stiff back as she stalked off toward the house. She was right. Two days just wasn't going to cut it. But she seemed to have Texas indelibly burned into her brain. He didn't know how he was going to get past that. He pushed away from the fence. And what the hell was so damn alluring about Texas, anyway?

When Santee entered the house, the four boys were waiting, properly attired in shorts and tees. They stood in line before a wooden chair that awaited her. Their hands were held up like little surgeons as they awaited inspection.

"I see two familiar faces and two that I don't know."

A pretty mahogany-colored girl pushed up front. "That's my brother, Simon," she stated, "and he oughta be first since these ones don't belong here."

Santee pulled off her dark glasses and slid the bow down into her minimal cleavage. "I don't believe I was talking to you, little missy. And they do belong here. Just as much or more than you do." Though she couldn't be positive about that. Maybe Sinclair had sired the two beautiful light-skinned black kids.

The girl planted her hands on her skinny little hips, chin lifted, haughty like a princess. "My mommy says we're to always be first."

"I don't care what your mommy says. Around here, now, we take turns being first."

Maddie's eyes narrowed. In a flash, her tiny foot flashed out, aimed at Santee's Sunny.

Santee shot to her feet, grabbed the girl under her pits, and picked her, kicking and squealing, up. "No one kicks my dog."

Seventeen jaws dropped at the nanosecond it took for Santee to launch off the chair; grab the flailing child, holding her at arm's length; avoiding her kicks and teeth but little pink nails dug at Santee's exposed arms. Mutely they watched Santee carry the screeching girl across the living room, down the two steps to the nearly empty family room, and across to one of the few chairs. In an instant, she put the child down, got the chair turned so it faced the wall, and put a hand on the little sundress-covered shoulder to hold the girl there.

The tantrum was a sight. The screams and shrieks made Ruarke cringe. But Santee remained stoic as time inched past and the raving rebellion wore itself out. Finally, when Maddie quieted into sobbing exhaustion, Santee left her huddled on the chair and walked back toward the dining room, tension around her mouth and glittering eyes the only outward signs that she had been affected by the ruckus.

"I'm telling my mommy on you!" Maddie screamed.

Santee forced her hands to remain open lest she punch something or someone. Her teeth ground together, head pounding as she marched past the seven ineffective adults and ten wide-eyed children and out the front door. The dogs scrambled through with her into the healing sunlight. Her lungs sucked in the heated cut-lumber-scented air. Suddenly exhausted, a little weak-kneed, she dropped her hands to her knees as she bent over.

How had she managed to not mete out the punishment of her childhood? The urge had attacked her so hard. A shudder raced down her spine at the mere thought of what would have been done to herself or her sisters had they dared to act even remotely like that. Bile erupted up her throat, but she swallowed it down. With a deep breath, she straightened and turned.

Through the window, she saw all the spectators frozen in place. If someone had rushed to comfort the brat, she'd have been gone like a gust of wind. But they'd remained as she'd left them, the only movement was their heads as they looked at her, eyed each other, and then turned to where Maddie still sobbed.

Santee walked back in and sat down. Tears showed on all four boys' faces, but they'd remained in place, hands held upward.

"Thank you, boys," she said quietly. "You did just the right thing, waiting here. I'm proud of you."

Wails resounded from the other room.

Santee motioned Trev closer. "Remember that we take turns being first so everyone gets a chance." Two blond heads, one black straight-haired one, and one black buzz cut one nodded solemnly.

Santee checked Trev's soap-scented hands. Then Trey's. Next was Maddie's brother, the boy with the buzz cut, head bowed as if unsure if he was to be part of this.

"And you are?" Santee said gently.

"Th-imon," he whispered.

"Pleased to meet you, Simon. I'm Santee."

He sniffed, twisting to wipe his nose on his shoulder, and nodded. "Mommy Tee," he said. "Is you our Mommy Tee too? Me'n Petey?"

She'd forgotten that the boys had started calling her that. She guessed it would be all right for the next couple of days. "If it's okay with your mommy and your daddy."

Simon seemed doubtful and close to tears that the others would be able to call her Mommy Tee and he wouldn't. Ruarke walked up, took a hand off his crutch, and put it on Simon's shoulder. "I'll talk to your mommy. It'll be okay."

"Weally, Unka Work?"

"Really." He ruffled Simon's prickly scalp.

Petey, the last in line, turned toward his parents, who stood arm in arm. Rosarita seemed close to tears for some reason. Pete pulled her close and dropped a kiss to her head. They both nodded, making Petey grin broadly.

From the far room, a chair was knocked to the concrete floor. It went ignored. A wail resounded, which was also ignored.

After Petey's hands were cleanliness checked, Santee was surprised to see the line had reformed.

"Ethmo kithes?" Trev asked.

Eskimo kisses. The one way Santee was able to fulfill their need for skin-on-skin contact and her need to avoid touching them in any way that could be deemed improper.

She carefully took each face in turn between her hands and lightly brushed the tip of her nose against theirs.

"One more thing," she said. "Do you remember what I said about pee-pee and poopy not going in the potty where it belongs?"

Trev and Trey eyed each other guiltily. They nodded, unable to meet her eyes.

"Do you remember that if the pee-pee and poopy get on the floor or on the walls that the people who put it there have to clean it up?"

They nodded solemnly.

Ruarke looked at the ladies in the room as they were exchanging glances. He hadn't realized that that was a problem, but apparently, somehow, Santee did.

"And do you remember how that stinky, yucky mess would have to be cleaned up?"

They nodded. "Crawling on the floor like babies and with an old toothbrush. Cuzz only babies do stuff like that." That punishment was mild compared to what she'd endured, when, sick as a dog, she'd messed the bathroom floor. She almost gagged just remembering it.

"Exactly. But that's not a problem here, is it?"

The four looked guilty as sin, but they shook their heads. "No, Mommy Tee."

"Fantastic. Now go sit down for dinner."

The Hispanic girl hesitantly stepped forward, eyeing the other room where the sounds of anger were lessening. "I'm Sophie," she whispered. "Petey is my little brother."

Whispering also, Santee said, "I'm Santee."

"Mommy Tee," Sophie amended.

"Right." Out of the corner of her eye, she saw Rosarita smiling tearfully, hands clasped almost prayerfully. What was up with that, Santee wondered briefly, before turning back to Sophie. Still whispering, she said, "Do you have a favorite color?"

She nodded as she warily glanced toward the family room. "Pink," she whispered as she leaned closer.

Santee help up a finger and turned toward Jamie. "Jamie, I need my bag."

He hugged it tighter to his chest but at her lifted brow reluctantly brought it to her. It was like removing duct tape getting it from his arms. His face scrunched as if in bodily pain.

Santee dug in a pocket, searching through the contents, before removing a fuchsia bandana. "Like this?"

Sophie's eyes got huge as her long ponytail bobbed enthusiastically.

"Now," Santee said as she carefully folded and refolded the large square into a long narrow band. She held it up stretched between her hands. "This is yours. If you want it?"

"Really?" she said softly.

"Really." Santee put it around Sophie's head and tied it into a headband. "But you have to remember that this is yours and nobody else's. If I see it on someone else, I'll know you didn't really want it, and I'll take it back."

Sophie looked worriedly toward where Maddie was lurking, unseen but not forgotten.

"You have to stand up for yourself, Sophie," Santee said gently. "She's not your friend if she's always first and forces you to give in to her all the time. That's a bully. Not a friend."

Sophie didn't look convinced.

"You are just as pretty, just as smart, and just as loved as Maddie is. Stick up for yourself. You'll be a lot happier. I promise."

Just then, sandals clattered across the concrete and up the steps into the living room. Maddie froze, her eyes narrowing on the bright band around Sophie's forehead. "That's mine!" She stalked over and made to grab it, but Santee blocked her greedy little hands. "My mommy gave it to me! You stole it!"

Sophie reached up to gently touch it, casting a glance at Santee before squaring up to face Maddie. "No, it's not," she stated. "Mommy Tee just gives it to me."

"You're lying! You stole it! My mommy—!"

"No," Santee said the word softly but firmly. She looked at Maddie's reddened outraged face. "I gave it to Sophie. It's hers, not yours. However, I do have a similar one for you. If you want it?"

Greedily, Maddie nodded, bouncing in place and clapping her hands. She froze at the sight of the pale pink bandana. She stuck a finger at Sophie. "That one's mine!"

"Okay," Santee said as she went to put the pink one back into her pack. "I guess you don't want one. But this one would look so nice on you."

Maddie grabbed at Santee's arm. "I want it! I want it!"

"Really?"

Maddie nodded, her long naturally curly hair bouncing.

"No fighting about colors, or I'll take them both back."

Maddie eyed the fuchsia one, made as if to say something, but the look in Santee's eyes silenced her. "'Kay," she said meekly. But everyone in the room wondered how long that would last.

But a promise was a promise, so Santee fashioned the band and tied it around Maddie's forehead.

"Can we go see?" Sophie asked.

"Yes, but remember this, I don't want to hear any arguing. And no saying one of you is prettier than the other. In other words…no fighting."

They both nodded and raced away hand in hand, friends again, at least for the moment.

The four boys looked so sad until Santee pulled out four more—two shades of green for the twins, a red one for Simon, and a blue one for Petey. She fashioned triangles and tied them around their necks cowboy style.

Though she wasn't sure if Remmy and Rio would want one, she'd gotten an orange one for Remmy and a black one for Rio. They did and wanted them tied around their necks, also.

Out came another red one with black designs for Jamie and two aqua ones, one with white accents and the other with pink accents. Surprisingly Shaynee and Shawnee seemed to each want one too.

"Well," Santee said as she zippered her pack shut, "makes my bag a lot lighter."

A round of thank-yous made Santee flush. It hadn't been her intention to try to ingratiate herself on the children. On a whim, she'd seen them and picked out a variety of colors, which, surprisingly, seemed to have matched each child's favorite…with the exception of Maddie, but Santee figured if she'd given Maddie the fuchsia one then she'd have wanted the pink one—a hard kid to please.

During dinner, laughter and talking were enthusiastic. Several times Santee flinched, the noise cutting through her brain. Meals in her childhood had been silent affairs. No one wanted to attract His attention. They were "out of sight, out of mind" kind of kids, but no matter how quiet, how obedient…

Santee swallowed hard. The bite of ham sandwich felt like glue in her mouth. Her hand trembled as she put it down. Her left hand reached across to still her right.

Show no fear.

Easy to think…nearly impossible to do.

A reddish nose bumped up under her arm. Warm breath bathed her shin. Quivering inside, lunch threatening to reappear, Santee fought it down. (Once and only once it had happened. Re-eating regurgitation had cured her of ever giving in to vomitus.)

Santee shoved the chair back, her head banging like a tom-tom. Her abrupt movement silenced the hubbub. "I'm sorry," she said as she untangled herself from the chair and her worried dogs and grabbed her pack. "I, um…thank you for a wonderful lunch. I, um…suddenly snoozy-poozy time has hit me like it will the boys in a little while. I…um…can I help you with the dishes before—?"

"No, of course not," Rosarita said. "You go, *pobrecito.*"

Sir Rob stood as she passed. "Are you ill?"

The concern in his blue eyes seemed so real, yet he barely knew her. If he did know the real her, he wouldn't be so gentlehearted.

"I'm fine." She rushed out into the blinding light, grabbing her dark glasses to cut off the sunshine shards stabbing through to her brain. The sawdust-scented air calmed her riled-up innards.

If they knew…

They'd kick her ass to the curb so fast.

If it came down to it, maybe she'd have to reveal a small piece of her inner self.

Not a big one. She didn't want them to revile her. Just enough so they'd be happy to get rid of her.

So she could finally find that elusive Texas, her final frontier.

Dusk had fallen on the southern Black Hills. Ruarke sat on the porch looking south toward the darker shadow that was Santee's camper.

She hadn't returned to the house. Not even when Jamie went to announce supper.

The little boys' good behavior continued even in her absence. When snoozy-poozy time was announced, the boys never argued, never even moaned. They just got up and got their pillows and blankets, found a spot on the floor, and lay down. Bedtime was a breeze also.

Maddie, not so much. Her strident protests resounded the entire walk to Pete and Rosarita's two-story house.

"She's going to leave, isn't she," Jamie said.

"We don't know that," Rob said.

Jamie shot to his feet. "She is, and you know it! Then everything will go back to just the way it was." Reggie arose and tried to put her hands on his rigid shoulders, but he ducked away.

"It will!" he cried as he backed away. "And you know it too!" At the door, he paused. "When she leaves, I'm going with her so you won't have to be stuck with me anymore!" The door slammed behind him; Buddy, his dog, barely managed to bumble his old self through with his master.

A wavery sigh escaped from behind Reggie's hands. "Oh, Jamie," she whispered.

Rob went to her and wrapped his arms around her, drawing her into his chest. Reggie looked up, teary-eyed. "I knew he was unhappy, but for him to think he's imposing? Is that the way we treat him, because it's not how I feel…not at all."

He kissed her temple, heart hurting because hers hurt. "That's not how we treat him, and you know it."

She pushed back in his arms. "If she doesn't take him, he'll run. I just know it."

"Reggie—"

"Listen to me, both of you," Reggie said. "The boy is terribly unhappy. If he thinks he's unwanted and unloved…a burden to us… he'll run away the first chance." She glared at her husband and son. "You and I know what will happen to a child his age out there in the big bad world!"

"So, my love, we need to come up with something to keep them both here."

"What?" she asked dispiritedly.

"Yeah, Dad, what's the plan? Because for some reason she's bound and determined to go to Texas."

Rob rested his chin on the top of his wife's head. "Why, do you suppose?"

Ruarke levered himself out of the chair to stand beside his parents. "Another question ought to be why she is here in the first place. How did she find us? Did you give her directions, Dad?"

"No."

"Nor me," Reggie said.

"So how—?"

"The same way all your groupies find you. The internet."

Maybe, Ruarke had to acknowledge. But Santee didn't strike him as much of an internet browser.

"So," Reggie said. "What's the plan?"

"I've got a couple of ideas."

"Like what, Dad?"

"Patience."

Ruarke didn't much like that approach. He wanted something concrete, preferably written in a contract…a long-term contract. Say sixteen- to twenty-year commitment. Signed in indelible ink…or even blood.

Maybe that was the way to go? A lucrative contract.

He looked out at the still-darkened camper.

Somehow, he really didn't think the way to her was through her pocketbook.

He sighed. God, he hoped his dad had a really good plan. Or they were sunk.

Chapter 10

The dusty track Santee jogged was designed for a vehicle, not a person pushing a double-wide stroller. Sunny sat in the stroller, lolling tongue and bright eyes attesting to her happiness to be alive despite her injuries. At Santee's side, the long-legged, heavy-bodied Rufus gamboled, a huge doggy smile was on his doofusy face.

The front wheel of the stroller rolled in the beaten path. The two backside wheels bucked on the grassy verges. Santee's arms were getting as much of a workout trying to control the stroller as her legs were. She could have gone out to the gravel road and had an easier run, but the dappled light strewn by the pines, the bounding of the insects, and the smell of cow in the air was far preferable to stale car exhaust.

Plus, though she could have probably gotten out of the motorized gate, she didn't have the code to get back in. And she didn't want to wake anyone by ringing the bell.

The altitude, though not really mountainous, was still killing her flatlander's lungs. Santee slowed, gasping as if out of shape. Planning to walk awhile, she got Sunny out so she could roam with Rufus.

Half an hour later, Santee and the dogs simultaneously heard the vehicle. The curve in the path through the pines blocked it from view. She and the dogs were hemmed in on both sides by barbwire. There was nowhere to hide. Shoving the stroller off to the side, Santee abandoned it, grabbing her pack. Both dogs caught her urgency and huddled closely. To the right, the pasture was too flat and open. To the left were a few trees and some small outcropping of rocks.

The best defensible spot was ahead, a towering jumble of stone, but the approaching sounds made it clear that they'd never make it.

She stepped to the left side and tossed her pack over the fence, parted the bottom two wires with her foot, and motioned the dogs through. At the wooden post, she clambered up and over. She grabbed her pack and ran, the dogs loping easily beside her.

The growling engine forced her to stop long before she'd have liked. A smallish freckled boulder about the size of a wheelbarrow was her best choice. She motioned the dogs into its protection, joined them, and began digging into her pack.

The first Ruger, startlingly purple, she stuck into her waistband. The black Ruger she laid on the ground beside her knee. The illegal shotgun, shoved barrel down in the pack, was pulled out. She checked that it was loaded and leaned against the sun-heated granite. The AK came out last, was checked, and set between the shotgun and her knee.

Motioning both dogs down, she huddled close to the already-hot-to-the-touch boulder.

The growl of the diesel changed to a soft rumble as it idled. Doors nicked open. Boots thudded to the dirt. Sunny's head lifted, nostrils working as she tested the currents. Her tail gave a tentative flip as she looked at Santee out of her one eye.

Rufus's tail was not tentative. It began raising a dust cloud sure to be seen.

"Santee?"

Oh, nuts. That sounded like Pete and where Pete was... She peeked around the boulder. Sure as heck there was Ruarke. She swiveled back into concealment. Dang it! She looked at her armament. All set and no one to shoot.

"Santee?" Ruarke sounded like he'd made a megaphone from his hands.

The dogs looked at her, panting softly.

It was pretty obvious she couldn't wait this out until they went away. They'd found the stroller. They knew she was here.

Dang it! She knew what they were going to think she was doing out here. Her cheeks heated. They certainly weren't thinking she'd set up to refight the Alamo in their back pasture. Oh nooo! They'd think she was out here taking a dump.

Double dang.

She started securing her weapons into their proper slots in the pack.

"Santeeee!"

She rolled her eyes at the dogs, who were grinning at her. "It's not funny."

But their thumping tails said they thought it was simply hilarious.

"You don't think it's so funny when you're taking a dump and I'm watching you so I can pick it up."

"Sannnteeee!"

"All right, already!" she called as she stood up. Rufus jumped up on the boulder, while Sunny looked around the hunk of rock. She and the dogs started back toward the fence.

Ruarke, with his crutches, belligerently moved up to the fence. Pete held his hand out to steady him if necessary. "Where the hell have you been!"

Sunny stopped in front of Santee, keeping her from going nose to nose with Sinclair and causing a nuclear reaction.

Santee motioned her hand like a game show model toward the stroller. "I'd say it's pretty plain where I've been."

"Without telling anyone!" His deep voice rose a few decibels.

Rufus let out a soft growl. Ruarke cast the big bully dog a glare.

Santee held up a finger to silence him. "Don't you dare tell him to shut up. Not when you're screaming at me." She pulled her dark glasses off, wincing as ice picks shoved into her brain. "And what makes you"—she poked across the fence into his chest—"think you have the right"—*poke, poke*—"to scream"—*poke, poke*—"at me?" *Poke, poke.*

It was very satisfying to see his azure eyes widen and then narrow. The big jock was way too used to ruling the roost.

Pete put his hand on Ruarke's arm. Ruarke blinked at him as if coming out of a trance. He gave Pete a nod as he inhaled then held it to a count of ten. Santee counted it out in her head with him.

He cleared his throat, red anger draining away from his face. "I'm, uh, sorry." He avoided her glacial gaze. "We were, uh, worried."

Santee settled her sunglasses back onto her nose, grateful for the relief. "We?"

"Yes, well, um, the kids. Jamie."

"The camper was still there," Santee said reasonably.

Ruarke shrugged; his muscular shoulders were showcased under the fine white silk shirt. "Well, you know kids."

Actually she didn't and had no plans to ever remedy that.

Santee set the pack over the fence, parted the wires for the dogs, and climbed over. Ruarke stood there almost nose to nose, his hand absently rubbing the spot on his chest where her finger had repeatedly impacted.

"You could have left a note."

She just shook her head and stepped around him.

He made to catch her arm, but she jerked away with a snake-like warning hiss. She held her finger up and shook her head.

"Santee."

She slung the pack into the stroller and patted the seat. Sunny climbed in with only a little boost from Santee.

She turned as Pete stepped to Ruarke's side to help him if need be out of the little ditch by the fence. Ruarke stiffened at the tough of Pete's hand but didn't shrug him off.

"You don't own me, Mr. Ruarke Sinclair."

He nodded. "But—"

"No buts. You may own the majority of this 'not Texas' state, but you don't own me."

He nodded again. "But—"

"Nor am I in your employ, so I don't owe you an accounting of my time." She grabbed the stroller's handle.

Pete stepped into her path, hands held out placatingly. "Would you and the dogs like a ride home? In nice air-conditioned comfort?"

The sun beat down on her almost nude shoulders; the narrow straps of the tight tee did little to shield her pale skin. The tight tee actually gave very little frontal support, not that she had much that needed support. However, the ogling of the two men would have been a huge boost to her vanity…if she gave a rat's ass. Just like men the world over, she thought with a snort and shake of her head. So locked in on the nipples denting the clingy fabric that she could have gutted them both like hooked trout before either could react. And she had zilch to ogle compared with Pete's Rosarita. Heck, even Sinclair's teenage daughters were more endowed than she was.

"Um, guys." Santee bent her knees, lowering her face into their sightline.

Both men jerked as if stung by wasps. They at least had the decency to blush as they looked sheepishly at each other.

"Sorry," they mumbled.

"Jeez, guys," Santee said. "It's not like they're anything to write home about. And you, Pete, have better right in your own home."

He grinned rakishly. "A guy can still admire what's kind of sticking out there."

Santee squatted, reaching for a fair-sized rock. With a laugh, Pete hunkered down behind the stroller as best as a big man could and pulled it way to the pickup bed. When he bent to lift it in, she let the rock fly, not nearly as hard as she could have, and plunked him in the butt.

Pete jumped and turned wide eyes at her as his hand touched the spot. "Nice throw."

Sinclair was eyeing her, brows lifted in surprise.

"What?" she demanded, hands on slim hips. "Girls can't throw worth a darn?"

He held up his hands as best he could from the crutches. "Didn't say that."

"Then what?"

"I'm just glad you didn't aim at his head and put some oomph behind it. Knock him out and I kind of doubt you and I could get the big guy into the pickup to haul his sorry ass home."

She shrugged. "Just tie him on behind and drag him."

"Hey!" Pete said. The stroller was in, and he slammed the tailgate. "Now that's just plain mean." He laughed. "Come on. Let's load up. They're holding breakfast for us." He swung open the rear door for her. "I'll try to reach Joe or one of the others and call off the search."

"Others?" Santee turned on Ruarke. "What the heck? What did you do?"

Again, he held up his hands to ward her off. He flinched away from her glare. "Don't blame me. Jamie's the one who raised such a fuss. You should have left a note."

Which would have been next to impossible for her to do, but she wasn't about to tell him that. "For pity's sake, the camper's still there!"

With a grunt, Ruarke levered himself into the tall 4×4 truck cab. "We tried to explain that, but Jamie was sure you'd taken your bags and headed out on foot like you did in Florida."

"I never left Florida before you drove off into the sunset." Santee motioned Rufus into the backseat. Sunny got her front foot up on the door jamb. Santee put one arm under the dog's chest and the other around her haunches and lifted the forty-five-pound dog in.

"Logic doesn't matter to a kid." Sinclair looked around at the dogs trying to get comfortable on the floor. "They're welcome to sit on the seat. Wouldn't be the worst these seats have seen."

So Santee patted the seat, and both dogs happily climbed up so they could look out the windows.

Santee slammed the door just as Pete climbed in behind the wheel. "Got ahold of Joe," he said. "He'll notify the others that the lost is found." He cast her a twinkly grin in the rearview mirror.

Santee just shook her head. Where were these people's brains? To actually think she'd walk off with two dogs, one of which was crippled, and leave a perfectly good house-on-wheels behind? Get real! She didn't like to think it, but actually, in the short time she'd had the camper, she'd gotten soft. The thought of hiking with two packs no longer appealed. Of course, it was all the dogs' faults. Hauling enough water and food for them would be pretty much impossible even with the stroller. It wasn't that she was getting soft. No way.

It seemed like the entire Sinclair ranch population was waiting in the yard when the pickup pulled in. Jamie, eyes swollen and red, raced to open the door and throw himself at her before her feet even hit the ground. Had the truck not been behind her, they'd have both ended up rolling in the dust. He was making some kind of garbled noises as he tried to crush her ribs. The rest of the boys huddled close, the girls hanging back.

"Jamie." Santee tried to pry his arms loose, but he merely melded tighter. "Jamie, come on now." Awkwardly she patted his shoulder. "What's all the fuss about?"

Finally, he looked up from her tear-and-snot-blotched tee. "I thought you'd left!"

Santee straightened his tilted steamed-up glasses. "I told you I'd stay until Monday."

He nodded. "I know."

"And today is…?"

"Saturday."

"Right. So there is no reason to be upset. Is there?"

"But…"

"Jamie. I promised. Either you believe me or you don't. But I'm telling you now I don't break my promises. Okay?"

He nodded but still didn't look happy or completely convinced.

"Good. So let's get the dogs out."

Jamie moved out of the doorway so Rufus could squeeze past. Santee lifted Sunny out and carefully put the gimpy dog down.

"Mommy Tee," one of the little boys cried. "Ooo gots pitcher." His little finger pointed at her back.

Santee winced, the heat making her lightheaded.

"It's a number, dummy," Maddie sneered. "It's a 4."

Santee grabbed the door as her knees got wobbly. Occasionally, there were days when she could forget that her back was marred. This had been one of those days. Until now.

"An' you even gots stars!" chirped another voice.

Santee forced herself to exhale and then draw in a ragged new breath.

"One." The light touch of a small finger seared her flesh.

"Two." Her stomach churned.

"Three." Bile charged up her throat.

"Four." She swallowed hard and stood, pulling away from the gentle poke.

"Wow!" Childlike awe resounded.

Sophie, in all innocence, said, "Four stars! You must a been very, very good to get four stars!"

Santee fought the swirling black memories. "Isn't it time for breakfast?"

Instantly Rosarita was there shooing the kids toward the house, ignoring their protests.

"Santee?"

Pulling herself out of the black vortex that sucked at her, Santee straightened just in time to prevent Jamie from sneaking her pack out of the truck. "Uh-uh." She grabbed it and waved him toward the house.

"Santee," Sir Rob said again.

The dogs were pressing so tight to her, almost shoving her over. Sunny stretched her nose up toward Santee's face, her doggy breath helping to blow away the remaining noxious memories. Thankful, Santee ran her fingers into the reddish-blond ruff.

The concern she felt radiating from the remaining adults stabbed at her. Silent questions, none of which she intended to answer, hovered like heat motes in the air.

"I need a shower."

She turned away. Her hand slid along the truck's hot fender as she went to the rear where Pete had the stroller unloaded. With a nod of thanks, she tossed her pack into it and pushed away from the well-intentioned people.

She didn't see them turn to each other. Although she walked straight and tall, there was a stiffness to her normally lithe movements. The crowding dogs showed their worry.

Joe and Pete looked at each other. "I feel a hunting expedition coming on," Joe said. His black eyes held about as much warmth as a rattler's.

"Count me in," Pete said.

"And me," Ruarke said.

"And us." Reggie grabbed Rob's hand.

"Nobody," Rob said, "does that to one of ours and gets away with it."

Chapter 11

Santee didn't go to the house for breakfast. Instead she sat in a lawn chair letting the sun dry her hair, which took all of a couple of seconds. The dogs lay nearby, each on their own rug with a fuzzy toy.

About an hour ago, the dogs had raised their heads, ears pricked. Jamie crept around the truck. Avoiding her eyes, he sat in the other lawn chair and opened a book.

He didn't say anything or disturb her in any way, but his presence changed the quiet. Maybe the airflow was altered just enough to throw the quiet into a slightly off-kilter pattern.

Ten minutes later, the dogs alerted again! Around the truck, Remmy and Rio silently tiptoed. Without a word, they each chose a dog and lay down on their rug, Remmy with Sunny and Rio with Rufus. Each got a very thorough face cleaning, which elicited some soft giggles before they opened their books, and silence was once more shifted to a different route.

Not long after, the dogs' heads came up again. Santee rolled her eyes. For pity's sakes! Not quite so quietly, four little boys marched around the truck. Remmy started to rise up, an angry inhalation ready to spew forth, but Santee dropped her hand to his shoulder. Beneath slitted lids, she watched as the boys settled to the ground, cars and trucks disgorging from their pockets. Soft putting sounds accompanied their playing, with a few diesel rumbles thrown in.

Jamie started to push up, face red with anger at their intrusive noise, but Santee cleared her throat and shook her head. For four little two- or three-year-olds, they were amazingly quiet.

Nearly noon, the noisiest intruder came. Ruarke on his crutches stopped, drawing all eyes to him. "Guys. Time to get ready for dinner."

They looked at Santee.

"We'll be coming in just a couple of minutes," he said.

Still they looked to her.

"You heard your dad."

They reluctantly gathered their stuff and left.

Ruarke peg-legged to the vacated chair, and just as he lowered into it, a big fart sound erupted. Startled, he dropped into the wimpy aluminum chair, making it creak ominously.

Rufus raised his head and chomped twice more on his fuzzy toad, emitting a nice fart each time.

"Jeez Louise," Ruarke said. He straightened his braced leg out. Rufus pranced over and deposited the frog in Ruarke's lap. Ruarke raised his slot in Santee's estimation by tossing the slobbery mess for the gangly overgrown puppy.

"You will come up for dinner, won't you?" He tossed the toad a second time. "Dad wants to talk to you."

"Look," Santee said sharply. Both dogs looked accusingly at Ruarke. "Give me fifteen minutes and I can be outta here."

"Wait! What?"

She jerked to her feet, grabbed her chair, and slapped it shut. "Save y'all the discomfort of kicking me out."

Ruarke stood up, balanced mainly on his one leg. "Will you wait a doggone minute?" His toe caught on Sunny's rug. Arms flailing for balance, he teetered. Santee got her shoulder in his armpit and arms around his waist, easily stabilizing him.

Ruarke was intensely aware of her fresh clean scent. Her long body pressed the length of his. His body responded with a force that hadn't been evident in a very long time. He didn't know if she'd felt his arousal, but she edged away to ease him back into the chair.

"Thank you."

She gave a curt nod, expression hidden behind those damn reflectorized sunglasses.

"Look." He spread his hands placatingly. "Please sit and listen a moment."

She stared down at him for a moment before reopening her chair and sitting down. The dogs relaxed back on their rugs but still eyed him closely.

"We don't want you to leave early."

Slowly, Santee relaxed back in the chair. "Then what?"

"Dad's got something he wants to talk to you about."

"What?"

"I don't know. He just wanted to make sure you were coming up for dinner."

"You don't have to feed me. I can come up after."

"Santee, they already have a place set for you. It was there at breakfast too, but you didn't show up."

She'd been too embarrassed at the spectacle she'd made of herself in front of the men this morning. That ratty tee had left nothing to the imagination. And they'd noticed. Oh, yes, they had. She knew better than to show that much skin...attract that much attention. But sometimes she just felt like being a normal person, unhampered by the past.

Now she wore sensible jeans, a sleeveless western shirt, and cheap tennies. Nothing of note was exposed. But could they ever forget how *He'd* marked *His* ownership of her...of all of them.

"Fine." She shrugged. "I'll be up in a couple of minutes. After I feed the dogs."

"I'll wait."

She tensed, glaring down at him again. "I said I'd be there."

He looked up at her, seemingly unaware of her hard-as-stone tone. "Just thought I'd walk up with you."

Still she glared down at him.

"So if I try to fall on my face again, you can catch me."

Finally, with a huff, Santee strode past him to the horse trailers' dressing room. The dogs knew what that meant and arose, tails wagging. She returned with a red and a blue bowl. Sunny sat and got the blue bowl. Rufus sat and got the red one. At Santee's okay, they began snarfing their dinner down. Since Rufus was still a puppy, they'd both get fed a third time this evening. Santee gathered up the bowls, encouraged the dogs to get drinks, then put everything away in the trailer.

As they headed toward the house, Ruarke commented, "That's quite the trailer you've got there."

"Oh?" She looked back at it.

"The former owners must have had tall horses because they raised the top about a foot."

"Hmmmm." She shrugged. Didn't much matter to her. She had no intention of hauling a horse in it. It had all been a package deal in the storage facility in Egan. So she'd just kept it…for now. It at least gave her a place to store the two bags of dog food, one for puppies and one for adult dogs. If she didn't have the dogs, she really wouldn't need the storage space or the trailer. And maybe the atrocious gas mileage would be minutely better.

"I've seen you standing out here looking at the house."

Santee tensed. "Oh?"

"I'd like to hear your ideas on it. Maybe after your talk with Dad."

"I really don't have any ideas." Not true, but he didn't need to know that.

"Oh, honey."

It was her turn to stumble a bit at the sexy rumble in his voice.

"I think your brain is working all the time, and I'd like to pick it a little bit."

Santee lifted her chin as she stepped up the porch steps. "I don't know what you mean."

"Oh, I think you do." She turned at the top, looking down at him.

He looked up and paused. "That would not be a bit nice, shoving me down the steps."

"And you think it's nice watching someone's every move so closely that she can't even pause for a moment without you reading something into it?" She turned toward the door. "I'm not near as smart as you're giving me credit for."

"On the contrary," Ruarke said into her ear. He reached around to open the door for her—so totally unexpected that she just stood there with her hand out to do it herself. "I think you are way smarter than you want anyone to realize."

"For a retard, you mean."

Ruarke kept the door closed. "What are you talking about? You're not retarded."

"Well, I sure as hell can't read. So what does that make me?"

Ruarke felt her pain as she shoved past into the house. He felt it for her too, because it was obviously a sore point for her.

But retarded?

No way.

Santee picked at the delicious casserole, or hot dish as they called it.

The voices were chipping away at her brain, burrowing past the walls she'd erected. Maddie's "me, me, me" and "my mommy says" were so strident, crushing out all other conversation. Her fingers scrunched around the fork's handle.

Rio and Remmy sat on either side of her, pressed close. Too close. Their little thighs were scorching her right through her jeans. Their very breath seemed to create a vortex, sucking oxygen from her area, leaving her lungs to strain for any tiny leftover atoms.

An insistent nose worked up under her vibrating arm. Sunny's warm tongue flicked at her sweaty wrist. When that failed, she wriggled until she was half into Santee's lap. Her gentle worried gaze locked on Santee's face, as if begging her mistress to let her ease some of the stress.

But Santee's gaze was locked on the fork trembling in her fist. There was so much she could do to alleviate the problem, and it didn't even involve child-cide. If only she weren't such a wuss. Stab and drag. Tear all the vessels. Spray bright-red blood all over. Feel the delicious release of all angst, the nightmare gone. Just blessed oblivion. A nip on her neck jerked Santee out of the delightful reverie. Sunny stopped scrambling to get into Santee's lap. Eye to eye they stared at each other.

Santee caved first. Now was not the time. Nor was this the place. Her aching fingers released the fork to clatter to the table. For just a moment, she let her nose sink into the soft doggy scented ruff.

The adult voices nearby were stilled. Santee could feel their gazes. Did they realize the mayhem she'd been contemplating?

Not likely.

These were nice, normal people.

Not damaged the way she was.

"My mommy says I don't have to make my bed in the morning if I don't want to," Maddie crowed.

Santee flinched. She didn't even remember what minor infraction she'd made as a child. Nothing remotely like what Maddie was doing.

The closet had been small. Stifling. Oh so dark, day and night. He'd stuffed a towel at the bottom so even that meager light was cut off.

How many days?

She had no idea.

The tiny space stank with urine and feces. Until, without food or water, her body just quit making any.

The darkness had been the worst. It clawed at her imagination. Or maybe ghost people really had visited her, people that she thought she had once known and loved. A shaggy brown dog had lain with her, curled up in the corner away from the sewage.

When the foul air and darkness had become too overwhelming, she'd shoved her fingers at the blocked crack under the door. If only a tiny draft of fresh air could be gotten. But somehow He'd known and stomped on her fingertips, stuffing the towel even tighter.

The doggy had tried to lead her away.

But suddenly eye-piercing light had broken through. And her chance at peace was gone.

Even worse, that was not a one-off incident. No matter how hard she tried, she just couldn't seem to abide by the rules. The others fared much better.

But not #4.

"Santee, honey?" Sir Rob leaned across to gently place his hand over her arm. "Why don't you take your plate and sit on the porch?"

She shook her head, aware that she was sweat-soaked through. "I'm not very hungry. I'll just—"

"That's an excellent idea, Dad," Ruarke said as he pushed back from the table. "I'll join you."

Shaynee arose. "I'll bring your plate, Dad."

"Thanks, hon." His azure eyes fell gently on Santee. "Coming?"

Rio and Remmy looked crestfallen as she arose. They made a motion to follow, but their grandfather shook his head.

"Me too! Me too!" Maddie screamed. "I wanna eat outside too!"

Santee stiffened. She knew if Maddie came, there were only two possible outcomes. Mayhem or full retreat, and she wasn't much for showing any weakness to the wolf pack.

"Oh no, you don't, little Miss Maddie." Mrs. Reggie grabbed the girl's chair, preventing it from being shoved back. When Maddie tried to scramble out, Reggie grabbed her and put her back in the chair.

"My mommy says I can eat outside if I want to!"

"Your mommy isn't here now. I am, and I say no."

Tears flowed as small toes kicked at the underside of the table, doing more damage to her flip-flop-covered feet than the table.

"I'm telling!" she wailed. "I'm telling Mommy you was mean to me!" She grabbed for the filled plate, but Reggie and Rosarita got everything throwable out of range.

Santee looked to Sir Rob, ready to apologize for causing the ruckus, but he held up his hand and shook his head.

"This has been a long time coming. We're all to blame. Not you. We've been too lenient on the child. So go. Eat outside in peace. We'll handle things here."

Squeals of rage followed them to the porch. Shaynee, Shawnee, Jamie, Rio, and Remmy also were excused to eat outside. The closed door barely muffled the battle inside.

"Wow," Jamie said. "I'd have gotten my butt spanked if I'd acted like that."

"Or worse," Santee said with a shudder.

Ruarke saw the thousand-mile stare in her eyes. He wondered what she had endured that was worse than a spanking but decided he was probably better off not knowing.

The adults looked frazzled as they staggered out after dinner. Maddie had finally cried herself to sleep. The little boys and Sophie were having snoozie poozie time with Mrs. Wilson overseeing.

Rob came out with a fairly large booklet in hand. He motioned Rio and Remmy off the glider and settled with a sigh beside Santee.

He shook his head. "That child…"

"It's our own fault," Mrs. Reggie said. "We felt sorry for her, being left behind like she and Simon are. But we let it go too far."

"She's a brat," Shaynee said.

"Now, girls…"

"She is," Shawnee said. "She goes in our room and goes through our stuff."

"She even takes stuff," Shaynee said.

"Like jewelry," Shawnee said.

"And when we see her wearing it and try to get it back, she screams bloody murder claiming it's hers."

Rosarita said, "Why didn't you tell us?"

The girls shrugged. "We didn't think there was anything you could do."

Pete was affronted. "And Sophie?"

"Oh no," they chorused. "Not Sophie. She's fine. It's just Maddie."

Jamie, Rio, and Remmy exchanged looks.

"You guys too?" Rob said.

They nodded. "She goes through our stuff too, taking whatever she wants."

"Well, that's going to stop right now." Rob jabbed his finger into the wooded arm of the glider. "Anytime this happens, we want to know. I don't care if it's a dozen times in one day or even in the middle of the night. You tell the nearest adult and let us take care of it."

They all nodded but still looked a bit skeptical.

The girls arose and motioned to the boys. "Come on, guys. Let's go and let the adults talk about us in private."

"Oh, Shawnee—" Ruarke called to his daughter. "Do you still have that drawing pad?"

Her honey-blond ponytail bobbed.

"Do you think I could have a couple of sheets?"

Shaynee's eyes twinkled. "Thinking of being an artist when you grow up, Dad?"

"Very funny, number 1 daughter."

Shawnee elbowed Shaynee toward the door. "Sure, Dad. I wasn't very good, so I gave it up. I'll get it for you."

"Thanks, hon."

Now with space on the glider, Sunny crawled up between Santee and Sir Rob, settling her chin on Santee's thigh and edging her nose under her hand. Her eye closed when the hand began to gently smooth her hair back, always careful of the scarred side of her face.

Rob kept the glider rocking slowly, soothingly. The afternoon, though hot, was peaceful without the screech of saws, the rumble of air compressors, and the *snap, snap, snap* of air-driven nails.

"Santee," Rob said. He brought the booklet forward. "I was wondering if I could ask a favor of you?"

Ruarke looked questioningly at his mother, but she shook her head and shrugged.

"A horse breeder I know is having a production sale." He flattened the book to show the glossy picture of a beautiful blood bay horse on the front. "I was wondering if you'd take a look at—"

Santee pushed herself back into the glider's corner, holding up her hand as if to shield herself from the mere sight of the horse. Sunny immediately squirmed into her lap. Rufus moved to press solidly against her knees. "I don't do horses." She gave a definite, firm headshake.

Ruarke saw his mother's eyes widen in surprise, a smile widening her lips. So that was what his dad and the contractor were talking about this morning, in the area where the former enclosed arena had stood before an arsonist burned it and the stables along with seven screaming horses to the ground. That had been the third strike against the Sinclair's in about a week, and it had been the last blow. His dad had never recovered enough to return to his first love—horse training. That had been going on fifteen years ago. What had suddenly healed the wound now?

But then he looked at Santee and knew. His father had seen Santee and how the horses fawned all over her and was betting it all on getting Santee to join him.

"I'm not asking you to 'do' horses. Just take a look. Find me some nice stable animals that I can make into good, steady, reliable family horses."

"I don't know anything about bloodlines and stuff."

"I don't care about that. Pretty horses do sell better, but my main concern is reliability. I want horses that people could be confident putting their two-year-old on, knowing that the horse will bring the kid safely back home."

Santee flipped through a few pages then finally gave a soft huffing sigh of defeat. "Okay. Not that I know anything about horses, but I can get through this before Monday morning."

Rob flinched, his smile freezing. "Okay, great," he said with a little less enthusiasm. "Just turn down the corner of the page. As many as you like since we won't get everyone we bid on."

Ruarke wondered what his dad's backup plan was. Would he still restart his training business without Santee?

"Um, Santee," Pete said, drawing her away from the glossy pictures. "If you don't mind me asking, what have you got going on down there in Texas?" At her frown, he continued quickly, ignoring Rosarita's quelling hand on his arm. "I mean do have kinfolk down there?"

Santee took a moment to try to ferret out exactly where Pete was going with this. "No." And she got back to the beautiful horses.

Rosarita shook her head at him, but Pete labored on. "A job waiting on you?"

Santee took her forefinger and pulled the sunglasses low enough so she could nail Pete with those icy eyes. "No, why?"

Rosarita's knuckles whitened with her warning grip. Pete winced as his wife's short nails dug in. "It's just that you seem real single-minded in getting to Texas, and I wondered—"

Shawnee came bouncing out of the house and stopped, aware she'd interrupted something. Her big smile faltered, and she lifted the oversized art book in front of her like a shield. "I'm sorry. I—"

Santee let Pete off the hook, pushing the dark glasses up, and returned to the book. Rosarita softly hissed something in Spanish in Pete's ear. Santee's lips twitched, leaving Ruarke certain she had understood exactly how badly Pete was being reamed out. Joe was also hiding a grin at his buddy's expense.

"It's fine, honey," her grandmother said, motioning her toward the group. "You're not interrupting."

Still, Shawnee hesitated, only relaxing when Santee gave her a nod. Shawnee sidled through the maze of legs to Ruarke's chair. She was careful near his outstretched leg and settled onto the arm of his chair. Handing him the sketchbook, she innocently said, "Going to be an artist for your second career?"

Ruarke froze. As did everyone else. Santee looked questioningly at him.

"Maybe," he forced out, hoping it sounded halfway normal. "You never know."

"Yuh, right, Dad." She laughed and kissed his cheek. "I've seen you try to draw. It's pathetic!" She flitted away to the house.

A sock to the gut would have been less of a shock. Ruarke felt their concern, and it drove him to his feet. He detested the awkwardness as he maneuvered crutches and a bum leg out of the group and down the steps to the yard. He gimped out into the sunlight back unbowed until he got to one of the carpenters' trailers and could hide behind it.

The metal was hot against his backside as he fell back against the trailer. His eyes stung. He'd been working so hard, doing everything the therapist and trainer wanted, biting back the agony that caused as he fought the odds of ever getting back on the diamond.

This was supposed to be his year…again. Most valuable player, gold glove, batting champ. There was no reason this wouldn't have been a continuation of that glorious last year. He was only thirty. Still in his prime.

And then he had to go into that damned mini-mart just to get some hot dogs.

They said he was lucky to be alive. That the unknown person had saved his life.

But he didn't feel lucky.

Sunny came around the trailer. Compassionately, the golden leaned against his good leg, her scarred face turned up to him. He worked his hand free of the crutch and laid his fingers over the ridged scars that didn't seem to bother her. The once beautiful dog wasn't concerned that she had burn scars down her right side from nose to flank. She didn't care that her eye was now a sewn-up slit. And she managed quite nicely, thank-you-very-kindly, on three legs.

So what did he have to whine about?

"Oh, Sunny." He ruffled her ear and a half. "Life just isn't fair."

He sensed Santee before she leaned beside him, the sketchbook in hand. He knew how he must seem to her. A spoiled, entitled rich guy boo-hooing because he wasn't going to win a few more awards.

"You wanted this sketchbook for me, didn't you?"

He nodded, drawing a deep, power-building breath. "I was hoping you could draw out what you envision for the house when you look at it."

"I can try, but I'm warning you, I've never had any lessons."

"I don't care. Just something to give me some ideas."

"For the family you have here, now?"

"Well, Miri and Sam would probably stay more if they had their own space. And Max, my manager and other best friend, and his husband, Bobby John, would spend more time with their own space. At least Bobby John would during football's offseason. My suite's out back on the north. You've seen them working there. And we'll have to replace the garage space we lost when we turned the garage into a family room and a second story for bedrooms."

She nodded and pushed away. "I'll give it a try." She started away toward her camper then paused without turning back. "I, um…" She paused, as if deciding whether or not to continue. "I might be able to help you with that tightness if you're willing to trust me with that leg."

A cramp darted up his leg, making him gasp. He grabbed at it, but the bulky brace prevented him from actually touching flesh. "Shit," he groaned between clenched teeth. How had she known, he wondered, as he watched her walk away?

Half an hour later, a Ranger rumbled toward Santee's place, disrupting her solitude. She and the dogs looked up as the red machine rolled around the pickup. Pete was driving, and Ruarke sat on the back seat, leg stretched. His face was tight, white lines of pain etched around his mouth.

Pete got out to help Ruarke. Santee set aside the auction pamphlet then pulled the other chair deeper into the shade.

With Pete carefully guarding his every lurching move, Ruarke made it to the chair and would have dropped into the flimsy thing if Pete and Santee hadn't each grabbed an arm and eased him down. Ruarke was covered in sweat and panting as if he had run a 5K.

"I didn't want to take any more pain pills. I hate how they make me feel."

Santee pulled the other chair over in front of Ruarke. "Easy to get hooked too." She grasped Ruarke's heel, and Pete maneuvered the chair under as Ruarke arched back, teeth clenched against the raging agony.

"What can I do?" Pete asked.

"Get some cool water," Santee said as she began unhooking the Velcro that held the brace tight around Ruarke's bared thigh. "There's a pail under the sink and a towel hanging over the oven door handle."

"I can go in your house?"

Santee looked up at him, surprised that he would have realized that she didn't like anyone invading her space. She'd never known privacy before and guarded it, not even really wanting to share it with the dogs at first.

"If you promise to be good."

He snorted and held up his right hand in a three-fingered Boy Scout salute. He chuckled aside her glare and fairly sprinted up the steps into the camper.

"Your friend there can be a wiseass."

Through clenched teeth, Ruarke said, "Don't I know it." Even the slight jarring of the releasing Velcro was painful. His big hands had death grips on the thin aluminum arms.

The camper door slammed shut behind Pete as he returned with a small plastic pail, an ice cream bucket in its former life, full of water.

"Keep him cool," Santee said to Pete, who set the bucket down and wet the towel, placing it around Ruarke's neck and wiping his face.

Santee knelt beside the outstretched leg and pushed the jean cutoff's cuff higher. "This is going to hurt some."

Ruarke's body was vibrating through waves of pain. Teeth clenched, he nodded.

Santee rubbed her hands together until the palms were hot. She winced at the scarred mess. Slowly she laid her hands down. Ruarke bucked at the lightest touch, breath hissing through his teeth. Very slowly, barely making contact, she slid her palms away from each other, one toward his knee and the other toward his hip.

Then back together.

The out again, increasing the pressure infinitesimally each time.

And slowly the tension in the leg eased as did the tension in Ruarke's body. With a sigh he dropped his head back, the white lines around his mouth easing away.

Pete watched, amazed, as magic seemed to flow from Santee's fingers. Her hands would stop, the fingers gently kneading a certain spot before moving.

She was getting pale under her tan. Sweat dripped off her chin. Her arms were beginning to tremble.

Pete grabbed the towel, wet it, and draped it around Santee's neck. She glanced around in surprise then gave a tight twitch of her lips.

Not understanding what was transpiring, Pete nevertheless realized that Santee was wearing out. But she wouldn't quit…or couldn't.

Pete reached across her and grabbed her wrists, surprised by the tingle he felt, and pulled her hands away from Ruarke's reddened leg.

With a little sigh, her ass dropped onto her heels. He eased her back against his legs, her sweat leaching through his jeans.

What the hell had he just witnessed?

He'd watched Ruarke get a massage before, but nothing like this.

Ruarke was laid out, breathing peacefully for maybe the first time in months.

And Santee looked like she's just finished a triathlon.

What the hell?

––––––––––––––––––

Chapter 12

Santee headed up to the big house after her run and shower. The atmosphere in the house was lighter than yesterday when Jamie had everyone worked up into a tizzy over her absence.

Inside, a slight shifting of shadows by the corner of the huge stone fireplace tried to draw her in, but she turned away toward the line of little boys awaiting her.

"You guys are all spiffed up today," she said as she inspected them.

"Ith Thunday," Trey said.

"Oh?"

Petey nodded. "We's all goes to church."

Ah, so that's why everyone was in their Sunday's best, leaving her extremely underdressed in shorts and a baggy tee.

Remmy leaned close. "You'll have to change. Grandma makes us all dress up in our good clothes for church."

"And we always eat out after," Rio said from her other side. "What's that called, Jamie?"

"Brunch."

"Oh, yuh, brunch. It's real good."

"Well, you guys can tell me all about it when you get home."

Jamie coughed out a piece of toast. "You're coming."

"No, I'm not."

"You have to."

"No, Jamie. I don't have to."

He shoved to his feet. "Then I'm not going."

"Why not?" Santee asked.

"Because—" Tears shimmered in his lashes. He looked to the others seated at the table for help.

"You could… You could…"

"And if I give you my word that I'll be here when you get back?"

"I'll take your bag with me."

Santee shook her head. Just what she needed was to send a kid off to church with a bag full of weapons. "We've been through this already. Do you trust me, or don't you?"

Sir Rob cleared his throat. "Of course we trust you. Don't we, Jamie?"

"But…" Remmy looked worried. "You'll be hungry."

His concern fanned a warm spark in her icy heart. "I'll be fine."

"Don't worry," Mrs. Reggie said. "There's plenty of food in the fridge. But we will miss you."

Yuh, right, Santee thought. The church would probably spontaneously combust if she were to walk through the door. She was way beyond redemption.

The kids were sent off for a last bathroom trip. The girls, including Maddie, after a glare from Santee that silenced a "My mommy says," and Sophie, quickly cleared the table, but when Santee started to arise to help, Sir Rob motioned her back into her seat.

This couldn't be good, she thought. A look at Ruarke didn't cast any illumination.

"I saw the clothesline—"

"Oh!" Santee hopped up. "Sorry. I should have asked. I'll take it down."

"No. No." He again motioned her to sit back down. "It's fine. But I don't imagine you have a washing machine in your camper."

Santee shook her head, wondering where in that tiny space the builders could have put one.

"Honey, you don't need to wash your clothes by hand. We have perfectly good machines here that you're welcome to use."

These people were just too much, Santee thought. They probably wouldn't even lock up the house when they left. They welcome a complete stranger into their midst then leave and just expect everything to be in its place when they returned.

"Thanks, but it's better this way."

They didn't understand, these good people. Way too trusting for their own good. Even the bodyguards had let her slip past, a wolf into a sheep shed. Pete and Joe had been through it. Their instincts should have fired off rockets, sounded the klaxons when she showed up.

Did they not question how she got here?

Because she sure as heck did. She remembered stopping in Egan for the camper. The night she found Sunny and Rufus near Mitchell was clear in her mind. But after their release from the vet hospital and her heading the camper south, there was nothing to show why she turned west and ended up in the Black Hills of western South Dakota.

She looked around at these good people. People who seemed to actually, maybe, liked her. Little did they know. And she knew she had to cut this off. Now. Before someone really got hurt.

"Um, Sir Rob." She slid the sale book across the table. "For what it's worth, I marked some horses."

"Thank you, hon. I'd like to discuss your choices sometime before the sale. Have you show me what you saw that made you choose the ones you did. And even why you didn't choose others that maybe I had my eye on."

"It'll have to be today then, since I'll be leaving first thing tomorrow."

She was picking the sketch pad up from where it leaned against her leg and didn't see Rob wince. She handed it across to Ruarke.

"I don't know beans about drawing buildings and all that prospectus stuff, but..." She shrugged. "I did what I could."

Ruarke opened it and was stunned.

Mrs. Reggie paused behind him and gave a little gasp, her hand covering her mouth. "Oh my!"

Her reaction gathered the other adults in an arc behind Ruarke.

Santee felt her face heating up. "I know it's not good."

"Not good?" Sir Rob said.

"It's beautiful!" Rosarita breathed.

Santee's sharp gaze searched for falsehood but could see only surprise and awe.

Ruarke turned to point at the main part, which looked nothing like the old square farmhouse it was now. It looked so modern, like a log house. "This?"

"I changed the roof, front and back to a big gable [a term she'd looked up on the computer that came with the camper] and pulled it out some, giving more room in the dining and living rooms and making a deep covered entrance porch. Above would be one of your friends' suite. The expansion out the back is a wide breakfast room or three-season porch. Above it is the other friend's expanded-out suite."

Ruarke pointed to the left of the front.

"A new office. Bigger so your secretary and bookkeeper have some elbow room."

Further left beyond that was a double garage. To the right was the former four-car garage now turned into family room and bedrooms above. Beyond that were two jut-outs with high peaks and lots of glass.

"Two small apartments," she said as Ruarke pointed. He looked questioningly, but she could only shrug. It had felt right and necessary when she was drawing it. They could obviously do anything they dang well wanted with it.

Beyond the apartments, barely visible was the roof to more garage stalls.

Ruarke flipped the page to the rendering of the back of the house.

His parents' wing showed a glass door opening onto the patio rounding the pool. The gable end was mostly glass up into the peak, not the most ideal, facing the north, but it would let in a lot of light on bleak winter days.

The three-season porch was glassed in on three sides. Above was the high peak, all windows, and a small deck under the extended eave, the same as in the front.

And then there was his room, a two-story affair, again with a high peak of glass facing north.

"Wow!" Mrs. Reggie said. She hurried around the table and threw her arms around Santee before she could duck away. "I love it!"

she softly squealed. She rocked Santee from side to side. "Love..."
She rocked them the other way. "Love..." Then rocked back again.
"Love it!" She planted a firm kiss on Santee's cheek.

"And to think," Mrs. Reggie said with a laugh, "all the money
we paid to that architect for something we didn't even really like. And
here"—she waved gracefully at Santee—"this young woman outdoes
them and it's something I actually like."

"Are there floorplans?" Sir Rob asked.

"Well, sure, but they're rough. I don't know about supporting
walls and this has to go here and that can't go there."

Sir Rob waved it away. "That's what we pay contractors for. I
just hope we're not too late to make some of these changes."

He came around the table just as Mrs. Reggie was relinquishing
her hold and nabbed Santee in a hug before she could escape.

Ruarke had turned back to the front of the house. "And this
space above the apartments?"

She shrugged. "More bedrooms. Bathrooms. If you can't use
them now, you'll need sleeping space when your kids get married and
come home with the grandkids."

Ruarke winced at the grandkids bit. His girls were almost their
mother's age when he'd gotten her pregnant and made his parents
young grandparents. A terrifying thought.

Santee had had no idea that her little drawings would cause
such a stir. They looked pretty amateurish to her. She was sure they'd
draw some eye-rolling and derogatory snickers when the Sinclairs
showed them to the architects. But it didn't matter. She wouldn't be
here to endure it.

For once, church went off without a hitch. Ruarke marveled at
the little boys', normally so restive and devilish, quietness. Not that
they paid the service any mind, but at least they weren't chucking
songbooks into the aisles and crawling under the pews to grab at the
other parishioners' ankles, drawing more than one outraged shriek
and a few curse words. Recently the pews around the Sinclair brood
had remained empty until all the others were filled. Only then did

anyone take the row in front or behind them. Today the kids were perfect Santee-inspired angels.

"Can we go home to Santee now?" Remmy asked, leaning his head against Ruarke's shoulder.

"Hey, Dad," Shaynee called. "We'll be right back."

Ruarke expected to see them going off to practice their flirting on some boys, but instead they were headed toward their mother, Heather, some strange guy, and their other grandparents.

"Da-ad." Remmy bumped Ruarke slightly onto his bum leg. For the first time in a long time, the jarring didn't cause him any pain.

"We were going to go out for brunch."

"Do we gotta?"

"Yah, Dad," Rio said. "Can't we just go home?"

Ruarke was so surprised at the words "Dad" and "home" being used by his boys that he was tongue-tied. He'd about given up hope that they would ever come to see him as Dad.

"Don't you want to go out and eat?" The restaurant was across the street from a park with a playground. In their little town, they felt comfortable letting the kids go play on their own after eating as long as the older kids, groaning all the way, kept watch over them. The adults could oversee from the big windows in the restaurant.

A boy on each side leaned against him. "We'd rather go be with Santee."

"We'll see." He watched as they bounded off to talk to the others, who also seemed excited about going home, except Maddie, of course, whose protest was loud and shrill.

He really wasn't looking forward to tomorrow morning and the fallout it was sure to bring.

Pete came up to Ruarke. He inclined his head toward the kids. "What's up with them?"

"They want to go home," Ruarke said. "So they can be with Santee."

"Well, I can't say I wouldn't mind that myself. I'm kinda liking that pretty little gal more and more all the time. Even when she scares the bejesus out of me."

Ruarke was shocked at the big man beside him. He was built like a professional wrestler, with huge biceps and pecs that threatened every shirt he ever wore. And he knew both Pete and Joe were always armed, even here in church. Yet he admitted he was scared of a skinny string bean like Santee.

"Man, you've had her locked eyes on you, haven't you?" Pete shivered but smiled. "Never thought I'd trust a woman to guard my back in a firefight, but she's the one. And Joe's the same way."

"Really."

"Yup. Really. And best of all, my Rosie girl likes her too." Pete's restless gaze searched through the exiting throng for any sign of a threat. "Kind of miss her now when there're so many directions to watch." Pete looked down at Ruarke's leg. He'd been standing an unusually long time. "Leg better today?"

"Actually, it is. What did she do, hypnotize me or something? Because I think I slept through it all from the moment she laid her hands on it."

Pete's beefy shoulders lifted. "Beats the hell out of me." Ruarke might have gone to sleep, but whatever she'd done, it'd about wiped her out. "Guess maybe you oughta get another treatment before you let her get away tomorrow, huh."

"Let—?" But Pete was moving off toward their parked vans. He and Joe would closely inspect each one to make sure they hadn't been tampered with while everyone had been in church.

Jamie stumbled up, his growth spurt leaving his legs too long and his feet too big for him. "Are we really going back, Ruarke?"

Ruarke read the fear in the boy's eyes, terrified that Santee wouldn't abide by her promise to be there when they got home. "We'll see what your grandparents say."

Jamie spotted them and went to plead his case but tangled his feet, landed on his knees, and bounced back up, red-faced, before actually getting going.

Rosarita's citrusy scent preceded her to Ruarke's side. Her dark eyes twinkled. "So are we going home?"

"I don't want you and the ladies to have to line up something for brunch and then this evening's barbecue too."

"Everything's ready for the barbecue," she said. "We could eat that early and line up a snack for later. Maybe break out the leftovers."

Ruarke nodded, rather relieved to be heading back also. "Okay with me if it's okay with everyone else."

Rosarita nodded. Her eyes lost a little of their normal sparkle. "Have you seen how she lets all the kids, even mine, call her Mommy Tee?"

"Does that bother you?"

"Oh no. No, no, no." Her graceful hands fluttered before her magnificent bust. "I just… She's white, and my Sophie and Pete Jr. are not. And I never thought anyone like that would treat my *niños* like their own. If something happened to me…" She whispered a prayer in Spanish and made the sign of the cross. "I'd be comforted knowing that a woman like that would raise my babies."

Hell and damnation, Ruarke thought as Rosarita swished away, her brightly flowered dress and full swaying hips gathering many appreciative male stares and narrowed female eyes. How had his life gotten so complicated so fast? It had only been forty-eight hours since the woman materialized and turned his household on its ear. Would the good she'd wrought survive the dust settling behind her camper tomorrow?

His eyes turned to the twenty-foot cross in the churchyard. *God, we might need a little help around here tomorrow.*

Santee was surprised by the caravan's return far earlier than Mrs. Reggie's estimate. The vehicle carrying Jamie must have stopped before reaching the house to let him off because moments later he raced around her camper, tangled his feet, and skidded on his face.

Santee shot to his side as he blindly patted the grass for his glasses. She found them a good three feet from where his patting hands searched.

"Here, Jamie."

He grabbed the ugly thick black framed things and perched them crookedly on his scuffed nose. He launched himself at her crouched form and bowled her over into the dirt. The dogs joined the game, dancing and barking around them as Jamie sobbed into her shoulder.

Emotional displays were not Santee's forte. All her life she'd buried feelings deep lest they be used against her. Awkwardly, she patted his back, which did seem to calm him down.

Pushing back, Jamie swiped at his cheeks and nose. He tried to straighten the ugly smeared glasses. Santee gently took them off his face and looked through the thick lens. The poor kid had to be about blind without them, and the heavily scratched glass didn't help. She pulled a purple bandanna from her pocket, huffed on the lenses, and cleaned them as best as she could.

"Did I hurt you?" Jamie asked shyly.

"No," Santee said as she arose and pulled him up too. "But who knew you were such a good tackler?"

He blushed bright red but grinned up at her. "If I just weren't so darn clumsy."

"That'll change," Santee assured him.

"Really?"

She forced herself to ruffle his silky brown hair. "You'll get the hang of this new tall body." She didn't add "eventually." She didn't want to depress the poor kid. "Let's sit down and take a look at those scrapes."

They'd called all the ranch workers, who hadn't been in their church to alert them of the change of plans. They were barbecuing early today. It was something they liked to do—get everyone together for a meal at least one Sunday a month, sometimes more often. Summers were easiest. Who didn't like a barbecue? Winters space got tight with everyone stuck in the house.

Ruarke sat on the glider on the front porch. He had never been around much in the summer, off playing baseball, so he wasn't the head grill master. He glared at his leg, which still, remarkably, didn't really hurt. He wasn't ready to take over from his dad. Not yet. He still had plans. Dreams. The itch to be back on the field, deafened by the adulation and the boos still too strong. The stench of sweaty testosterone-charged men. The heat pounding down on his head. The smell of the perfectly mown grass. The crack of the bats. Even the umpires' "Safe!" or "Out!" calls. His dreams were still filled with these things.

Joe and Pete slammed through the door, their broad shoulders hitting the jambs as they battled to get through. The house creaked at the attack.

"Someone's coming!" Joe called as he headed out the sidewalk, his hand going to his hip holster.

Pete came to get Ruarke up on his shoulder, under Ruarke's pit, to half-carry him inside. The Glock, already in his huge mitt, looked like a toy.

Shaynee and Shawnee raced out, hands waving up and down "Wait! Wait!"

"Get back inside!" Pete yelled. "Someone's coming!"

"Wait!" They held up their hands to stop them. "It's…" They looked at each other.

"Who, girls?" Pete barked.

"It, um, could be…probably is…"

Pete was about ready to boil over. Joe had already taken up a defensive position by one of the construction trailers.

"Shaynee, who is it?" Ruarke demanded.

"Mom," she finally said.

Ruarke heard Pete say, "Oh crap," under his breath. Heather tended to be not so nice to the help. She was too much of a princess. Employees were merely peasants, way beneath her need to be polite to. She disliked Rosarita mainly because of her brown skin. Sniping about illegal aliens and INS didn't sit well with the Sinclairs and enraged Pete. Rosarita's family had been in the US for generations, far longer than either the Hendersons or Sinclairs.

Heather and Regina Sinclair had never seen eye to eye, even before Heather dumped two squalling babies on the Sinclairs' doorstep in the middle of the night. Then when Ruarke hit the big time, she had the gall to sue for alimony. Little did she know the outcome was going to be her owing child support, of which he hadn't seen dime one.

So there was not a lot of love lost between the Sinclairs and the Hendersons. But then there were Shaynee and Shawnee, and it was necessary to make nice through gritted teeth.

Shawnee said, "And maybe Grandpa and Grandma." She looked to her sister. Softy she added, "And Mom's new boyfriend."

"Double crap," Pete muttered.

"Girls!" Rob and Reggie stood in the doorway.

"We're sorry," they exclaimed, "but we were talking, and they kind of—"

"Invited themselves over," Shawnee finished.

"That was before we knew we were barbecuing early," Shaynee said miserably.

"We went to tell them not to come," Shawnee said. "But they'd already left."

"And you know Grandpa Henderson doesn't allow phones on when he's driving."

There were a lot of things that Lawrence Henderson didn't allow. Like his beloved daughter openly dating the neighbor's kid. They had threatened statutory rape charges if Ruarke didn't marry her and then refused to allow her to live with her husband or him to visit. The annulment after the babies' births was a relief to everyone.

As the dust cloud neared, Pete went off to warn Joe. Reggie gave Ruarke and Rob a gloomy look before heading inside to warn the women to set out four more plates.

Shaynee and Shawnee had their heads together psst-psst-psst-ing. When the Lexus SUV rolled to a stop, Shawnee pranced down the sidewalk while Shaynee raced into the house.

Rob looked questioningly at Ruarke, but he could only shrug. The workings of his daughters' minds left him clueless.

"Well," Rob said as the Hendersons came toward the house. Sharron picked her way along as if afraid she'd step in something nasty on her expensive heels. Lawrence, never Larry, held on to her arm as if afraid someone might steal her or that she'd get lost on the short walk.

The women wore bright summer dresses that probably cost a little less than the national debt and enough diamonds to choke a horse. Sharron's face was so tight that she looked out at the world in constant surprise. Heather's face appeared to have had its first session with the plastic surgeon.

Lawrence wore a beautiful silk western-cut suit. He doffed his Stetson as he held his hand out to Rob.

"Robert." His beady eyes were cool as they switched to Ruarke's leg as Ruarke arose also. His grip on Ruarke's hand was meant to dominate, but Ruarke met his grip just as firmly as always, meeting the older man's arrogant gaze.

"Oh, Ruarke!" Heather gushed as she bus-kissed his cheeks. Her perfume was almost overpowering and probably just that expensive too. "Oh, your poor leg!"

This was not the first time she'd seen his "poor" leg. She made a move to touch it, but her companion stepped up. He looked familiar. Suave, smooth, pampered skin, and sharp eyes, he held out his hand and tried to crush Ruarke's. "Grant Marshal," he stated with pride, as if assured that the mere mention of his name would be all the introduction he'd ever need. He put his arm possessively around Heather's slim waist and hauled her close.

Ruarke kept his face blank, not giving the man the recognition he craved. The name did tinkle a tiny bell. Some TV actor, but since he rarely watched TV, he didn't really know more than the name.

As everyone was getting seated, stealthy movement around the corner of the house drew Ruarke's attention. Shaynee, with a bundle clutched to her chest, slunk on tiptoes until she reached the drive, then she took off.

Rob raised his brows to Ruarke, but Ruarke didn't have any answers.

Lawrence stretched his legs across the porch like a blockade. Sharron's lip curled as she brushed off the cushions with a delicate hanky before perching on the edge. Heather sat on Grant's lap though there were other chairs. His hand rested possessively on her shapely hip.

"So, Ruarke," Lawrence boomed, "how's rehab going? Gonna be able to play ever again?"

Ruarke didn't give the man the satisfaction of wincing. "That's the plan, Lawrence."

"That's right," Grant said, leaning too eagerly forward. "You were that ballplayer that got shot, weren't you? So tragic. Heather mentioned it, but I don't follow much sports, so it never made any impression, sorry."

Ruarke just bet the man didn't know anything about it. Grant probably loved the opportunity to twist the knife a little. Ruarke shrugged. "I've had a good run. If I never step foot on a diamond again, I've got good memories, a ton of awards, and enough money to last a lifetime. So I'm good."

"Really?" Sharron said. "With those—what is it—five more children? Are you sure you're able to financially handle it? We'd hate to think of our darling girls having to scrimp for anything because you took in those orphans."

"Two of those orphans happen to be my sons with Rachel and the other three are fantastic kids. Rachel and her husband left a big house that I sold and plenty of life insurance, so they're financially set."

"But they have to share a bedroom," Heather said with a shudder. "At their age—"

"We like to share a room, Mother," Shawnee said.

They'd been so locked into picking at each other that they hadn't noticed the girls' return. And the almost unrecognizable vision that tucked the bow of her sunglasses into her cleavage and gave him a sly wink.

Ruarke and Rob stood, Lawrence turned around sharply, and Grant shot to his feet, almost dumping Heather to the floor.

Santee wore a touch of makeup, just enough to accent her eyes and lips. She had a gauzy white blouse open to the waist, where it was tied. Beneath it peaked out a lacy chemise. The skirt she wore was reminiscent of the one Sandra Bullock wore in *Speed* in pale purple, lightweight enough that, in the right angle of light, her strong thighs were visible. The skirt was short, exposing a mile of slender legs down to the lace-topped anklets showing over the top of short brown boots.

Rob leaned close. "Shut your mouth, son, and be damn appreciative. She's doing this for you."

Santee stepped into the group, hand held out to Lawrence. "Hello, I'm Santee."

She did the same to each, having to jerk her hand out of Grant's grasp. Her mouth tightened warningly at his avaricious gaze roaming slow as a caress over her. He grinned like the Cheshire Cat when Santee, who was a couple of inches taller, put her lips to his ear. The smile froze, and he paled as Santee's breath whispered against his ear. She pulled back and looked closely at him. He gave a sharp nod then forced a shit-eating smile as if he'd just made a conquest.

But Ruarke knew differently. Santee had just put the man in his place, probably with the threat of dire repercussions. He noted Grant's glance at the girls and the way Santee shifted to block his lascivious gaze. Ruarke's hands locked on the crutches' grip. Damn him! If he so much as—!

Santee was at his side, now using her body to block his view of the SOB Grant. "Easy," she whispered, her lips grazing his cheek. "Just a warning to a lecher. I think it took. Don't you?"

Grant seemed to have lost his arrogant machismo and looked surprised and deflated by its loss. His hands shook just a bit as he hauled Heather onto his lap. He jerked his hand away from her worried, questioning touch. "I'm fine," he growled, making Heather pull back from this unseen side of him. Knowing he'd gone too far, he grabbed her hand and noisily kissed her palm, making her giggle. All was again right in her world.

Ruarke couldn't help but grin. Oh, yes, whatever Santee had said to the bastard had indeed had its desired effect.

Santee motioned for Ruarke to sit and bent over to help his leg onto the stool, giving him a sweat-popping glance down at the small mounds half-hidden within the lace. Her narrow behind just happened to be pointed at Grant, and damned if she didn't give it a little wiggle. Grant went beet red, and he swallowed hard. Heather noticed and turned to see what had so distracted him, but Santee had already settled tight to Ruarke's side, pressing those lovely breasts against his arm as she slithered her fingers around his wrist, over his palm, and interlacing their digits.

Ruarke felt his own heart rate kick it up a notch. Santee wiggled her eyebrows at him as if laughing at the ease with which she'd riled him up. Her fresh Ivory-Soap scent overlaid with a vanilla-y fragrance that probably cost pennies compared with Heather's designer perfume all went straight to his groin. It had been a long time since he'd felt this level of activity below the belt.

He saw the twinkle of amusement in her normally icy eyes before she put the dark glasses on. He wasn't used to women having that reaction to him. It put a hell of a big damper on his ardor, to have the woman think he was the silliest thing ever.

"Oh god!" Heather squealed. She pointed at Sunny as the dog hopped up next to Santee.

"How awful!" She glared at Ruarke. "You should have shot it and put it out of its misery!"

Rufus squeezed past a bunch of knees until he found a preferred one.

"A pit bull!" Heather screeched. She pulled her legs up into Grant's lap, preventing him from retreating himself.

Santee slid her hand from Ruarke's and ruffled both dogs' ears.

"My God, Ruarke!" Heather shrieked. "You can't have a pit bull around the girls! It could kill them in their sleep!"

"Rufus," Santee said, amusement in her voice. The dog's long tail slapped powerfully side to side, making Grant wince at the impact with his shins. "Would you do that?" He put his head up to Santee's face, broad tongue flicking at her. "Would you kill someone in their sleep?"

Santee eased her sunglasses down to look at Heather huddled upon her boyfriend's lap. "Rufus wouldn't hurt a fly. And he is mine. Not Ruarke's." She hugged Sunny. "As for Sunny, whether she lives or dies is my decision. If I thought she was in pain, I'd do something about it. My decision. My responsibility."

"Surely," Lawrence stated, "even you [Santee stiffened at the sanctimonious tone, and she turned her laser eyes directly on him] can understand that a dog like that has no place anywhere near our grandchildren."

Shaynee and Shawnee watched, wide-eyed. Santee cleared her throat to get their attention and jerked her head toward the house, sending them inside.

"I can agree with wanting to shield and protect those two beautiful young ladies for as long as possible."

Lawrence puffed out his chest and nodded regally.

"However, even I can see that you're not looking close enough to home." She inclined her head toward where Heather was huddled, her hiked-up skirt showing a hint of bare cheeks. "Is your daughter and her boyfriend sharing a bed? Is that the message you want to send to your teenage granddaughters, that it's okay to sleep with just anyone?"

Heather squeaked, "We're not doing anything wrong!"

"Maybe not for someone, um, your age."

Ruarke hid a huge grin behind his hand as a couple of snorts sounded.

"Also, you might want to check for some white powder, smokeable green leafy stuff, or some other illegal substance in pill form as Mr. Marshal is famous for enjoying."

Both Marshall and Lawrence went beet red as the Henderson women exchanged questioning looks. Ruarke hoped they didn't have two heart attacks to handle at the same time.

Marshal shoved upright, all but dumping Heather, who squealed in protest. "How dare you!" Grant raged. "I could sue for libel."

Slowly, majestically, Santee arose and leaned into Marshal's contorted but guilty face. "It's slander, numb nuts." Again came the snorts. "Even I know that." She turned to Lawrence, who'd also jerked upright, hauling Sharron with him. "I would suggest you look to manage your own bad or harmful influences before you come over here and try to tell us what to do."

"Daddy!" Heather cried.

Henderson was in a staring contest with Santee. Her small smile fanned the flames even more. He jerked toward Rob. "Are you going to let that-that—?"

Rob shot to his feet. "Careful, Henderson."

Heather tried to get in Santee's face, but Rufus, with his goofy show of very long, very white teeth, sat on his mistress's toes. "How dare you talk to us like that!" She stamped her foot and angled it back as if to kick.

"I wouldn't," Santee stated.

Heather met her gaze, eyes widening at the look in Santee's eyes, and carefully put her foot down. "Daddy?"

"We're leaving," he declared.

"So soon?" Santee trilled. "That's so sad. And after you invited yourselves to dinner."

Lawrence grabbed Sharron's arm, whipping a startled cry out of her. They stalked past Pete and Joe, who weren't being very successful in hiding their amusement.

Heather tried to intrude into Santee's space again, but Rufus, sensing the antagonism, had shifted, forcing Heather farther away. "I hope you burn in hell!"

Santee leaned over Rufus, forcing Heather to draw back, almost knocking Marshal down onto the chair. "Been there." Heather's jaw dropped. "Done that." Santee winked. "Learned a lot of dirty survival techniques, if you get my drift."

Heather's mouth worked like a goldfish out of water and was just as bug-eyed.

"In other words," Santee sibilantly whispered, "you do not want to screw with me. I fight dirty. Dirtier than some pampered piece of fluff like you could ever imagine."

Heather whimpered, whether in fear or frustration. She looked to pasty-faced Grant.

"Shut up," he hissed. He grabbed her arm, making her squeal in pain.

"Grant!" Her stiletto heels made her mince as she struggled to keep up. "Grant?"

"Shut the fuck up, Heather!"

"Don't leave mad!" Santee called, hands around her mouth to form a megaphone.

Car doors slammed. The big engine roared. Tires spun, shooting gravel and dust as the SUV fishtailed into a turn and shot out the driveway.

Silence settled on the porch, the only sound the slight creaking of the glider as Sunny shifted tight to the back of Santee's legs.

Then a chuckle burst, breaking up Santee's second thoughts about how badly she'd overstepped her place. All heads turned toward Rob. Rob looked at their surprised faces and snorted; guffaws rocked him as tears streamed down his cheeks.

Santee looked at Ruarke, eyebrows wiggling a question about Rob's sanity. Ruarke's chuckle painted her cheeks red. Pete and Joe whooped, slapping each other ungently on the back.

Santee shook her head at them. "Sir Rob, I—"

Rob held up his hand as he fought for breath. "Don't you dare apologize." He planted his hands on his knees as he gasped. "I only have one regret."

Santee waited for him to put her in her place. After all, she wasn't a Sinclair. She'd had no right to say what she did to their former in-laws, the twins' mother and grandparents, for Pete's sake.

"I wish we'd gotten that on tape so w-we c-could have s-see their expressions—" He snorted out another burst of guffaws.

"Um, Grandpa," Shawnee said from the open living room window. "We, um, kind of did tape it. Just in case."

Roars reverberated on the patio.

Santee shot a glare at the girls huddled just beyond the screens. She hadn't sent them into the house so they could turn around and listen at the window. There was movement behind as Mrs. Reggie and Rosarita moved into view, tears streaming from their dancing eyes.

"It was Grandma's idea," Shawnee said.

"Mrs. Reggie!" Santee turned to the girls. "I should not have spoken to them like that. They are my elders. I should have been more polite."

Shaynee said, "But they were dissing you first."

Dissing?

Ruarke laid a hesitant hand on Santee's shoulder. It tensed at his touch but didn't shrug him away. "Quit kicking yourself. You only said what we've wanted to for years."

Rob moved to her and gave her a firm hug. Then he headed for the door, chuckles following in his wake.

"And, Santee?" Ruarke said. "Thank you for all—" He motioned up and down at her garb.

Her cheeks flushed. "Thank your girls. It was all their ideas."

"But you didn't have to do it."

"I couldn't just let you flounder among the sharks, and my usual attire wouldn't have had the desired effect."

Joe snorted. "That's for sure."

Santee jerked toward him. His appreciative look made her blush. "I think I'd better change."

"Oh," Pete said. "Do you have to?"

Rosarita came out and slapped her husband's arm, still laughing. "Come on, everyone. Let's eat."

The others went inside, their laughing voices resounding. It was far different than the funeral-like atmosphere if the Hendersons had stayed.

Ruarke dared to slide his arm around Santee's waist. "Don't change."

Danged if he didn't take her breath away and make her very aware of his raw maleness. It was a strange feeling, not something she'd ever allowed herself to notice before. Actually, she thought that had been killed a long time ago.

Santee still wore the flirty skirt that evening and felt daring doing so. It was probably something she'd never do again in this lifetime.

She had the sale booklet and approached Sir Rob. "I hate to bother you."

He smiled gently up at her and took her hand. "You could never bother me." His smile widened as his eyes twinkled in memory. "Especially not after today."

Dang it, she could feel her cheeks flame again. She hadn't blushed in years, and that's all she seemed to do. She showed him the booklet. "Would now be a good time?"

His smile froze. "Wouldn't you like to wait until tomorrow?"

She just shook her head and turned toward the huge dining room table that was actually two tables with all the leaves they could hold. She took her normal seat then shifted to Rio's, which was on her left between hers and Sir Rob.

Surprisingly, all the adults wandered in also. Coffee scented the air, and the ladies, Rosarita, Mrs. Reggie and Mrs. Wilson, opened Tupperware containers of leftovers, cookies, and cakes.

She'd hoped this would be a private meeting where they could go over her choices and she could thank him for everything and…

Ruarke sat across from her in his normal spot. The other adults, normally seated with kids separating them, had moved down to Sir Rob's end of the table.

Coffee was poured for everyone except her. An unopened can of Dr. Pepper was placed before her by Rosarita. Dang it, they even knew that she didn't drink coffee and didn't trust anyone else to open her drinks. These people were worming into her brain, but if they really knew her, they'd be only too happy to see her taillights tomorrow.

"Santee, honey." Mrs. Reggie was behind her and gently caught Santee's hand, easing it away from the back of her neck. She tsk-tsked and gave the red-topped spray can a quick shake. Icy coolness floated across inflamed skin.

"The gnats really did a number on your neck," Mrs. Reggie said and set the can beside the Dr. Pepper. "Take this and spray it whenever your neck starts to itch." She patted Santee's shoulder and turned away before Santee could protest.

These people! Santee gulped the sweet drink. They were just too…too…well, nice. Way too nice for the likes of her.

Santee reached for the booklet to get this over with, but Sir Rob slid it away.

"Before we do that, I'd like to talk to you."

Oh, crap!

"Do you have a reason for going to Texas?"

Oh, she had a reason all right. But it wasn't something she could share with these goody-two-shoes people. "Yes."

"A job?"

She shook her head, not liking where this conversation seemed to be going.

"Relatives to visit?"

She covered a snort with her hand. The only relatives she had had made it plain they'd just as soon see her dead. So again, she shook her head.

"Good!" He slapped his palms on the table. "So you can stay here!"

It shouldn't have been a shock, but his statement still shot her to her feet. "Sir Rob! No!"

He motioned her to sit, which she reluctantly did. "Why not?" he asked reasonably. "If you have no reason to go to Texas, and we want you to stay here, why don't you just stay with us?"

Santee knew her mouth gaped open as she looked around at the people nodding and grinning. Even Ruarke seemed to be in favor, the fool. She thought he'd at least have more sense.

"I can think of several."

Sir Rob leaned back. "So let's see if we"—he motioned toward the others at the table—"can counteract your misgivings."

Santee arose and started to pace. She wanted out of this so badly, but she respected these people too much to just tell them to f—— off. It was her life, and it didn't include them.

"First." She held up a finger. "I don't do horses. I never intend to do horses. Yet somehow I feel you have included me in your horsey plans."

Sir Rob at least had the decency to flush a bit.

"Second." Two fingers went up. "Other than that, you don't really need me without inventing a job for me."

"Not true," Sir Rob stated. "I need an assistant. Someone to drive when I have to visit our other properties, giving me time to work on other stuff during the drive."

"Rob's right," Mrs. Reggie spoke up. "I always worry whenever he heads off on his own to the pig farm or all the way east to Mitchell and the grain farm. I'd feel so much more at peace knowing you were with him."

"Sooo," Santee drawled. "Y'all'd be willing to send your husband off with a much younger female on what sounds like a two-or-more day excursion?"

Mrs. Reggie took a calm sip of coffee before setting the cup down. "Do you have designs on my Robert?" She smiled at Santee's reaction. "Didn't think so." She looked balefully at her husband. "Are you thinking of tossing me aside for a younger model?"

Sir Rob was beet red. "God, no." He lurched around to his wife of thirty-two years and crushed her into a kiss.

Mrs. Reggie smiled serenely. "Didn't think so. So, no, I have no objection to sending my husband off with a young beautiful chickie like you."

It took Santee a moment to get past their open display of affection and trust in each other. In her place, Santee knew she'd never let it happen. It'd just be asking for trouble.

"Three." A third finger raised. "I don't do snow and cold." She knew she had him there. Even he couldn't change South Dakota's climate.

"We do get some cold and some snow, but the Black Hills is often called the banana belt. The envy of the rest of South Dakota because the cold and snow are usually short-lived. Here and gone while the rest of the state still suffers. So we could do a trial run of, say, until the first measurable snow and then talk again."

"I seem to remember, not too long ago, that you had a major blizzard the first part of October."

They winced at the memory of cattle buried in snow up to their bellies and smothered by the wind-driven fury. They'd lost a third of their Angus cattle, many only days away from being shipped out to the sale barn. At least they'd had Ruarke's baseball money to fall back on and see them through the rebuilding. Others hadn't been so lucky.

"Sooo," Santee said, "if that were the case I'd be here a little over a month. Hardly worth it."

"Oh, honey," Sir Rob said. "I think you'd be so overcome with pity that you'd stick around."

Santee shook her head. "You don't know me near as well as you think. I'm more of a cut-and-run kinda gal than a 'stand by your man on a sinking ship' kinda gal."

Sir Rob smiled. "I think you're wrong there, child, but continue on."

Did these people never accept defeat? Santee held up a fourth finger. "Probably the most compelling is the kids. And I think this is a Mrs. Wilson question. How do you think another month of me hanging around will affect the kids, given how attached they already seem to be getting?"

The retired teacher took a moment and a sip of coffee before saying, "You're right, the children are going to be deeply affected whether you leave now or later. I personally don't think they could get any more attached. And I remember how they were before you arrived here. Their behavior, their happiness, their comfort in these new circumstances are very high right now. I fear a serious setback if you leave."

"Would that setback be any less if I stayed another month?"

"Probably not," she admitted.

"If I left now, they'd have time to settle back down before school starts."

She nodded. "True. But staying could give the children a good start in school and another month to settle in here." She shrugged. "There's no way to know for sure what's best, one way or the other."

Not exactly what Santee wanted to hear. She'd thought it would fall more toward her getting out of their lives so they could settle in and get over her.

"Number five." She drew a deep breath, forcing herself to reveal a morsel if it meant they'd push her out. "If you really knew me, you'd kick me out rather than trying to keep me here." She looked at each attentive listener. "I was not brought up in the best of environments." A major understatement. "Corporal punishment was meted out without mercy even for the most minor of wrong doings." She shrugged. "You hear about how adults grow up to reflect their upbringing. Well, that's me."

Fists clenched, she turned away from the sympathetic looks, drew a resolute breath, and turned back. "You have no idea how many times I've had to fight off the overwhelming urge to smack one of these kids. I can't stand their noise, the running around, the clinginess." She shuddered. "In my life, a touch involved pain, always."

"Santee..." Sir Rob tried to move in to give a hug of comfort, but she held her hand out to stop him.

"That is a prime example. Your first instinct is to hug and comfort. Mine is to give a slap upside the head or worse, probably much worse. And—" She cleared her throat. "And if that ever happened... if I ever fell back on my past and actually hit one of these kids, I could never live with myself." Her eyes were bleak. "And I would expect, no, I would demand that I be put down with all the sympathy you'd show a rabid dog."

Sunny was nudging anxiously at Santee's fist. Rufus whined up at her on the other side as he pressed heavily against her leg.

"In fact," Santee stated. "This." She waved her hands at the dogs. "This is enough to drive me over the edge. It would kill me to do something hurtful to these two really great dogs, which I've come oh so close to many times. So..." She jerked her sunglasses down over her stinging eyes. "So I need you to take them off my hands too. For their sakes. And for mine."

She spun for the door, tangling into Rufus, catching herself, and rushing out. The two dogs barely made it through the doorway before the door slammed.

That hadn't been so hard.

It just took slicing open a vein.

No big deal.

———————————

Chapter 13

Santee pushed the stroller toward the house. The dogs danced around her, anticipating a run. They had watched her load all their belongings: two kinds of dog food, tennis balls, bowls, blankets, and Sunny's meds into the stroller.

It was early, the sun barely up. All was packed and ready to pull out. She'd just dump the dogs. No need for goodbyes. Enough had been said last night.

As soon as she opened the door, six people looked at her from their chairs at the table. So much for the easy way out.

Sir Rob stood and faced her, his normal bonhomie hidden behind a serious facade. "Santee. Come in. We've been waiting for you."

Not good. Not good at all. Those were not the faces of people who'd gotten up extra early to see someone off.

"Sit down." Sir Rob motioned to her seat. "We need to talk."

Stubbornly, Santee waited at the door. "I think it was all said last night."

"Oh no, dear," Mrs. Reggie said. "You didn't give us a chance to rebut all your points. So sit down."

Obedience was so ingrained that her knees actually buckled as different parts of her moved in obedience while others tried to stay put.

Everyone turned at a pair of feet banging down the stairs, as Jamie burst around the doorway into the dining room. A stuffed backpack dangled from his arm as he struggled with a crammed pillowcase. Buddy danced at his side, eyes locked on the case with his belongings, especially his beloved tennis balls.

"We're ready!"

A fist closed around her gut. "Jamie," Santee said, shaking her head.

"You need me!" he insisted. "I can do all the reading and writing for you. All you'd have to do is sign your name." He pushed Buddy away from the ball-shaped bulge in the corner of the pillow case. "We won't be any trouble. And I don't eat much. And Buddy... Well, I could get a job after school to pay for his food. And—"

Santee didn't remember moving, but she was standing in front of the boy. Her hands shook as she laid them on his trembling shoulders. "Jamie," she said softly, only too aware that what she said right now could have a huge impact on this child. "That is a wonderful sacrifice you're willing to make and I am unbelievably honored, but—"

"No!" he moaned as he dropped the pillowcase and flung his arms around her, crushing the breath from her lungs.

Carefully Santee pried his chin up. "Jamie—"

"Jamie," Sir Rob cut in. "Santee is staying for a while longer, so you don't have to worry."

Santee's head torqued around, hitting its limit with a chiropractic-inducing crack. "Sir Rob," she warned.

"We voted," he said. "And it was unanimous. Until the first snow flies."

Jamie was watching her so closely, hope shining. She had to be so careful. "I see Mrs. Wilson isn't here. Was hers a dissenting vote?"

"Nope," Sir Rob said. "She's down at Pete's in case the girls wake up, but she voted as we did. We're keeping you."

"Didn't you hear what I said?"

Pete said, "We heard. Rosarita and I talked." He grabbed Rosarita's hand, kissing it before pulling her down onto his lap. "We're going to change our wills so that you and Ruarke inherit our kids if anything should happen to us. That's how worried we are by what you said."

Santee rocked as if an explosion's shockwave walloped her. Never all that voluble, she was at a loss for words, her poor brain racing around like a squirrel in a cage.

Joe came around and held out his big black hand. "Keys."

She just blinked, still befuddled. He noticed the bulge in her pocket and carefully, with two fingers, fished them out. "I'll get the camper set back up. And if it came to it, I give you my word should you ever turn rabid, I would put you down. It would kill me, but I'd do it." He tossed her keys into the air. He caught them, then he gave her a wink and strode out, grabbing the stroller as he went past.

Santee looked around at the remaining people but found no ally to her cause. When her gaze landed on Ruarke…was that a smirk? She narrowed her eyes on him, but he deflected them, not bothering to hide a smile.

"Is it true, Santee?" Jamie looked up at her, his chin fit perfectly between her boobs. "Are we staying?"

We?

The knot in her gut tightened. They'd cornered her so slickly. Just when she'd thought she had it whipped.

Oh, well, Texas would always be there. Somewhere.

In the blink of an eye, Santee found herself in possession of a credit card for ranch expenses and a credit card from Ruarke for the kids' expenses. When she asked about a limit, he'd shrugged it away, telling her he'd let her know if he felt she was overspending. Oh, the tribulations of being rich. She'd also had to get her wages, the amount still a mystery, direct deposited to her bank in Egan. Her poor brain reeled from trying to see so many wormy lines and get her name on them. Thank goodness her name was short. She'd felt so conspicuous, leaning close, trying to tame the restless lines and knowing that the perfectly coffered woman, who'd greeted Sir Rob as Mr. Sinclair and Ruarke by his first name, was eyeing her, probably wondering how the Sinclairs had ended up with such a loser. Santee wondered that herself more than once.

"Umm, Dad," Shawnee said at breakfast.

Ruarke had been looking out at the arriving carpenters. But he was actually looking beyond and dreading the arrival of the physical therapist, a sadist if ever there was one. "What, hon?"

"School starts Monday."

"Really?"

"Yes, and we still haven't gotten our back-to-school stuff yet."

Oh, joy. He'd never done it, taken the girls to get their supplies or new clothes, and his mom never complained, but the horror stories his teammates had told made him glad that his kids were his mother's responsibility, coward that he was. And now with five more? Just fantastic!

"Maybe," Shaynee said, "Santee could take us?"

Santee looked up from stewing about how worthless she'd been so far. She shrugged. "If they know what they need?"

"There'll be flyers that list what each grade requires," Mrs. Reggie said.

Santee eyed her suspiciously. Was that relief on her guileless face?

"And if it's okay with your grandpa."

Why wouldn't it be okay? Sir Rob needed an assistant about as much as Shaq needed to grow another twelve inches.

"It's fine with me. Just be sure you shop in town first before you head off to Walmart in Rapid."

"Wouldn't it be cheaper at Walmart?" Santee said. "Considering how many kids you've got here?"

"Maybe," Sir Rob admitted. "But we shop locally as much as possible. If our local businesses close up, the town starts to die. And we don't want that."

Santee shrugged. "Makes no difference to me. Do I need to change clothes?"

"Stand up! Stand up!" Joe exclaimed with a huge grin.

The supercilious look she gave him only made his grin broaden. She arose and stuck a hip-shot model pose. The jean shorts were faded but clean and holeless. The sleeveless snap-buttoned shirt had tails that hung down over her shapely rump. Snap shut another button and the hint of a lace chemise would be concealed. The cheap rubber Walmart sandals were still serviceable, but she could easily swap them for tennies. Laced through her belt was a smallish leather rectangular pouch just large enough to carry the essentials.

"Turn around." Joe rotated his finger in a twirling motion.

Santee would have liked to tell him what he could do with that finger, but there were little ears taking it all in. She hoped the yellow lenses didn't cover the look she gave him, but apparently it did because the fool didn't seem fazed.

"You look fine," Sir Rob said. "Joe, maybe you could go along and help out."

The strong beefy black man's face froze. "Um, just the two of us?"

Santee looked at the eleven young innocent faces. How hard could it be? But then she looked at Maddie.

The clerks' eyes widened when the eleven kids, two adults, and one service dog entered the general store. (Sunny proudly wore the vest that Sir Rob had put on her.) Already the store reverberated with the screams of an irate toddler and the wail of a baby. And here were four little boys coming in. They envisioned the toy department destroyed when they left.

Santee felt naked walking around without her full pack and only one dog. Though neither dog was a guard dog, they were watchful. Sunny was allowed in, though Santee had wondered where that service dog vest had come from.

"Hi," Shawnee called to the very pregnant teenage clerk. Both clerks recognized who she was, just not which one she was. Surprisingly Santee never had that problem. "Back-to-school shopping."

"Hope you still have some supplies," Shaynee said.

"Oh, yes, girls," the older woman said. "But you're cutting it rather close."

"I know." Shawnee laughed. "We had to remind Dad."

"How is your father doing?"

"Yuh." The younger one's eyes gleamed at the expected secret info. "Heard tell he'll never play ball again."

Santee started to bristle, but Shaynee merrily deflected the nosiness with a laugh. "He's rehabbing hard every day."

Joe and Jamie grabbed carts. The Fabulous Four boys attached, two to a side, to the cart Jamie handed off to Santee. Rio pushed the other cart while Remmy steered Santee's. Shaynee and Shawnee each held the hand of a little girl and led the way. The school supplies were in the same place as every year.

"Um, Santee," Jamie said. "They've got a box for donated school supplies, if you're interested.'

She nodded. "Thanks for noticing that." And since there was no limit on the credit card, the Sinclairs would be donating.

"Okay, the Fab Four will go first."

Maddie stamped her little foot. "I'm supposed to go first! My mommy says so."

"Then your mommy should be here herself. I'm here, and it's my rules."

Maddie's mouth opened to scream, but Santee held up her finger. "One word and you'll go to school without anything."

"My m—"

"Joe, can you handle this while Maddie and I wait in the van?"

"Sure can."

Maddie's mouth pouted shut. Tears glimmered in her lovely angry eyes. She stamped her Sunday-best hard-soled white shoes on the worn wooden floor, but she didn't dare to speak out.

"All righty, then. The Fab Four go first."

Backpacks were first on the list so each boy could pile his booty inside. There was a wide range of prices, anywhere from a couple of bucks to fifty. Santee got the boys situated in front of the low end but not cheapest ones. "Jamie, will you pick out an extra backpack? We'll fill it to donate."

Shaynee had the list and checked off each item with five slashes. Shawnee took a Sharpie and wrote names on the backpack tag since all four packs were the same color blue with dinosaurs! Later at home, each item would be marked with the proper name.

The full packs were put in the cart, the donation one in the child seat.

"Okay, girls."

Maddie launched as if hit with a cattle prod. Santee winced at the remembrance. Maddie nabbed a huge backpack out of the most expensive pile. She whirled around triumphantly, but Santee slipped it free and tossed it back.

Her mouth opened to wail, but Santee help up her finger. "We can still go sit in the van if that's what you want."

The mouth closed, eyes blazing and little fists clenching.

There are several nice Disney-themed bags. Sophie happily made her choice. Maddie's eyes gleamed with covetousness. She reached out to grab it away, but again Santee stepped between them, preventing the tenderhearted Sophie from giving it up. "Choose another one."

Hard soles sounded like cracks of thunder as Maddie stamped to the pile. Her shoulders trembled, and she sniffed noisily, looking over her shoulder to see if she was melting any cold hard hearts. Finally, after three were picked, only to be rejected just before her name went on the tag, Santee prevented the return of the fourth and gave it to Shawnee. The little mouth opened to protest but remained silent beneath Santee's stare.

"From now on, girls, your first choice is the one you get. We're not spending all day here."

Maddie could have spent twenty minutes just choosing and rejecting notebook colors.

Then came the battle over crayons. Maddie wanted the sixty-four pack with the built-in sharpener. The kindergarten list called for a smaller pack. Maddie ended up with the much smaller pack. And finally, their packs were closed as well as the one Jamie had filled for donation and put in the carts.

It took a fraction of the time for the remaining kids to pick and fill a backpack, plus three more to donate.

The carts and kids were rolling toward the front past the other last-minute school shoppers, most of whom were having as much fun dealing with their kids as Santee had with Maddie.

The draining of adrenaline made Santee's knees wobbly. She leaned down, and Sunny put her face up, warm breath breathing calming strength into Santee's face. A big black hand fell on her shoulder and squeezed.

"You done good, girl," he rumbled and went off after the kids.

It was all the kids, Santee thought. Entitled brats were taking over the world demanding and getting anything they wanted. The harried women here were willing to give anything just to get it over and done with. She'd only had Maddie to stand firm with, and she was exhausted. How did parents do this twenty-four hours a day, day after day after day?

This was an excellent reason for good birth control. Or in her case, not being able to get pregnant. Good thing, that. She'd have made a terrible parent.

*****

The sadistic therapist was gone, though he'd seemed surprised, shocked even, by the progress since last week. But it hadn't made him go any easier on Ruarke, though achy the leg wasn't knifing his breath away.

After a hot tub soak and a shower, Ruarke felt at loose ends. The kids were gone. Santee was gone. Work continued on the house… The carpenters had been warned of changes to the plans. They had Santee's renderings and were consulting with the architect, who had faxed copies waiting in his office this morning.

"I sure am glad you sent Joe with Santee," Pete said.

Ruarke knew Pete was referring to Maddie. He hadn't realized what a brat she could be. His mom had never complained, but then she wouldn't. She'd always wanted a whole house full of kids.

A memory of another little girl threatened to bubble up, but Ruarke squelched it. Not today. Life was too good today to let that spoil it.

"How do you suppose it's going?" Ruarke said.

Pete whipped out his phone to call Joe. There was a lot of uh-huhs and reallys and more than a few appreciative chuckles.

Ruarke poked Pete. "What's up?"

"Hold on." Pete put the phone to his chest. "They're all done."

"Really?"

"Really. They're just heading out to the drive-in for a treat before—"

Ruarke·shoved to his feet. "Tell them to wait. Go to the park for a while. We'll drive in and join them. Have lunch instead of just a treat."

Pete relayed the message. "Joe says okay. We're to meet them at the park."

"Great! Let's tell the ladies to save dinner. Grab Rosarita and see if the folks want to come along and head into town."

*****

The municipal park included a softly bubbling creek within the picnic area. Several small shelter houses covered individual tables, plus there was a large shelter with a stone fireplace and approximately thirty tables. Nearby, the playground, complete with swings, slides, monkey bars, teeter-totters, an old-fashioned merry-go-round, and rocking animals for the little tykes, awaited their kids.

Farther away were two basketball/tennis courts, a small skate-board park, and a baseball diamond.

Santee, Joe, and Jamie sat at a table near the play equipment. The sun beat mercilessly on their heads and shoulders. It was going to be another hot one. Good thing they had a pack of bottled water for the sweaty kids and panting dog.

There were a few other kids on the playthings. Their mothers grouped together, eyeing Santee and Joe distrustfully.

The boys didn't know any of the other kids but integrated easily. Shawnee and Shaynee pushed Maddie and Sophie on the swings; Maddie's demands for "higher! higher!" grated in the quiet.

"I think we're a major topic of conversation," Joe said.

Santee nodded, distracted by the sensation of being watched by someone or something other than the women. Restlessly she searched, but there were too many hiding places, too many trees, too many picnic shelters, and too many boulders along the creek.

Joe bopped Santee's shoulder with his. "You'd almost think they'd never seen an interracial couple before."

Full raven brows lifted over the sunglasses. Santee folded her hands over her heart and in a sweet girly voice said, "Are y'all asking me to go steady?"

His chuckle rumbled. "Truth to tell, I doubt I could handle a young chickie like you."

"Believe me," Santee said. "I'm better when seen from afar."

Where the heck was that watcher? Santee kept scanning but couldn't find the source. Sunny crawled out from the shade and gently laid her scarred snout on Santee's thigh.

Joe caught Santee's hand, drawing it away from her scraped neck. He could feel her disquiet but could find no reason. The mothers seemed relatively nonthreatening. The kids definitely not. So what had her panties in such a wad? Her hand twitched to get back at her nape, but Joe held on, folding his big black ham fist over her long delicate pianist's fingers and covering it with his other hand. Tension vibrated down her arm and into her hand.

He'd never had a white girlfriend. Never even wanted one. In high school, it had been like trophy hunting—who bagged the best white girl. And the white girls were out doing their own hunting for the best, baddest, blackest dude they could find.

Not him.

Yet here he found himself with Santee and felt perfectly comfortable with her. This smart, beautiful, eerie woman was becoming his second-best friend, which surprised the hell out of him. He knew she carried even though he'd never seen the gun. He was comfortable having her at his back, if she let him take the lead, or he'd gladly cover her ass if she led.

He chuckled, which drew her gaze. He couldn't help the huge grin. She drew her sunglasses down far enough to look over the top. Those strange pale eyes sent a shiver through him…him, a military vet who'd seen more than his share of dangerous situations and people. Goddamn but he liked this girl—woman, he quickly amended, lest she be reading his thoughts, took umbrage, and decided to kick his chauvinistic ass, which he had no doubt she'd be able to do…or die trying.

"Stop it." She shoved the glasses back. She jerked her hand loose, almost smacking herself in the face when it popped free. From the hard look, Joe knew he'd have been blamed if she had.

"We'd better get the kids to the bathroom," she said, shoving to her feet, still scanning for danger. "They'll be here soon."

Joe didn't question how she knew, just arose and called for the kids. Maddie, of course, was the only complainer, fighting Shawnee to hang on to the swing chain. Santee took one step in their direction. Maddie pulled a pout and stamped the not-so-white-anymore shoes in the dirt. "It's not fair!" she wailed but let Shawnee lead her toward the bathrooms. "I'm telling my mommy!"

Joe snorted.

Santee's lips twitched. She wasn't much for out and out smiling. He wondered what had been done to her to kill that emotion? He was probably better off not knowing. The list of retributions he wanted to perpetrate on that faceless son of a bitch was already long.

They were loading the kids into the van when Santee caught the hint of shadowy motion on a perfectly windless day. The length of a football field away, in the cottonwoods down by the creek, a form stepped out. The distance was too far and the shadow too dark to see him clearly. The pants seemed baggy, probably falling off his skinny ass.

There'd been a kid, early teens, hanging around outside the general store when they'd exited with their bootie. He'd had baggy pants and untied hightops on. His shaggy hair dangled in his glowering eyes. He'd leaned his shoulder insolently against the wall, watching. And if he'd turned to watch the girls like that, Santee would have been all over him. But he didn't. Nor did he look lasciviously at Jamie or the littler boys.

So what was up with him? If it was the same kid?

The Sinclair ranch pickup pulling in distracted her for a moment. When she glanced back he was gone.

If he ever was.

The drive-in was fairly busy on this hot noontime.

There were three carhops, but the Sinclair brood headed to the outside tables, under the trees.

Sir Rob and Mrs. Reggie waited at the order window for the kids to be sent in groups. The Fab Four was first, but Maddie launched herself crying, "Me first! Me first!" She shot around the table where Santee sat. Santee merely held her arm out, and the girl snared herself. Santee pointed back to the table where Sophie, Pete, and Rosarita sat. Tears shimmered in her beautiful dark eyes, and her bottom lip pursed. Maddie's little feet stomped the pavers as she marched back. Over her shoulder, she glared at Santee and said, "I'm telling my mommy!"

Santee had to give the kid credit. She tenaciously hung onto her "divaness" for all she was worth.

"I had no idea Maddie was such a brat," Ruarke said for the millionth time. "My girls didn't turn out like that."

"You're lucky," Santee said. "Your folks did a good job, but a girl like Maddie just wears a person down."

"But not you."

Santee snorted. "You have no idea how many times I've—"

Her attention diverted to a table on the other side of the patio. A heavyset woman sat hunched while a man stood over her. The ugly look on his face matched the ugly-sounding words coming from him. Her kids were wide-eyed, scared, their ice cream cones forgotten, puddling on the table.

Santee didn't know who the man was or what his connection to the woman was and didn't care. She wove her way through the tables and their gaping diners.

"Hello!" Santee said brightly. She edged herself between the vitriol-spewing man and the embarrassed woman. "I thought that was you!" She leaned down and gave the woman a one-armed hug.

The man was sputtering behind her. "I weren't done."

Santee pulled her sunglasses off, sticking the bow down her cleavage—such as it was. "I'm sorry to interrupt, but we haven't seen each other in a long time. I knew you'd understand."

She turned to the kids, who were near tears. "We're sitting over there." She pointed. "Take your ice cream and sit with the kids."

The kids hesitated, but their mother nodded and tried to smile bravely. "You go ahead. I'll be just a moment."

Santee could feel the woman trembling against her legs. She laid a hand on the quivering shoulder and gave it a gentle squeeze.

The man was grumbling behind them as the woman stepped out of the picnic table.

"Chin up," Santee whispered. She winked and gave her a steady, bolstering look.

The cutest dimple creased the woman's cheek. She was eight or nine years older and outweighed Santee by maybe seventy-five pounds but she was so perky cute. Santee didn't do perky or pink as the woman did. Her golden hair was in a high ponytail held with a pink bow. She wore pink capris and a whiter-than-white tee. Just too perky and cute for words.

"Hey." The man's skinny dirty-nailed finger tried to poke at the woman, but Santee shifted her shoulders, deflecting his arm.

"I know you'll excuse us," Santee said brightly, her cold gaze nailing his angry face.

He backed off, mouth working.

Santee turned and followed the woman, glaring at the others who'd been closer but hadn't helped. Rabid idiots were taking over the world, aided and abetted by the sheep who wouldn't do anything.

The men were standing when they approached. Ruarke motioned her to sit. The woman stopped short. Santee plowed into her back, almost sending her face-first into the table. The woman gaped at Ruarke, having recognized him. Ruarke gave her his best smile, which made her fair skin blush deep red.

"My husband is going to be so jealous," she sputtered.

"Stop," Santee said as she joined her on the bench. "The man's head is big enough as is without another pretty woman fawning all over him."

Ruarke sat, a little awkward due to the brace. "A man can never have too much fawning by pretty women."

She looked suspiciously at him, but his smile and twinkly blue eyes made her blush again.

Santee held out her hand. "I'm Santee, by the way." She motioned toward Ruarke. "I guess you know who he is." The pony-tail bobbed. Santee motioned to the rest of the Sinclair bunch. "And these are all the Sinclairs' extended family."

"I'm Sherril Albertson and my kids Amber and Landon. And my husband, Loren, is going to be so jealous." She checked on her kids, who were both a bit on the chubby side. Landon was sitting with Rio and Remmy, while Amber, a tomboy with short yellow hair, dirty yellow T-shirt, and skinned knees, had settled in with the age-matched Fab Four and seemed to be accepted despite her being "a girl."

"Does your husband work in town?" Ruarke asked. "Could he join us?"

Sherril perked up and looked at her watch. "Maybe. For just a minute."

"Call him," Ruarke urged. He'd been recognized by a bunch of the diners. If he could get the whole Albertson family here, their status in town would shoot up and maybe they'd be spared any more of this weight prejudice shit.

Sherril hauled out her phone and walked away. "Honey, you'll never believe—"

Santee rolled her eyes, making Ruarke chuckle. She gave him a glare and shoved her dark glasses back into place.

"You done good, girl," Sir Rob said as he slid a loaded tray onto the table. The S-twins and Jaimie had also hauled trays.

Sherril all but bounced back, a huge grin on her lips. It was almost as if the nastiness of before had never happened.

Not five minutes later, an implement-shop-logo'd truck pulled in. A big bear of a man with a full beard stepped out. His teeth flashed within the whiskers at the sight of Sherril rushing to him. But she halted three feet from him and held out her hands to hold him; he was dirty, greasy, sweaty, and smelly, off, but he hauled her in despite the squealed protest.

Ruarke arose and held his hand out to the man. Loren Albertson was shorter but probably outweighed Ruarke by fifty pounds. His arms were huge with work muscles, not gym muscles.

"Sorry about that." He waved a hand at his grimy clothes. "Tearing a truck apart. Guy's gotta have it by tomorrow."

"Don't worry about it," Sir Rob said, introducing himself and Mrs. Reggie. "Have a seat. How about something to eat?"

"Well…" He touched the gut. "I could eat," he admitted. His brown eyes twinkled at his wife. "The little woman's got me on this crazy diet. Hardly enough to keep a lil ole bunny rabbit alive."

"Now, Loren—"

He grabbed her to him and bussed her soundly on the lips to the laughter of the adults and the eeewwws of the kids. His chuckle rumbled at the brilliant shade of vermillion his wife turned. "But I've only got a few minutes."

Sherril started toward the order window, but Sir Rob motioned her back. "Let me."

Ruarke and Loren bonded immediately over sports, both having played for the local high school.

Sherril glowed with love and pride at the grease-stained man across from her. He paused and gave her a wink, which pinked her cheeks.

"Are you happy?" Santee asked, a stupid question because the answer was so obvious.

"Oh, yes!"

"Does he love you just the way you are?"

Sherril frowned at Santee. "I think so, yes."

"Then why let some jackass you don't even know, whose opinion means less than nothing…why let him drive you to tears and scare your kids?"

Santee could see Sherril thinking seriously about that.

Sir Rob dragged Santee, Ruarke, Pete, and Sunny, of course, to the feed / saddlery / western wear / grain store while the rest of the family went home, including Jamie, who lobbied strongly to come along.

The door jangled as Sir Rob led the way inside. People in the checkout line came over to shake hands with Ruarke and Rob. They tried to introduce Pete and Santee, but the neighbors talked over them, not much interested in the hired help. They were all too interested in whether or when Ruarke was going to play again…the hometown sports star who'd made the big time.

Santee leaned into Pete. "Do they have a sign proclaiming this as the hometown of the famous Ruarke Sinclair?"

Pete snorted. "Not that I've noticed."

From the left, a man hurried from behind the jewelry case, hand encrusted with turquoise held out. "Robert Sinclair! It's been a while."

"Al," Rob said, his face not betraying how the huge gaudy rocks had to have dug into his hand. Again Rob tried to introduce Pete and Santee, but Al shouldered his way to Ruarke.

"Ruarke!" He pumped his hand. "How're they hanging?"

Santee rolled her eyes at Pete and wandered off, drawn by the heady scent of leather that permeated the store. Passing the shirts, she paused at the men's clearance rack. She pulled a shirt out with some purple in the western plaid. She fished out the sale tag, had no trouble deciphering numbers, dropped it as if scorched, and shoved it back onto the rack.

It was back to Goodwill or some other used store, or she'd go naked before she paid that for a shirt, no matter how pretty.

In the back corner was a nice display of weapons: handguns, hunting rifles, and shotguns. The two men behind the counter were sneering at her. Finally one deigned to approach her as she roamed down the case.

"Got a cute little .380 1911 here," the smarmy guy said.

"Oh, really?" Santee's voice trilled. "Is it purple? I just love, love, love everything purple!"

The two salesmen smirked. "No, little lady, it's not purple. We do actually have a pink camo automatic in here." He made a show of taking out his ring of keys and working his way through them, leaving her standing.

Finally, he lifted the gun out, laid it across both palms, and presented it to her like a waiter in a fine restaurant.

"Oooh!" Santee made her fingers tremble slightly as she hesitantly touched it. "It's so pretty!"

"Santee."

She stilled looked over her shoulder at Ruarke and a widely grinning Pete.

"Dad's looking for you."

The two gun sellers were all agog at having Ruarke Sinclair in their midst. It made her want to kick them where it would hurt the most. This was getting ridiculous.

Voice back in normal range, she asked, "Where is Sir Rob?"

Pete pointed toward the opposite corner of the building.

Santee and Sunny headed off, away from the excited adulations. She just shook her head. Men and their sports figures.

The aroma of leather became stronger the closer she got to the wood-rail encircled saddlery.

Sir Rob and Al were in the back corner.

Santee threaded her way past some beautiful new saddles. Several stands were loaded with silver-parade saddles, not working saddles but beautiful nonetheless. Her nostrils worked overtime. There really was nothing like the smell of leather…unless it was the smell of horse, but she wasn't going there.

The men were standing in the used saddle area. Al was loudly expounding about the saddle that looked like it had been dragged behind a galloping horse through a lava patch and stomped on by an elephant.

Sir Rob saw her and looked relieved. "Al, this is Santee."

Al's eye boldly roamed Santee's assets. He held out that turquoise-studded hand.

Santee turned her shoulder to the man. "You wanted to see me, Sir Rob?" From the corner of her eye, she saw Al's face darken, eyes narrowing.

"Yes. We—I mean, I am going to need a variety of saddles. Several good used ones will work just fine. I'd like you to look them over and give me your opinion."

Santee looked hard at Sir Rob, but she wouldn't give Al the satisfaction of voicing a protest.

"Now this one here, little lady"—Al patted the busted-down hunk of junk—"is perfect for your needs."

"Might as well bury it," she said. "It's dead."

Sir Rob snorted.

"Now see here—"

She walked away from his blustering. At a glance, she saw four that didn't look too bad. The leather wasn't beat up too badly, some saddle soap and some Neats and they'd supple back up. But putting her hands on them took the number down by one. Lifting them up and another dropped off the list. She looked at the sales tag and almost had to pick her jaw up off the floor.

Composing her face, she returned to the men, who'd been joined by Pete and Ruarke.

"I see two that aren't too bad, but I'm thinking you might be better off waiting."

"Waiting!" Al exclaimed. "And only two! There're a dozen good saddles here. You won't find any better."

"Two," she told Sir Rob.

"Why wait?"

"Because they're way overpriced."

"What the hell you say!"

"Come fall, people'll be trying to get out of the horse biz, not wanting to feed them over and whatnot, so they'll be selling their tack dirt cheap and"—she looked square at Al—"be better cared for."

"Why, you—"

Pete stepped between Santee and the affronted store owner, saving the overweight, out-of-shape man a thrashing at the hands of a "little lady."

"So," Sir Rob drawled. "What would it take for you to want those two saddles?"

She eyed him suspiciously, but he seemed to honestly want her opinion. "Two bridles of your choice. Two saddle blankets of your choice. New cinches and latigos for each, a can of saddle soap, and a big container of Neats foot oil. Throw in a couple of brushes and curry combs. And knock, oh, say, a hundred bucks off per and it might be worth it.

A strangled sound came from behind her. If Pete weren't there, she might have something to worry about.

Sir Rob's eyes twinkled. "Okay. Thank you. So, Al, you heard the lady."

Santee moved out of the way to let the negotiations begin. Ruarke and Pete joined her by the faux fence.

"So," Pete said. "Were there really only two decent ones, or were you just jerking the asshole's chain?"

Santee blinked wide eyes at him, "Me? Jerk his chain? Not me. But there really were only two worthwhile ones. The rest were junk."

Sir Rob did his own choosing of bridles, blankets, etc.

Santee didn't hear the final price but didn't care. It was none of her business. She was ready to help haul the saddles upfront, but Sir Rob made Al call for help.

Sir Rob made sure his choices made it into the carts, and he followed close behind as they were pushed to the front just so nothing accidentally got switched between the rear of the store and the front.

Al Baker paused to glare at Santee, but she'd been glared at by worse men.

"Are all men in this town chauvinistic pigs?"

Ruarke chuckled. "I think you bring it out of them. If only you were more retiring and demure." He grinned at her.

She had to fight to keep from kicking him. With a sniff and toss of her shorn head, she passed both grinning men and marched away. Sunny paused long enough to give them a warning glance before trotting off after her mistress.

"You're playing with fire, my friend," Pete said.

Ruarke chuckled. "I know, but it's good to see her vibrant and alive rather than all cold and closed off."

"Just don't think I'm going to protect you if you push her off the edge. I doubt if Joe and I together could protect your ass. Unless I'm way off base, I think our little Santee fights dirty and takes no prisoners."

Ruarke bopped Pete's shoulder with his fist. "This next month or so could prove to be most interesting."

"You can say that again."

Pete didn't like to separate from Ruarke, but he left to pick up some things that Ruarke had pointed out.

Ruarke followed Santee, zeroing in on the lighted case that she'd paused in front of for a couple of minutes.

Hmmm. So maybe Santee did have a weakness.

———————————————

Chapter 14

The biker bar they'd passed by the other day might have possibilities, Santee mused. If she could get a job there, bartending, not waitressing, she just might find the solution to her problems. Surely a biker bar would have the right kind of rowdy action that she needed.

She swirled the small orange juice carton. If only she weren't such a wuss, she could solve her own problem and not have to rely on someone else.

Breakfast had already been eaten. The Fab Four were in the bathroom for the last time. Jamie was sulking. He'd made yet another foray into the battle to stay home...be homeschooled by Mrs. Wilson. It wasn't just new-school, first-day jitters. He wanted to make sure that Santee would remain here.

A horn sounded outside from the huge van that Ruarke had gotten to ferry the kids to town, his and the employees' kids. Joe was the designated driver and impatient to get going.

Santee did the final check starting with the Fab Four and sent them off with their new backpacks. Rio and Remmy followed Sophie and Maddie out the door. Jamie remained seated, a sullen pout on his lips.

"We're not going through it again," Santee said.

"But—"

"No. You can't stay home. No, Mrs. Wilson is not going to homeschool you. Yes, I'll be here when you return. Now go to school."

He looked ready to cry, but he arose, avoided looking at anyone, and lumbered out.

Mrs. Reggie was outside taking first-day pictures. Jamie's was going to be quite the keepsake with his gloom-and-doom expression.

Mrs. Reggie was the school nurse. Her Jeep followed the van out the driveway.

Ruarke's phone chirped. He smiled. "Hello, Miri. You just missed the kids. Mom took—"

"What the fuck, Ruarke!" Her screech blasted the whole room. "Who's that bitch Santee, and what gives her the right to tell my Madison that she can't have this or do that?"

Ruarke gave Santee an apologetic grimace as he said, "Hold on while—" He started to get up, but Santee waved him to stay put. She left with her dogs and sat on the glider.

"I demand you fire that bitch!" Miri screamed. In the background, Sam's voice rumbled, but Miri hissed him to shut up. "I want her gone!"

"That's going to be hard since I didn't hire her."

"Then what's she doing there?"

"Dad hired her. She's merely helping out with the kids."

"Let me talk to Rob," she demanded. "He'll get rid of her if I ask."

A glance at his father showed Rob shaking his head. "Dad says Santee stays."

"Ruarke! What does that bitch have on you that you'd even want someone like that around?"

This Miri was nothing like the Miri he'd grown up with, best friends since kindergarten. Something happened their senior year that changed her…something she refused to talk about, even with him.

"Maddie is at the point of being an insufferable brat, Miri."

"What!"

"That's right. Santee merely made us all wake up to the fact that we were letting her get away with stuff none of the other kids were allowed to do."

"But—"

"I told you how bad things were with the boys after Rachel's kids came. We all thank God every day that Santee showed up and got them straightened out. So, as long as she's willing, Santee will have a place here. And that's all there is to it."

"But, Ruarke, Maddie's different. She's sensitive."

"She needs her mother to get a backbone, or when she gets a little bigger, she's really going to be uncontrollable."

"Uncontrollable! Come on! She's five!"

In the background, Ruarke heard Sam say, "I tried to tell you." Miri hissed him to silence.

"Maddie is just a little girl."

"Right. A little girl with a nasty temper. Who treats the adults like they're beneath her and doesn't have to be polite to. That they're there to answer her every whim, clean her room, make her bed, put away her clothes."

"Is that so wrong? That is, after all, what they're hired to do."

"They're not her personal slaves. And they deserve to be treated with respect and listened to as authority figures. Instead, she tells people to shut up. She threatens to tell her mommy on them and get them fired. Even this morning, there was a battle over what she was wearing to school. I'm telling you, Miri, she looked like a five-year-old hooker, makeup smeared all over her face. The waistband of her skirt rolled over so many times that her panties flashed under the hem and her shirttails were knotted practically at her throat."

"And I suppose your precious Santee objected to that."

"No, actually it was Mom who wouldn't let her go to school like that. Maddie threw a full-scale hissy fit on the floor, a first-class tantrum. I think one of the girls taped it, so I can send you a copy after they get home. It was awful."

He didn't tell Miri that his mother had been in tears, and Santee did step in, hauling the squalling kid under her arm to the bathroom. Madison had come out pouting and still angry but clean faced and decently clothed. Santee, on the other hand, showed red streaks on her arms and cheek and what might have been teeth marks on her hand. She'd dumped the "threatening to call Mommy" kid into a chair and, hands fisted, had walked out.

"I don't believe it could have been that bad. Not my little girl."

"Tell me that after you see the video."

Sam's deep voice rumbled out. The man was six feet, six inches, tall and lean, a star-wide receiver, but Miri pretty much ran their marriage. She'd married a black man in part to spite her parents, who'd immediately disowned her and had never even seen the kids.

"Sam says we're coming home during our bye week. I wanted to go somewhere fun—" Sam's voice sounded again in the background. "But he—we think it might be more important to come home and see the kids."

"Good," Ruarke said. "Then you and Sam can look over the new plans for a suite for the two of you."

"A suite? Really? Where?"

"The entire second story of the old house is going to be expanded and made over into two suites, one for you and one for Max."

"Really! When did you decide that?"

"It was Santee's idea."

"Santee," she said flatly.

"Yes, Santee. And you'd better get your head around the fact that she's here, and if Dad has his way, she won't be going anywhere anytime soon."

"And what about you, Ruarke? Your money keeps the ranch afloat. You ought to have the final say over who works there or who doesn't."

"Actually, Miri, right now we need Santee. So I'm praying that she stays."

He looked at his dad, who was flipping through the horse sale booklet, a seldom-seen grin on his face. A lot of factors had contributed to Robert Sinclair's lack of smiles. Ruarke had been one… getting Heather pregnant at fifteen among other things…the loss of his daughter. Ruarke'd do just about anything to keep easy smiles on his dad's much younger-seeming face.

Midmorning, the call came in from one of the hands that the neighbor's motley bunch of cattle were on Sinclair land.

They took off, Ruarke and Pete in the pickup, Santee and Rob in the Ranger with the fence repair equipment, and two hands-on ATVs. It wasn't a long distance as the crow flies, which was how they went. By road, it would have been fifteen miles. However, their way didn't have a road, so they bumped and zigzagged their way across the pastures.

Jerry Graham's no-name-breed cattle were scattered in the tall winter grass, pulling at it as if they hadn't had a square meal in weeks, and judging by their protruding hips, that probably wasn't far wrong.

In the distance came the hair-on-the-back-of-your-neck-raising howls of the wolf hybrids the old man bred. At one time there'd been quite a market for the mentally unstable beasts. It seemed all the wannabe tough guys wanted a wolf. Now they seemed to have gravitated to pit bulls. But the old man still had his breeding stock sounding like the hounds of hell.

Santee stopped the Ranger and stepped out, telling her dogs to stay. She stood listening to the eerie howls.

Pete pulled the truck up beside her. Ruarke rolled his window down. Rob came around to Santee's side.

"What's wrong?" Rob asked.

"Hmm?"

Rob grabbed her hand from the back of her neck. It was a wonder she had any skin left the way she attacked it whenever she was unsettled.

Santee seemed to come back from a far place. She looked at Sir Rob holding her wrist. It twitched to get back to her neck. She forced her hands down and shoved them into her shorts' pockets.

Uncle Sol and the hands drove off to help the lone horseman try to ease the reluctant cattle off their winter graze. But Santee's attention kept turning toward where the Grahams' homestead sat unseen behind a hill.

"Why don't we go over there and see what kind of mess the fence is in?"

Santee nodded. She'd barely heard Sir Rob, but the pull from that direction was inexorable.

The howls grew louder as they cleared the last hill. Below was the sorry sight of a property left to rot. Though still lived in the sun, blistered, shingle-ripped, wind-tilted buildings struggled to remain upright in the weed-choked yard.

The ground went from lush graze on this side to trampled dust on the other. Near the leaning fence posts were two vehicles, lights strobing red and blue. Several men could be seen moving around near the sheriff's vehicles.

Santee shivered, as if the howls were racing down her spine. Something bad had happened down there.

Sir Rob sighed. "Let's get it over with."

The two Sinclair Ranch vehicles rolled slowly down the slope. Two men in sheriff uniforms, two men in suits, and a woman in a dark-blue dress stood around a blue tarp on the ground. The woman was pressing a tissue carefully to the corners of her eyes. One of the sheriff's men strutted around the tarp, one hand held out to stop them, the other resting on his freed gun butt.

Sunny, sitting in the middle, turned to Santee and rested her chin on Santee's shoulder, breath puffing in Santee's ear. It didn't have the calming effect it normally did.

Sir Rob reached around the dog and laid his hand on Santee, stopping her hand's move toward the pack on her belt. He could only assume that she had a gun in there. She was as stiffly alert as the sheriff's deputy who stood blocking their way.

"Arrest them!" the woman wailed. "They murdered my daddy!"

The two suited men were in earnest, loud conversation with the other officer. The sheriff nodded as if in agreement to every word.

The howling continued unabated. Both dogs were rumbling deep in their chests.

An errant breeze ruffled the splotch of color enough to uncover a booted foot and part of a frayed-jean-clad leg. The body was maybe ten feet onto Sinclair property, lying in the lush grass. The fence line behind the people was sprung, posts akimbo and wire coiled nastily as if the starving cattle had forced their way through.

Sir Rob slowly eased his phone out and called Sol. "We've got a situation over at the Graham place. Hold the cattle where they are and send a couple of guys home to get some hay brought over here."

"Do you need help?"

"No. Just stay well back. The sheriff is here."

"Not good."

"No, it's not. Looks like a body on the ground."

"Old man Graham?"

"Could be."

The sheriff broke away from the seemingly distraught three-some and circled to the Sinclair vehicles. His thumbs were tucked in his service belt that sat high on slim hips. His aggressive stride took mere moments to bring him around to the front of the vehicles, where he planted his feet wide as if preparing for a gunfight.

Dark sunglasses covered his eyes, shielding his expression as he looked first at the Ranger occupants and then at the pickup. "Wanna tell me what you're doing here?"

"Sheriff Armstrong. Mind if I join you?" Sir Rob said.

"You armed?"

"No."

There was a long pause as if the sheriff was deciding whether or not to believe the older man. Santee bristled at the disrespect, but Rob held out a quelling hand.

Rob stepped out, and the pickup door also opened.

The sheriff pointed at Pete. "Not you."

Pete raised his fingers from the steering wheel to indicate his understanding.

Santee eased out. Her movement was noted by a smug, dismissive grin. She felt the pressure of both men's gazes. Then they turned away from her, dismissing her as a danger—a gross misjudgment on their part. She loosened the flap on the holster/wallet and leaned her hip against the Ranger's fender.

There was major tension in the air as the four men faced each other. Sheriff Armstrong eyed Ruarke's crutches with seeming pleasure.

"Don't look like you'll be back playing ball ever again."

"Maybe," Ruarke acknowledged. "Maybe not. Verdict's still out on that. But either way, I've made enough to last me pretty much forever."

The sheriff's cheeks darkened. He turned to his deputy and jerked his head toward the Graham children.

The deputy turned then said, "Looks like the coroner's here."

"Take care of it," Armstrong barked. "And get the Grahams out of there."

Armstrong's attention had never really wavered from the Sinclairs. "So'd you come all this way just to visit old Jerry?"

"We came to return his cattle to his side of the fence."

Santee watched as the Graham heirs were motioned away from the body so the coroner could pull in. They began circling toward the sheriff.

"Heard you and old man Graham didn't much like each other. So maybe you came over earlier. Had words. Things got outta hand, with the old man ending up shot dead, and then you made up a reason to be here by setting his cows loose on your property."

Ruarke stiffened. He and Lance Armstrong had a long history. They'd hated each other in elementary school. Fought each other for leader of every sport. Competed for the girls, especially Heather. Went in every school vote from class president to prom and homecoming king. The majority of the time Ruarke won, mainly, he thought, because Lance Armstrong was not nice to women, a bully of men, and a sore loser. But he was handsome in a brown hair, weasel-faced way.

The Graham heirs arrived out of breath and out of sorts. The woman again sent off a wail as if her world had just shattered when, in fact, none of them had been home in years.

"Arrest them, Sheriff," the oldest, bald as a cue ball, Stan Graham, said. He'd managed to get a law degree from a no-name school. He moved to Pierre and now sucked from the government's tit in some way, shape, or form.

"Yuh, Sheriff," the younger son, Marvin, said. He was a shyster real estate developer/contractor in Sioux Falls, whose houses had a tendency to start falling apart the day after they sold.

Cissy's sobs were about as real as her brothers' concerns. She'd skipped out before graduation, rumored pregnant, went to LA, and was never seen in South Dakota again...at least not in this part of South Dakota.

"Why would we want to kill Jerry Graham?" Sir Rob said. "We—"

Stan stuck his chin out belligerently, "Because you wanted Dad's land. Always have. But Dad wouldn't have nothing to do with you almighty Sinclairs."

"Yuh." Marvin snorted. "Dad'd call me and tell how you come crawling over here with a lowball bid and he'd chase you off with a shotgun."

"Really," Sir Rob said. He inclined his head toward the poor excuse of a ranch yard and the overgrazed dirt ground. "And why would I even want this?"

Marvin hooked his thumbs in his suspenders, the only thing keeping his pants over his pop-belly. "The land. That's why. Any dumbass knows the Hills land is premium right now. More buyers than there are acreages. This here"—he waved his arm, almost taking his sister's head off—"is worth a fortune."

Cissy, a bottle-blond hard-lived woman, stepped forward. "And it's ours now. All ours. You want it, you'll have to deal with us now."

Stan laughed. "Hell, Cissy. Even the almighty Sinclairs ain't got that much money, not what we'll get once we divide it up into ranchettes. And—" He poked his foot as if to kick Ruarke's crutch, then he saw the pickup door start to open and thought better of it.

Armstrong saw the girl set to launch, a tigress if ever he saw one. Stan Graham was looking at the wrong danger source. This one would have gotten there first, and he'd have been a dead duck before the bodyguard even got his ass out of the truck.

Stan cleared his throat. "And don't look like no more multimillion-dollar contracts'll be coming your way ever again."

Ruarke looked at Sir Rob and nodded.

"We really don't have any reason to harm Jerry," Rob said.

"Right," Marvin sneered. "Cuz you knew there was no way he'd sell to no damned Sinclairs."

"Actually," Rob said, "as of yesterday, the land and all that is on it are now Sinclair property."

"What the fuck!" Stan shouted.

"No fucking way!" Marvin screeched. "I was going to break it up and make us a fortune."

"Which is why Jerry came to us. This ranch was in the Graham family for generations. He did not want it broken up into little bits and sold off."

"That's a f—!"

Santee launched into Stan's face, pulling her mirrored sunglasses off with her left hand. Nose to nose, she glared at the weasel. "Careful how you finish that sentence," she said.

Stan's Adam's apple bobbed as he swallowed hard. He glanced at Marvin, but the idiot just gaped, worthless as always.

"Apologize."

His bowels gurgled, and he had to tighten his bladder hold it in.

"I won't ask twice."

He didn't want to, but damned if he didn't hear himself say, "Sorry."

"Sorry what?" she pressed.

It was those damned almost colorless eyes. He felt them knifing into him like an icicle riding a vein straight to his thundering heart. His lungs couldn't seem to draw in anything but overheated, oxygen-depleted air.

"Sorry what?" she repeated. Her eyes narrowed in warning.

"Santee." Sir Rob gently laid his hand on her stiff shoulder. "Let's all take a breath here."

Lance Armstrong, high school track star, Minneapolis cop, and county sheriff for the last three years, had been caught flat-footed. Maybe it was those damned eyes—cold and mesmerizing as a snake. He'd seen warmer, more human eyes on serial killers on death row. He knew if she hadn't stopped herself, he'd never have been able to save Stan, and he'd been standing right beside the man.

Marvin grabbed the frozen Stan's arm. "You haven't heard the last of this," he warned as he half-dragged his sibling away.

Violence still danced on the heat motes. Santee stared after the Graham trio, only easing off when they crossed the fence line. They'd passed their father's body without so much as a glance.

Lance Armstrong took off his cowboy hat and mopped his brow. It didn't get much closer than that. He'd faced down Sturgis revelers and not been caught flat-footed like this. "What you say, true?"

Santee stiffened and turned on him, obviously not afraid of his badge in the least. The scarred dog came from the Ranger and nuzzled into Santee's palm. She drew a deep wavery breath, her fingers lacing into the silky reddish hair. With a last warning glare at the sheriff, she shoved her sunglasses on and stepped back.

"It's true," Rob said. "Jerry and his attorney came to us. We agreed on a price and that he could live out his days here."

"So you'd have no reason to kill him."

"None at all."

"Hmmmm." Sheriff Armstrong turned toward the three retreating figures. "So who would?"

"If they didn't know…" Ruarke said.

"Really," Lance said flatly. "Think I couldn't come up with that on my own?"

"I wouldn't know," Ruarke said. "Seems like you were always trying to ride my coattails all our lives."

Lance sailed his hat aside like a frisbee. "The hell you say! If you weren't—"

The wolf dog howls took on a new frenzied tone.

One of the Grahams was walking toward the tied-out animals. He pointed at them.

Bang!

Yip!

Bang!

Yip!

Santee streaked across the pasture, the terrified howls spurring her on. Each bang, each yip signaled another dead wolf dog.

She heard an engine rumbling closer behind when she hit the hardpacked yard. The pickup was trying to pass her, but a final spurt launched her.

Stan Graham, as if sensing her, tried to turn the rifle, but Santee dove in under it. The rifle discharged into the air over her shoulder. She drove into him as hard as she could. His stale cigarette breath expelled in her face when her shoulder drove into his gut. His grunt of pain was very satisfying.

She was up on her knees, pulling him up by his tie, right fist drawn back...

But it ran into a barrier.

She tried again.

Same barrier.

She swiveled on her knee, burying it deeper into the groaning man's gut—balanced and ready to take on the new adversary.

Pete pulled back. Hands in the air.

The shock of seeing him made her blink, her rage doused.

Then the first dog hit her, knocking her off the man. Rufus panted happily as he danced on the downed man's stomach, ignoring the groans his fifty pounds elicited. Sunny hit next, knocking Santee flat, her hot, wet tongue cooling the rest of Santee's rage.

The Ranger slewed to a stop as Rob stepped out and took the rifle. He held his hand into the mass of wriggling canines. A hand grasped his, and he pulled Santee up.

Stan was sputtering as the sheriff got out of the Ranger. "I want that bitch arrested!" Rufus took exception at his tone and rumbled a growl. Stan crabbed backward on his butt, eyeing the big white teeth. "She assaulted me!"

Lance looked at Santee. Pete took half a step in front of her, arm out to either guard her from him or prevent her from attacking. Lance turned to Rob and his bitter rival, Ruarke. "Do you want to press charges?"

"What!" Stan screeched. "I'm the injured party here!" He pointed a trembling finger at Rufus. "And I want that vicious animal shot!"

Santee lurched to go after him, but Pete kept her barred in. So she kicked him instead, making him grunt in protest.

"Those mutts had to have some monetary value. I can charge him with theft. Willful destruction of property. Trespassing. Any number of things."

The men looked at Santee as she stood staring at the carnage. Sir Rob shook his head. "Just get them all out of here."

Rob held the rifle out to Armstrong. "Guy's a pretty good shot with this. Wonder what killed the old man?"

Stan sputtered as he scrambled to his feet. The rear end of his silk suit had split in the fall, exposing his dingy tighty-not-so-whit-eys. He shouted for his siblings, and their car sped off in a cloud of dust.

The stench of blood tried to clot Santee's nostrils. There were ten dog houses scattered in the field. She walked out, flies buzzing past, already drawn to the blood.

Ten houses. She could see eight lumps of gray/white in the dirt. Eight perfectly still forms that only moments ago had been warm, breathing, serenading animals.

Her dogs pressed tight to her legs. The wild scent of the dogs added to the stink of blood and fear kept them from exploring nearer.

A soft whimper turned all three of their heads. Santee told the dogs to stay and went on alone to one of the farthest houses.

Each dog had worn a circle path the extent of their chain. The dog house was at the circumference of the circle. They had enough chain to get inside but that was about it.

Careful to stay outside of his circle, Santee eased around to the side of the doghouse. The beautiful dog lay panting, his back legs splayed out behind, useless, his intestines looped out into the bloody dirt.

Santee's eyes stung, and her throat threatened to close up. Heavy panting filled the silence.

"Shit."

She turned to find Pete at her side.

The dog coughed up a wad of blood.

"I'll go sit with him."

Pete grabbed her arm. "You're not going in there!"

"Pete."

"No. That's a wild animal. Hurt and in pain. You're not going in there."

"He won't hurt me."

Pete believed her 95 percent. But it was that extra five percent and the ass-whipping he'd get if he let anything happen to her that made him stand firm. "You go check out that last house. I'll take care of this."

Finally, she sighed and walked on. Moments later, the bang made her flinch. She didn't know what the Sinclairs would have done with the wolf dogs. There were so many tales about how unpredictable and untrustworthy they were, but still…

The chain shimmered by the last doghouse. There was no sign of a dog, no body, and no sounds of an injured one hiding. She circled the beaten track to the far side of the house where the chain laid. But no dog hid in the shadows there. Carefully, she edged into the circle. Step by hesitant step, she went to the chain…which ended in a broken link. She stood there holding the chain and looked out into the pine forest.

Somewhere out there was a wolf dog. Possibly injured. Comfortable enough with humans to not be afraid. Used to being fed by humans.

Never having had to hunt to feed himself, he'd turn to the easiest sources: calves, chickens, lambs, and possibly people.

––––––––––––––––––––––––––

Chapter 15

Santee stood before the fireless fireplace looking at the framed family photos on the mantle. Her hands were locked together behind her like a child looking but knowing she dare not touch.

Ruarke watched as she leaned sideways into the pictures, not moving her feet any closer to the antique rocker in the corner—the rocking chair that no one ever sat in, not because it was uncomfortable but because it was always chilly in that corner even when the fireplace was blazing.

He was seated at the table. Breakfast was over. The ladies were cleaning up. Kids were off to school with a minimum of muss and fuss. Pete was in the kitchen making the ladies giggle. Joe was off God knows where. And his dad, Sir Rob, he thought with a smile, was conferring with the ranch secretary/bookkeeper before he and Santee set off. While, oh joy, he awaited the therapist and later the masseuse.

Right now, he was just enjoying the view: the long tanned and toned legs encased in the modest-cut jean shorts, the long-tailed western shirt that accented the narrow hips, and the slender torso with its undone snaps, allowing the pale purple tee to peek out.

Santee seemed to flinch slightly.

Had the rocker moved a millimeter? Must have been a shadow.

Ruarke arose and grabbed the four-footed cane he had graduated to. Still in the heavy brace, he rounded the table and crossed the living room.

Santee's head turned slightly, aware of his approach.

Somehow, Ruarke knew which photo had captured her attention. It wasn't the one where he held the division football trophy or him wearing the dopey homecoming king crown with Heather beaming at his side or him balancing a tiny baby girl in each arm looking both proud and scared to death. Oh no, she couldn't be fixated on any of those. It had to be that one.

The one that made both his parents cry whenever they looked at it. The one he avoided looking at. The one that he'd come close to ripping out of the frame and tearing into itty-bitty bits and burning in the fireplace.

The one that showed the four of them. His parents, him at fifteen, and the little five-year-old raven-haired girl holding his hand, looking up at him with adoring eyes. It was her first day of kindergarten. Her first day of riding the bus with her big brother…much to his deep embarrassment. The kids rode him mercilessly when she wanted to sit in the back of the bus with him and every time she called him Wookie.

Ruarke reached past Santee and took down the picture. The day was burned into his memory…though not as much as the one a couple of months later.

"That's Savannah. My sister."

"Didn't know you had a sister. She doesn't look much like you."

Ruarke let his finger touch the still image of the little girl who'd seldom stood still. "She wouldn't." He sighed and replaced the frame. "She was adopted. Her parents worked for us. A young couple in their twenties. He was a ranch hand. She was going to school to be a CPA while working as Dad's secretary/bookkeeper."

"They went out one night, date night don't you know, and left their two-year-old with Mom and Dad. Sheriff's officers showed up around three a.m. to inform us that they've been hit by a drunk driver and were both dead."

He could feel Santee's sympathetic gaze. She wouldn't be so sympathetic if she knew the rest.

"For two young people, they really had it all together. They each had a will, which stated if they both died, Mom and Dad got their daughter." He cleared his throat. "So that's how I got a little sister."

"But she'd not here now."

"No, she's not. But that's a story for another time." He motioned back toward the table. "Will you sit for a moment?"

Wariness glared in her pale eyes, but she nodded. She took her normal seat, two over on Rob's right. He pulled out the chair on her right that Rio claimed.

"We've got a problem."

She stilled. He could see her mind flashing through trying to pick out what she'd done now.

"It's not you," he said quickly. "Sam's bye week is next week. Miri and Sam will be coming home for six days."

"Ah." Santee nodded. "Sounds like you're the one with the problem. Not me."

"Damn it, Santee!"

She stuck her nose in his face, icy eyes narrowed. "Don't you swear at me," she ground out.

It was a strange sensation having his balls try to hide in his scrotum. And not a pleasant one at that. "Santee—"

Her untamed raven brows arched.

"I'm sorry. All right?"

She gave a terse nod and leaned back out of his space, giving his sphincter a breather. "She's your BFF."

"D—"

Her brows arched.

Ruarke cleared his throat and started over. "Santee. When Miri comes, the shit's—I'm allowed to say 'shit'?" Her lips twitched. "The shit's going to hit the fan. Maddie is going to revert to the old Maddie, and Miri is going to aid and abet it."

"So what's your plan?"

He looked at her.

Santee shot to her feet, her hands held out to fend him off. "Oh, no! Not me! She's your friend. Not mine."

"That's why it's perfect. You don't have the background with her."

"Or you don't have the backbone," Santee stated.

A couple of snorts sounded, evidence of an audience.

"Santee—"

"No. Huh-uh. I've already overstepped by dealing with that little out-of-control brat. It's about time you stepped up." Her knuckles whitened on the back of the wooden chair. A soft whine sounded from Sunny. "You leave me dangling, alone, and this is not going to end pretty."

Ruarke watched her stalk out. Her worried companions scrambling after her.

"Shoulda seen that one coming," Pete said.

Ruarke looked suspiciously at the big man in time to see him hiding a grin.

"Pete's right," Rob said. "We're the ones who'd let this situation entrench. You're the one who's got to get us out of it."

"Me? Why me? Why not us?"

Rob walked around the table and laid his hand on Ruarke's shoulder. "Because, son, she's your BFF."

Pete snorted, and Rob's lips twitched and then broke into a broad smile. He patted Ruarke's shoulder and walked out.

"Thanks a lot, Dad."

Rob waved over his shoulder as he closed the door.

He glared at his amused constant companion. "And you're no help either!"

A lonely howl echoed in the night. Santee had heard it ever since the wolf dogs had been killed. It seemed to be getting closer every night.

Both dogs raised their heads. Sunny's chest rumbled against Santee's inner thighs, where the dog lay. Rufus sat up, head cocked to listen to the lonely eerie sound. With a grumble, he lay back down and put his head heavily on her leg.

A 6×6-foot hunk of fake grass carpet acted as their patio. Old couch cushions picked up at a rummage sale were spread together to be lounged on, one leaning against the trailer tires as a backrest for Santee. When she moved on, leaving the dogs behind, she'd be able to use the lawn chair again, since there'd be no one wanting to sit on her lap anymore. That kind of hurt to think about.

They became aware of someone approaching. Santee reached for her bag, but the dogs' tails began to wag, indicating a friend was coming. Where they sat, they were in the shadow of the trailer. Dim light from inside the camper shone through the window, casting a glow across the yard by the door.

Ruarke came around the truck. This late at night he moved stiffly. He paused and leaned down to lay his hand on his leg. A soft groan was exhaled.

Santee patted Sunny to get her off her lap. She arose, startling him. She grabbed a lawn chair and moved it onto the patio. A plastic end table was placed for an ottoman.

With a sigh, Ruarke lowered himself. With both hands he lifted the leg onto the table. "I saw the light. Hope you don't mind."

Santee hid a grin at his worried tone. "Nope."

He looked sharply at her. "That's all you've got to say?"

"Good luck?"

He snorted. "Thanks a heap."

"I will say this…" She waited until he gave her his attention. "If you let Miri ruin Maddie again, I'm done."

"Santee."

"Don't Santee me, Ruarke Sinclair. The kid was coming around until she found out her mother's coming home. She's already back-sliding, talking back to Rosarita, arguing with me and Mrs. Reggie, and being disrespectful to the ladies."

He sighed heavily. "I know." The ache in his leg sharpened. Ruarke squeezed at the brace for a little relief.

"Let me." Carefully Santee eased the Velcro loose. One hand under his leg, she pulled the brace free. He'd worn shorts as if anticipating her taking pity on him.

She rubbed her palms together until the skin was hot. Softly, she settled her hands onto the heavily scarred thigh.

His body arched and his breath hissed at her gentle touch. His fingers dug into the aluminum chair arms.

"Easy," Santee whispered. Her hands remained immobile until he breathed. The leg felt swollen and hot, the skin taut. She slowly formed her fingers around the contours of his leg…and tightened them. Carefully she began kneading and massaging as, gradually, her energy rushed from her fingers into his leg.

The world narrowed down to just the two of them. Their breathing synced.

Ruarke felt his blood pounding, breaths speeding up. He slumped back as the pain released him.

Rufus knocked into Santee, breaking the meld. Knees wobbling, she leaned over and fell into the other chair. Her limbs shook as if she'd been electrocuted. Santee laid her head back, breathing hard. Ruarke's soft snores lulled her into an unusually deep sleep.

Santee awoke with a start. Both dogs were whining, pointing toward the trees. Slinking from tree to tree and boulder to boulder, a pale shape edged down. Then he froze, turning toward the road, and disappeared as if he'd been a figment of her imagination.

Headlights broke the wee-hour darkness even before the birds were thinking of announcing the new day. A form separated from Joe's dark house. Pete cut across from his, taking up defensive positions as the vehicle rolled in.

Santee laid her hand on Ruarke's chilly arm. He started, "Wha—?"

"I think your BFF just drove in."

He sighed and reached for his brace. Santee got it and helped him get it around his leg, surprisingly aware of the feel of his skin and his masculine scent. Their hands tangled over the Velcro. Their gazes looked, but slamming car doors jerked them almost guiltily apart.

He arose without help. "Um, thanks. I don't think I've slept that well in a very long time…at least not since you last performed your magic on my leg."

Magic? More like a curse that never took her far enough over the edge so she couldn't recover.

"Mommy said I get to stay home today. Just me an' her."

Her mommy must have also said she could play the little hooker again too; her top and bottom were micro bikini small, and she'd been into the makeup again, big time. Her lips were garishly red and her eyes were surrounded by black as if she'd lost a prizefight.

Santee looked at Ruarke, who, too, appeared as if he wished he'd never gotten up. Miri and Sam were still asleep, but Santee knew if she stepped into this that Miri would explode, whereas if Ruarke handled it…

"Maddie, you know the rules. You only get to stay home if you're sick."

Maddie put the back of her hand to her forehead and faked a cough. "I am sick, Uncle Ruarke. Really I am."

"In that case, young lady, you'll be spending the day in bed."

Huge tears gushed, creating rivers of mud down Maddie's cheeks. "But my mommy said…"

"Well, honey, you live in this house, with us, and you have to live by our rules."

A pout poofed out her bottom lip. "I hate you."

"And you need to change clothes and wash your face."

The door opened, and Maddie's face lit up. "Mommy! Daddy!" she screeched as she flew across the dining room and into the petite highlighted blond woman's arms.

Miri gathered Maddie up, hugging, kissing, and cooing.

Simon ran to his father and threw his arms around his knees. The tall black man grabbed his son and tossed him up, almost putting his head through the ceiling.

Miri and Sam knew the boys, having been here when they arrived from Florida. Only Santee was a stranger. She arose as the Adamses approached the table. Miri's hazel eyes nailed Santee. She seemed surprised when Santee didn't wither away at her glare.

Ruarke made the introductions. Miri tossed her head, but Sam came around, long fingers closed warmly and gently around Santee's. His smile seemed genuine, or he was one heck of an actor.

"Mommy! Mommy! What are we going to do today?"

"Well, I thought—"

"Maddie has school today, Miri," Ruarke said.

"I know." She clutched Maddie tighter. "But since it's only kindergarten, I thought we'd have a girls' day out."

"Yeah!"

"No, Miri."

"What do you mean, 'No, Miri'? This is my kid. I'm her mother. If I say she's staying home, she's staying home." She glared at Santee as if this was all her doing.

"You are her mother, but she lives here. My house. My rules. Only the sick get to stay home."

Still glaring at Santee, she replied, "But just this once won't hurt. They don't really have school, just playtime, socializing. Stuff like that."

"Maybe in our day, but now they have homework every night."

"She's five, for heaven's sake!"

"Yes, and nowadays kindergarten is serious school. She needs to go today. Her face needs to be cleaned, and she has to change into something suitable for school. And she needs to do it fast or she'll miss her ride."

"Mommy, please! You promised!" The running black eye goop smeared Miri's pale neck and all over the collar of her white polo shirt.

"Miri," Ruarke said, "the rules are the rules. If you break this one, be prepared to take Maddie with you when you go."

Miri gaped at him. Then her eyes shot to Santee, but Ruarke shifted so that his body blocked Miri's view of Santee. "She put you up to this," she hissed, loud enough for everyone to hear.

The children were bug-eyed. The Fab Four slipped from their chairs and scuttled around to crawl into Santee's lap. Even Simon had slipped away from his dad to be comforted by Santee.

Her arms had to tighten around the boys to prevent them from falling off. Remmy and Rio pressed in tight from their chairs on either side of her. She felt a presence behind her, tilted her head back, and found Jamie there, angry-faced.

"We don't want you to leave," Rio choked.

Santee felt like the center of a little boy sandwich. The six little ones were hugging her so tight. "I'm here until first snow." She bounced her legs. "Is it snowing?"

They all craned their necks to look out at the beautiful, sunshiny September morning. "No," they said in near unison.

"So I guess you're stuck with me for a while yet."

Miri glared up at Ruarke. "I never thought you'd turn on me too. And for the likes of…of that." She glared at Santee. "Until other arrangements can be made, I guess I'll have to abide by your rules. But I don't like being treated like this!"

Miri whirled, Maddie wailing in her arms, and headed outside. Rosarita scrambled to follow since Maddie was sleeping in her house and would go there to change, but Sam motioned her to stop.

"If you don't mind us alone in your house, I'd like to handle this."

"*Por supuesto.*"

"Thank you." He half bowed to Rosarita and acknowledged everyone, including the ladies peeking out from the kitchen. "And thanks to all of you for taking such good care of our Madison and Simon. I hope you'll be amenable to keeping both of them again when Miri and I have to fly back to Atlanta." Tall and dignified, he followed his wife and daughter out.

Outside, Miri turned on him, the rumble of their angry voices carried inside. Moments later, Miri whirled in a huff and marched off with Sam following.

"Well," Shaynee said, "that went well."

Laughter broke the tension.

Sir Rob caught Jamie before he escaped out the door after the rest of the kids. "Did you get me that address?"

Jamie shifted uneasily, clearly wishing he'd managed to evade the man again. He nodded. "But I don't know… I don't want her to get mad at me."

Sir Rob gently put his hand on the boy's slumped shoulder. "Why would she get mad?"

"Because she trusted me to fill out the check and make out the envelope. Can't you ask her?"

"It's a surprise."

"Oh." Jamie looked up at the graying-haired man who wanted very much to be called Grandpa. "You're scared to ask her too."

Rob snorted a laugh and hauled the boy, huge book pack and all, into his arms. "Too true. But I promise. If there's any fallout from this, I'll take the blame."

Jamie looked hard at him for a moment before shrugging out of the pack and digging into one of a dozen zippers. He held the slip of paper, holding it tight for a moment before sighing and releasing it. "She's not going to like this," he warned as he hurried outside.

"Who's not going to like what?" Ruarke asked.

"Jamie had the name of the veterinarian that Santee is still making payments to because of Sunny and paying God only knows what kind of interest rate. I'm going to call him, find out what the outstanding bill plus interest is, and send him a check or charge my credit card if he will."

Pete snorted. "Jamie's right. She's not going to like it."

"I'll have to take that chance."

"Better you than me," Ruarke said.

"You can say that again," Pete said.

"What are you up to today, Dad?"

"I thought Santee and I'd make a run over to the Graham place. See how Clay and John are doing on cleaning up that mess. The ladies are packaging up food for the guys. Why?"

"Do you think you could hold off a couple of hours?"

"I suppose. Why?"

"I thought I'd like to go along."

"You going to feel up to that after therapy?"

"I think so. I've been feeling pretty good of late." He didn't say that he thought it was all due to Santee's massages.

"Okay, if you're sure."

Sam and Miri, who was still miffed and sulking, joined them.

Five people and two good-sized dogs made for tight quarters. Sam, Santee, and Sir Rob sat in back, with Rufus sitting between Sam and Santee. Sunny had started out sitting on Santee's lap but now had fallen over on her back paws bouncing in the air at every bump, snoring softly. Miri snuggled into Ruarke's side.

Pete looked in the rearview mirror and grinned.

"I saw that, Pete Jackson," Santee said. "You'd better be nice to me or I'll tell Rosarita on you."

He scuffed a big hand across his face, but the dancing eyes wouldn't let the smile die.

The ranch driveway from the gravel pounded the pickup and trailer with the two ATVs. Their progress slowed to a crawl.

Sir Rob pulled out his phone and ordered a load of gravel to be spread down the drive.

At the sight of the rundown spread, Sir Rob had Pete stop. The cattle were gone, shipped out at a loss. The buildings needed major repairs: listing at all angles, siding unpainted for eons, and shingles balding on the swaybacked roofs.

"Wow," Sam said. He was a city boy, Chicago born and bred, and even he could see the ratty condition. "Is it worth repairing?"

"That's a very good question," Rob admitted. "There are times when we'd need a couple guys here, but we could get a trailer house brought in for them. I'd like to save either the barn or that shed so we'd have a place to put stuff out of the weather and out of sight. But we'll see."

The skid loader came out of the barn with a load of manure, dumped it in the spreader, and immediately went back for more. The manure had been halfway up to the windows in spots, and two horse skeletons had been found so far.

"So what about the dead guy?" Sam asked.

Pete started the truck forward as Rob said, "I hear they're looking real close at the kids. The rifle matches up, but which one did it? They all three needed the money, or so I hear. And no one's ratting on anybody, yet."

The pickup was assaulted by a wall of nose-hair curling stench when they rolled the opened the doors. And it was only partly from manure. The other part was sewer gas. The ammonia seemed to kill the oxygen, making it hard to breathe through the nose, but mouth breathing collected stink particles on the tongue.

Santee shifted Sunny enough so she could reach her hip pocket. She pulled out a pale purple bandana, triangled it, and tied it around her face. "Anybody else want a bandana? I've got more."

All four men wanted one. Her pack had ridden in the bed; it was so heavy there was no chance of it blowing out. It took some digging, but she found four. It seemed to help, but that might have been psychosomatic.

"The guys didn't tell me the sewer was a problem too," Rob said. He walked off toward the barn where the two hands worked.

Santee stood looking at the corral where the wolf dogs had been kept. The bodies were gone, either buried or dragged out away from the yard and dumped for scavenger food. She didn't know and didn't want to know. Their slapdash houses were dumped on a pile along with other refuse, awaiting the right conditions for a match.

The dogs' noses were working double time. Santee put a hand under each jaw and arched their heads up toward hers. "You roll in anything super stinky and you're riding in the back."

They didn't look too worried. Riding in the open truck bed sounded like fun...tons of smells flying by.

Santee turned toward the narrow shotgun-style house. The porch roof hung low on the left-hand corner; one of the support posts had rotted off and lay in the dust. The steps were bowed downward so deep that the nails were popping out of the stringers. The guys' bedrolls were spread out on the porch; apparently the sewery air was preferable to sleeping inside the house.

Santee paused at the top of the steps, hand out to grab that idiot Ruarke who was negotiating the ominously cracking treads. His triumphant grin upon reaching the relative safety of the rotting deck made her want to slap him upside the head. The fool wanted to get back on a baseball field, yet he risked falling through the dang splintery boards full of rusty nails. And for what?

"What?" he asked.

She just shook her head. Sometimes there just were no words. Dumb was just plain dumb.

The door squeaked like the entrance to a haunted house. Fetid, hot air wafted out, carrying the scents of wood rot, ancient onions, and backed-up toilet.

The dogs pressed in eagerly, but Santee grabbed both collars, hauled them outside, and ordered them to stay. They both looked crestfallen at being excluded from the fun.

Ceiling tile, yellowed from rain seepage, dangled in several places. Ancient linoleum rolled in the toe-catching curls.

Sam said, "Oh my God! And to think someone actually lived here."

The living room and dining room were across the front of the house. A hall ran straight through the middle to the back door. It separated the kitchen, piled high with baked on, cooked in, and eaten off pots, pans, and plates, from the bathroom.

Santee dared to brave the stench, took one look into the bathroom, and backed out. "I'm not using these facilities even if I have to pee behind a bush."

Pete grunted. "Me either, and I'm not that picky."

The bedroom on the left of the hall had a bed piled high with soiled bedding. The one on the right was a little bigger than a closet. A single open-spring iron bedstead took up so much space that a person would have to sidestep between it and the wall to get into it.

Santee grabbed the back door and tugged, but it wouldn't budge. Pete added his strength, and with a great groan, the door capitulated and dragged over the warped floorboards.

The back stoop had rotted away, leaving a two-foot drop to the ground and a pile of rotted planks and rusty nails. The open door, however, created a nice, if stinky, breeze through.

"Looks like a burn down to me," Ruarke commented. "Probably not enough good wood to warrant the time and effort to tear it down."

Sam said, "And they managed to raise how any children here?"

"Three," Ruarke said as he led the way back up the hallway. "It was different before Mrs. Graham died."

"How long has she been gone?" Sam asked.

Ruarke paused in the living room among the damp-rotted couch and butt sprung recliner. An ancient thirteen-inch black-and-white TV, complete with rabbit ears, sat on an old peach crate. That wooden peach crate was probably the only thing in the whole house worth salvaging.

"I was pretty young, ten or so. So that'd be about twenty years. I remember seeing them in church. Mr. Graham always wore a suit and tie. Mrs. Graham was pretty nice-looking and always had a hat on."

Santee stepped to a hole in the ceiling and looked up into the dimness.

"What do you see?" Sam asked as he peered up with her.

"Bats."

"What!" He jumped back, caught his heel on the linoleum, and fell into Pete's arms.

"It's fine," Santee said. "They're asleep now. But I wouldn't recommend the guys sleep in here."

Sam shuddered. "No kidding!"

"You'd better watch it, though," Santee said.

"Why?" His dark eyes widened, showing white all around the irises.

"All those lovely dreadlocks would be a perfect nesting ground." She fluttered her fingers at his head.

He ducked and squeaked, slapping at her hands. "Stop that! It's not funny!"

The broad grins on Ruarke's and Pete's faces said otherwise.

"It's okay," Santee said as she patted his arm and headed him toward the door. "If ESPN or TMZ hears about your fear of little old harmless bats, you can be assured none of us told."

"Unless the money's right," Pete said solemnly.

Sam jerked around, caught his foot on the threshold, and slammed into Santee. She managed to brace and prevent both of them from pitching face-first off the porch.

"For a first-class black athlete," Santee said, her arms still around the tall black man, "you certainly are clumsy."

Sam gaped at her then caught the twinkle in her pale eyes. His teeth flashed brilliant white against his ebony skin.

Santee went down the steps and turned, arms spread and feet braced. "Ready."

Sam snorted. "Very funny." He carefully went down the rickety steps.

Pete looked at Ruarke, a broad grin on his face. "She made a joke."

Ruarke nodded. He watched as Santee called to her dogs and walked with Sam toward the barn. Sam said something and gave Santee a shove. She retaliated and rocked the bigger guy.

"She's loosening up with us," Pete said. "Hope that means she's going to be sticking around."

Ruarke's stomach dropped. If they had another early blizzard like a few years ago, he had a feeling she'd be gone as soon as she could get her truck dug out.

That just couldn't happen.

———————————————

Chapter 16

Miri walked into the house wearing a cranberry-red sheath that looked simple but probably cost at least a month's salary for normal people. She was going to blast away all the other parents at the school open house. Her five-inch stilettos ticked as she sashayed across the wooden floor.

Sam wore dark jeans that looked like they'd been ironed and an open-neck pale-blue shirt with the sleeves rolled up to accentuate his muscular forearms.

Ruarke had been awaiting them, knowing they'd be early. Miri was never late and also never on time, often way early. He motioned them to the table where he had the new house plans spread out.

"You look beautiful," Ruarke told Miri.

She beamed at him. "You clean up pretty good yourself." She looked around, didn't see "her," and relaxed.

He was dressed casually in jeans and a polo shirt. "I'm glad we've got a few minutes. I wanted to show you the new designs."

The exterior architecture hauled the old square farmhouse into the twenty-first century, with deep covered patios, big dormers, and huge windows. Rob had vetoed the log or half log siding, opting instead for dark-gray steel siding, lighter-gray steel roof, and white no-maintenance trim. They lived in a semiwooded area. The possibility of wildfire was too real. So the area around the houses and buildings was kept meticulously weed and chaff-free and trees trimmed back. Every building, as its roof needed to be replaced, got steel rather than asbestos.

"Wow!" Miri exclaimed at the artist's rendition.

Then came the floor plans for the farmhouse's second story.

"As you can see, there will be two suites. Each with its own bathroom, walk-in closet, nook for a small fridge, tiny table, microwave, and coffee maker. We can open up into the attic if you'd like a loft. There's plenty of room for a king bed and a couple of easy chairs. And there's a covered deck."

Miri was poking her finger at the bathroom. "No tub? We have a big soaker tub in Atlanta."

"Hon—" Sam said. "It's wonderful what they're doing for us. Giving us a home…family."

"I know, but…"

Ruarke had known this would be a stickler. Miri had always been a bath as opposed to a shower person. "These old walls can't support that kind of weight, and our wells can't stand the kind of drawdown daily that a large tub would require, but—" He poked his finger at the rectangle on the new deck. "Out here, with all the new construction, a small hot tub could be supported. Something that doesn't have to be drained and refilled every time you use it."

"But no bubble baths," she said sadly.

"No bubble baths," Ruarke acknowledged. "The only other option would be for you to build a house of your own and sink another well."

"I like the idea of being here. In this house. With you."

Ruarke looked quickly at Sam, hoping the man didn't get the wrong idea. By now Sam ought to know that flirting for Miri was like breathing; she did it unconsciously and even with Ruarke, whom she knew would never take her up on anything.

Miri was not a cook or a housekeeper. To have the ranch's crew of women, ranch hands' wives mostly, who handled all those tasks plus laundry, was ideal. Plus, Rosarita handled the staff, so Miri wouldn't have to do a thing.

Miri nodded. "I could live with a good soak. I don't necessarily need bubbles."

Sam smiled and winked at Ruarke. Miri also wasn't good with the day-to-day child-rearing, wanting to always be the "good time" guy rather than the adult. Living in the house here would give her kids lots of adults to raise them.

Miri launched at Ruarke and squeezed him so tightly. "Oh, Ruarke, this is so thoughtful of you and your parents. I—" She looked at Sam. "We love it." Sam nodded and took her outstretched hand.

Sam's parents weren't happy with the biracial marriage. They were polite but unwelcoming with Miri. But at least they hadn't cut him off the way Miri's parents had. The kids got to see his parents a couple of times a year and received presents for birthdays and Christmas.

"How did you ever think of all this?" Miri gushed, eyes glowing.

"I didn't."

"Oh?" She nodded. "Of course the architect came up with this wonderful plan."

"Umm… Well, actually Santee had the concept."

Miri's mouth pruned as if she'd bitten into a lemon. "Santee," she said flatly.

"That's right, Miri. Santee. I'd planned a bedroom with an en suite bath over Mom and Dad's room, but Santee said if you were going to live here, you needed a space to call your own."

Both men could see Miri edging toward letting her dislike of Santee color her choice.

Sam said, "We gratefully accept your offer. I think we'd like to open up into the attic for a loft. And I insist on paying for this."

Sam was always more than generous, paying to have his kids stay here.

"And I will accept you paying for this. That's what Max and Bobby John are doing for their suite. They're giving you first dibs. Do you want the front suite or the rear suite?"

Sam looked at Miri. Her mouth was still pruny. "I'm leaning toward the rear. I'm sure Bobby John, being a ranch kid, would rather look out at the animals than I would."

Sulkily, Miri lifted her shoulders. "Whatever."

Ruarke started to say something to jolly her out of her funk, but Sam gave a short shake of his head. So Ruarke let it go. This was something the Adamses were going to work through themselves.

Ruarke just couldn't understand this intense dislike Miri had for Santee. She hadn't even met her but trashtalked her whenever he phoned or Messengered.

This is not a good idea, Santee thought as she and Sunny crossed the ranch yard to the waiting vehicles. Sunny pressed warmly against her leg, but it did little to quell the inner unrest.

Ruarke stood beside the smaller van, the sliding door open. From inside, Miri's strident voice sounded, "Surely we're not going to be stuck with that stinky damn dog too."

Santee looked down at the golden's freshly washed and brushed hair. She'd even brushed her teeth midweek when it was normally a Sunday task. She ruffled Sunny's one good ear. She could hear Sam hushing his wife.

"This is not a good idea," Santee said.

"Ignore her," Ruarke said.

Santee shook her head. "I don't do well in crowds."

The kids were all in the big van that Joe was driving along with Sir Rob and Mrs. Reggie. Other ranch parents and their kids had already taken off for town. Santee was the last to load. And she wouldn't even be here if Jamie hadn't lobbied so hard. He was watching her closely, ready to spring out if she turned away.

"Are we going or what?" Miri grumbled.

Rosarita gave Santee a commiserating half smile. Normally, she bore the brunt of Miri's nastiness. She felt guilty to feel relieved that the acid tongue had found another target. She considered Santee a friend and didn't want to see her treated that way either, though Santee seemed to take it better, letting the digs slide right off her, which probably added to Miri's temper. Rosarita had always thought that Miri got some kind of perverse pleasure out of seeing her zings draw blood.

"You could wait in the car until later then go in. There'll be an early rush, then they'll thin out by eight or so," Ruarke said.

"Maybe."

"If not, you can tell the kids, truthfully, that you tried."

"What a dang fuss."

Ruarke snorted. "Come on." He held his hand out to her as if she weren't capable of stepping into the van unassisted. Santee settled on the seat beside Rosarita. Sunny, wearing her orange vest, settled on her feet, nudging the backpack aside so she had more room.

"Sorry," Santee said and reached for the bag, but Rosarita just laughed it off.

The van started and headed out the drive.

"You look lovely tonight," Santee said. A snort sounded behind, but when she would have whirled on the bitch, Rosarita patted her arm.

"Thank you. You look nice too."

Santee felt dowdy next to Rosarita's vibrantly patterned dress that showed off her womanly assets to perfection. Santee, technically, didn't own a dress. She still had that filmy skirt that the twins had raced down to her when their mother unexpectedly showed up that day. They'd seemed to think it was important that she gussy up. But now a clean, barely worn pair of Goodwill jeans and her best pre-owned purple western shirt over a partially visible lacy chemise was the best she could do.

"We are three very lucky guys this evening," Pete said. He winked at Rosarita in the mirror, making her blush.

"Yes, we are," Sam said from behind.

Santee wanted to clarify that they were not three couples, but Ruarke half turned and winked at her. He winked! At her! She had to fight the urge to turn around and see who he'd actually been winking at, but he'd seemed to be looking straight at her.

What's up with that? she questioned the back of his head.

Parking was nonexistent at the school. Joe pulled the big van into the no-parking sign in front and expelled the passengers before heading to find a parking spot. Pete pulled in behind.

Crowds of people cut around the van headed for the elementary school. Santee's heart began to pound, and her lungs constricted. She looked at the bodies blocking the doorway, knowing that there were hundreds more inside breathing up all the oxygen. Jamie came to her, but Santee sadly shook her head.

"Jamie, I just can't."

"Then I'm staying too."

"No, you're not. If the crowd's clear enough later, I'll come in. You go. Find your Hannah." He blushed. "I'm sure she's looking for you. Pete, I'll park the van."

He looked surprised but didn't argue. He gave Santee the keys and assisted Rosarita out around Sunny and the bulky backpack. Grabbing her around the waist, he easily swung her out.

Sam unpacked his long-legged body and turned to Miri. With a quick grab, he had her wrist and pulled her around to face him. "Don't you dare."

Santee couldn't see what had almost happened, but she could guess.

Miri stepped to the door, chin high. She looked imperiously down at Santee before gracefully alighting to the cracked pavement.

Santee stepped close, mouth to ear, almost overcome by the expensive perfume wafting around the other woman. "Mess with me, bitch, that's one thing. Mess with my dog and your ass is mine. Clear?"

Miri's eyes widened when she looked into those icy eyes. She swallowed hard and nodded.

"Excellent. Have fun."

She motioned for Sunny to stay; told the kids she'd try to come in later, ignoring their protests; and jingled the keys in her hand as she walked around the front.

Joe was returning and looked surprised that Santee was getting behind the wheel. He came up to the driver's side door. He could understand how she felt. He didn't much like crowds either. "I found a spot way down there on the street." He pointed off ahead of her. "Want me to come with?"

Santee smiled. "Thanks, but I managed a truck camper and a twenty-some-foot trailer. I think I've got this."

He reached and patted her shoulder.

"Never doubted it. Just thought you could get me out of this."

"Sorry 'bout that." She started the van and put it in gear.

"No, you're not," he called.

She smiled as she threaded the big vehicle between pedestrians, who seemed set on getting run over. With a sigh of relief at not mowing anyone down, she got to the street and headed off to find the other van.

Ruarke had been right. Eight o'clock must have been the witching hour. People poured out of the building, and parking spaces opened up. Santee turned the van around and moved it closer to the old two-story brick building. She wished she'd gotten the keys to the other van. She could have moved them both.

Sunny sat in the passenger seat watching the school. Two figures came out the door attracting the dog's attention. She stood up and began wagging, tongue lolling.

Jamie and his friend, a girl who had to be the infamously smart Hannah, searched the cars. Santee flipped on the van's headlights for an instant. Jamie saw, and his tense shoulders relaxed. He lifted a hand and started across the street.

Santee got out with Sunny, making sure the dog stayed safely between her and the van.

The girl with Jamie was slightly pudgy and unkempt. Her jeans were too long for her and unraveled on the ground. Her tee bagged at the neck and had a ketchup stain on the bodice. Her blond hair (what was it with all these blondes in this country?) looked clean but billowed around her head as if electrified. And her glasses. The heavy black frames listed across her pert nose at a severe angle.

The poor kid had so many strikes against her. But she had Jamie. So she was lucky.

"Santee. This is Hannah," he said proudly, making the girl blush and lower her eyes.

"Pleased to meet you, Mrs.—ah…"

"Santee," she said. "Jamie talks about you all the time." Both kids were blushing, and Hannah glanced shyly at Jamie.

Jamie said, "I think you could try it now. A lot of people have gone home already."

Santee looked at the innocuous building, dread weighing heavily. She'd never had much of a formal education. They'd always claimed they were homeschooling the girls. Actually, Santee figured they were scared that one of the girls would let slip about the abuse. So when the pressure to enroll the kids in school got too hard, they'd just pack up and move on. He never had trouble finding a job. His reputation as a horse trainer was A-1. His employers never suspected what He did to the fractious horses.

"Hannah, before we go, I have a bandana that would look lovely in your beautiful hair. Would you like it?"

Hannah's hands went to her head, eyes widening at the unexpected compliment.

Santee hauled the backpack onto the van's seat and rummaged inside, past the weapons and other life necessities. "I've got a pretty blue one that will match your pretty eyes."

She showed Hannah the deep blue one. Hannah nodded excitedly. Santee folded it into a narrow ribbon and, while Hannah held her hair, put it on top of her head and tied it under at the nape of her neck. When her hair was released, it no longer swirled around her face like a cloud.

Hannah patted at her hair, looking nervously at Jamie. "Looks good," he said.

Santee didn't have a mirror, but the van did. "Climb in and see for yourself."

The oversized pants made movement difficult, but Hannah managed to get in and face the mirror. Hannah's smile made the hours waiting in the van worth it. Jamie leaned over and gave Santee a quick one-armed hug.

A whole different girl walked back into the school after Santee made just a couple of clothing adjustments. She rolled up the pants legs and waistband so the jeans fit her better and used an assortment of safety pins to secure them. For the shirt, Santee gathered the tails around to one side and knotted them at her waist, which was actually smaller than the overlarge clothing had indicated. Sadly there wasn't anything that could be done about the glasses. Not tonight anyway.

The Fab Four awaited her in the hall outside their room. They raced up, giving Sunny hugs first, which showed where Santee rated in the grand scheme of things.

Simon and Trev were first and second today and got to hold her hand and lead her into their room. Trey and RePete led Sunny in by her collar. Their excited voices seemed to echo in the room. Santee motioned them to quieter tones, and the pounding in her head lessened with the decreased volume.

Ruarke was chatting with the woman who turned out to be the boys' teacher. He and the woman seemed very comfortable with each other. They seemed about the same age so could possibly have gone to school together.

"Santee," he called, motioning her over. "This is Heidi Cameron."

"Gonzales."

"Oh, right, Gonzales. I forgot that you got married recently."

She laughed, brown eyes twinkling. "It's been over two years. And you sent us a lovely crystal vase as a present."

Ruarke laughed. "I wanted to send a microwave. But Mom vetoed that in a hurry."

Heidi laughed. "We actually could have used a microwave."

Heidi turned to Santee. "So you are Mommy Tee, the inventor of 'snoozy-poozy' time."

"Yay-ess," Santee said warily.

"What a wonderful idea! I hope you don't mind, but I use it with all the kids and have no trouble getting them to at least lie down and be quiet. Because everyone knows—"

"Only babies take naps," Santee said.

"Exactly," Heidi agreed then excused herself to talk to some other parents.

Santee breathed a sigh of relief.

"That wasn't so hard."

"Easy for you to say. You know all these people."

After a quick look at the artwork on the walls and an in-depth exploration of the play area and the toys, they were off to a quick tour of kindergarten, led by Sophie and a beaming Rosarita.

Remmy was a first grader. Rio was in second grade. Santee was shown their desks and their books and their papers on the walls. Their friends had already come and gone. Their teachers eyed Santee speculatively, as if wondering who the heck this woman was being escorted around by the town's "claim to fame"?

Outside the sixth grade room, a "bad" boy leaned against the lockers. His malevolent stare made everyone give him a wide berth. He dressed like a black gangster: baggie-assed pants hanging low, untied high tops, and a long hoodie on a warm evening. He had shaggy brown hair that dangled into his dark eyes. And there was a hint of darkness to his cheeks, as if his beard was starting to sprout.

His leering eyes nailed Santee. Jamie tried to pull her into the room, but she stared down the little punk until he finally caved, but not before his mean eyes nailed both Jamie and Hannah. Then he pushed away from the wall, sauntering down the center of the hall, shoulders busting aside any kid who got in his way. Not many did. They saw him coming and scattered.

"I wish I could do that."

Santee turned to the older woman who'd come out of the room. The gray-haired woman said, "He hasn't backed down for me, not once."

Santee watched the little miscreant stalk away. Something seemed familiar. The slouch or the baggy hoodlum clothes. She'd seen that kid somewhere before.

Finally, after what seemed like hours, Santee drew a deep breath of air that had not already been through another's lungs. She leaned down and ruffled Sunny's neck. The canine pressure against her legs had helped get her through this night and allowed her to be dragged all over the school: the cafeteria ("where we get our food"), the gym ("where we get to run and play"), the office ("where the puh-puh, head of all the teachers, lives"), and even the bathrooms ("where the pee-pee and poopy go in the potty, not on the floor").

Ruarke snorted. If he'd heard that once, he'd heard it a dozen times. Santee had drilled that into those four little boys' heads. There also had not been any problems with them keeping their clothes on. They knew it bothered their Mommy Tee and so didn't do it any-more, whereas before, it hadn't mattered that a dozen people had been upset by it and sternly talked to them. One time. Santee turned and walked out, and that's all it took.

Sir Rob came up to the van where Santee was loading Sunny. "Why don't you let Reggie and me take the kids home. You seven go have some fun on this lovely Friday evening."

"I'll go with you," Santee said.

"No," Mrs. Reggie said. "You need some time off too. Rob and I can get the kids to bed."

Santee looked back toward the school to where Hannah still stood looking lost and alone.

"Jamie," she said, "are Hannah's parents picking her up, or does she need a ride home?"

"Her parents are off on some trip. Seems like they're always gone. Her brother and sister are supposed to be watching her, but…" He shrugged.

The S-twins looked at each other and nodded. "Maybe Hannah could spend the weekend at our place. We could stop by her place—"

"Her brother's having a party there. That's why she doesn't want to go home," Jamie said.

"So she can borrow some stuff of ours," Shaynee said.

"Couldn't look any worse than what she's got on now," Shawnee said. "At least how it looked before someone"—she looked pointedly at Santee—"got their pins in her."

Santee looked up to the sky. "I don't have a clue what you're talking about."

The S-twins giggled and hugged Santee. It was amazing, Santee thought, how nice these girls were. They hadn't had the most stable of lives—a mother who abandoned them and a father gone playing ball for six to eight months a year. And then at fourteen, they'd had five brothers shoved on them. Yet here they were, after having spent a whole evening wrangling their little siblings through an elementary open house, still able to empathize with poor Hannah.

"Jamie, see if Hannah would like to spend the weekend with us," Mrs. Reggie said.

"You wouldn't know her parents are probably two of the wealthiest people in this end of the state," Bob said. "They're the ones buying up the ranches, subdividing them into ranchettes, and making a fortune doing it."

"Hannah sure doesn't take after her siblings," Mrs. Reggie said. "They got the athletic ability, and Hannah got the brains."

"And the shaft."

"Robert Sinclair!" Mrs. Reggie exclaimed.

"Well, it's the truth. They go to every one of the sporting events, but I've never seen them at anything to do with this girl."

"Shh," Mrs. Reggie hissed. "Here she comes."

The bounce in her step was their answer, the smile the icing. "I called and put a message on the machine letting them know where I'll be." She clapped her hands excitedly. "Thank you so, so much."

"We're glad to have you," Mrs. Reggie assured her. "Now let's get loaded up, and maybe we can talk Sir Rob, here, into stopping by the drive-in for a treat."

Sir Rob linked his arm through his wife's. He winked at the others. "I don't think that will take too much convincing."

At the schoolhouse door, another unkempt figure appeared to watch the Sinclair caravan leave.

"I can get us a table at the Bucking Bull," Joe said.

"Take it," Ruarke said. Friday nights even in a small town could be lively. This time of night they were lucky to get a table.

Santee was going to be sick. Sunny knew it and was doing her level best to calm Santee down, but all her kisses, panting in the face, and laying like a warm blanket across her legs was not solving the problem.

The parking lot was packed with pickups. Music blasted the air. Cowboys with their cowgirls on their arms laced around the trucks, set on having a good old time.

The van's interior lights came on. Miri and Sam slid past and out the door. Miri's hips were already swaying as she led Sam off.

"Santee?" Rosarita looked concerned at her.

"Go on. Have fun."

Rosarita looked torn, but she took Pete's hand and stepped out.

Joe hesitated, but Ruarke waved him off. Even bodyguards needed to blow off some steam. He left Ruarke only because there hadn't been a problem in quite a while.

"You go," Santee said.

"Wouldn't be much fun," Ruarke said, surprised at how truthful that seemed.

"I'm sure Miri will save some dances for you."

"True, but dancing with Miri is like dancing with my sister." At Santee's askance look, he said, "Sure she flirts with me. She flirts with all men. It's just her. But we both know nothing's going to come of it."

"Never did?"

Ruarke winced at the memory of the month when they'd tried to be more than friends. They'd discovered real fast that they made better friends than lovers.

"Does Sam know?"

Ruarke shrugged. "I don't know if Miri told him or not. I haven't. And there's really nothing to tell. We gave it a try, but there was no real sexual attraction."

"You were a teenager, and there was nothing sexual."

Ruarke laughed. "I know. Surprised us both, but it was for the best. So?" Ruarke inclined his head toward the neon flashing sign of the Bucking Bull.

Santee shook her head. "You go."

He patted the braced lag. "How much dancing could I do with this? Besides—" He got out and stood before the side door holding out his hand to her. "We've got music right here."

"I can't." She'd never danced in her life.

"I can't really either, so we'll just kind of sway." He wriggled his fingers at her.

Her hand seemed to have a mind of its own as it settled into his warm palm. She allowed herself to be gently tugged out past Sunny.

She stood there so awkwardly. She had no clue what to do in a situation like this, with a man like this. This was so far beyond her realm of experience.

"Now," Ruarke said softly. "If you would loop your arms around my neck like so." He took her limp arms and put them on his shoulders.

"And I will put my hands like this." He settled his big paws on the point of her hips. He'd have liked to have put them elsewhere, but he figured she'd deck him.

He started to sway, his hands guiding her tense body. Then he started to slowly move in a circle as they moved to the music. By the end of the song, when she jerked away, she'd actually been relaxing into him.

Santee felt like such an idiot! Dancing out here with the likes of Ruarke Sinclair! There was only one possible reason he'd be doing this, and he was going to be sorely disappointed because it just wasn't going to happen.

Santee went and sat on the door ledge. Sunny came and licked her ear.

Ruarke made a short phone call and eased himself down beside her, leg outstretched.

Maybe he'd come to his senses and was calling a taxi or one of those Uber cars to take her home. Then he'd be free to find someone who'd be happy to be a woman for him.

They sat there for several minutes when a car cruised slowly through the parking lot. Santee started to get up, thinking it was her ride, but the car went on past. She looked at Sinclair, waiting for him to holler and flag down the car, but he just looked quizzically at her.

"Who did you think that was?"

"My ride."

"Your what?"

If she were the eye-rolling type, she'd do it now. "The car you called to take me to the ranch."

He smiled at her, a smile that would have made a lesser woman weak in the knees. "Now why would I call a car and send you home? We just got here. And besides, you're the designated driver."

"The phone call—"

Joe came with a tray of goodies. "Sorry it took so long. They're really busy."

He unloaded the tray's contents onto the running board: a frosty mug of foamy beer, a dripping unopened can of Dr. Pepper, a basket of wings and a basket of fries, along with a handful of ketchup packets and two containers of dipping sauce.

"Anything else right now?"

"We're good for now," Ruarke said and held out fifty dollars to Joe. He tried to wave it off, but Ruarke said, "Buy a round for the others. And thanks."

"Call when you need a refill." And he was off.

"That was the call you made?"

"Yes. Dig in."

Santee felt like an ass. But what else should she think?

While they were eating, Ruarke asked, "You honestly thought I'd called for a car to take you home."

Santee shrugged, avoiding looking at him.

"Why would I do that?"

Again she shrugged.

"Santee, I'm not that kind of guy."

She raised those pale eyes to his. "You're all 'that kind of guy.'"

"Ouch!" What had happened to give her such a low opinion of men?

Before he could try to delve deeper, Pete and Rosarita appeared with another tray. They were both flushed and laughing, clearly feeling no pain. Pete dug in his jeans and pulled out the van keys. Holding them out to Santee, he said, "I hear you're the designated driver."

"I seem to have heard that also," she said as she took charge of the keys.

The party had apparently moved out by the van. Pete and Rosarita made no move to return inside. They danced tight together, voices soft, giggles suggestive.

Ruarke held his hand out to Santee.

She looked pointedly at his leg.

"It feels surprisingly good." He wiggled his fingers in a "come hither" motion.

Santee arose, made sure Sunny knew that the food was not fair game, and moved into Ruarke's arms. Once more he kept his hands polite, their body spacing friendly, not lover-like.

The beery scent was not too appealing, but she knew he was far from inebriated. His scent tickled her senses, unfamiliar pheromones attacking her reticence.

Joe's arrival gave Santee the excuse to back out of Ruarke's hands. A big-haired blonde, with big attributes, giggled as she was dragged behind him. "Boss, are you going to need me any more tonight?"

Ruarke laughed. "No, go ahead, but you'll have to get your own ride home."

"I'll figure something out. Thanks." He went back toward the bar with the woman flapping along behind.

Joe and his lady detoured between two other cars rather than run into Miri and Sam. "What's going on?" Miri demanded. "What's everyone doing out here?" She grabbed Ruarke's arm, well aware that those hands had just been on Santee and not liking it. "Come on, Ruarke. Let's go dance."

Ruarke pulled free. "I'm not much of a dancer right now. You need to dance with your husband."

"But it's no fun if you're not there!" she whined.

Time seemed to stand still as eyes flicked between her and Sam.

"Oh!" She turned to her stiffened, cold-eyed husband. "You know I didn't mean it like that!" She leaned into Sam, running her hand under his shirt. "It's just more fun with the two of you to dance with."

Sam grabbed her wrists and threw them away from him. He spun on his heel and marched off.

"Oh, come on, Sammy!" Miri cried. "Don't be like that." She teetered after him and cried out when she twisted off her heels and bumped up against a dusty pickup. She called to Sam as she again went after him. "You know I only did it so he could get away from her!" She stumbled and cried out, but he refused to turn back to her. "Sammy, come on. Don't be like this!"

"Santee," Ruarke said.

185

She waved away whatever he would have said. "Sunny needs a walk."

As she and the dog headed off to find a weed to water, she heard Rosarita say, "I never did like that woman."

"Rosie," Peter warned.

"It's okay," Ruarke said. There were times that he didn't like her very much either.

When Santee and Sunny returned, the party debris had been cleaned up. Rosarita and Pete were already in the van. Pete called to Sunny and got the dog down by his feet.

Nearby, Sam stood stiff as a corpse, his hands tucked into his pits.

Miri was in the van, her sobs resounded into the night.

Ruarke looked like he wanted to go to Sam but didn't know how receptive the man would be. He looked pleadingly at Santee and inclined his head toward Sam.

Santee knew that she wasn't good at this touchy-feely stuff. She didn't know what to say, so she just stood beside him. The air vibrated with his anger.

Sam glanced down at her. "I'm so sorry."

"It's not your fault. I bet she's jealous of every female that comes close to him."

He nodded. "This is getting ridiculous. I should have put a stop to it a long time ago."

"It doesn't mean she doesn't love you."

"Doesn't it?"

Santee put her hand on his arm. "No. It doesn't. Maybe all you need is to make it plain that enough is enough."

"You think that will work?"

"It can't hurt to try. You've got her all to yourself in the back of the van. Talk to her. Put your oversized foot down."

He snorted, teeth flashing against his dark skin. He looked over her toward the van.

"I truthfully don't think he leads her on," Santee said.

He sighed. "I know. They're like brother and sister, yet they aren't." He put his hand on her shoulder and gave it a gentle squeeze, then he ducked into the van and moved to the back. Miri's voice sounded shrill, but Sam's sharp retort silenced her.

The drive home was tense. Sunny whined occasionally. From the back came a deep voice mixed with higher-pitched pleas. From the middle seat came smooching sounds. A glance in the rearview mirror made Santee flip it up so she couldn't see what was going on back there.

"Take the next right," Ruarke said.

"What? Why?" Santee said. That narrow dirt road wouldn't take them to the ranch.

"Just do it, please."

So Santee flipped on the blinker and turned off the highway onto a two-track dirt road that led into the pines, over a cattle guard around several tight curves and under branches that scraped the roof and sides of the van. Granite boulders the size of VW bugs lined the road, making a U-turn impossible.

At least a mile later, the claustrophobic trees fell away. A clearing appeared like magic, with half a dozen cars scattered throughout. Country music twanged softly.

What the heck?

"Pull up over here." Ruarke pointed to an open spot.

Santee shut off the van and the headlights. "Where are we?"

There was enough of a moon to show Ruarke's broad smile. "Lover's Lane."

"You're sh—"

The sounds in the back of the van were sounding more and more urgent, both male and female.

Crap! Santee exited fast, pausing only long enough for Sunny to jump out. The other door slammed, also.

She and Ruarke met at the front of the van. "You guys do this together all the time?"

He grinned at the unspoken "yuck" in her voice.

"Miri and I double-dated all the time. If we wanted to you-know, and we always wanted to you-know, we had to. It got so we didn't even notice, and actually, it kind of became like an aphrodisiac…not that teenage boys needed it, but it sure got the girls' juices flowing."

Again she shot him that "yuck" look.

Santee shuddered and wrapped her arms around herself as frigid memories threatened to escape. The feel of the bed rocking. The sound of another sister's cry. The grunting triumph as—

"Santee!"

She blinked back. Icy sweat drenched her. Her teeth chattered as she hugged the dog who was trying to climb into her arms. Warmth enveloped her as Ruarke's jacket descended onto her shoulders.

"I'm going to hug you now," he warned as he pulled her against him. His scent clogged her olfactory glands, similar but not like the other.

"I'm okay." She tried to wriggle free, but he held on, gentle but firm.

"Not yet."

Sunny dropped to the ground but planted her feet on Ruarke's toes.

He put his hands on either side of Santee's pale icy face. For a moment there, she'd been gone from him, and it scared the crap out of him. What would he do if she didn't come back from that scary place in her mind?

The van picked up a rhythm of hops and jerks. Sounds of pleasure resounded.

At Santee's dour look, Ruarke had to laugh. "Looking them in the face tomorrow is going to be difficult."

Ruarke leaned in and pressed his lips to hers, catching her by surprise. Her mouth O'd, but he didn't press his advantage.

"Don't," Santee warned. His breath felt so warm against her icy skin, his palms like little heaters on her cheeks.

"Why?" he whispered, lips brushing hers.

Santee eased back. "You don't know me. I could be an ax murderer for all you know."

"Do you have an ax in that bag of yours?"

"That's not the point!"

"Hard to be an ax murderer without an ax."

Her eyes narrowed on him. "I could hurt you really bad right now and you wouldn't even be able to yell for help."

"I'm really not into that sadomasochistic stuff, but if you are, I'm willing to give it a whirl."

"You're being way too cavalier about this. I'm not a one-night-stand kind of girl."

"Never thought you were."

"Then what is this? A test to see if the great Ruarke Sinclair still has it? You still have it." She twisted away. "Now leave me alone."

"And if I don't?" He moved up behind her. He wanted to slide his arms around her but thought better of it.

She turned on him, but the van door sliding open cut her off.

Pete stepped out, fully dressed, but shirt hanging open. "Been a while since we've come here. I missed it."

Santee went to the door and got Sunny in.

"If y'all're finished, we'll be going."

The interior smelled of musky sex. Soft voices sounded from the back. Sam and Miri must have worked it out. Santee jumped when Rosarita's arms came around the seat to hug her.

"Gracias for stopping, *mi amiga*." She sounded sleepy, happy, and very satisfied. With a giggle, she withdrew and settled into her husband's arms.

This evening certainly hadn't turned out as expected. There was no way in a million years she'd have ever dreamed she'd end up in Lover's Lane. Seemed like a bucket list kind of event.

Sam and Miri seemed relaxed and happy as they headed out for Atlanta.

Rosarita was blushing and all atwitter; the other ladies cast knowing looks at each other and giggling.

Joe returned, very relaxed.

Even Sir Rob and Mrs. Reggie seemed uncommonly affectionate.

The only tension was between Santee and Ruarke. She wanted to slap him upside the head with a 2×4, knock some sense into that idiot.

She'd told him she wasn't a one-night-stand girl.

She was leaving with the first snow, which could be most anytime.

So how was he reconciling those two facts with the way he was acting?

It just didn't make sense.

————————————

Chapter 17

Something was different. Santee's hands were on him, but the scorching heat wasn't there.

He tried to visualize his leg healing with each knead, but the connection wasn't there.

Her hands slid so silky soft tighter and higher until they—

His eyes popped open.

Long blond hair fanned over his groin. Long fingers strongly stroked—

"Stop!"

His masseuse raised her head, her tongue slid the circumference of her full red lips.

"Liza. No."

She smiled, her hands still folded around him. "The insurance company never needs to know." She began to lower her face once more.

"No!" Ruarke leaned up and almost nose to nose caught her wrists.

The squeak of the opening door turned both their heads. Santee stood silhouetted in the sunlight. She paused, pulling her dark glasses off. "Ruarke? Sir Rob wan—"

He felt the impact of her gaze and knew the erroneous picture he and Liza painted.

Without a word, she backed and squeaked the door shut.

"Goddamn it!"

The Cheshire Cat smile froze. "Really, Ruarke. I wouldn't mind—"

"Back off."

Her hands were shoved away, hurt in her eyes.

Ruarke swung his legs over the side of the table, hauling the towel into coverage.

"Ruarke, I'm sorry. I didn't mean—"

Didn't she? he really wondered. Apparently his "type" was well-known. And here she was, natural or not honey-gold hair; blue-eyed, possibly with the help of colored contacts; and buxom, definitely with augmentations. And now she had an eye witness who'd truthfully testify to the compromising situation.

Had this been planned, he thought sourly, just hopeful for a witness, or perhaps there was a video camera someplace taking damning evidence of sexual exploitation in expectation of a lawsuit and a huge payoff?

Her bag was sitting nearby on the weight bench. The narrow end seemed to be angled toward where he'd lain. Or was it just a figment of his suspicious mind.

He grabbed his phone and punched Pete's number. Liza seemed nonchalant about it all, but it could be a ploy. "Pete, can you come here?" He clicked off, knowing Pete would be but a moment.

The woman looked tanned and lovely in her tight white tank and short white skirt, as she quickly started packing her bag.

The door whipped open, and Pete burst in. His suspicious eyes scanned for trouble. His gaze flitted between his boss and the beautiful woman, feeling the tension in the air. In just a couple of strides, he was at his angry boss's side. He grabbed Ruarke's arm, knowing he wasn't supposed to be on his feet without the leg brace yet.

Ruarke turned tired, sad eyes his way. "Can you check Liza's bag?" He inclined his head toward where it sat innocently enough. At Pete's silent question, he added, "Make sure there isn't a recording device in it."

Pete stiffened. He had no idea what had sparked this suspicion after all these months, but it was his job to protect Ruarke from any kind of attack.

"Here," Pete said, moving to the pile of Liza's stuff. "Let me help you."

"No, I've—" She made a grab for the bag.

But Pete got it first and turned his back to the woman.

"Give it to me!" She pounded on Pete's back, but she might as well have been brushing her knuckles on a steel-reinforced wall.

By contract, they had the right to search everyone as they came or left but so far had never felt the need. Something happened. Pete noticed what looked like a tiny lens fitted into the leather.

"I'll sue!" She turned as if to go at Ruarke, but Pete blocked her. "Ruarke, please, it's not what you think!"

Ruarke sighed as Pete pulled a small video recorder out of the bag. Liza dropped to her knees, sobbing. Ruarke said, "I don't know how you planned to edit this, but you should know that this room is also being taped. Every session with you and every therapy."

Running mascara coursed black trails down her pale cheeks. "I'm begging you." She made as if to crawl to him, but Pete blocked her. "I need this job!" she shrieked. "Please!"

"How many others have you pulled this same shit on?" Ruarke asked.

Her eyes shifted away.

Ruarke got his phone's directory up, found the right number, and listened to the ringing. It didn't take long for the insurance company to react.

Sheriff Lance Armstrong showed up in person along with a female deputy. Pete had made copies of all the ranch's pertinent recordings, plus he'd managed to make a copy off Liza's camera for themselves. Knowing Armstrong as he did, Ruarke would not have put it past the man to accidentally on purpose lose the videos or tamper with them in such a way that threw Ruarke in a bad light.

"Wow," Lance said as his deputy put Liza into the car. He took off his hat and wiped the leather band with his handkerchief before resettling it on his head. "You've really had a bad year."

Ruarke pulled his gaze from the woman leaning against the fence by the barn. The horses had come trotting up the minute Santee stopped there.

"At least this one's your type," Lance said, nodding at the woman straining to look out the rear window of the cruiser. Her tearstained face pleaded with Ruarke.

Ruarke was getting extremely tired of being told about his type.

"More so than that serial-killer-eyed one." The sheriff gave a fake shudder. "Can you imagine looking into those icy eyes at that…climatic moment?" He shuddered again. "I bet a guy'd shrivel up every damn time."

Ruarke could imagine it, had been imagining it when Liza screwed everything up. He'd be lucky if Santee ever spoke to him again without visualizing that damning instant.

Goddamn it!

Lance chuckled. He clapped Ruarke on the shoulder with just a little push to unbalance him, but Ruarke's leg was strong enough now to take it. Lance gave him that shit-eating grin that he had shown every time he'd done something to undercut Ruarke.

"Well," Lance said, holding up the evidence bag, "guess I'd better get these safely back to the station."

Rob walked out of the house. "Can you stay for a cup of coffee, Sheriff?"

"No, thank you, sir," Lance said politely, which was how he got elected. He was polite to the older folks, good-looking and flirty to ladies, and managed to not kick any dogs or run over any cats…at least not while anyone was looking. And sadly he'd probably be the county sheriff for a long, long time, unless he decided to ride his looks into the state legislature.

The sheriff's car headed out, but before it left the yard, it pulled up to where Santee stood. Ruarke could see Santee responding to something Lance said and gritted his teeth. At least he knew Lance's gambit with Santee couldn't be too blatant. But Ruarke was relieved to see Joe heading across toward the barn. Lance must have also and sped away before the big black man got to Santee's side—not that she needed backup, but Lance was snake enough to slither through the best defenses.

"I wish you wouldn't do that, offer him coffee. You know I can't stand the man."

Rob clapped his hand on Ruarke's shoulder. "Doesn't hurt to make nice to local law enforcement. Never know when we might need the dirty, rotten, slimy bastard."

"Dad!"

Rob's eyes twinkled. "You think I'm clueless, but I see and know way more than you think." He nodded toward Santee and eyed Ruarke. Then he turned and headed across the yard toward the crew working on the new arena.

Santee and her dogs went to meet up with him. Ruarke watched as his dad got animated, his hands expressing what he was saying. Santee walked beside him, intent on his words.

Ruarke wished he could get Santee to listen that easily to his tale of woe, but somehow he didn't think it would go that smoothly for him.

Santee sat outside beside the trailer as usual. She was wrapped in a blanket, but soon even that wouldn't be enough. The nights were getting decidedly nippy.

Both dogs lay with her, a third creeping closer every evening. Sunny and Rufus wore kids' tees, safety pinned so that it fit around the belly and so Rufus could still pee. It wouldn't be long before she'd have to go doggie jacket shopping. Never would she have guessed she'd be shopping for clothes for a dang dog. But then she'd never intended to have a dang dog, much less two of them…maybe three.

Sir Rob could never understand why she wanted to be dropped at the thrift store when they were in town. "Just go to Walmart," he'd say. "I'll buy my granddogs' duds." He didn't realize that she could afford to buy new. What else did she have to spend her more-than-generous wages on? She never drove her truck anywhere, so no gas expense. All her meals were provided. She didn't need much for clothes unless she was still here when it really got cold. Plus her utilities were all provided. What else was there to spend her money on but the dogs?

Just today she'd gone in for breakfast and to get the kids off to school. Rosarita handed her an envelope. "You got a letter," she'd said brightly. A rare occurrence. "Ees from the doggies' doctor."

Santee had wondered why, when the next payment wasn't due. Then Sir Rob tried to slip it out of her hand, saying he'd see what was up, when normally it was Jamie's job to read for her.

Suspiciouser and suspiciouser.

So she'd held tight to the point where one of them had to give or the letter was going to rip down the middle.

"Please," Sir Rob had said, which just deepened her suspicions. At her head shake, he'd finally given in.

It didn't take a reader to see the bottom line of the bill with a bunch of zeros on it.

Further up the sheet was her last payment followed by a much larger payment, which brought the amount she owed down to zero.

She looked at her boss. At least he had the grace to look guilty about going behind her back.

"I'll write you out a check."

He shot off the chair. "You will not!"

Silence descended as the rare raised voice resounded.

"Those are my granddogs. If I want to pay off their medical bills, I will. And besides he was charging an astronomical interest rate."

"I was lucky he let me pay on time, or Sunny'd have been put down and Rufus would have been in a shelter. Who'd have wanted this big dumb dog that looks so pit bully? He'd have been put down too. But you still shouldn't have gone behind my back…"

Jamie came in and looked decidedly guilty also. So, Santee knew where Sir Rob had gotten the vet's name and address.

"Or take advantage of innocent kids like that."

Jamie'd looked relieved. Sir Rob seemed a little embarrassed but not nearly as chastened as he should have.

"Men!"

Rufus raised his head and gave a thump of his tail as if to say, "Not me."

Sunny and Rufus alerted, tails dancing at a friend's visit. The wolf dog eased warily to his feet.

Santee knew by the uneven tread who was coming. Her cheeks heated at what she'd walked in on. It was none of her business who Ruarke Sinclair did it with.

"Santee?"

She sighed. "Yes?"

"May I?"

Her mouth opened to say something snarky, but she snapped her teeth down on it. The consequences of voicing that, at one time in her life, would have been brutal.

"Sure," she said. "Why not?"

From her feet, the wolf dog slunk away into the night. He'd only recently gotten brave enough to creep in close.

"What the hell!"

"It's okay." But was she telling the canine or the man?

Ruarke edged nearer. The wolf dog's eyes glowed red like a hellhound.

Santee pulled the cushion from behind her back and shoved it under Ruarke as he warily lowered himself down.

"When did he show up?"

"It's been a while now." Santee didn't want to admit that the dog had shown up within two days of the incident at the Graham ranch. He still dragged a piece of chain. She hadn't gotten close enough to unhook it from his collar. Besides, she wasn't getting that involved. It was one thing to put out some food for an animal who'd never had to find his own... She was, after all, just preventing him from going after a Sinclair calf or chicken.

"What's his name?"

Santee opened her mouth then clamped it shut. She saw him smiling at her. He thought he knew her so well. "Not my dog."

"Looks pretty well-fed."

"So."

"Seems pretty content here."

"So."

"Sooo," he drawled, "one would expect that the person who was the object of the dog's trust and affection...the one who'd been feeding him...might also have given him a name. Rather than always thinking of him as 'that dog.'"

She rolled her eyes. "Duke."

"He does remind me a little bit of John Wayne."

Her glare earned her a resonating chuckle that settled deep into her gut, an unusual but not unpleasant sensation.

"Santee, we need to talk."

Oh, crap. The four worst words in the English language. "I couldn't just let him starve."

"Not about the dog."

She'd known that but had hoped to divert him onto another topic. "I can't think of anything else that needs to be talked about." She determinedly averted her gaze from the handsomest man she'd ever been this close to…and his smell that seemed to overpower the piney woods scent and headed straight to her groin.

"How about what you walked in on?"

"None of my business what goes on between two consenting adults." She sounded like such a sanctimonious prick.

"The sheriff wouldn't have been there if it had been consensual."

"Really. I heard it had more to do with blackmail or selling off the lurid pictures. So you are charging her with rape?"

That made him pause.

"Boys will be boys." Santee went to get up, but Ruarke caught her wrist and kept her in place.

"What's that supposed to mean?"

Santee jerked her hand free. Rufus and Sunny moved away, upset by their humans' tenseness.

"I never had sex with that woman. It wouldn't be ethical, me being more or less her boss."

"No sex of any kind?"

"No."

"No little hand job?"

"No."

"No little oral job?"

"Santee!"

"Come on, Ruarke. You don't need to paint yourself lily white for me. You're a guy in your prime. That's all that needs to be said."

"You don't have a very high opinion of men."

She wasn't going into her reasons for her opinions. She spent the vast majority of her life subjugated to the power of men who'd used and abused that power at every opportunity and in every way, shape, or form their nasty, shitty little minds could conjure up. No, no, her opinion of men was not very high.

"You've been married twice and divorced twice." "Not because of my infidelity!"

"You're off on away games for ten to fourteen days, and you're telling me you never hooked up with some groupie and got your rocks off?"

"Not while I was married."

Santee snorted in disbelief.

"Ask Pete."

"And he wouldn't lie for you? You guys rally together. Cover each other's backs. He's got a good thing here. He's not going to screw it up by telling the whole truth and nothing but the truth."

"So if I can't keep my pants on, what about Pete? Do you really see him cheating on Rosarita?"

No, she didn't, but… "He probably wouldn't even think of it as cheating. It's only sex after all."

"Goddamn it!"

Duke went sharply on alert. His glowing eyes locked on Ruarke.

"Easy," Santee said softly. Poor Rufus was trembling against her leg, torn between being a good dog and his human's protector. Sunny, gentle, ladylike Sunny, had no qualms. Her lips lifted to show nice white fangs. Santee laid a soothing hand on each dog.

Ruarke rubbed his hands over his head and down his cheeks. Santee could feel his need to move around, but his bum leg and a dog ready to tear him a new one kept him seated.

"God," Ruarke groaned and sighed. "When I was a free man, sure, I had one-night stands. And I suffered for it by getting myself a stalker, a woman who'd built this whole lie about us until she believed it and was ready to kill me and my family rather than lose me. That is when Pete and Joe came into my life and security cameras and living behind gates. It made me think twice about screwing around. But then I never really enjoyed it anyway. It was simply a need, like eating or sleeping."

"Right," Santee said, letting the disbelief drip through.

Ruarke ignored it. "After I was shot, even that urge was gone. It's very disconcerting to a man when he isn't getting...stimulated several times a day the way he used to."

Santee kept her face frozen, though it was way too much information.

"Yesterday, I was not aroused by Liza or by the massage." He swallowed hard. "I was daydreaming about another woman's hands on me." He turned to Santee. "Someone so out of my usual attractant zone. Someone tall and slender. Someone with not-blonde hair. Someone who thinks way too much for my good. Someone who makes it very plain that her opinion of me and men in general ranks a tad higher than raw sewage. Someone that I feel this desperate need to prove to that I can be a nice guy, one she can trust, who would never hurt her if for no other reason than because I know she could and would kick my butt. Someone who is bound and determined to leave me in the dust as she speeds off, for some God-only-knows reason, to goddamned Texas!"

Santee's heart thudded so loud it was amazing she could hear what she wished she could un-hear. How the heck had she gotten herself into this situation? She'd been going along, minding her own business, and whammo changeo, here she was stuck in an episode of the *Twilight Zone*. Her whole dang life was an episode of the *Twilight Zone*. One would think that she'd earned a break from it. If only—

"I should leave."

"God, no!"

"Look, man—"

"Ruarke."

"I know your name," she said shortly.

"You're trying to distance yourself by not using my name."

She narrowed her eyes at him. "You a shrink or something?"

"No, but—"

"So shut up and listen. Really listen to me."

He gave a nod, but Santee didn't think he meant it or that it would do any good.

"You don't know me." He opened his mouth, but her upheld hand silenced him. "I'm not a nice person. Not the kind of person you need to—" She frowned. "Have you noticed the bruises on Jamie lately?"

The sudden topic change threw Ruarke for a moment. "I did. He said he'd fallen at school."

"Fallen or was shoved?"

"What are you thinking?"

Santee turned those blazing eyes on Ruarke, but they weren't blazing at him for a change. "I think someone is beating up on Jamie. Or Hannah and he's defending her. Or both."

"So what do we do about that? Talk to his teacher, Mrs. Helling? I had her in sixth grade. She's one heck of a teacher.

"She looked worn out to me."

"Well, she's not a spring chicken. And it was late on a Friday. All the teachers looked beat."

True, Santee thought. But not like that. She had looked like a woman on the verge of a breakdown.

"I think we need to shelve this other unnecessary discussion and find out what the heck's happening with your eldest son," Santee said.

The next evening, Santee put her arm out to prevent Jamie from disappearing after supper and hiding a new bruise on his cheek. "Jamie," Santee said. "Let's go outside for a minute." He looked to the safety of the kids, who were scattered around the family room, then his shoulders slumped, and he nodded.

Santee led the way to the glider. She shook open a blanket for him to slide under and covered their legs.

"What did I do?"

"Nothing. Well, I take that back." She felt Jamie tense up. "I don't think you're being totally honest with me."

"I would never lie to you!"

"Not lying per se. But definitely fudging the truth."

"About what?"

Santee pointed to the new purple spot on his jaw and the older greenish one on his cheek.

"Oh."

"Who did that to you?"

He opened his mouth, denial in his eyes, but he stopped as her black brows were raised warningly. "I can't tell you," he said miserably.

"Are you being threatened?"

His thin shoulders lifted.

"The little kids?"

He shrugged again.

"Hannah?"

He slumped as if he'd been punctured and all his stuffing was seeping out. From the corner of his eye, he looked at her.

"Me?"

"Everyone," he mumbled.

Santee put her arm around his skinny shoulders and pulled him close. "Tell me who it is. I'll take care of it."

"I can't. He's too mean. He'll hurt you." His teary face lifted. "I can't let that happen."

"Oh, sweetie." She pressed his head to her shoulder. "You can't let a bully rule you. Let me take care of this."

Her jean jacket was soaking up a gallon of tears. She just held him until the fury lessened.

"It's that gang banger punk, isn't it?"

Jamie tensed.

"That Deke kid."

He shuddered. A single bob of his head answered her.

Unfortunately, she didn't have quite enough time.

Chapter 18

A raw wind blasted out of the northwest. It smelled of moisture, rain and possibly snow. The temperature hovered in the mid to upper thirties, but the windchill was knocking the temps into the single digits.

Santee was sniffing the wind like a wild creature—like that scary wolf dog that hovered around her. If it snowed, she'd be able to leave…her promise fulfilled, but was she able to leave? She still didn't know where to find that Deke kid and put the fear of Santee into the little shit's black heart.

Sir Rob was talking to the contractor working on the arena. Luckily the walls and roof were sheeted. No way would they be hauling those gigantic sheets of steel in this wind.

Surely they could have moved the discussion inside the arena instead of out here. Santee's legs felt prickly from the wind through her jeans. She had a zip hoodie under her jean jacket but wasn't overly warm on top either. Her toes were cold in tennies, and her bare hands were raw from being constantly out of her pockets rubbing at the back of her neck.

Only Sunny and Rufus seemed warm in the new nylon kids' jackets, red for Rufus and blue for Sunny, that Sir Rob had Rosarita pick up for them on her last trip to town. Duke didn't need a jacket. His grayish white fur coat was thick and soft, rippling in the wind, designed for weather like this.

Santee pulled the black hood over her short hair and huddled like a turtle under the shell. Jeez, how did people stand this? If she didn't still have unfulfilled responsibilities, she'd be out of here in a flash and find that danged elusive warm Texas.

Sir Rob's phone rang. He looked at the caller ID and smiled, so Santee knew who was on the other end. The yin to his yang, the peanut butter to his jelly, salt to his pepper. It was a new concept for her, that maybe love really did exist in rare instances.

"Hi, hon." His smile faltered. "Yes, she's right here." He held out the phone to Santee.

She eyed it. She didn't do phones. Had no real use for one and no one to call. Yet someone had tracked her down. Warily she took it. "Yes?"

"Mommy T—"

Santee frowned at Jamie's blubbery voice using the term only the younger kids ever called her. "What's wrong? Is Hannah all right?"

"Umm, not r-really."

"What happened?" Sir Rob pulled her hand from under the hood, the nails bloody. Santee gave him the look, but it bounced right off him.

"We-we're in trouble. C-can you c-come?"

"Yes! Of course. Is Mrs. Reggie there with you?"

"Y-yes."

"So you're safe."

"Yes. And um, I need, um, Ruarke too."

"Okay. Hang tough. I'll get Ruarke, and we'll be there as soon as possible."

She handed the phone back.

Sir Rob shut it as he watched the rage build in Santee.

"What happened?"

She shrugged. "Jamie didn't say, only that he's in trouble. But dollar to donuts I'd bet it involves that little shit Deke."

Santee stomped off toward the shed / workout room. Her faithful hounds followed on her heels. Duke looked over his shoulder at Sir Rob, his pale yellow eyes calculating whether Sir Rob was the cause of his human's upset. A sharp whistle jerked Duke around breaking the sphincter-clenching stare.

"Shit, man. Wouldn't catch me living with that beast," the contractor said.

Rob exhaled. He'd live with it and a dozen more if that kept her here. He had to get this building up and stocked with trainable horses. Something, anything, to make her want to stay.

Pete came out and hurried to the van. Moments later, Santee and Ruarke emerged. Side by side they waited for the van to pull up. Sir Rob had seen the way Ruarke looked at Santee, the yearning there, of which she seemed totally oblivious. Now, if only Ruarke would get on the ball. Rob could then quit worrying.

Three people and three dogs loaded into the van and raced off. Sir Rob didn't envy that Deke kid at all.

All the dogs stayed in the van because Sunny didn't have her vest. Santee was simmering, ready to blow, and could have used Sunny's calming influence.

Ruarke and Pete trailed behind. They were both worried about what would happen when she saw the kid.

Santee shoved into the school office. Jamie and Hannah shouted her name and raced to her. They hugged her waist so tight, muttering unintelligibly. The quick glimpse she'd gotten had shown busted glasses for both kids held together with white tape. Jamie had new bruises and a fat lip. Hannah's chin was abraded, as if she'd face-planted and skidded on it.

"Hannah, my sweet, look at me." She nudged the girl's chin up, showing more than just a scrape. The whole right side of her face was scratched. "Do your teeth hurt? Show me."

"They're okay, I think, but my beautiful glasses!"

On one of Hannah's stays at the ranch, the Sinclairs had had enough of those crappy black rimmed glasses, but they had no authority to make decisions of this kind for her. So they'd given her two hundred dollars, over her protests, and sent her into the optometrist to get her eyes checked and put a down payment on a new pair. Shaynee and Shawnee just happened to go in a little later ostensibly to get Shawnee's glasses adjusted. They'd helped her pick out the new ones with bright-blue frames that matched her eyes.

"Hannah, we'll get you new glasses, but your pretty face and your teeth and no broken bones, that's what's important." Hannah crushed against Santee again. "Are your parents coming?"

Her head rocked. "They're gone. Again."

They're lucky they were gone. Santee steamed.

"Jamie, let's see." Besides new bruises, his shirt was torn, showing fingernail scratches on his shoulder. The knees were out of his almost new jeans, showing deep scrapes. And his new glasses, of course, were toast.

"I'm sorry…"

The principal's office door opened, and a bespeckled college-professor-type man stepped out. His black suit looked like it'd have cost a normal person a month's wages. "Mr. Sinclair." He nodded at Ruarke. "Mr. Jones." He nodded at the bear-like man leaning his shoulder against the wall. The little SOB Deke stood a foot away from his old man. The kid had his hand on his stomach, wincing at the touch, but otherwise seemed unmarred.

"Please come in." He motioned to the four chairs. "Be seated." Once more behind his desk, he turned, spotted Santee, and opened his mouth to send her out but closed it quickly, shuddering at her narrow-eyed frosty glare.

The Joneses took standing positions near the door. Ruarke and Santee took two chairs as far from them as possible. Santee pulled Hannah onto her leg. Jamie stood behind her, his hand gripping her shoulder. Both kids were trembling like leaves in a brisk wind.

"My name is Dr. Richard Clark. Mr. Sinclair and Mr. Jones I've met before." He turned his mud-brown eyes on Santee, who was less than impressed by the stressed title. "I don't believe I've had the pleasure."

"Santee Smith," she ground out.

"And your relationship would be—?"

"None of your business."

His bushy brow shot up. "I, um, see." Beneath her cold stare, he lost his train of thought, unnerved more by the young woman than by Deke Jones's brute of a father, whom he'd already met with many times over the course of Deke's nine years (retained twice) in elementary school. Thank God the boy would be going to high school next year, no matter what.

"I, um…" He tapped a wad of papers into alignment and cleared his throat. "I have here the reports of the adults who witnessed the altercation. The fight between the boys over the girl—"

"What!" Jamie sputtered. He pointed at Deke. "He shoved Hannah down and kicked her books across the hall."

Hannah was nodding. "I thought he was going to kick me. If Jamie hadn't been there…"

The pompous ass said, "So you hit him."

"He hit me too," Jamie said.

"You could have reported this to an adult, but you didn't."

"We've tried! Dozens of times!" Jamie said.

Hannah was nodding. "No one did anything!"

"So you took matters in your own hands despite our strict no-fighting policy. You did know about that, correct?"

Both Jamie and Hannah nodded miserably.

"I'm afraid the leaves me no option but to suspend the three of you for a week."

Very calmly, Santee got Hannah off her lap, and she stood up. "Let me get this straight," she said reasonably as she leaned over the desk, planting her knuckles on the glossy oak surface.

Ruarke got Hannah out of the way so he could make a grab for Santee if…when it became necessary.

"This bully was sexually harassing our Hannah. Our boy, Jamie, comes to her defense, preventing the bully from further injuring our Hannah." Santee leaned further over the desk, driving Dr. Clark's roller chair backward. "And they're being punished! Look at their faces!" She was practically prone across the desk, trapping the good doctor in his chair.

"We, ah. I—ah?"

"What is the school's policy on sexual harassment, doctor?"

"I—that is, we—"

"Sounds like a nasty lawsuit if you ask me, and be assured we will be informing Hannah's parents of that."

"I—now you just wait a minute. You can't threaten me!"

"No? You let that little monster threaten everyone in this school. Now that the shoe's on the other foot, it's not so all right, is it?"

Old man Jones was chuckling cruelly at the doctor's expense. A hint of admiration glinted in his lecherous eyes as he let his gaze roam over Santee's tight-jeans-accented ass. His ham-fist grabbed Deke by the back of the neck, drawing a squeak of pain, and marched him out—for the last fucking time.

Dr. Clark blinked owlishly at Ruarke.

Ruarke arose and carefully laid his hand on Santee's quivering back. He could feel the urge to leap the desk and rip into Clark surging through her. "Santee," he said softly. "Kids. Let's go." He got a fistful of Santee's jacket and eased backward, drawing her off the desk.

Santee cast a last malevolent glare that slapped Clark into rocking backward in his chair. "Come on, kids."

Ruarke paused at the door. "Oh, and by the way, I double everything Ms. Smith said. You'll be hearing from my lawyer."

The principal sputtered, but Ruarke had the satisfaction of shutting the door in his face.

Jamie and Hannah were facing Santee. "We're so sorry!"

Santee shook her head. Ruarke noticed the new scratches on her nape. "You've got nothing to be sorry about." She awkwardly hugged each child. "You stuck up for each other. You took on a kid half again your size. You were extremely brave."

They gave her tremulous smiles.

"Maybe not too smart," Santee said, earning a bark of laughter. "But very brave." She leaned into their faces. "I'm very proud of you."

"As am I," Ruarke said.

"We thought you'd be so mad," Jamie admitted.

"And with our broken-up brand-new glasses," Hannah said, "we were sure you'd be mad."

"Like Santee said." Ruarke moved in front of the kids. "You are what's important. Glasses are cheap. Now go get your stuff and let's head for home. Hannah," Ruarke continued, "I'm sorry, but both of my little felons will have to do their time out at the ranch." Hannah lit up. "I'm sure we can come up with some suitably nasty punishment when we get you home."

Hannah flung herself at him, squeezing him so hard. "Going home sounds really good." Close to his ear, she whispered, "Daddy," and took off, leaving Ruarke with a heart full to bursting.

Jamie shyly kind of leaned into him. "Thanks, R—Dad." And he hurried off.

He felt a hand on his arm and expected it to be Santee's, but it was his mother's, the school nurse. "You are a really good man," she said, eyes shining.

"A lot of it is Santee. She brings out the best in us Sinclairs."

He looked around with a smile. Where was Santee? He saw her stalking down the narrow hallway between the principal's office and the nurse's office.

Deke leaned against the wall where his dad had slammed him. His neck hurt from the fist lock his dad had put on him as he hauled Deke down the hall.

"You just won't learn, you little bastard." His breath smelled of onions, bad teeth, and his noon-hour whiskey shots. Deke had tried to turn away, but his chin had been clamped in vice-like fingers and jerked around. Spittle spattered Deke's face. "Three goddamned times since school started. You think I got nothin' better to do than come here cuz you had to go fuck around with that son of a bitch Sinclair's kid? You think he couldn't get me fired if'n he wants to? One fucking word and I'm outta there. Don't matter I'm the best damned mechanic they got. As is I get docked pay every goddamned time I gotta come down here!" He stuck his nose so close that it touched Deke's. "You just wait, you little son of a bitch!" he snarled. He shoved Deke so hard the big boy would have toppled over if not for the cement block wall.

Deke watched his father slam out the door. He could see Jamie and Hannah with the Sinclairs. How much different their reaction had been from his old man's.

Then he saw her. Her locked stare kept his feet hypnotized and frozen in place. His mind raced like a squirrel he'd once caught and locked in a cage. It had panic-raced around and around and up and down and around again until it just died. Deke now understood why.

She glided up to him, so much like a comic book superhero but without the boobs. Her eyes! He shuddered. God, her eyes! They froze him to his soul. Don't pee. Don't pee.

They were almost the same height, but Deke shrank downward as if she'd be more lenient on a smaller kid. His heart thumped so loudly it echoed in the narrow hall…or maybe it was just in his brain.

"You ever touch one of my kids again, and I'll come looking for you." She jabbed her finger into his chest. "Do"—jab—"you"—jab—"believe"—jab—"me"?

He could only jerk his head up and down. He had no spit to make his mouth work.

"You"—jab—"do"—jab—"not"—jab—"want"—jab— "that"—jab, jab.

God, no! He shook his head vehemently side to side. He'd rather face Dracula with a toothpick than this woman.

"Good," she snarled. "Then we're clear?"

He nodded. Definitely clear. He'd thought his old man was terrifying. He was a wuss compared to this woman.

She turned away as Hannah and Jamie returned with their coats and loaded backpacks. The woman's long strides carried her so gracefully down the hall to the reception area. They fell into that woman's warm, safe embrace. She cast one more glacial look at him, making a warm dribble course down his thigh. Then she turned them away, her arms around them like a fierce momma hen's wings around her chicks.

He hated them all. Especially her!

The weather had turned nasty the very next day, but it didn't snow…yet. Sleet pounded down like rain, covering everything in a glittery, icy frosting. The pine trees' boughs hung heavy to the point of breakage. Mrs. Wilson had Jamie and Hannah at the dining room table. They might have been kicked out of school, but they didn't get to miss out on school.

"Thank God!" Sir Rob said. "Buses have left, and Reggie is on her way too. Ladies, the kids should be home for dinner. Could you throw together some sandwiches and such?"

"*Por su puesto*, of course," Rosarita answered him. "We begin immediately."

"Thank you."

Ruarke said, "Never should have had school in the first place. Those top-heavy buses on these icy hills?"

Santee stood at the window, her reflection looking back at her hands digging into the back of her neck. Her eyes shifted to Ruarke walking up behind her. She shifted aside so he didn't hold that superior position over her. His hand reached slowly toward her face. Warily she watched it, but it went for her hand with the bloody nails.

"What's wrong?"

He said it so earnestly, as if he really wanted to hear her thoughts…as if he actually believed that she had thoughts worth a man's time to listen to.

She shrugged.

"The kids will be fine." He folded her hand into his. "The buses have gotten through in worse."

"The gate."

"The gate is open."

She shook her head. Something… "The gate."

Ruarke pulled his phone out. "Let's have Joe go check it out."

Santee pulled her hand from his warm grasp. She waved away that idea. "It's stupid."

"Joe, can you check out the gate? See if anything's wrong?"

"Sure thing. But I didn't see anything on camera."

"It's a waste of time," Santee said.

There were monitors in three places, Rob's office there at the house, Joe's house, and Pete's house, plus they could be accessed by cell phone. Ruarke didn't know how it all worked. He didn't have to. That was Pete and Joe's department.

Ruarke and Santee stood side by side as Joe exited his place and climbed into his ice-covered Jeep. It took a few minutes for him to scrape the windshield and get the defroster warmed up enough to keep the windshield at least partially clear.

Ruarke marveled at being able to stand so pain-free. He lifted onto his toes just a touch. Still no pain. His huge grin made Santee look suspiciously at him. He wanted to haul her into his arms and twirl her around the room, but her narrowed eyes made him think twice. Maybe he could at least leave the damned brace off more.

Santee looked at Sir Rob an instant before his phone rang. Sir Rob's face grew serious.

"Okay. We'll be right there. Call Sol and let him know."

Sir Rob put his phone in his pocket. "Maria!"

The pretty young Hispanic woman came out of the kitchen, wiping her hands on a towel. "*Sí*, Señor Rob?"

"Do you want some more goats?"

"Oh, *sí*! We are, um, how you say, ready for *las cabras*, Juan and I."

"Good. We've got four adults and three little ones out at the gate. Call Juan. Tell him to take the truck out and at least one other guy to help him load them. Have him pick you up to help get them settled in."

"Oh, *sí*! Gracias! Gracias!"

"Santee."

She had known there was more.

"There are two giant black horses out there. And they're scared."

"I'll lead them in."

She hurried toward the mudroom, Sir Rob and Ruarke following. She paused, eyebrows raised.

"I'll wait in the truck."

Her narrowed gaze told him he'd better.

As they pulled on their coats, Sir Rob commented, "That's not much of a coat."

Santee had zipped the black hoodie and was forcing the metal buttons of the jean jacket through the tight holes. "I'm good."

Sir Rob looked at Ruarke and shook his head slightly. "Grab a slicker," Rob said. "If you're riding."

"Leading."

"Either way, you're going to get wet."

Santee pulled out three slickers from the closet and handed them out. If there was any wind out there at all, two already skittish horses were not going to tolerate flapping green plastic.

Pete pulled the 4×4 pickup as close as possible and hurried to help Ruarke, slipping but safely into the truck.

Santee just shook her head at the dumbass. Then she went to Duke, who had been sitting out of the weather on the porch. She took his face in her hands and said, "You have to stay here, boy. You'll scare the horses." His tail wagged low and slow, unhappy to be left behind.

The big truck fishtailed its way up the hill to the gate. The underlying gravel barely gave it enough traction to climb.

Three men were loading the bleating goats into a rusty old Ford pickup. Maria hovered, hands clasped as if in prayer, her eyes sparkling. A lot of Spanish and some English cuss words accompanied the struggles.

The two giant black horses drew Santee out of the truck. Grass blades crunched beneath her tennies as she slip-slided, one hand pressed to the side of the pickup. Joe waited at the cattle crossing, hand out to her. Without hesitation, she slid her bare hand into his leather-gloved one.

The horses were huge, easily sixteen or seventeen hands. Their coats were dull, and they shivered as the sleet soaked through to their bones. Their hips, ribs, and backbones jutted with no fat layer for insulation. They were huge but finer boned than a standard workhorse.

Sir Rob joined her, hanging on to the gate post for dear life. He couldn't risk a broken bone. He had way too many irons in the fire right now.

"What are they, Sir Rob?"

"I don't know."

Santee wiped ice from her lashes. A word popped into her head. "Friesians?"

"Could be. Never heard of any around here, though. Can't even imagine how much they'll eat."

213

"Probably why they got dumped on you."

Sir Rob sighed sadly, knowing that some fool hadn't taken the cost of feed into consideration when he got the two giant horses. Sometimes he'd like to just shake people.

Santee said, "Kick 'em where the sun don't shine."

Sir Rob snorted. He hadn't realized he'd been speaking aloud, but Santee sure hit the nail on the head with that one.

The horses' heads had jerked up, eyes showing white and nostrils flaring, at Santee's approach.

"Easy, now. Easy." Slowly she eased closer, talking all the way. The sleet plinked on the slicker. Her tennies were already soaked through, her feet sloshing.

The mare snorted, stamping a dinner plate-sized hoof.

"Easy, girl." Santee held her fist out to the trembling nostrils. Tentatively the mare stretched her neck out; her huge teeth could easily have crunched the delicate bones. The mare snorted and snuffled. Santee held still, letting the mare choose.

Slowly the wild eyes lost their white halo. The reared-up head lowered as she shifted closer. Her relaxing demeanor made her brother calmer.

Santee moved in, the smell of wet horse unpleasantly pungent. She laid her hand on the horse's icy neck. "What a good girl, Blue." Her hands sluiced sleety water off the black neck.

The gelding nickered softly as he stretched his nose past his sister. His eyes closed contentedly at the gentle touch to his sensitive nose.

"You're very lucky, Black," Santee said as she fondled the black nose. "These people will take really good care of you. You'll get fat and sassy and never have to worry about being hungry ever again.

Joe came up on the other side of the fence to untie ropes so Santee wouldn't have to slide down into the ditch to do it.

Santee reeled in the lines, both horses snuffling at her back. "Thanks, Joe."

"The guys don't think they can get the trailer up here," Joe said.

"I'll lead them, but they're not going to walk over that cattle guard."

"There's a gate this side of the drive. I've got it standing open."

Santee unhooked Black's lead. He would follow Blue, Santee sensed, so she squelched off with Blue's lead in her hand. Squishy clumps sounded behind her as first Blue and then Black followed.

The ditch had a culvert and flattened path at the walk-through gate, so no one had to slip-slide down the two-foot drop into the ditch. They clumped in through the gate.

Santee kept them off the super slick drive. The wet ground gave their raggedy overgrown hooves more traction than the ice-covered gravel would have.

She slipped and skidded in her almost smooth-soled tennies. Blue clumped beside her, Black following.

By the time they reached the yard, Santee could barely feel her feet and legs. Her face also stung at the repeated plinking. Her bare right hand holding the lead was numb.

This day had few redeeming qualities. The only good thing was the fall had been so dry the county had enacted no-burn rules. Now people wouldn't have to worry so about wildfires.

Now as long as the family got home safely.

Uncle Sol stood at the open corral gate. The pickup had already eased past to park by the house.

Slowly, Santee led Blue across the gravel courtyard toward Sol. The horses were steadier on the slick surface than she was.

"I've got the infirmary ready," Sol said.

Santee led the horses to the small barn that was set far apart from the other buildings and the other animals. At the moment it stood empty. There hadn't been any horses dumped in a while that had to be quarantined.

Thick rain pattered on the roof. But inside it was warm and dry. Fresh hay scented the air. The horses' nostrils flared at the scent of food.

"This is Blue." Santee handed the rope to Sol, who handed it off to one of his workers. Blue walked off obediently but turned to watch Santee. Santee patted her haunch as she passed by.

Santee caught Black's halter and snapped on the lead. "This is Black."

Again Sol handed Black off to a worker, who led him off to be dried off and blanketed.

"I've seen worse," Sol commented. He tsked, shook his head, and went to check on his new charges.

A truck rumbled up outside with a puff of diesel exhaust. Duke's displeasure drifted eerily on the airwaves.

"Santee."

She stiffened at Sir Rob's sharp tone. Her brain flipped quickly through the past hour but couldn't find an instance that would have ticked the man off. "Sir?" She turned warily to face him.

"Good God, child!" he exclaimed. "You've got to be frozen."

Shivers flared at the reminder.

"Where were your boots?"

"Since I am supposed to be in sunny, hot Texas now, I don't have any need for boots. Now, if you'll excuse me."

"Santee." His voice was gentle, contrite. He reached out to her, but she lifted her shoulder and pulled away, eyes filled with the same icy sleet that was coming down outside. "I'm sorry. Of course you wouldn't be prepared for this kind of weather. Would you please bring your wet clothes up to the house and use the clothes dryer?"

She was about to protest. She hadn't used their laundry facilities, though they'd offered several times. She handwashed and hung them out to dry on a line tied between the trees.

"They'll never dry even hanging in the camper. At least not until this weather clears, and by then everything will smell musty or even moldy. Get some dry clothes and come up to the house. Take a hot shower and wash and dry your clothes."

She didn't want to. It made her feel beholding to them. The easy life she'd been living here was going to make the transition back to being on her own very difficult.

"Please."

Santee looked out the open door at the miserable weather and sighed. A shower where the hot water lasted more than a couple of minutes sure sounded good. She sighed and nodded. "Okay."

"Good! Pete can take you—"

"I can walk. Doubt I could get much wetter."

Sir Rob chuckled. "Funny girl. No, the truck's already warmed up. Won't take but a minute."

"Fine." The cold must be addling her brain. "But I'm going to get the truck seats all wet."

"Pete's already put a blanket on the seat."

Santee eyed Sir Rob. "Pretty doggone sure of yourself."

Sir Rob grinned but shook his head. "Not at all. But I know a sensible woman when I see one." He swept his arm out for her to precede him.

Santee felt warmed clear through when she shut off the shower, but the instant it wasn't pounding heat into her, the cold once more seeped from her bones. The towel was thick and fluffy unlike the "ready for the rag bag" ones she had. She winced as she toweled her head and touched the nape of her neck.

Her clothes were already in the washing machine. Rosarita had insisted on waiting outside for them, and Rosarita, being Rosarita, got her way. Santee just hoped she didn't examine her saggy underwear. Someone who didn't plan on being around too long didn't go out and buy new duds.

She pulled a baggy gray sweatshirt and saggy-assed gray sweatpants on. Her socks were not very white anymore, but they were fairly thick as she went sock-footed out of the laundry room's bathroom and promptly tripped over Rufus as he popped up from his watchful place by the door. Sunny was smarter and had lain out of the pathway.

Children's voices drifted from the dining room. They'd gotten home while she was in the shower.

When they spotted her, the Fab Four followed by Remmy and Rio rushed her. They hugged her so tightly, six pairs of arms like octopus tentacles around her. Each took a turn telling her about their morning before going to their chair for their noon meal. Remmy and Rio didn't have to go as far since their chairs were on either side of hers.

Dinner was tomato soup made with milk from the ranch's own rescued milk cows and grilled cheese sandwiches. How the ladies kept up with sandwich demands from so many eaters was amazing.

After dinner and snoozy-poozy time, Mrs. Wilson would have all the kids at the table. An experienced teacher, she'd gone online and printed activities for each child. If nothing else, they'd read aloud to the littler kids.

Rosarita brought Santee's clothes fresh and warm from the dryer...or was it from an iron? If so, it must have been a huge shock to the clothes since Santee didn't own an iron. Her tennies still leaned near the wood fireplace in the living room, still not completely dry.

"Gracias, Rosarita," Santee said as she took the pile.

"*Da nada*. We be happy to wash your clothes always. No problema."

"Thank you, but you ladies have enough to do without my laundry too."

Put her clothes through too many washing machine cycles and she'd end up with a pile of threads.

Santee put the pile near the door and went to stand by the windows looking out over the glittering yard. Duke sat on the outside of the window, sensed her, and looked over his shoulder at her. His golden eyes seemed to sear into her soul.

Reflected movement broke their gazes apart. Ruarke came up behind her. He took her hand away from the back of her neck again. "Come with me." Her eyes narrowed suspiciously. "Please. I need your advice."

Still suspicious, Santee pulled her hand free and told the dogs to stay.

"They're welcome to come too."

So she released them, and the three of them followed him across the family room, stepping around the kids napping on the floor.

She stopped when Ruarke opened the door to his suite and held it for her. Santee had never been beyond that door. She knew where it went, but she'd never seen it.

His eyebrows raised in a challenge, eyes smiling at her hesitation. It goaded her into advancing, which his smile said he'd known would happen. Her elbow just happened to flail out a bit and catch him in the midriff. He woofed a grunt. She could have really hurt him if she'd wanted.

A four-foot-wide hall extended about twenty feet, a wall of windows on the left showing a backyard and pool; on the right, two open doors showed a massive walk-in closet, the entire right side of which was empty, and a bathroom larger than her entire camper.

Past a circular staircase that led to the loft was his bedroom.

Ahead was a wall of windows, two stories plus the peak. A patio outside held a covered hot tub.

To the right was his huge blond, pine-post bed. Sitting in bed he could look out that wall of windows. Beside the bed was a whole wall of bookshelves filled with paperback books neatly arranged. In the left corner was a gas fireplace with a sofa facing it. Were those dog beds on the floor? Must be cushions to sit on the floor with, Santee decided.

Wow! she thought. A microwave and a refrigerator! A person could live right here like a little house.

He was smiling at her reactions.

"Kind of like a bug under glass," Santee commented.

"One-way glass," Ruarke said.

Double wow! That must have cost a fortune.

She turned to the loft but couldn't see anything. Ruarke held his hand out, indicating she should proceed him up the circular stairs.

Santee was too aware of him behind her saggy-ass sweats. She could almost feel his amusement, which made her want to kick back, accidentally of course, right into his smug face.

The dogs whined at the bottom of the stairs. They'd never seen a circular staircase and didn't know how it worked.

"Stay there. I'll be right back."

"Or maybe not."

She stepped off the stairs and turned on him. "What did you say?"

He looked at her, the epitome of innocence. "When?"

"On the stairway there." She pointed at the metal structure.

He shrugged and turned away but not before a smile peaked out. "I may have just been commenting, favorably I might add, on the view."

The view? The only view was…!

"Ruarke Sinclair!" She stomped after him.

He turned. He was definitely laughing now. "Yes?"

She glared at him, almost nose to nose. He put his hand on the back of her head and lifted just a little, bringing her onto her toes. Her eyes widened as his gaze shifted to her lips.

She was too stunned to move when he lowered his lips to hers and gently eased them apart. His lips played hers, fogging her brain.

Santee was no virgin, but she's never been kissed before, not like this! She blinked at his closed eyes as he gave a soft moan, tongue darting into her mouth.

His arm went around her waist, hauling her tight to him. Their bodies fit together so perfectly, his arousal pressing hard between the juncture of her thighs.

When his lips released hers and ventured to her neck, she managed a ragged breath.

"Sinclair!" Did she actually whisper that, or had it merely been in her head? Her hands fluttered ineffectively, loosely at her sides.

"Ruarke."

"Mmm." His mouth found a spot in the left side of her neck that sent an electrical charge through her. Her knees buckled, sending him even more intimately against her.

She gasped as warm hands slid over her bare butt, gripped, and lifted. She couldn't get any higher on her toes without a ballerina's toe shoes.

"Holy—"

His lips found that spot again.

"Ruarke!" It came out as a squeak with as much power as a mouse's death squawk.

He drew back, blue eyes blazing as they roved her face. His thumbs rubbed lazily on her rump. "What?" he said with a wicked grin.

"Stop that."

He leaned in and brushed his nose against hers, a danged Eskimo kiss. "Stop what?"

She forced her hands to touch his waist and pushed. He budged about as much as a twenty-ton boulder.

His fingers started a foray into her cleft, making her gasp again. "Ruarke, dang it!"

He moved to claim her lips.

Knock! Knock!

They both froze guiltily.

Knock! Knock!

Both the upstairs door from his loft area that led to the kids' bedrooms and the door they'd entered through downstairs were being pounded on.

"Shit!" Ruarke barked.

"Santee! Come quick!" Shaynee called.

"Dad!" Shawnee screamed from downstairs.

Santee twisted free, hiking up her pants as she flew downstairs. The dogs were barking excitedly as her sock feet spun out. She caught herself one-handed on the floor and surged upright.

"Santee!"

She barreled through the door and into Shawnee, catching the girl before she fell to the floor.

"What's wrong?"

Her mouth worked, but nothing came out. She pointed toward where the rest of the kids were gathered, gaping at something at the front door.

Santee raced across the family room and up the three steps to the living room.

Jamie stood holding the front door open. He turned to her, eyes wide with shock.

Santee froze.

It couldn't be!

Chapter 19

Standing at the front door, dripping melting sleet all over the old oaken floor, flanked by both Joe and Pete, stood the little shit Deke Jones.

Santee felt the other kids' eyes ping-ponging from her to Deke and back. She sensed Ruarke's approach and heard him whisper, "What the hell?" But her gaze was frozen on the gutsy little shit who stood head bowed and shoulders slumped, eyes seemingly locked on the rivulets of water running away from his untied boots.

Jamie and Hannah stood off to Deke's side. Their eyes wide behind their Deke-broken glasses, locked on her.

Slowly she stalked up the three steps from the family room. She took perverse pleasure from Deke's hesitant glance at her. He was trembling, whether from being half frozen or from fear. Santee thought it had better be the latter, because the rage burning inside her warranted that response.

Stringy black strands of hair dangled to shield the kid's face, hiding his quick glances.

Santee stopped close enough to hear his ragged breathing. His slumped shoulders and bowed head did nothing to quench her fiery insides.

"Talk!" she snarled.

Deke flinched. "Don't got no place to go. You seen to that," he mumbled.

"So this is all my fault?"

He looked up for a moment, showing a fat split lip, a swollen-shut goopy eye, the other eye blackened, and a swollen nose and cheek, then he shook his head.

"I'll get the Jeep out and haul him back to town," Joe stated.

Deke's head popped up, eye wild. He shook his head. "No! Please!" His gaze swept the adults but landed on Santee, as if knowing she was the one to convince. "Please. I'll be good."

Santee snorted. She was so rigid her muscles seemed to be vibrating. Kids like that didn't change. A hand slid into hers. She turned to find Jamie at her side. He was still bruised and scraped at the hands of this bully, but there was a gentle plea in his eyes.

"He needs us."

Santee shook her head sharply.

Jamie tagged her hand to his chest, covering it with his other one. "You have said over and over again that it's our responsibility to look after those who are smaller and weaker and need our help."

A fine credo came back to bite her in the butt. "I was talking about your little brothers and sisters. Not this." Her sneer had the desired effect of making Deke cringe. She didn't feel more than a twinge of remorse at bullying the bully.

"What about that time at the drive-in when that guy was picking on—?"

Santee with her free hand waved it away. It was extremely irritating to have things thrown back in her face like that. She didn't want to be jollied out of this rage. It felt good. Her blood was boiling like hot crude again.

"Jamie—"

"Mom."

She arched an eyebrow to let Jamie know that she knew he was pushing her buttons. He never called her mom.

"He can sleep in my room. At least until we see how it works out."

"And what about Hannah? How does she feel about having that little miscreant in the house?"

Jamie motioned Hannah over. Warily she circled around the teeth-chattering lump.

Santee slipped her hand free to cup Hannah's chin. "What do you say?"

Sad blue eyes lifted to Santee's. "I guess I feel like Jamie does. Maybe he deserves a second chance."

Santee snorted. "You're both way too softhearted. People like that never change."

Jamie said, "That could have been me."

Santee shook her head. "Not hardly."

He nodded firmly. "It could have. With Rachael treating me the way she did. I was filling up with so much hate, I felt like I could explode. And you know who I would have exploded on…my little brothers. If you and the Sinclairs hadn't come along… It changed me. The pressure building up in me just sort of oozed away. Don't you think we should at least try that with Deke?"

"Deacon." The big kid straightened his shoulders and looked at Santee. "Deke is dead. Deacon is here, now."

Kind of like a split personality, Santee thought. That was something she could fathom. The Santee before Sunny and Rufus versus the Santee now.

A whining bark sounded.

"Remmy, honey, would you see where the dogs are locked up?"

Moments later the two dogs came barreling up. Sunny shoved Jamie aside to get on Santee's right. Santee fingered the soft hair as she looked questioningly at Jamie. He nodded and looked pityingly at Deke-Deacon. Santee wasn't sure a leopard could change its spots so easily. Her spots were still very much evident, only a tad faded.

Santee looked around at each adult. They gave a lot of shrugs, which kind of indicated it was her call. She didn't like that. She didn't plan to be here long term. What she decided now they'd be stuck with after she was long gone.

Drawing a deep breath, Santee stepped up to the kid who was almost as tall as she and probably outweighed her by fifty pounds. He looked warily at her out of one bloodshot blackened eye.

"These people are much kinder than I am. Me? I'd kick your ass to the curb so fast. But these are nice, trusting people, so here's the deal…"

For the first time, hope shone in that painful eye.

"Your old man beat the crap out of you and kicked you out."

"Yes, ma'am."

"You had nowhere else to go, so you thought, 'Hey, those Sinclairs are such schmucks. They'll feel sorry for me and take me in.'"

He flinched as the iota of truthfulness in that statement hit home.

"But I'm not a Sinclair. Kindness is not my middle name, nor is gullibility. They may be all nicey-nicey, but I will be watching. Am I clear?"

Deke-Deacon bobbed his head.

"Plus there are only about a thousand rules you'll have to live with here. One of the main ones is respect. There are older people here. There are little kids. There are dogs and cats and horses and cows. There are young women who will be treated like sisters. There are adult women who take care of us, doing our laundry and cooking our meals and cleaning up after us. And they come in a variety of sizes, shapes, and colors. The men here also come in a variety of sizes, shapes, and colors. All will be spoken to with respect and excellent manners. Is that clear?"

His head bobbed.

Mrs. Reggie made a move, but Santee held up her hand. She was far from done.

"There are a ton of chores you'll be given, which could range from picking eggs, cleaning manure out of barns, milking cows, helping little kids with their homework, helping them in the bathroom, or even putting them to bed. All without a single complaint."

"I won't." Santee's raised brow flustered him. "I will. I—"

She held up her hand. "School is a priority. Therefore homework is a priority. And good grades. And most of all, respect for your teachers. There will be no more calls from the principal. No more being kicked out of school. And no letters home from your teacher. Clear?"

"Yes, ma'am."

"I'm sure I'm forgetting something." Santee looked around. Pete, Joe, Ruarke, and Sir Rob were all fighting off smiles. Mrs. Reggie and Rosarita were looking way too compassionate. They were the ones who could be taken in by this little shit.

Joe was talking on the phone, lots of nodding and okaying. He hung up and said, "I was talking to my sister, Dez, Desiree. She's a social worker. Not in our county, but she'd come if the weather weren't so awful. She says we need to document the kid's injuries. I'll Skype it to her so she'll be a witness if need be. Lots of pictures and video."

Mrs. Reggie moved up to take over. She sent Rob for a blanket. The S-twins gathered the Fab Four to get them ready for bed. Pete and Rosarita headed for their house with Maddie and Sophie, after Rosarita reminded them that there were leftovers in the fridge for Deacon's snack.

Deacon stripped to his underwear while concealed by the blanket, leaving the wet mess by the door. Wrapped up tight, he padded in wet socks after Mrs. Reggie. Joe followed.

"Jamie," Santee said. "You're on picture duty. Take a bunch and video too."

"Ruarke!" Mrs. Reggie hollered. "We're going to need some dry clothes. Warm them up in the dryer first."

Ruarke headed off.

Hannah took Remmy and Rio into the family room, leaving Sir Rob and Santee.

"Are you sure about this?" Santee said.

He shrugged. "Couldn't very well kick him out into this weather."

"I could have."

Rob laughed, put his arm around her shoulders, and hauled her to him. "You're not that heartless."

He really didn't know her at all, Santee decided. Santee eased away from his warmth. "Sir Rob, do you mind if I sleep in this house tonight?"

His face lit up. "Of course not! We'd love for you to move in here. Take any—" Then his face fell. "There aren't any beds in the rooms over Reggie and my bedroom. Reggie has been after me, but—"

"That's okay. I won't be needing a bed or a room."

"Aah." He nodded. "You plan on keeping an eye on our newest member."

She nodded.

"As soon as the weather clears up, we'll go get bedroom sets for the two rooms over our room and furniture for the two apartments.

"They'll have their own," Santee said.

"Who?"

Santee blinked at Sir Rob. "What?"

"Who will have what?"

She had no clue what he was talking about and must have looked it.

He laughed it off. "Never mind. You go do what you've got to do."

She looked quizzically at him before heading off into the elements to get some necessities for herself and the dogs from the camper.

Sir Rob shrugged. Maybe he was hearing things.

Two unhappy dogs were left behind when she headed out for the camper. Duke trotted out from wherever he'd found shelter. He'd made it plain he wasn't a house dog, so he stayed nearby but outside. He thought it was great fun gamboling on the ice. At least the sleet had let up some, but the overcast sky was black and gloomy. The lighter-colored icy path showed her the way. Normally she liked being so far away. A night like this, with sleet pinging off the slicker hood, not so much.

The camper latch was iced shut. Two good whacks of her fist managed to shatter the covering. The hinges resisted opening, but Santee was tougher.

She was gathering stuff into garbage bags when lights shone in the iced-over windows. A howl-bark sounded a warning as the vehicle pulled up alongside the pickup camper. She opened the door to look out and found Joe and his Jeep there. The interior lights showed Joe unmoving behind the wheel. He didn't trust Duke, but when he saw Santee, he popped the Jeep's tailgate and got out.

"You should have hollered," he said as he pushed up the tailgate.

"You were busy."

"I would have given you the keys."

Santee was touched. The Jeep was his baby. "Never thought of it."

"Well, you should have."

But that wasn't how her mind worked. She was a true soloist in this life. Always had been.

Santee handed out the dog beds and a garbage bag with food bowls, blankets, breakfast stored in Cool Whip bowls, Sunny's meds in a baggie, and a couple of fuzzy toys, Rufus's beloved brown bear and Sunny's stuffed lion. Her own necessities, toothbrush and paste, deodorant, and clean undies, fit in her pocket.

It always killed her to leave the door unlocked. A good thing she had, or the keyhole would have been frozen shut. She didn't have anything worth stealing anyway. And the Sinclair Ranch people seemed unnaturally lawful.

Except at night, when the bogeymen came out. Then the lock was turned.

Huddled in the Jeep's warmth for the drive back, Santee said, "I didn't know you had a sister."

"Yuh. Sort of." The Jeep skidded, but Joe easily steered into the slide and got it straightened out. "We're not blood related. We were in the foster system together. We got housed together twice for a total of about three years. When she aged out, she kept in contact. When I aged out, she was there for me until she kicked my butt out of the hole I was drilling for myself. She pretty much strong-armed me into joining the Marines. Best thing I ever did. After the Marines, I bounced around some. Raised some hell. When I got this job and it turned into a permanent gig, she moved out from the Cities. She's all the family I've got."

"Until now," Santee said. "I think the Sinclairs consider you family."

His teeth shone brilliant white against his ebony skin. "Yuh. Who'd a thunk."

Joe parked close and helped haul stuff upstairs into the hall outside Jamie's room while Santee dealt with the happy dogs.

"Thanks, Joe."

"No problema." He gave her that devastating smile. It really was no wonder that he, so easily, got rides home after nights out tomcatting around. The area women had to be falling all over themselves to be of service to him. "By the way. Dez can't wait to meet you."

"Me?" Santee said. "She doesn't know about me."

"Sure does," Joe said. "I've told her all about your escapades."

"Escapades? What escapades?"

But he gave her a lazy salute and headed out to the still idling Jeep.

"It'd be real easy to be jealous of that guy," Ruarke said. He'd been at the table with Deacon and the kids having a late snack. He was getting around so well—the limp was mostly gone—that he could almost sneak up on people.

"How's he doing?" Santee said, eyeing Deacon.

"Tired. Sore. Still chilled. Kind of quiet."

"The quiet before the storm," Santee said.

Jamie led Deacon off. Their steps clumped up the hardwood stairs.

Remmy and Rio came for a good-night hug before heading upstairs also.

"You're planning on keeping watch in the hall tonight?" Ruarke asked.

"Do you really want to trust an unknown fourteen-year-old boy upstairs with your three daughters?"

"Not so much, but the shape he's in, I kind of doubt he could do anything."

"Or it's all a ruse."

"Oh, it's no ruse. You'd know if you'd seen—"

Santee was frowning, staring past him into the past. The color drained from her face. Her arms encircled her body protectively. She winced, head snapping around as if from a slap.

Sunny whined and butted against Santee's leg. Rufus hopped on his back legs, trying to reach her hands.

"Santee!"

She inhaled sharply and was back. Her scary eyes focused on him. "Yes?" Her hands lowered to the anxious dogs.

The creaking overhead drew her attention. "Pain without obvious bruising is a skill."

She wandered off, leaving Ruarke with his jaw dropping.

There were three boys' bedrooms upstairs and one boys' bathroom. The huge double bathroom was actually two bathrooms side by side, a toilet and a double sink vanity on either side with one side having a shower big enough for four little boys at once and the other a tub/shower combo. Handy with seven and now eight boys trying to get ready every morning. A dim nightlight lit the hallway, guiding their little treks to the toilet in the night.

There were two girls' bedrooms and another double bathroom, just like the boys, only with a smaller shower which allowed for, a conveniently located washer and dryer. The S-twins shared a room, and the other had been planned for Maddie, but she still stayed with Rosarita's Sophie, so it was now Hannah's room whenever she stayed over…which was more and more often.

This was all above the former garage now family room. There were two exits, the original set of stairs into the dining room and the other stairs leading down to the family room. Also, they could access Ruarke's loft, but only under extreme circumstances were they allowed to intrude there.

Santee and the dogs settled across the hall from Jamie's room. The dim nightlight left the area along Hannah's bedroom wall in shadow.

Soft footsteps brought all three heads to attention, not toward Jamie's room but to the end leading to Ruarke's loft. A light bobbed, growing brighter as it neared. He came around the corner like a cyclops, a light strapped around his forehead.

The dogs growled, and Santee held her hand up at the blinding light. She murmured calmly to the dogs; her hand dropped into her backpack and closed around a familiar grip.

Ruarke killed the light quickly, but not before leaving dancing orbs in Santee's eyes. One arm full of pillows and quilts, he slowly came closer. The dogs came sniffing out to him. Santee grabbed their blankets off them before they could drag them away.

The dogs had blankets, Ruarke noted, but Santee's legs were uncovered.

"Think Rufus would mind if I—?" Ruarke motioned moving the dog bed over.

"I can—" Santee made a move to arise.

"I've got it." He dropped his bounty on Santee's legs and moved the bed, making an unhappy dog. With a huff, Rufus climbed in, circled twice, and settled again with a huff.

"Here." Santee held out a blanket. "Cover him up, would you?"

So Ruarke did something he'd never done before or thought he ever would. He tucked a dog in for the night and got his nose licked in thanks.

Santee had tucked in Sunny and placed a pillow beside her on the floor for Ruarke to sit on and the other leaning against the wall for his back.

"Take that one." He poked his cane at the one against the wall. "Sit on it."

Santee started to protest, but he held up a finger, and his eyebrows rose. She wrinkled her nose at him but, in a huff, grabbed it and shoved it under her butt.

Ruarke settled slowly, his back sliding down the wall, the damned leg stuck out like a broken wing.

Santee flipped a quilt over his legs and would have the second one, but he stopped her.

"You take that one."

"I'm fine." And she started to flip it over him but again was stopped by his outheld hand.

"Take it."

With a huffy sniff, she tossed it over her chilly legs.

"The dogs have blankets, but you don't," Ruarke commented.

"So?" She gave him an eyebrow-arched look.

"Just an observation."

They sat close enough that their shoulders touched with the least little movement. Santee carefully edged a fraction away, but Ruarke sadly noted it.

"I hope you don't mind my joining you."

Santee shrugged. "Your hallway."

"Our hallway," Ruarke said softly.

"I don't think Sir Rob would object."

That hadn't been the "our" he was referring to. "I was hoping we could continue where we left off earlier."

Santee leaned exaggeratedly away, eyeing him.

Ruarke snorted. "I meant that I never got a chance to ask you—"

"Too busy grabbing my ass."

Ruarke threw his head back to laugh, but Santee slapped a hand over his mouth, flicking her eyes to indicate the room across from them. He took her hand, chuckling softly.

Santee pulled to free her hand, so Ruarke quickly slid his arm around her waist and pulled her hip to hip. Her eyes narrowed as she lined up a protest, but he held up his hand and inclined his head toward the bedroom.

A silvery glare sent a chill thrill through him, though his entire left side burned with their combined heat. His nostrils flared on the sleet-fresh scent still wafting from her short hair.

Chin set, ignoring the caress of his gaze, Santee said, "So what was the all-fired-important question?"

Ruarke smiled at her ingenuity. For most women, an "all-fired-important question" would be a proposal. If that even crossed her mind, Ruarke knew she'd be out of there in a cloud of dust and a Road Runner's "beep, beep" in her wake.

"I wanted your opinion of whether you preferred the bed on the main floor, like I have it, or would you like it better in the loft?"

She arched away from him, eyeing him as if he'd lost his mind. "My opinion doesn't mean squat."

She'd be surprised how much it meant.

"But if it was yours," he pressed, "how would you like it. Bed down or in the loft?"

She sighed and folded her arms across her breasts with a huff. "I would guess you'll go in more often from the family room, and the bathroom is down there, along with your multitude of clothes in the closet, so it makes the most sense downstairs. Fewer steps."

"Yes, but the view on those steps...ooo-lah-lah."

Santee jerked around so fast she almost tore his rotator cuff. He held his hand up to quell the outburst.

Her eyes narrowed at his pompous grin. Hissing, she said, "I knew you were staring at my ass!"

"And a mighty fine ass it is, even in saggy-assed sweats."

She leaned in, teeth clenched, making Ruarke arch away a tad. "I could really hurt you, you know."

His head bobbed like a bobblehead doggie in a car's back window.

"You wouldn't have time to scream for help."

His nuts were scrambling to hide in his scrotum, a most unpleasant sensation, especially when his penis was trying to follow.

"I meant no disrespect, but it was right there…and so admirable."

She snorted and shook her head. "Men," she hissed, and not in a complimentary tone at all.

Ruarke put his hand up toward her face, embarrassed at the tremors running through his fingers. She arched suspiciously away, tensing as he placed his palm against her cheek. It knifed his soul the wary way she eyed his hand as if fully expecting a slap.

"I would never hurt you," he whispered.

She snorted like a spooked horse.

"I'm nothing like the other men who mistreated you."

"Yuh, right." She knocked his hand away. "You're twice my size. Twice my strength."

"But you fight dirty."

She nodded, eyes staring into his. "I do. I also don't turn the other cheek. Never ever." Her glacial glare nailed him. "I get even."

Ruarke read the veracity in her eyes. "If I ever hurt you, I would deserve anything you did."

"Yuh, right." She hugged her right arm close, away from the merest contact with him. With a sniff, she turned away to stare at the wall. "You say that now."

"I have never hit or even hurt a woman."

"Is that what your two ex-wives would say?"

"If they were truthful, yes, that's what they'd say. Just ask Heather." He reached for his phone, but he'd left it charging. "We'll call tomorrow."

"None of my business," Santee said primly.

"So this afternoon, in the loft…"

"Not going there."

"Tell me I didn't turn you on." He held his hand out as if to enfold her and ease her closer, drawing her narrowed eyes to his arm.

"Truthfully?"

Ruarke nodded.

"Truthfully I'd really like to rip that arm off."

Ruarke wriggled his eyebrows and grinned. "And miss out on all the pleasure"—he wriggled his fingers in front of her—"these could give?"

It was too gloomy to see, but Santee felt the heat in her cheeks. TV and movies were all about sex, but Santee had never experienced that melting sensation before. As pleasant as it had been, it also scared the hell out of her. With a sniff, she turned her shoulder toward him and settled down to not sleep.

"Ruarke!"

He jerked awake and groaned. Sleeping on the floor was not as much fun at thirty as it had been at ten.

If Pete found it strange finding him alone in the hallway, tucked in like a little kid, Santee's pillow under his bum leg, Pete showed no indication. He held his hand out and hauled Ruarke to his feet.

"Hurry up!" he urged.

"I haven't even—" "It'll be over if you stop and do all that."

"What will?" Ruarke asked as he was being hustled downstairs and out to Joe's idling Jeep. Overnight, the sleet had stopped, and the temps had started to climb. Even in the dull predawn, the *drip, drip, drip* of melting ice could be heard.

Ruarke barely got in before Pete slammed the door shut and hurried around the Jeep. Too fast, he skidded it across the yard to the exercise shed, barely managing to stop it before it slid into the metal siding. Pete hurried around, got Ruarke out, and supported him across the icy gravel to the door.

"Sssh." Pete put his finger to his lips before opening the door. The *stump, thump* of a dribbling basketball flooded out the door.

The near end of the building held every piece of exercise equipment a man could want, from a weight bench, to a treadmill, to a stationary bike, to the latest Bowflex, and everything in between.

The far end was a full-size basketball court complete with hardwood floor and a scoreboard all taken out of a nearby gymnasium whose school was being closed. There were even collapsible bleachers that now stood open for the game's watchers.

On the floor were Joe and Santee. Joe's ebony torso glistened with sweat. Santee had a crop top tee and short shorts on. Both showed redness on knees and elbows where they'd skidded on the unforgiving floor.

The S-twins sat on the bleachers; Shawnee's camera was up filming. Deacon and Jamie sat at the scorekeeper's table, notching up the baskets. The score was 42. Home was leading, whoever home was.

Santee ducked a shoulder into Joe's check, bulling ahead. She stopped at the top of the key, letting Joe stumble back, and put up a beautiful shot. Swoosh. Nothing but net—44 points.

"How long's this been going on?" Ruarke asked as he sat down on the weight bench.

"'Bout forty-five minutes or so. Started real friendly, but Joe tripped her up, maybe accidentally, I don't know, but Santee took exception. It's like watching a pickup game in Harlem, dirty and physical." His grin was huge. "It's been great."

Joe was like a bull using his power, but Santee avoided being pushed around by him, using her lithe quickness to evade him. But she wasn't afraid to stick a hand in and steal the ball or be called for a foul by accidentally on purpose tangling her toe around Joe's ankle. And Joe wasn't averse to ramming his shoulder into her, knocking her on her ass, just as he would a man.

The free throw line was Santee's domain. Two shots, two points. Joe was lucky to sink one of two.

A horn sounded. Joe shot and missed. Santee smirked. He wrapped his tree-trunk-like arm around her bare midriff and hauled her to the bench where towels, water, and Gatorade bottles sat.

Ruarke made to rise, but Pete put his hand on Ruarke's shoulder. "They're not done."

Just a few moments later, the horn sounded, and they came off the bench. Santee jogged toward where the ball had ended up, while Joe just stared and shook his head. He was moving like a punch-drunk boxer at the end of his rope.

Santee trotted back and two-handed the ball hard at Joe's chest.

Ruarke couldn't take his eyes off those long legs and flat belly. Santee moved with such strength and agility. Her long fingers easily controlled the large ball.

Butt to Joe, Santee worked her way toward her basket. He tried to slap around her, but her long arms kept the ball out of reach. She planted, turned left, and lifted the ball. Joe leaped to block, but Santee spun on the planted foot, came around, and shot.

The score was 67, Santee, 63, Joe.

"How long are they going to play?"

Pete looked at the scoreboard. "There's three minutes left. Or until Joe collapses."

The ball got loose. Both scrambled after it. They went down, both struggling for control.

A whistle sounded.

Shaynee came down, got the ball, and moved to the center court. Santee was up first. She held her hand down for Joe. For a moment, he looked up at her then smiled and grasped her hand. She said something that widened Joe's eyes, then he laughed as Santee smiled over her shoulder.

A real smile, Ruarke noted. Not that quirk of the lips like he got.

Shaynee tossed the ball up.

Santee got in tight and knocked it away from Joe's hands. The ball went out of bounds. She jogged over to get it and, no argument, tossed it to Joe.

He came in fast, dodged around her using his shoulder to knock her back, and drove into a layup. Swoosh. Two points.

Score was now 67, Santee, 65, Joe.

Santee glanced at the clock distracting Joe. She cruised by him for her own layup—65.

Joe made four quick points. One on his "in" and the second Santee fouled him and he actually made both shots—69.

The girls started a count down.

Ten.

Santee brought the ball in.

Five.

Santee worked it down court fighting past Joe's flailing hands.

Four.

At midcourt, Santee moved hard right. But Joe was there.

Three.

She backed up, dribbling slowly.

Two.

She drove hard as Joe backed up.

One.

She stopped at the three-point line and put up a beautiful arc-ing shot.

Bzzzzz.

Swoosh.

Three points!

Hoots resounded, echoing in the metal building.

Joe dropped his hands to his knees. Shaking his head but smiling, he held out a hand to Santee. She took it, and he hauled her into his sweaty embrace, slapping her back as vehemently as he would have a man.

Apparently that was different, Ruarke thought, from him merely reaching out to touch her. Joe got a smile. He got the icy stink eye.

A telephone sounded.

Shawnee dug her phone out, her huge smile dying away into a grimace as she said hello.

Her eyes widened in horror.

Chapter 20

Two vans made the trip to Rapid City over sloppy roads. Trees on the hills had caved to the weight of the ice, exposing the honey-colored cores of shattered branches.

The van that Pete drove headed straight to the hospital. The Sinclairs and Hendersons may not have been buddies, but they were united by granddaughters. Shaynee and Shawnee held hands the entire way to Rapid City despite being told by their nurse grandmother that Grandpa Henderson's procedure was safe and non-life-threatening.

The second van with Joe driving carried Santee; the Fab Four, who hadn't taken the hint that it was going to be a long boring day; Hannah and Jamie, whose glasses were in; Remmy; Rio; and Deacon. Sophie and Maddie were the only smart ones and opted to stay home.

At the optometrist's, Hannah was again given cash to pay for her glasses. Joe went in with Jamie and Ruarke's credit card.

Santee waited in the van, keeping an eye on the bruised and stiff Deacon. He had seemed to go a shade paler when they pulled up to the optometrist's office. His fingers plucked at a thread on his oversized jeans. If the kid kept worrying that thread, he could end up wearing a floppy kilt rather than pants.

"I, um, am really sorry," Deacon mumbled around his swollen lip.

"You are now," Santee said. "We'll see how long those feelings of remorsefulness last."

He shifted around stiffly on the seat. The dry-ice heat of her gaze kept him staring at his clenched hands. "I promise you—"

"Words are easy to spit out. Actions aren't so easy to fake."

Deacon's shoulders slumped. He'd thought no one could ever be as tough as his old man...he'd been wrong.

Hannah came bouncing out with the exact same frame as the wrecked ones. Her blue eyes sparkled as she crawled into the van and flung herself into Santee's arms. "Thank you so much!"

Awkwardly Santee patted her back. "You are so welcome, but the Sinclairs deserve the big hug."

"I will," she promised. "But you're the one who thought I should come stay."

"Everyone thinks you should stay at the ranch. Not just me."

"But you got them to let me stay."

"Hannah—"

Jamie slid in, his glasses were also the same silver wire-rimmed frames. "Wow," he said. "Two pairs of glasses in just a couple of months is some kind of record for me."

"Me too," Hannah said as she settled into her seat and buckled in.

Deacon sat staring, with his one semigood eye and one swollen-shut eye, out the window. His reflection showed in the glass. If Santee weren't the suspicious cuss she was, she'd almost be taken in by the shimmer in Deacon's eye and the contrite, sad expression on his face. Almost.

As early as it was, Walmart was already hopping. Sunny's vest got her in the store. The passel of kids got the stink eye from the door attendant, but it was Joe and Santee, as a biracial couple, who really got the old biddy's goat. She didn't say a word, but her sneery face said it all.

Santee halted, but Joe grabbed her arm, and Sunny pushed her legs and forced her past. With a huff, she planted her hands on her hips and glared at Joe.

The kids looked from Santee to Joe and back, not understanding. But Deacon knew. As Deke, he'd been followed around every store he'd ever entered. And with good reason. If he wanted it, he took it. Not now, though. He looked at Santee and knew that she'd know, and his ass would be grass. She was just looking for an excuse.

"What wrong, Mommy Tee?" Simon said.

Joe just shook his head.

Still steaming, Santee rubbed her hand over Simon's spiky head. "Just big people's stuff."

That was enough to satisfy the Fab Four and Remmy and Rio. But Hannah and Jamie knew better. Something very wrong had happened. They just didn't know what. But they were ready to back Santee if need be, positive she was right.

"Okay, guys. Onward and upward. Deacon needs new duds."

"No, I—"

Santee's look silenced him. "Deacon's pants are way too big. We wear our pants up where they belong and not..." She looked at Jamie.

He grinned. "And not hanging off our butts."

"And we don't wear jeans with ratty holes in them unless...?" She looked at Hannah.

She beamed. "Unless we wear a hole in them. And then Rosarita will see that they get patched."

Hannah looked at Jamie, and simultaneously they said, "And we do not, never ever under penalty of death and dismemberment, take scissors and cut holes in them."

"Wow!" Santee said to Joe. "They actually listen once in a while."

In perfect harmony, they continued, "We don't spend good money on holey pants." They high-fived each other.

"Practically word for word," Joe said.

They were caravanning through the aisles. Hannah held the hands of Simon and Trey. Jamie had RePete and Trev. Deacon shuffled along, looking as if he'd rather be anywhere but here, his blackened eyes garnering a lot of attention. Rio and Remmy were each pushing a cart. Joe and Santee with Sunny followed.

Deacon had just finished trying on jeans, and two choices had been made when the first cop showed up. He was in his thirties, but his eyes looked older. His name tag read Murphy. His narrowed gaze took in Deacon's bruised and swollen face. If Deacon were forced to strip, he'd find a ton more bruises from his shoulders down to his knees.

"I'd like to ask you some questions, son. Come with me."

Deacon flared, but a soft clearing of a throat stopped him. "Here is fine."

Murphy glared at the daring woman. "All right, then." He noted the gawkers gathering and waved them on. "Who did this to you?"

A clearing throat stopped Deacon from saying he'd fallen. "My old man."

Murphy's eyes jerked to Joe.

Deacon snorted. "Do I look—"

The air suddenly seemed to vacuum out of the area. Deacon felt eyes boring at him and knew they didn't belong to the cop. He stood on a precipice… Santee's warnings about respect for all the ranch people regardless of color or sex. It all rushed through his mind like a dizzying vortex. He couldn't get his tongue untied to extricate himself from this, and he desperately wanted to…needed to.

"Is there some problem here?"

The city cop jerked around to face the sheriff from the neighboring county. His hand eased away from his pistol. "Concerned citizens reported a kid who looked like he'd been beaten up. Just checking."

Lance Armstrong nodded. He and Deke Jones were old adversaries. Any petty problems from pickpocketing to petty theft had had him searching out Deke or his old man.

Deacon stood slump-shouldered, praying that the damned sheriff didn't spoil this for him. One excuse. That's all she'd need.

Lance said to Deke. "Your old man do this?"

Deacon nodded.

"Heard you got in trouble in school," Sheriff Armstrong said. At Deke's nod, he said, "That the reason?"

"Don't need no reason," Deacon said surly. "But yuh."

"So," Armstrong said, "you and the Sinclair kid buddies?"

"Yes," Jamie spoke up. He moved to Deacon's side. "Yes, we are."

Armstrong's gaze shifted to Santee. She coolly looked back. Most people, especially women, were either awed or intimidated by him. Santee Smith was neither. Nor was she bedazzled by the sight of his sexy body in a well-cut uniform. How could she not be?

"He's staying with the Sinclairs?"

"For now anyhow," Santee said.

Armstrong shrugged. "Hope you know what you're doing."

"Me too."

Armstrong cleared it with the cop, gave a jaunty salute, and sauntered off. Santee didn't know whether to thank him or kick him…the arrogant ass. But he'd gotten them out of a sticky situation.

The kids were wide-eyed. RePete said, "Is Deacon goin' away?"

"No." Santee hunkered down to their level. "The nice policeman just wanted to make sure we weren't the ones who hurt Deacon."

"Oh. Okay." And all was right with their world.

Santee looked at Joe. His eyes smoldered. She elbowed him. "Buck up, buttercup. I'd have come visit you in the slammer."

Joe snorted. He'd expected her to say she'd have taken the fall. "Conjugal visits?"

Her cool gaze was accompanied by a slow smile. "Be careful what you wish for." She wriggled her eyebrows at him before heading the kids off in search of underwear, much to Deacon's red-faced chagrin.

"Could I speak to Santee?"

"Sure. Hang on."

Over the open line came the hissed argument. Ruarke had to smile at the sound of Santee flat-out refusing and Joe telling her "Buck up, buttercup" (Where did that come from?) and take the damn phone. He heard what sounded like a raspberry, which made him snort. His inflection showed a smiling man where before had stood a depressed one.

"Hello."

The grudging sound made him chuckle, "How goes it?"

"Well, other than having a cop confront us in Walmart about abusing Deacon and having your buddy Armstrong come to our rescue, just peachy."

"What?" He wanted to keep that SOB Armstrong as far away from Santee as possible, even though he didn't think she'd fall for his line of BS. Would she?

A rustle of excitement sounded behind him. Mirrored in the window, a doctor walked tiredly into the waiting room, but a weary smile told them that it had gone well.

"I've got to go." Dead air sounded before he could tell her he'd call back.

Half an hour later, Ruarke called again. "Hey, Boss. How's Mr. Henderson?"

"Out of surgery. Put a stent in. Doctor says he'll be out making life miserable—"

Joe snorted. "I'm guessing he didn't use those exact words."

"Probably not." Ruarke looked at Sharron Henderson, his former mother-in-law, who looked exhausted. Shaynee and Shawnee clung to each other, so relieved that their seldom-seen grandfather was going to be all right. Heather hung on the arm of her newest boy toy, a model-handsome guy who looked like he'd rather be anywhere but here and whose eyes seemed to stray way too often toward the twins for comfort.

"So, you're outta the hospital?" Joe said.

"The girls and I are. Heather and Sharron are staying. Can I speak to Santee?"

"She ain't here."

Surprisingly he felt as if he'd sprung a slow leak. "Where is she?"

"Goodwill."

He should have known. Get her into town and the first place she asked to be dropped was a thrift store.

"Oh," Joe said. "Here they come."

"What did she buy? Can you tell?"

"Well, the kids all have at least one book. Jamie and Hannah each have an armful. Santee's got a couple of bags of stuff."

"And Deacon?"

Joe looked into the back at the sulky teenager. "Santee took pity on the poor schmuck and let him wait in the van with me."

"Hurting pretty badly?"

"Seems like it."

"Serves the little miscreant right. So where are you headed next?"

"Well, there's got a long list for Sam's Club, and Santee mentioned PetSmart."

"Send us the Sam's list. We'll swing by there. You take Santee to PetSmart. Then it'll be almost noon, we'll meet for dinner."

"Sounds good. If you don't mind, though, I think I'll ask Santee rather than tell her."

Ruarke snorted. "Smart man. See you soon."

"You're sleeping in the hall!" Deacon squelched.

Santee continued to place the dogs' beds and the pillows Ruarke provided, apparently for the two of them again.

"Looks that way."

"Why?"

Santee rotated on her toes to face him. "Why do you think?"

For a moment, his eyes seemed to tear up. "If I gave you my word?"

"How much your word is worth?"

"A week ago I'd have said not very much." His dark eyes sought hers. "Now, I'd say everything."

"Prove it."

"I intend to." He turned and walked into the room he shared with Jamie.

"I hope so," Santee said. "I really do."

Ruarke settled down next to Santee. His butt already hurt. "How long are we going to do this?"

Her glacial eyes nailed him. "No one said you had to. I've got this."

"Just wondering if I should have my mattress hauled up here. We could at least sit in comfort."

"Go to bed."

"Join me."

"You have no idea what you'd be letting yourself in for."

His beautiful blue eyes twinkled as a grin spread across his lips. "I have somewhat of an idea, and I wouldn't fight you off if you wanted to give me a clearer picture." He wriggled eyebrows lecherously.

"Go to sleep, you idiot."

"Seriously—"

Santee held up her hand and shook her head.

Ruarke wanted to put his arm around her and pull her against his chest so that it wasn't him and her standing separate watches, but them, together. Her stiffness warned him that now was not the time.

With a sigh, he tried to squirm into a more comfortable position. This was going to get old in a big hurry.

———————————————

Chapter 21

Deacon looked at himself in the mirror, running his hand over his head. Gone were the shaggy locks he could hide behind. No more bad boy glowering for him. A new Deacon Jones had been created…a bouncing fourteen-year-old baby boy. One who was scared to death that he was going to blow this, that Santee's eagle eyes would discover some transgression and he'd be "kicked to the curb" as she called it.

His new jeans, shirt, shoes, and even underwear and socks were only camouflage hiding the old Deke. It had only been a week since his rebirth, but it was a constant battle to keep the old thoughts and actions from rising.

He'd caught himself, just last night, staring at Shaynee and Shawnee. They were just so beautiful and graceful and smart. And they were supposed to be his sisters. Somehow he didn't think that brothers were supposed to have physical reactions like he had when looking at one's "sisters." And there had sat Santee, all sharp-eyed, watching him…waiting for him to make a fatal mistake.

"Come on, Deacon." Jamie poked his head into the other side of the bathroom where Deacon loitered. "We're going to miss the bus."

Can't have that, Deacon thought sourly. Not on the first day after being expelled for fighting. Another strike against him. His stomach was tied in knots. The orange juice, all he'd managed for breakfast, sat sourly in his churning gut.

He pounded down the steps and raced for the door. "Have a good day" and "good luck" sounded but were barely heard, surely not intended for him.

Outside Santee waited, of course.

She looked him over and nodded approval. It was enough to make his cheeks heat up.

"I don't know what you owe for your lunch, but Jamie has a credit card. Go with him to the office and settle up, then pay up to the first of the month. You'll then be on the same schedule as the rest of the kids."

"Didn't trust me with it, huh?" Her eyebrows arched. God, he hated it when she looked at him like he was some disgusting stink bug. She didn't look at precious Jamie or Hannah like that.

"Should I?"

Deacon's shoulders slumped, seemingly under the weight of the brand-new backpack loaded with all the school supplies he hadn't had at the start of the school year.

"The school knows Jamie has the right to the credit card. He pays all the elementary lunch bills. Hannah's included."

"Oh."

"So you know what's expected."

He nodded.

"Treat everyone with respect, the way you'd like to be treated. No calls from the ja—um, principal."

Deacon's head jerked up. Santee's lips quirked, which made him smile.

"And no notes from Mrs. Helling."

"Right."

"Okay, then. Go have a good day. I expect a ton of homework for you three if Mrs. Helling lets you make up what you missed."

Old lady Helling.

Right.

The day was just looking better and better.

Sir Rob was holding court in the dining room. The ladies were gliding in and out, refilling coffee cups and cleaning the table, which was now three wooden tables shoved together to accommodate the newly expanded clan.

"It's going to be a busy week," Sir Rob said. "Bobby John's team is having their bye week, so he and Max will be coming in later today and staying over through the weekend.

"This is Tuesday. Friday is the lead-up to the horse sale. Friday afternoon we can walk through the fairgrounds and look at the horses. Friday night, there's going to be the show and tell where they'll bring each horse out into the arena and show them off. Saturday at noon the sale starts.

"We'll be taking the van on Friday night and Saturday. Plus we'll take the six-horse trailer. Don't know that we'll get that many, but"—he grinned at Santee—"between the two of us, we've got a bunch of possibilities picked out. Anything else?"

Ruarke raised his hand. "Sam and Miri are coming in today also for a couple of days."

"Great!" Rob said. "The more the merrier."

Santee couldn't believe that he actually seemed happy to have four more people mobbing his house.

Sir Rob chuckled. "Good thing we got some furniture in those spare bedrooms so they'll have a place to sleep. Anybody else?"

Reluctantly Santee raised her hand.

"Yes, Santee."

She hated this. Now everyone was looking at her. "Could I borrow a vehicle to run into town?"

"Of course," he said immediately. "Is there anything we can help with?"

"No, I can get the tanks off myself."

"Tanks?" Sir Rob said. He already had the guys lined up to wrap her waterline and sewer hose with heat tapes so they wouldn't freeze. "As in propane tanks?"

Santee nodded. "It won't take long."

The nights had been cool…just above freezing. Rob could have kicked himself. Of course she'd have to have the furnace running, and those small tanks didn't last long.

"May I ask how long you've been avoiding getting the tanks refilled?"

Her reddened cheeks were answer enough.

"Dang it, Santee—"

But she was up and gone, her dogs scrambling to avoid being left behind.

Dead silence reigned. Even the kitchen clatter was silent.

"Good going, Dad."

Rob glared at Ruarke, but he was right. Santee never asked for anything. Her vehicle was tied to the camper, so unless she unhooked everything and took the pickup and camper, she was stuck out here with no transportation.

"I'll call and get a big tank brought out for her."

"She could still just shut off the tank and unhook the tubing to take off," Joe commented. He held up his hands when everyone glared at him. "Hey! Don't kill the messenger. You know as well as me the girl has a stubborn streak a mile wide."

After her morning run, Santee walked into the ranch yard, her breathing slowing and the chilly air drying her sweat-drenched hair. The air buzzed with normal construction noises and the excited whickering of hungry horses. Normal, yet Santee felt the weight of eyes upon her. Carefully, she looked around but couldn't see any overt starers…but they were out there somewhere.

She rounded the almost completed training arena and stumbled to a stop. Ahead, beside her camper now sat a fat silver propane tank. Her teeth ground together. She'd known she never should have mentioned the need for propane, but it was such a hassle to uproot the camper in order to take the truck anywhere.

A Ranger pulled up beside her. "Santee," Sir Rob said. "I had them fill your tanks when they hooked up the big one. All you have to do is unhook the hose should you ever decide to leave. Please don't just shut off the big tank to spite me."

"Me?" Santee pulled her glasses off and leaned down to look at Sir Rob and Ruarke. "Spiteful and vindictive? Hah!" She shook her head and walked on, pushing Sunny in the stroller.

"So do you think she'll leave it hooked up?" Rob said.

"Your guess is as good as mine," Ruarke said. Women were impossible to understand in the first place, and Santee was even worse because she didn't follow typical female pathways.

Max Gold, Ruarke's good friend and manager, and his husband, Bobby John Johnston, drove in just as dinner was being served.

Ruarke left the table and went outside. "Max!" he called. "Get your bags later. Soup's on!"

Max wore his typical three-piece suit and shiny leather Italian loafers. The cost of his outfit could have fed a family of four for a month. "Ruarke!" They hugged and slapped each other's backs. "You look—" He spotted the big gray dog and froze.

Ruarke laughed. "Relax. It's just Duke."

"Duke."

"Yuh, I told you about the wolf dogs on the Graham place. How one got away?"

"Yes?"

"Well, ta-da."

"You have a wolf dog."

"Santee has a wolf dog." Over Max's shoulder, Ruarke watched Bobby John approach. "Hey, Bobby John."

They shook hands, Ruarke's fine-boned fingers lost in the catcher's mitt of the football lineman's grip. Had he wanted, Bobby John could have crushed Ruarke's hand. He stood maybe six feet, two inches, but he was a bull of a man. A Texan from his snake-skin-booted toes to his Stetson-covered head. He was so different from refined Max that the theory that opposites attract really applied to them.

"How's the leg man?" Bobby John said, warily eyeing the wolf. Growing up on a west Texas ranch made him anti-wolf to the core.

"Leg's doing remarkably well. Still hopeful."

Where they stood, above them was all new roof. The carpenters had gotten the gables added front and back to form the additions to the two suites. Work on the suites was made the priority over completing the first floor's dining room, living room, office expansion.

"Quite some changes," Max commented. "And you said it was all this Santee's idea?"

Ruarke motioned them inside. Both Max and Bobby John warily eyed the wolf dog as they edged past.

"Santee's plan. Everyone else thought it was a good idea considering the amount of time you two and Miri and Sam spend here. Give you a home base when the retirement bug bites you in the ass."

Bold as brass, Bobby John swept off his Stetson and walked up to the only stranger at the table, hand extended. "Bobby John Johnston."

Santee arose and hesitated just a fraction of a second before putting her slender hand in his. "Santee Smith."

"Pleased to make your acquaintance. Do you mind?" He inclined his head toward the chair on her left.

"I don't," she said. "But Rio might at suppertime."

"Santee," Ruarke said as he led Max up to the table. "My good friend, Max Gold. He handles all my affairs."

Ruarke sensed a coolness in their exchanged greetings that hadn't been there between Santee and Bobby John.

Max clapped Ruarke on the shoulder. "I make sure the big buy doesn't get taken to the cleaners by anyone." A warning sounded clearly in his voice.

Ruarke turned on Max.

Santee snorted. "Too bad he's not man enough to keep himself out of those kinds of situations."

"Santee!"

That damned half smile tugged at her lips. But her cool gaze remained locked on Max.

"Soup's on!" Rosarita declared as she walked in with the tureen in her hands. The tension broke as Pete rushed to carry the heavy bowl for her.

Bobby John patted the chair beside him, and Santee sat back down. "Don't you pay him no never mind. He just gets a touch over-protective with Ruarke." Bobby John eyed the two men as they sat down at the opposite side of the table. "Makes a body wonder if they could have been more than friends at one time." He wriggled his eyebrows.

Santee snorted at the thought. "I kind of doubt that."

"Yuh, me too. Ruarke's kind of a pansy."

Santee looked askance at him. "A pansy?"

"A' course. You know all them baseball players are a bunch of pansies. Real men play football."

Ruarke didn't know what was being said across the table, but Santee was giving Bobby John one of her full-on smiles. Ruarke had never understood Max's attraction to the big Texas oaf. They seemed so dissimilar. Consequently, he and Bobby John were not buddies. But here Max's husband was bonding so damn easily with Santee. And unless he misjudged the look she shot him, Ruarke guessed it was at his expense.

Jamie held the credit card out to Santee as he came in after school. Neither he nor Hannah seemed to have any more scrapes or bruises.

"How'd it go?"

"Okay, I think," Jamie said.

Hannah nodded. "Mrs. Helling kept looking at him as if waiting for him to blow up, but it never happened."

"Better not have. Got homework?"

They both groaned. "Tons," Hannah moaned. "Mrs. Helling expects us to do everything they did the whole time we were gone."

"See," Santee said. "Crime really doesn't pay."

"You can say that again," Jamie said as he trudged in.

Deacon plodded toward the house, head down and shoulders slumped, the brand-new backpack almost but not quite dragging in the dirt.

"Deacon."

He flinched and looked up.

Santee held her hand out indicating the porch swing. They settled on opposite ends, leaving a good three feet between them. Deacon plopped the stuffed backpack between his feet. Sunny edged up and gently laid her head on Deacon's knee. A moment later, his hand moved to the dog's soft head, but Santee doubted he was even aware of it. He sat staring off into space, and what he was seeing was not making him happy.

Deacon sighed. "Do you think Mrs. Helling's afraid of me?"

"Does she have reason to be scared?"

He sighed again. "Maybe."

"Why do you think she might have been afraid of you?"

His hand worked Sunny's head faster. "She's always watching me. Every time I'd look up there, she'd be eyeballing me like I was some freak or something."

"You know why, don't you?"

Deacon shook his head.

"Because angry, loner-type teenage boys are the ones who come to school with guns a'blazing. And the first one who dies is the teacher they hate."

Deacon's face went gray. "I should just drop out."

"Not and stay in this family you don't. No way."

"I can't go back. Not if she thinks I'm going to shoot her or something!"

"Yes, you can. And you will. Prove to her that you've changed."

"How?"

"By keeping your head down, doing the work without complaining, and gasp, maybe even raise your hand and answer a question on occasion. And don't give me any of that guff about not knowing the answers. I listened to you with Remmy and Rio. You have a whole lot of knowledge locked away in that brain of yours. Use it."

"You think that'll do it?"

"All you can do is try. And give it time."

Deacon realized he was petting Sunny and looked surprised. Sunny looked up at him, so calm and loving. He leaned down with both hands and ruffled her neck. "Thank you," he said to the dog but looked sideways at Santee.

A car pulled into the yard.

"Deacon. Ruarke has friends staying over this week. Act like you belong. Don't get defensive and don't get mad when this woman"— she nodded at Miri, who was just exiting the Lexus through the door Sam held open for her—"starts cross-examining you. If push comes to shove, let me do the shoving."

"You don't like her?"

"It's mutual. Just don't let her get to you."

Miri looked lovely in a skintight knit dress and four-inch heels. She minced up the walk hanging on to Sam's arm.

Sam saw them and smiled. "Santee!"

Santee arose and motioned Deacon with her.

"Sam." She smiled at him. Soberly she said, "Miri. This is Deacon Jones, a friend of Jamie's. He's staying with us for a while. Deacon, this is Sam and Miri Adams, Maddie and Simon's parents."

"Pleased to meet you."

Duke chose that moment to rise and shake.

Miri cried out and tried to climb into Sam's arms. Duke looked at her and ambled off in the direction of the corral that had become the doggie potty.

Miri disengaged from Sam and smoothed down the cocoa-colored dress. "That dog shouldn't be allowed around the children. Some day—"

"Duke is fine with the children," Santee said. "He just doesn't like people in four-inch heels."

Miri sniffed and stuck her nose in the air. "We'll see what Ruarke has to say before we leave Thursday." She turned for the door, her tightly encased ass swishing a little extra.

Santee elbowed Deacon.

"Oh, um, sorry." He blushed a nice dark red.

"It's okay," Sam said with a laugh. "If she didn't want to be ogled, she'd wear something entirely different. Just don't leer or drool." He winked and followed his wife into the house.

The loud noise of greetings between friends who hadn't seen each other in a long time blasted through the open doorway along with Maddie's strident demands for attention.

"Wow," Deacon said.

"And this is just the beginning."

Ruarke knew if Miri and Max were here more often or full-time, there'd be a lot less hubbub. The three of them sat together reminiscing while Sam read a book and Bobby John flipped through TV channels. Santee was doing her nightly thing getting the kids ready to go upstairs.

He was looking forward to sleeping in the hall, even though his ass was not. And then she did the unexpected.

Santee went to Deacon and had a short fierce conversation where all the boy did was nod in agreement. Then she went to the S-twins and Hannah. The girls looked at Deacon, who was tomato red, and nodded. Finally, she said good night to Sam and Bobby John as she went toward the mudroom and the exit.

Bobby John stopped her and gently talked to her. Santee was shaking her head no. Behind his back, Bobby John motioned Sam over. Whatever was being talked about involved Miri, Max, and himself, because they kept looking over and Santee kept shaking her head.

"What's going on over there?" Max asked.

Ruarke wished Max hadn't turned Miri's attention to Santee. He could feel her ire rising up immediately.

Bobby John went down on one knee, hands held playfully together. An actual snorted laugh sounded from Santee. Her face brightened in a seldom-seen actual uninhibited smile. Her laughter was like music. She gave Bobby John a shove that almost toppled him, grabbed his hand, and pulled him to his feet—no small task.

"You're going to regret this," she told them as they were bowing and thanking her.

Miri said, "What the hell?"

Santee and the dogs headed into the mudroom and soon exited out the front, where Duke came dancing up. The four of them walked off.

So much for together time in the hall, Ruarke thought.

"About that wolf," Miri said. She watched Santee and the dogs walk away, eyes narrowed with loathing.

What was he going to do with this animosity between his best friend and his—?

His what?

That was a very good question.

"Tell me you didn't invite her," Miri wailed again.

"Miri," Sam said tiredly.

"Come on!" she whined. "It would have been so much more fun just the five of us. Like always!"

Ruarke caught Rosarita's reaction further back in the van. Pete put his arm around her, but she wasn't overly consoled by it.

"Maybe for you," Sam said.

Miri turned on him in a huff. "What's that supposed to mean?"

"Miri," Sam said and shook his head.

"I mean it, Mr. Adams. What the hell is that snide comment supposed to mean."

Sam rarely had enough of Miri's attitude, but she'd just bumped him over the top. "It means, my love, that you, Ruarke, and Max have a good old time together while Bobby John and I sit off in some corner, forgotten."

"That's not true!"

Joe held open the camper door, shifting all the attention from Miri to the longest expanse of shapely legs this side of the Rockettes. Then came about the shortest most form-fitting denim skirt. A denim jacket covered whatever top Santee was wearing. Her hair was shiny and slicked back into place with gel.

A wolf whistle resounded in the metal interior, cut off with a jab from Max. "Hey," Bobby John protested. "I might be gay, but I ain't dead."

"Don't tell me she's bringing that ugly damn dog along!" Miri wailed.

"Okay, I won't tell you."

"Ruarke!"

"There's not much point in having a service dog and leaving it home."

Miri sniffed. "What's she need a service dog for? She just wants everyone to notice her with that ugly dog."

"That's not what they're gonna be looking at," Bobby John said dryly. He grunted again at the sharp poke in the ribs. "Well, it's true."

Sunny pottied and trotted back to Santee, tail bobbing. Santee told Duke goodbye, and Rufus was sleeping with Jamie tonight.

The interior light came on as Joe opened the door. Ruarke swiveled around, wishing he were going to be sitting beside Santee instead of in the front seat to accommodate his damned leg. He gave the brace a whack with his fist and winced when his leg complained.

Bobby John held his hand out from the third row of seats. Sam, in the second row with Miri, wouldn't have dared. Santee had to hike the tight skirt up indecently high so she could lift her booted foot onto the running board.

Ruarke envied Sam his view. Miri was swiveled half around so her back was to Sam and the door.

"Thank you," Santee said as she edged past to the rear seat where Pete and Rosarita sat. Pete half stood and, leaning over his wife, gave Santee a one-arm hug.

"Oh, Rosarita!" Santee exclaimed. "What a lovely dress! Love that scarlet color on you."

"Gracias! I make myself."

"Beautiful and talented," Santee said. "Pete, you're a very lucky man."

Rosarita's cheeks pinked, her spirits lifting after an afternoon of Miri's snide remarks about Rosarita's parenting skills, cooking skills, and dowdiness.

Ruarke followed Santee's progress via the makeup mirror in the visor. As she walked hunched over, the skirt slid precipitously higher, with no discernible flash of panties. So was she wearing a thong or nothing at all? Either way, Ruarke's throat went dry.

Sunny followed on Santee's heels and settled on the floor at her feet.

"Sophie and Maddie sure seemed happy enough to spend the night with the big girls."

"*Sí*," Rosarita said. "I just pray they sleep and can go to *la escuela* tomorrow."

The door slammed, and the light cut out on Miri's "Wouldn't hurt them to miss a day of kin-der-gar-ten."

The entire drive into town Miri sulked, refusing to be jollied out of it by Sam, Ruarke, or Max.

A lively conversational rumble drifted forward from Bobby John, Santee, Pete, and Rosarita.

Finally, Sam said, "Max, why don't we change places so you, Miri, and Ruarke can talk more easily?"

It was awkward trying to get super tall Sam to the back and the wiry Max to the second seat.

Only then did Ruarke realize that Sam had been right. This was the way it always was. The three of them glommed together, leaving Bobby John and Sam to fend for themselves. And there probably weren't two more mismatched men on the planet. The only thing they had in common was football, and even then their football positions did not lead them to think highly of the other—one was thought of as a knuckle-dragging fat thug while the other was thought of as a prima donna who spent most of the game just racing away from the action.

Ruarke felt guilty for all the hours the two men had been forced to suffer through each other's company. The rumble of both their voices and their mutual laughter sounded sadly strange.

Miri sniffed, and Max, ever the gentleman, dug out a handkerchief for her. "I still don't understand why she had to come along," she whined.

Joe's hands tightened on the steering wheel, while Ruarke wondered if his best friend had always been such a self-centered bitch.

The Bucking Bull's bullish outline rocked forward and backward in neon splendor. The parking lot was maybe a third full, typical for a midweek night. There wasn't a live band, and it must not be karaoke night, or the lot would be packed.

Miri looped her arms through Ruarke's and Max's as they walked toward the neon-Budweiser-sign lit windows. This seemed so natural. Again, Ruarke felt a twinge of shame knowing that, if not for Santee, Pete, and Rosarita, but especially Santee, Bobby John and Sam would have been trailing along behind. How unbelievably thoughtless they'd been.

Max pulled the door open, releasing a Kenny Chesney song. Miri stepped in like a queen, every movement designed to attract attention, and she got plenty of that. She slinked between chairs, nose stuck in the air, too hoity-toity to acknowledge any of the patrons, many of whom she'd probably gone to high school with. She commandeered a table that was surrounded by other taken tables.

"Let's sit over there," Ruarke said. Closer to the wall there were two tables already shoved together, which would easily have accommodated all of them.

"I want to sit here," she pouted.

Max pulled out a chair for her. Ruarke reluctantly sat, easing his leg under the table.

Santee entered, and the air was sucked up into every males', and a few females', lungs. She looked over the room, noted where Ruarke's threesome were seated, and headed to where Ruarke had wanted to go.

More than one cowboy arose and moved his chair aside so Santee and party could pass. Each received eye contact and a "thank you, sir," and she'd nod to the others at the table. Those who remained seated got an excellent view of long, long legs.

"Is this okay?" she asked as she went around to the wall side to get Sunny out of traffic zone.

"Looks good to me," Bobby John said and took the chair to her right. Rosarita sat down on the left with Pete beside her. Sam sat at the end beside Bobby John. Joe came from the bar with a tray held high: a pitcher of beer, frosted glasses, a bottle of water, and an unopened can of Dr. Pepper on it.

Miri was trying to flag down the waitress, but the apron-clad server was doing a good job of ignoring her highness. Max finally got up to go to the bar, his three-piece Italian suit a misnomer in this cattlemen's bar.

Miri called after him, "I'll have a strawberry daiquiri."

Max returned with a beer for Ruarke; a whisky, not a scotch, for himself; and a margarita for Miri. "They said no daiquiris."

Miri's full lips pulled into a pout. "I had my heart set on a strawberry daiquiri."

The beer was frosty and probably tasted good, but it was flat on Ruarke's tongue. Across the room, he could see the rest of his party laughing and having a good time, while at his table Miri held court to a rapt Max. Same old, same old.

Someone dropped a quarter in the jukebox. Miri turned to Ruarke, but he merely pointed to his braced leg. She pulled a pout and turned to Max. Country music wasn't his forte, but he gallantly held his hand out to her and led her to the packed dancefloor.

Pete led Rosarita out. Joe went in search of an unattached female. Bobby John held his hand out to Santee. She tried to wave him off, but he stood up with his hand out. She clearly said he'd regret it, but the big man's laugh rumbled throughout the room.

She said something to Bobby John that made his face get beet red. He laughed and said something smart back that earned him an elbow poked in his ribs.

Ruarke glared at Bobby John, wishing he'd been the recipient of that jab.

Santee wasn't a good dancer, not nearly in Miri's class, but laughed with Bobby John at her missteps. Unlike Miri, who seemed so focused on being perfect that Ruarke wondered if she even derived any pleasure out of it.

The next song was a slow one. Miri held out her hand to Ruarke. "Come on. You won't even have to move, just sway in place."

Santee was enticing Sam onto the floor. Ruarke got up and joined Miri.

Santee and Sam swayed together, but not skin tight together. Both tall and lanky, they looked like they were made for each other. Their arms looped around each other's bodies but loosely.

As opposed to Miri, who was squashed against Ruarke. Her full ruby lips moved constantly, but Ruarke didn't hear much of what she said, too tuned in to what Sam and Santee were doing.

Santee nodded toward Miri, as if encouraging Sam to cut in, but Sam gave a firm shake of his head.

Miri saw her husband with Santee and stiffened in outrage. "That little bitch!" she growled.

And so the night went. Miri got more and more irked whenever Sam and Santee danced. Every slow dance she got Ruarke up and onto the floor, which was when Sam and Santee seemed to be out also.

It was almost closing time. Joe had already passed the van keys to Santee, having found an alternate way home. Miri had Ruarke on the dance floor. Santee maneuvered Sam close. Santee tapped Miri's shoulder.

"Excuse me."

How she managed it, Ruarke had no clue, but in seconds Miri was out of his arms and spun into Sam's. The tall black man was just as surprised as Ruarke.

"Hope you don't mind," Santee said. She looped her arms around his neck but kept a very proper distance between them. Ruarke tried to draw her closer, the faint scents of Ivory Soap and some other soft cologne went straight to his libido. The warning in her eyes made him settle for her suppleness in his arms.

"That was awfully nice of you to dance with Sam and Bobby John like that."

"It was no great hardship. They're nice guys who deserve better from their spouses."

Ruarke sighed and nodded. "You're right."

"Then why didn't you ever do something about it?"

"I didn't realize it was such a big deal until just recently."

"Really!"

Ruarke nodded.

"You didn't realize that the three of you were a clique, that Sam and Bobby John weren't invited to join?"

"No."

She gave him that "I find that hard to believe" look and shook her head.

"Then you need to mend some fences real dang quick because they're both rethinking this whole 'one happy family all under one roof' thing. Sam especially."

Sam and Miri were quietly going at it. When the song ended, Sam walked away, leaving her standing, mouth agape and arms still in dance position.

"I think it's time to go," Santee said.

Ruarke left a generous tip for the waitress that had ignored them all evening. He would have done the same for the other table, but

Sam and Bobby John were waving aside Pete's offer and were both pulling cash out. The waitress had at least put them on her route.

The air in the van was tense. Only Pete and Rosarita seemed to have much of anything to say to each other.

The van's blinker came on. Sam stiffened sharply. "Santee—"

"Sunny's really restless and needs a potty break."

The dog lifted her head at the sound of her name. She had been sleeping soundly, not bothering anyone.

Santee pulled the van up where it had been parked the last time at Lovers' Lane. She got out and helped the tripod dog out and went to the front of the van, where the ticking engine would keep her warm.

Ruarke got out and joined her. His leg ached from all the dancing.

"Think it'll work?"

The half moon was enough to show Santee's shoulders lift. "Had to try something."

A half an hour ticked past with no bouncing inside the van. Santee's arms wrapped around herself. The jean jacket didn't provide much warmth.

"I can think of something that would warm you up," Ruarke said; his sexy smile would have melted the brass off a spittoon.

Santee looked askance up at him. "I'll just bet you could."

Ruarke moved in front of her just as she put her hand on the vibrating hood. Her lips twitched. "Someone is getting lucky."

Ruarke put his hands on her cool cheeks, startling her attention to him. He leaned in and brushed his lips across hers.

"Ruarke." Her hands flattened against his chest, but with a nudge from his wrists, they slid up his shoulders and around his neck as they had been less than an hour ago on the dancefloor.

He dropped his head to the sweet spot on the left side of her neck. The shiver that rocketed through her went straight to his groin.

Santee blinked at him, surprised by her body's traitorous reaction.

His foot edged her boots apart. He stepped between, settling himself naturally between her knees.

The skirt took but a moment to hike out of the way. His warm hands slid up her smooth ass to discover that she did indeed have underwear on in the form of a skimpy thong. He tightened his grip and pulled her tight to his straining erection.

"Sinclair."

He liked the breathy way her voice sounded. He slid his right hand down her thigh and lifted, urging her leg around his. He settled even deeper into her, his jeans stretched to their max.

A strong tug and the undies were not a hindrance.

"Dang it, Sinclair!" Her breath hissed as his fingers slid into her heat. Her leg tightened around him as she arched onto the toes of her other foot, meshing even closer.

The van began a rhythmic rock.

Ruarke grabbed her other leg, lifting it around his hip. Her elbows planted on the van's hood as her hips started to slow dance against him.

He reached between them to his zipper. His hand jerked the remainder of the thong off and tossed it aside. Her breath pounded his eardrums to the thumping of his heart.

The zipper was carefully edged down. He reached past her demanding groin—

Then she stopped.

Frozen.

Hands on his shoulders pushed him away.

God! No! What had—

She was looking over his shoulder, her sharp gaze searching the surrounding pine forest.

"Get in the van!" Santee hissed.

Her legs dropped from around him, her feet landing on the ground as her hand dipped for the leather pouch at her waist.

"Sunny, go with Ruarke!" The dog was instantly at his side.

Ruarke was yanking his zipper up as he moved his jittery hand across the cool metal, propping him up against the adrenaline's undermining retreat.

Suddenly, Pete was there. He got Sunny in with the hand that wasn't holding a gun. Bobby John came out, also armed.

"What it is?" Bobby John called.

"Don't know," Santee replied. Two hands braced her Ruger as she searched the woods.

"I've got you covered. Get in the van," Bobby John said.

Ruarke was in, the passenger-side front door slammed behind him.

Pete had taken a step aside so both he and Bobby John had an angle past Santee, their guns pointed at the blackness where hers had been.

Santee slid her backside along the vehicle. The side mirror forced her to dodge around.

She got the driver's door open and edged in to Miri's "what's wrong?" Santee got the engine started, headlights flooding the innocuous boulder-strewn hillside.

Was that movement at the edge of the trees?

The side door rammed shut. A hand rested on her shoulder as Pete leaned between the front seats.

"See anything?" he asked.

"Maybe." Santee maneuvered the van in a U-turn and headed out faster than they'd entered.

"What was it?" Pete was now turned to face the rear where Bobby John had moved Rosarita into the center seat with Max and watched out the back.

"I don't know," Santee said.

"That's because it was nothing!" Miri spat. "She just had to ruin our night by getting everyone to focus on her."

"Shut up, Miri," Ruarke ground out.

"What?"

"Miri," Sam said, "for once just shut the hell up."

Santee took her eyes from the snaky path for just a moment to mouth to Ruarke, "Sorry."

Not half as sorry as he was, but for vastly different reasons.

Chapter 22

"There's a rummage sale today," Sir Rob said as he looked through yesterday's paper. "There's supposed to be workhorse stuff on it including harnesses and horse-drawn equipment."

Bobby John said, "Speaking of workhorses, what are your plans for the blacks?"

"Try to sell them, I suppose, once they're fattened up."

"I'd like to buy them.'

"Really?"

Jamie was shifting nervously from foot to foot as he stood beside Sir Rob. The kids were already heading out the door on their way to the bus. He held his iPad in his hand. He looked worriedly at Santee.

Bobby John motioned to Sir Rob to talk to his grandson, knowing the boy was in a hurry.

Jamie held the iPad out to Sir Rob. On the screen, a big fat snowflake showed on the weather site. Fear shone in the boy's eyes.

Sir Rob looked at the screen and knew instantly what the boy's problem was. His own gut went sour. He nodded and patted the boy's hand, mouthing the words, "I'll take care of it."

Jamie frowned at him, close to tears. Sir Rob tried to look confident as he nodded that Jamie should leave it all to him. Santee was watching the exchange, which didn't help Rob's confidence any. She still hadn't committed to staying. The arena was almost built. Tomorrow was the presale at the fairgrounds. Saturday was the sale. If there was no Santee, what was he doing all this for?

He desperately needed something to make her want to stay.

Miri and Sam and Max had all headed out early this morning. Sam had to be back for Sunday's game, and Max had clients to appease. Miri and Sam were at least talking, though stiltedly. Their "backseat negotiations" had at least gotten them that far. Luckily Santee didn't return from her run before they left, so the banked embers of Miri's rage weren't reignited.

"So, Bobby John," Sir Rob said, "if you want the horses, are you interested in looking at the horse-drawn equipment? The ad doesn't say what kind. Could be for ponies for all I know, but we could take a trailer and go see."

"I'd like that, if it works in your schedule."

"Santee."

"Yes, sir?"

"Do we have anything pressing on our schedule that would prevent us from checking out that sale?"

Santee was surprised by the question. She wasn't Sir Rob's personal assistant. "Not to my knowledge."

"Good. Let's get a move on. Sale starts at ten, and it's on Nemo road, so it'll take us a while to get there from here."

A flatbed trailer was towed behind the crew cab dually pickup that Pete drove. Ruarke hated the damned leg, which kept him delegated to the front seat's legroom. From the rear came the easy conversation between Santee and Bobby John. Ruarke could barely get two words out of the woman and nothing of consequence, yet there they were chatting like a couple of magpies. He slapped the offending leg and softly cussed at the resultant stab of pain.

Pete gave him a knowing look.

"Watch the damn road," Ruarke growled softly.

The man had the audacity to chuckle as he easily negotiated the circuitous Nemo Road.

"Good help is hard to find," Ruarke mumbled.

Pete shot him a laughing glance. Pete knew very well why Ruarke's panties were in such a knot. Everyone else had gotten "some" last night except him. And the man's unexpressed testosterone was making him "testy."

"Quit that," Ruarke grumbled. It didn't help that Pete had seen Santee put an abrupt stop to Ruarke's seduction last night.

The GPS took that moment to advise them their destination was a hundred feet ahead on the left.

The house yard consisted of a Cape Cod-style house to the left, a fair-sized open area, and a small barn and corrals to the right. There weren't many lookers yet, so Pete was able to maneuver a U-turn and had the truck facing out, ready to leave if no dumbasses blocked him in.

The horse equipment was staged in the corral beside the barn.

Bobby John slipped out, followed by Santee. The resident dog barked from a chain-link enclosure. Santee stopped Sunny from following. A sharp bark told the world that she was affronted at being left behind.

A sad-eyed elderly gentleman was walking among the painstakingly restored equipment. "I had to get rid of my horses," he was telling another pair of lookers. "Couldn't afford to feed them anymore."

Bobby John roamed off into the equipment which was, indeed, designed to be worked with draft-sized horses, not ponies.

Santee headed toward the barn. Ruarke followed. She noticed him and waited so they walked side by side. The barn smelled luscious: hay, horse, and manure. Santee paused just inside to devour the aroma. The dimness allowed her to take off the dark glasses and hang them from one bow in her limited cleavage.

On the right, an open door showed a tackroom with saddles on stands and harnesses neatly hanging. To the left was the almost empty feed room. A lone partial bag of feed drooped.

A sharp-eyed man stood in the tackroom, almost daring anyone to just try to steal anything. Ruarke walked in, unaware that Santee had paused to look at the pictures and ribbons in the display case.

All the leather looked as if it had just been cleaned and oiled. It was supple and in excellent condition. Anything metal, bits and buckles, gleamed.

"Hey, Jack," a man called to the man in the tackroom.

Jack gave Ruarke a steely glare before stepping outside.

Santee looked at Ruarke through the door and gave her head a little jerk. Outside she tipped her head toward the showcase.

And there they were, two big black horses—as a team towing the carriage, one if the wagons, the baler, or under saddle. The old man beamed with pride as he handled the lines or reins. One picture had the horses' names…

Ruarke's breath caught, and he looked sharply at Santee, but she was looking at other photos. With her reading problems, he doubted she'd deciphered the names.

Santee turned toward Ruarke frowning slightly. He was looking at her so strangely. His hand seemed to shake slightly as he pointed at a photo with a caption. She raised her brows questioningly.

His fingers pointed at the first word. "Black," he said softly. Moving his finger to the other word, he said, "Blue."

Santee shook her head, a cold sweat breaking out. What were the odds that she'd come up with the correct names for the two horses, one in a gazillion? She'd thought she'd been so clever coming up with the two words for a bruise. And what were the odds that they were now at the horses' former home?

"Yuh, I got rid of them nags," the old man's son crowed.

"Slaughter?"

"Hell, time I got to them they were so skinny even the knackers wouldn't take 'em."

"Then what? Humane society?"

"Hell, no! They wanted me to pay them to take 'em. Said it'd be expensive gettin' them nags back up to weight so they could sell 'em. Hell, what'd they think? Nobody wanted them giant hay burners, or I'd a sold, made a few bucks. But folks know it costs too much to feed 'em. And I sure as hell wasn't paying no one to take 'em."

"Then what?"

"Heard tell in the bar one night how people was taking their unwanted animals out and dumping them in the country. So that's what I did. Drove around one night out in the middle of nowhere till I saw some goats tied to a fence. So I just stopped and tied the nags up there too."

"What'd you tell the old man?"

"Told pa I found 'em a real good home." He chuckled coldly. "Oughta make out real good on the rest of this shit. All gravy."

Santee's eyes narrowed on the old man's SOB of a son. "Wait here," she said. "I'll send Sir Rob and Bobby John in."

Settling her sunglasses into place, Santee went off. If ever she needed Sunny's stabilizing influence, it was today. She sure wanted to strangle a man.

"If you want the carriage too, son," Sir Rob was saying, "get it. We'll find room to store it."

Bobby John looked torn. He'd already pulled the tag for the buckboard, which he figured he could make use of hauling feed and seed. The carriage would be useless...but it was so beautiful.

"Sir Rob," Santee said, "Ruarke would like to see you in the barn."

He silently questioned her but left.

"What do you think?" Bobby John asked.

"I think if you ever want something like this, now's the time, but—"

"But what?"

She angled her head, and they moved out of earshot of the other lookers.

"I think it's entirely possible that your Black and Blue came from here."

Bobby John blinked at her. "Here?" She nodded. "As in right here?" He turned toward the old man who was reminiscing with some old cronies. "So that means—"

Santee laid her hand on Bobby John's arm. "His son dumped the horses. Ruarke and I overheard him crowing to some sleazy pal of his."

Ruarke and Sir Rob joined them.

"So now what?" Bobby John asked.

Sir Rob shrugged. "We could call the sheriff and file a complaint. It's illegal to dump animals like that."

"And run the chance of losing the horses," Ruarke said.

"Or," Santee said, "you could tell the old man you have his horses, don't say 'bought,' and never got the bill of sale as promised. Then buy up the harness that you know will fit them and the saddles and anything else you want now while you can."

Bobby John nodded. "I'd like to have them all legal like."

Sir Rob clapped him on the shoulder. "Let's do it then. I'll come with."

"Thanks."

Bobby John and Sir Rob had only been talking a few moments with the old man when his rheumy eyes let up. He grabbed Bobby John's hand and then Sir Rob's, pumping them hard. "Jack! Jack! Come here!"

When Jack came rushing up, his father's excited voice rang out. "These are the people you sold Black and Blue to!"

Jack staggered back a step, a sickly look on his face. He was nodding like a beaten boxer trying to clear the cobwebs out of his brain.

"They say they never got that bill of sale or the registration transfer for the horses."

"I, um, I'll do that right now." Jack staggered a little as he clumped toward the house, as if he was trying to work out just how much trouble he was in and how he was going to get out of it.

Ruarke wouldn't have been surprised if the weaselly man climbed into a vehicle and raced off. "Pete," Ruarke called, "would you mind making sure that guy doesn't escape out the back?"

"Sure thing." He jogged across the yard, drawing the ire of the penned dog who slammed into the chain-link fencing as it snarled.

After an interminable ten minutes, he came back out with a manila envelope in his hand. Ruarke phoned Pete to tell him the miscreant was back.

Sir Rob stepped away to make a call. Jack eyed him suspiciously as he handed the envelope to Bobby John. He put his best shit-eating smile on as he apologized for the delay…what with all the time that had gone in to getting ready for the sale and all. Right there on the hood of the truck, the papers were brought out, spaces filled in, and signed on the bottom line.

"Did you call the sheriff?" Santee asked.

Sir Rob shook his head. "Called Sol and told him I needed more trailers and guys for heavy lifting. He's going to send the two hay trailers and six guys."

Ruarke eyed the yard that seemed so large when they had pulled in and pictured the two big gooseneck trailers coming and making the U-turn.

"Bobby John," Sir Rob called, "write the man a check and take everything, equipment, wagons, harness, and saddles. Everything."

"We don't..." Jack sputtered to a stop under the combined glares of the Sinclair clan.

The old man was wringing Bobby John's hand in a double grip. Tears shone in his faded eyes. Bobby John pulled out his phone with pictures of the recovering horses for the old man to cry over.

Santee went into the corral and paused beside Jack, saying, "You might want to put a Sold Out sign on the fence." Then she jogged around to gather the tags from the carriage, sleigh, hay mower, rack and baler, manure spreader, and road grader/scraper. She gave them to Bobby John before going to the barn for the tags on the saddles and harness.

"Think you're pretty smart, don't you, bitch?" The room darkened as the door was pulled shut.

Santee turned to face the despicable weasel.

Her advanced hands clenched. She had her pouch on her belt but never even thought of pulling her gun.

Hands out, he dove as if to grapple with her. Santee drove her fist into his soft gut, crinkling her nose at the fetid air that whooshed out. He dropped hard to his knees, moaning.

Once she would have kicked in his ribs and gone for his nuts, but she danced aside, balanced for another attack.

The door flew open. Pete, white-faced, rushed in and stopped. Color returned along with his smile. His lip curled at the moaning man on the floor. "Need help with anything?"

"You could grab some gear and haul it out to the truck." When he got close, she said, "And, um, thanks for coming."

"Glad to, *mi amiga*. Glad to." He winked at her and grabbed a saddle, grunting at its heft.

"Wuss," Santee said, receiving a broad grin. She grabbed the other saddle. The heavy covered stirrups accidentally clunked the prostrate guy in the head. "Oh! So sorry."

Bobby John, Ruarke, and Sir Rob were still being regaled with tales of the good horse times. Sir Rob made as if to come help haul, but Santee waved him off. No way was the boss going to do scut work like this.

They set the saddles on the trailer temporarily until they brought out the horse blankets and saddle pads to put under the beautiful leather so it wouldn't get scratched.

It took all five, four pushers and Ruarke steering the tongue, to get the rubber-tired buckboard pushed up the ramps and onto the trailer. Not surprisingly Jack didn't offer to help, but his elderly father wanted to. So they had him eyeballing so the buckboard tires cleared the trailer fenders.

There were eight ratchet tie-downs, and they used all of them to secure Bobby John's load.

Before they left, the old man come out of the barn with a box. Tears ran down his face, but he was smiling as he handed the box to Bobby John. Inside were all the pictures and ribbons from the showcase.

"You'll want to keep these," Bobby John said, his voice choked.

"No, no. I've got more pictures." He clapped his arthritic hand on Bobby John's shoulder. "Just take good care of my babies."

"I will, sir."

"I know you will."

Sir Rob stepped to the man, hand out. "If you're ever out in our end of the hills, stop in. Your son knows the way."

Jack's ears reddened.

The first of the ranch's trucks and trailers turned in, claiming the limited space. Sir Rob went to tell the guys what needed to be loaded.

Pete honked as he pulled out onto the blacktop. The second truck/trailer waited to let them out before turning in.

"Don't you wonder," Pete said, "how a man like that got stuck with a son like that?"

Bobby John sat with the box of mementos on his lap. He looked so sad. "Only every day," he said softly. Santee nudged in close and laid her head against his muscle-bound shoulder. A moment later, his cheek pressed against the top of her head.

Ruarke angled the visor mirror so he could see into the back seat. He also looked sad…or was it mad?

Santee stood at the big windows overlooking the backyard. Her gaze strayed toward Ruarke's suite but hauled her eyes away, cheeks burning with the memory of her last visit to his sanctum.

A few snowflakes were slowly flitting down to the barren yard, devoid of tables, chairs, and chaise lounges. All had been loaded up and carted away to a shed. The swimming pool was drained and covered. For just a moment, Santee thought of the hot tub outside Ruarke's room, not visible from where she stood, and wondered if it, too, was put away for the winter or if he still slipped his long lean…

Not going there, either!

Sir Rob's reflection proceeded him. "Santee, honey." He stopped beside her. His gut clenched at the sight of the pretty, puffy flakes drifting lazily down. "Tomorrow's the sale." She nodded. "I need to know I can count on you to still be here and will go with me to pick out some appropriate horses.

"You know a whole heck of a lot more about horses than I do."

"But you have the instincts."

Santee drew in a deep breath, held it, and slowly exhaled. She felt as if she was a wild young filly, wanting to kick off the traces and run far, far away. But her mind kept bellowing at her "Are you crazy!" every time she even looked off into the inviting distance.

"Stay here," it cried. "Stay where it's warm and safe, for once never having to worry about where the next meal is coming from or whether it's safe to even close your eyes and sleep. Danger lurks out there! Don't go! Stay here where people have your back."

It was like a siren's song in her brain. It would be so easy to stay. So very easy.

But life was not easy for the likes of people like her. And the longer she stayed, the more her survival skills atrophied from disuse.

The longer she stayed, the harder it was to break free of the gentle ties these people tried to bind her down with.

The longer she stayed, the bigger the chance her bad luck would cause the boom to drop… On herself, it was fine, but not on these good, gullible people whose only fault was that they took her in. "I'll stay through the sale." She turned from the window to look the happy man in the eyes, not into his reflection. "Then I'll have to hit the road." The smile died quickly, making Santee feel like she'd just kicked a puppy. "We'll talk about that later." He turned away quickly, deftly avoiding her hand that tried to keep him there, to get this hashed out here and now, not mulled over and sleepless-tossed over for the next two days. But he escaped. Dang it! These Sinclairs were a wily lot.

Chapter 23

The fairground stables were wall-to-wall people, highfalutin people, dressed to the nines. Santee had never seen so much silver and turquoise in her life...including herself.

Her good jeans and nice relatively new shirt were not good enough. Oh, heck no! She'd been presented with a midilength plum skirt over slouchy black suede boots. A black silk blouse gave absolutely no warmth, nor did the plum-colored bolero jacket. The black maxi wool coat was plenty warm but cumbersome and had been shrugged off and thoughtfully hauled around by Bobby John.

She also was one of the silver and turquoise crowd. Around her slender waist rode a concho belt, each silver disc with a man's thumb-sized hunk of blue-green rock in the center. On her wrist was a wide silver-and-turquoise cuff bracelet, and around her neck dangled a heavy squash blossom necklace. It was all supposedly out of Mrs. Reggie's jewelry box, but Santee wondered since Mrs. Reggie had her own complete set as ostentatious or even more so than any of the other show-offy women.

The men looked equally as spectacular in their western cut suits, bolo ties with silver/turquoise clasps and tips.

The Sinclairs were well known and constantly being chatted up. Sir Rob tried to include her, but Santee made her escape with Sunny tight to her side.

The best of the best, the horses destined to be the biggest sellers, were warehoused in the arena's attached stables. But there were other barns open that housed the second-stringers.

Santee stepped out into the cold evening air. Her lungs hauled in great gasps of unprebreathed oxygen. The wool coat dropping onto her shoulders startled her. She jerked around to find Bobby John behind her.

He gently grasped her right hand and pulled it away from the back of her neck. Only then was she aware of the stinging skin.

"What's wrong?"

Santee shrugged. "Too many people. Too little air."

"Ain't that the truth. And ever' single one tryin' to one-up the next guy."

Santee struck a pose, her hand indicating the necklace like a model showing off her wares. "Y'all can't mean me!"

He laughed and wrapped his arm around her as they headed for the next barn. He dug out the catalog that Sir Rob had slipped him and a pen.

The horses here were tied in open narrow stalls as opposed to the box stalls in the other building. None of the owners stood at these stalls answering questions or going inside to shift the horse around for more advantageous viewing. Here, there were two bored stable-hands and all of half a dozen lookers.

"Gonna be some bargains here," Bobby John commented as he once again removed Santee's hand from digging at the back of her neck.

They went down the first aisle, leisurely able to check out the horses on either side.

Santee vetoed a horse she'd marked as a possibility. The look in the gelding's eyes turned her maybe to a definite no. But she added two more that looked a lot better in person. Both were nondescript brown horses, but the mare and gelding were both nice sound quarter horses who nickered at them and stretched their noses for a scratch.

At the far end, the big sliding doors were open to the cold night. Santee stepped out and found her hand clasped yet again. She turned to smile at Bobby John but found Ruarke holding her hand. Thunder rumbled as if in response to the uptick of her heart rhythm.

"Is everything okay?"

Drawing her hand from his warmth, Santee nodded, not exactly the truth, but… "We've got this other side to check out yet." She walked away from his delicious clean scent, all too aware of the man now walking beside her. His nearness made it hard for her to concentrate on the horses.

She liked the two prospects she'd marked in the catalog and added another. This one was just a yearling, younger than ideal because she wouldn't be ready to be ridden for another year, but there was something in those big brown eyes. Heck, in actuality, most of the horses in this barn would make good riding horses. The majority seemed sound of limb and temperament. However, there wasn't an eye-catcher in the bunch…all browns, bays, and a very few sorrels. Luckily Sir Rob didn't care about color, just temperament.

"You're doing better than Dad," Ruarke said. "I think he added at least six more to his list."

"He'll pay dearly for anything in that barn," Bobby John commented.

"I bet they're pretty, though," Santee said.

"A palomino and a buckskin," Ruarke said.

"Good thing the auction isn't tonight, or we'd be impulse-buying a whole herd."

They were between buildings when Santee stopped. "Do you really think Sir Rob has a chance with this horse-training thing? The horse business is such a boom-or-bust kind of thing. Just because it's booming now—"

"I haven't seen Dad so alive in years. Whether he makes money or not, I don't care." Ruarke wanted to say the odds of success really rested on her slender shoulders, whether she stayed or not. If she went, he was afraid his dad's bubble would burst once more, and Rob would be back to the husk he'd been when Savannah vanished. But Ruarke also didn't want to say anything that would scare Santee into running. God, what a mess!

People were streaming into the arena as the "show and brag" session was about to begin.

Joe was the designated bodyguard for the evening and looked very cowboyish. He'd been tasked with saving seats at the end of an aisle so Ruarke's leg could be straight. He looked relieved with he saw them coming. Their six seats were in two rows, so they could talk easily. Others had tried to claim the seats, but the big black man's scowl was generally enough to send them searching elsewhere. He motioned Ruarke to the end seat beside Sir Rob, but Ruarke shook his head indicating, he'd take the next row with Santee and Bobby John. Joe smiled. In Ruarke's position, he'd want to be as close to the pretty little filly as he could and fend off any rogue studs trying to separate her from the herd.

The show had barely begun when Santee asked to be let out. She gave him an apologetic half smile. She left her coat behind so she wouldn't be venturing outside, but still Ruarke didn't like it. As if sensing it, Joe got up and followed.

Santee turned with a smile as she and Joe headed out together.

They returned with beers, a can of Dr. Pepper, and nachos. Bobby John shot to his feet and easily stepped over Ruarke's leg to help Santee with the baskets.

"I didn't know if this was too gauche for this situation, but Joe assured me if y'all didn't want yours, he'd eat it, him being kind of a gauche type of guy."

"Hey!" Joe said. "I may be uncouth, but you don't have to advertise it to the whole world. Besides, I don't even know what 'gauche' means."

Santee winked and shoved a loaded chip into her mouth.

Ruarke watched his dad offer to repay Joe, but Joe shook his head, nodding toward Santee. Ruarke would bet money she hadn't used either the ranch or his credit card for this.

The horses were really beautiful. The grays, palominos, buckskins, Appaloosas, and even a couple of paints and pintos, all the eye-catching colors, paraded their stuff. The older broken stock were flamboyantly trotted in, ridden by smartly dressed cowboys or girls. The crowd oohed and ached at the cute little girl in her cowgirl duds and white boots as she led a docile black colt into the arena. A chestnut with some reining training came tearing in and did a sliding stop and some 360-degree spins. A buckskin ran a steer along the rail, keeping the bawling animal from escaping or turning back to the safety of his pals in the corrals. A few mares came out with a late colt at their sides. All were bathed, brushed, and shined.

Santee found her hand grabbed away from her neck. Ruarke's smile shot lava through her veins that, accompanied by his warm touch and the leathery scent of his cologne, made her heart thrum. She tried to pull her hand free, but Ruarke laced his fingers through hers.

With a soft huff, she savored his warmth with ill grace. Gee Whiz! All she was trying to do was pull that too-long hair out of her collar. First thing, when she left, she'd have to whack that off. Long, it was way too much trouble.

The heat that was kindling inside her was ridiculous! The guy was merely holding her hand for Pete's sake. No wonder parents didn't want their horny teenagers to even sit close, much less hold hands.

Santee tried to shake her hand free, but Ruarke held on. "Ruarke." She leaned close to whisper. "I've got to go. Sunny has to go out."

Ruarke looked down at the quiet dog lying in the aisle beside him. The dog hadn't moved, but his momentary distraction allowed Santee to pull free, arise, and grab her coat. He was forced to let her out.

He stood there watching that long skirt swish as she took the steps down. Sunny flanked her, easily negotiating the stairs on three legs.

Ruarke bent to sit down and almost bumped into Bobby John's head. He'd been leaning to watch Santee leave. He gave Ruarke an unapologetic grin before sitting back.

Joe was also practically falling into the aisle, also, for a last glimpse. He made a motion to get up, but Ruarke clamped a hand on his shoulder. Joe looked up, a shit-eating grin on his face. If anyone was going to follow Santee, it was going to be him.

Ruarke fumed as he went down the stairs. Santee wasn't even Joe's ditsy type. And Bobby John…the man was gay, for God's sake!

The concession area was crowded. Not only were there food sellers but displays of horse trailers with luxurious living areas nicer than Ruarke's house were on display, as well as clothing stands, jewelry vendors, saddlery sellers, and anything else remotely horsey.

"Ruarke Sinclair!" Acquaintances and well-wishers seemed to come out of the woodwork, making Ruarke's progress snail-slow. Ruarke wanted nothing more than to cut them off and find out where the hell Santee had gone, but hands had to be shaken and polite questions about family and ranch had to be asked and answered. These were his people. He was their claim to fame. He had to give them a moment with him.

He talked with half his brain while the other half searched beyond them. Being tall helped, but all the men and a lot of the women were wearing cowboy hats, which negated his height advantage.

And there she was, finally. Clear across the way at the exit doors. So maybe there had been some ESP working that told her that Sunny had to go out.

And there was that damned smarmy Sheriff Lance Armstrong, the dirty, rotten SOB. Standing there, hat in hand, smiling down at her like he'd like nothing more than to hustle her to the nearest motel and fuck her brains out.

Ruarke started apologizing and hurried through the throng. Of course he wasn't projecting his own feelings about Santee. But if Lance laid as much as his pinkie on her—

Lance saw him coming, and his smile faltered. Santee turned, that lip-twitching smile welcoming him, melting the icy rage that had festered.

The shoulders of Santee's coat were damp, and droplets glistened in her black slicked-back hair. Sunny took the moment to shake, spattering Lance's crisp khaki uniform, making his lips tighten.

"Sorry," Santee said.

The sheriff shrugged, but he was still miffed. "No worries." Reluctantly he held his hand out to Ruarke.

Ruarke switched the cane to his left hand and braced himself should Lance try to pull him off-balance. From past experience with the man, Ruarke wouldn't have put it past him. But instead it was a death-grip shake. Ruarke had excellent hand strength and matched him, pound for pound, eyes locked with the slightly shorter man's.

"Ahem, gentlemen!"

Neither wanted to be the first to give.

"On the count of three, if you still haven't released each other's hand, I'm going to kick one of you where the sun don't shine and Sunny is going to bite the other one in the same place. So here we go. One. Ease up a bit."

Their knuckles changed from white to red.

"Two. Ease off some more." When the knuckle color didn't change, Santee said, "I mean it. Ease off."

Finally their hands looked less red.

"And now, on three, you will both drop your hands or else. Look me in the eyes and see if I'm serious or not."

No one looked at her. She put her hands, one on each trembling wrist.

"Here we go. Three!"

Ungraciously the hands separated.

"Okay. Good. Saves me from an assault on an officer charge. Now if we can get back to what we were talking about."

Ruarke was not going to shake the feeling back into his hand or flex his fingers, noting that Lance didn't either.

"I hate to say this, gentlemen," Santee said, "but I've got four three-year-old boys at home with better interpersonal manners than you two. Now cut it out."

Lance hunched his shoulders up and then lowered them. "Okay, fine." He turned his snarky smile on extra-high wattage. "You were saying?"

"I was asking if there had been any complaints about..." Her cheeks reddened. "Strange goings-on out at Lover's Lane."

Lance's eyes shot to Ruarke's. Many times they'd gone there, sometimes even making out in the same vehicle. That was back in the day when the rivalry had been friendlier. Back before Ruarke had become the whole damn state's claim to fame.

"And you were there when?"

Santee's cheeks were pink, but she met Lance's gaze with her chin held high. "Wednesday night."

"And what happened?"

Santee sighed. "Nothing specific. A feeling we were being watched. Even Sunny's hackles raised. And where we were parked straight ahead, there's this Volkswagen bug-shaped rock with four trees growing at each corner, almost like a four-poster bed. I saw... movement."

"What kind of movement?"

"Like something lighter in color moving through the shadows."

"An animal?"

"Only if it was upright on two legs."

"I see." Lance turned to Ruarke. "And you saw this too?"

Ruarke felt his cheeks warm, damn it. "I was facing the other direction."

"Was anyone else there? Did they see anything?"

Santee's eyes hardened. "They took my word for it, and we got out of there."

"I see."

She stepped up into the Sheriff's space. "Just because no one else saw it, doesn't mean it didn't happen."

"No, of course not. And rest assured, I will check it out." He clapped his hat on and lifted his fingers to the brim as he turned to another constituent.

"Yuh, right," Santee growled. "When hell freezes over or when something happens out there. The jackass."

Ruarke chuckled. That's what he liked to hear. He took her hand, drawing a surprised look. She tried to pull free, but he closed his fingers around hers and drew her knuckles to his lips. She widened her eyes. His smile instantly narrowed on her eyes.

"Don't think I won't kick a gimpy man."

"I have no doubt."

Santee gave a firm nod. "Good."

He kept her hand despite sneaky attempts to slip free as he led her back into the fray. "By the way," Ruarke said. She arched a raven brow in his direction. "I like your hair grown out like that. Nothing as sexy as a ponytailed woman." He wriggled his brows suggestively. Her eyes narrowed, which made him pick up the pace.

Dang him, Santee groused. She had to give it to him. Ruarke used their clenched hands as a means to fend off the adoring, amorous women, with their "come hither, I'll do anything" smiles. The men he was pleasant to but didn't invite deep conversations. And when someone made a derogatory comment about Sunny's appearance, he cut them off with a sharp look and moved on.

They were trying to make their way up to their seats through a horde coming down.

Bobby John got Sunny up on his lap and out of the traffic zone. Santee sat down, but Ruarke remained standing, not willing to risk his leg stuck out in the aisle.

"What's happening?" Santee asked Sir Rob, sliding forward on her seat.

"Intermission while they bring in the horses out of the back barn."

"Ah, the second-stringers."

He chuckled. "Exactly. How many do you suppose will be back for the second half?"

Santee looked at the cowboy aristocracy and said, "Very dang few.

"Their loss," Sir Rob said. "Our gain."

Santee was right. Very few people remained in the arena. The horses were run through so fast that it was impossible to really note much about them.

Slam, bam, boom, and it was over.

Some of the others were grumbling about how slapdash it had been there at the end. So Rob Sinclair was not the only one interested in the cheaper horses.

On the drive home, the slapping of the wipers and pounding of rain on the roof was soporific. Ruarke's parents slumped together in the middle seat, sound asleep with Mrs. Reggie's head on Rob's shoulder.

Santee and Bobby John sat together in the third seat. Ruarke angled the mirrored visor so he could see them. They had talked for a while, but now Santee's head rested on Bobby John's shoulder.

If it weren't for this damned leg, he'd be the one sitting with Santee. He'd be the one smelling the Ivory soap freshness. And maybe there could even be a little hanky-panky behind his parents' back.

Chapter 24

The next day dawned gloomy and bone-chilling. Snow scented the air. The internet warned of something called thunder snow carrying the potential for mega snow. It was going to be spotty, inches here while a few miles away just a smattering.

Santee carefully folded the finery she had worn last night. Her hands smoothed the fine suede skirt and jacket. She'd never worn anything so fine…and probably never would again. The boots that had hugged her calves as if made for her she put in a Walmart bag to be hauled to the house.

And the jewelry…so beautiful and so expensive. She was surprised they hadn't wanted it all back last night when they dropped her off at the camper. The squash blossom necklace alone had to be worth big bucks. She carefully wrapped it in a used shopping bag and placed it on top of the pile of clothes. The silver and turquoise concho belt was placed in another sack.

Clothes and jewelry went into a larger Walmart bag. The coat and boots she'd have to carry as they wouldn't fit in the bag.

She got the dogs into their sweatshirts. And she pulled on her hoodie and jean jacket, pulling the hood over her as yet untrimmed hair, which felt good against the icy air.

Boy howdy, how she hated cold weather! And snow was really a four-letter word to her. The warmth of Texas beckoned ever stronger. After today, there'd be no more reason to stick around.

Duke came out from under the truck. Butt in the air, bushy tail wagging, he enticed the other two to come play. At first Santee had been wary. Coyotes did that, enticed a dog to play, luring him out to where the pack lay in wait to make dinner of him. But Duke acted more dog than wolf. And he was always so careful around Sunny.

He and Rufus might roll each other over or run into each other in a takedown. But never Sunny.

Santee carefully carried the borrowed duds to the house, entering through the mudroom. She took her own and the dogs' coats and hung them up before entering the family room.

It was quiet in the house. Saturday was the only day the kids got to sleep in. The Sinclairs liked to get to church early on Sundays, so the kids had to be up and dressed early that day also.

Only adults sat at the table, minus Rosarita, who remained at her house until Sophie and Maddie got up.

After "good mornings," Santee said to Mrs. Reggie, "I brought your clothes and jewelry back. Would you like me to put them in your room?"

Mrs. Reggie seemed at a loss for words. Maybe she wanted to check that everything was there without embarrassing anyone?

"I could show you—"

"But hon—" Mrs. Reggie said.

"That's fine," Ruarke said. "Just set it all there and come sit down to breakfast."

"O-kay." Santee felt she was missing something here, but she put the pile on a chair in the living room. Maybe Mrs. Reggie didn't want her in their room? That made sense. Wouldn't want just anyone scoping out her stuff.

The warming trays sat on the table, filling the air with the scents of bacon, sausage, pancakes, and eggs. The chair on Sir Rob's right had been left vacant. Bobby John pulled it out for her.

Santee felt conspicuous taking food from under the lids. She always felt like such a pig. She'd much rather wait to come to the house until after breakfast, but they had such a hissy if she didn't show up. Left to her own devices she probably wouldn't eat anything for breakfast. But that wasn't acceptable here either. A small unopened carton of orange juice had been set at her place. Bobby John pushed the ketchup toward her. The two of them were the only ones who put ketchup on their scrambled eggs.

"The sale starts at one," Sir Rob said. "I thought we'd leave at eleven."

Santee found her right hand being pulled away from her sore nape. Bobby John grinned at her wrinkled-nose look. She said, "Sir Rob, I don't think you'll need me today. I'll—"

"Of course I need you! Your young eyes are a lot keener than mine. You'll notice things about the horses that I won't."

There went that idea of getting packed up and out of here while no one was around. Dang these people!

Bobby John again pulled her hand away. The snotty look she gave him earned a smirk. "Eat with your left hand." His huge mitt closed warmly around hers. "I'll keep this one out of trouble."

Chuckles around the table heated her cheeks. Santee tried to slip her hand free, but his gentle vise was unbreakable. With a huff, she took the fork in her left hand. Dang it! If she wanted to scratch the heck out of her neck, she ought to be able to! It was her neck after all!

Santee hoped she wasn't too much of an embarrassment to the Sinclairs. They weren't dressed as high-toney as last night but were still several steps above her jeans, tennies, and hoodie with the jean jacket. At least they could truthfully say she was just the hired help.

There hadn't been any snow overnight, but the threat lingered. The gray sky glowered above. Scattered slick spots made driving and walking an adventure.

The wind bit straight through Santee's outerwear, making it plain, yet again, just how inadequate it was. She hunkered into the hood and tugged up the jacket's collar, but the damp chill still managed to trickle down her neck. Her toes in soggy tennies were like ten little frozen baby carrots.

Dang, but she hated this weather!

They'd had to park the truck with the six-slot horse trailer a fair distance from the arena. Who'd have thought there'd be so many early birds or that a horse auction would garner so much interest?

The parking lot was potted with crystally holes. The churned-up gravelly muck left half-frozen ruts running in all directions.

Ruarke's right foot slid on a ridge, cane flying out. Santee leaned hard into him, wrapping her arm around his waist. The cane clanged against a nearby trailer.

"I've got you," Santee said, snugging up close.

His hand fell over her shoulder, landing almost indecently over her breast. Her bare hand grabbed his calf-skin gloved one and held it.

Santee looked up, nerves still humming at how quick it had happened. Ruarke's eyebrows were lifted roguishly, eye twinkling as he looked from his hand to her eyes. Should have left the dumb shit fall on his ass, hurt his leg!

"Ruarke! Are you all right?"

"I'm fine, Mom. Thanks to Santee's quick reflexes."

Still, there was an impish gleam in his azure eyes. If she didn't know better, Santee would have thought he'd staged the near fall in order to cop a feel. But since she had so little in that department, she rather doubted he'd risk reinjuring his leg for that.

Mrs. Reggie came and gave Santee, still acting as Ruarke's brace, a squeeze. She didn't seem to notice where his son's hand had almost landed. "Thank you, hon."

Pete, who was today's driver, retrieved the cane and held it out to Ruarke. Ruarke took it with his left hand.

"I'm good like this," Ruarke drawled, eyes mischievous.

Santee ducked out. She held Ruarke's hand out to Pete. "I think he'd be better off with a sturdier support."

"Maybe," Pete said with a devilish grin. "But I doubt he'll enjoy it near as much." He took Ruarke's arm around his shoulder.

Ruarke stuck his tongue out at Santee before walking off. Santee stood stunned. Bobby John snorted. He took Santee's arm.

"Pete's right." Bobby John led her toward the arena. "I think Ruarke would much rather have you pressed up tight against him than big, old sturdy Pete."

"Bobby John Johnston!"

He shrugged. "Just sayin'."

A ratty, rusty, faded blue pickup rattled into the parking lot. An even more ancient trailer clattered behind it.

Santee stopped, eyes following it until it disappeared into the maze of parked vehicles.

"What's up?" Bobby John asked. He had noted the anomaly compared to all the shiny new or almost new trucks and trailers but didn't think much of it.

Santee frowned. Her right hand twitched, but Bobby John held it firmly. "Nothing, I guess."

There was a lot less swank and a lot more kids in the crowd today. All the Sinclair kids had opted to stay home when faced with hours of watching horse after horse parade by. They were the smart ones. These kids were already bored and running around. Teens were performing their mating dances, the boys preening and the girls pretending to not notice or care.

Sir Rob registered and got a bidding number, 244, and stuck it in his coat breast pocket so the number showed. Two number fours. Double the number tattooed on Santee's shoulder or the number plus the number of stars. That didn't seem like a good omen to her. He had been a good luck charm to her...just the opposite.

Thunder boomed overhead, rattling the steel roof. The lights flickered to the accompaniment of teenage squeals. Rain or possible hail ponged the roof like buckshot. Conversation was next to impossible.

The speakers crackled to life. "Sorry, folks, but we're going to be starting late. This weather is spooking the horses, and it's not fair to them or the Hutchinsons to bring them out now. So sit tight. The sale will go on. And don't forget the concessions or the vendors—"

Bobby John leaned over to Santee. "Wanna go on a grub run with me?"

Santee wondered if he had been reading her mind. She nodded and turned to Ruarke. He was gently talking to a little girl who was looking teary-eyed at Sunny's boo-boos.

"The puppy is all better now," he assured the child. Sunny sat up, tail wagging and tongue lolling happily. "See?" Ruarke ran his hand over Sunny's head. "It doesn't hurt her. Is it okay with Mommy if you pet the puppy?"

The young mother had this three-year-old and another child on her hip and might even have another in the hopper. No wonder she looked beat. She nodded. So the little girl was able to give the puppy a hug and a kiss and got her face washed too. She left giggling while her little brother kicked and screamed in his mother's arms.

Other little kids were being drawn to the Sunny magnet.

"Are you okay with this?" Santee asked. "We could go sit in the truck—"

"No!" Ruarke cleared his throat. "No, I'm fine as long as Sunny is."

"She'll be fine. Bobby John wants to check out the food. Do you want something?"

"Sure, whatever." Ruarke shifted to access his wallet.

Bobby John stopped him. "I've got this."

He and Santee stepped carefully over Ruarke's leg. Santee told Sunny to stay. Sir Rob also immediately went for his wallet, but Bobby John waved him off.

Again the vendors ran the gamut of fancy westerns duds to work clothes: silver embossed show saddles to plain leather tack; high-end living-area horse trailers to plain stock trailers; $100,000 diesel 4×4 trucks to down and dirty "throw your tools in the back and go fix some fence" workhorses.

The lines at the concessions showed that everyone had the same idea. Santee rolled her eyes at Bobby John, but he had his eye on something in a vendor's stall.

"Why don't y'all go get in line. I want to check out a couple of things."

"Okay," Santee said. "But you know they'll card me and won't sell me any beer."

"Ah'll be there long before you get up to the front of the line."

Santee hoped so since she wouldn't be able to read the danged menu. But by watching the food being carried past, she pretty much knew what was being offered.

"Hey!"

Santee turned to the twenty-something guy who'd pushed his way to her side. "Hello." Usually she had a good memory for faces, but she didn't have a clue who he was. And this was a good-looking face. And boy did he know it too.

He gave her a good looking over before turning his dazzling emerald green eyes on her. "You here all by your lonesome?" A lock of honey-blond hair dangled, just begging to be smoothed away from his eyes.

"No," Santee said. "I'm here with friends."

"Really?" He made a show of looking over the crowd. "Someone really let a hot babe like you out without a leash?"

Santee stiffened. Being called a babe was one thing. But a leash? "The guy I'm with knows I can take care of myself."

The guy pressed in closer. "I have no doubt a babe like you could take care of anything and everything a man desired." He waggled his eyebrows lewdly and grasped her arm above the elbow.

His smug "no way could you say no to a stud like me" grin made her teeth grind together.

"Take your hand off me."

Out of the corner of her eye, she saw three or four more guys joshing each other as they watched their buddy try to separate her from the herd. Then like wolves, they'd fall on her.

The grin widened, and the fingers tightened. "Come on. Don't be like that. I'll show you"—his eyes swept her up and down, paused at her breasts, and gave a little shrug before smiling devilishly into her eyes—"a real good time. Like you've never had before."

"Really?"

He nodded eagerly. "I've got some blow and some pills and a whole lotta booze."

"Where? In your mommy and daddy's basement?"

Color crept up his fair-skinned face.

"Let go of me." Santee grabbed his thumb and yanked it backward until his knees buckled and his fingers freed her. "I'm here with a real man." Her scathing gaze roamed him. "Not some little boy."

He shook out his stinging hand then leaned his sneering face into hers. "It'd a been a pity fuck anyway."

Santee slammed her foot onto the side of his knee, hearing a satisfying crunch.

He went down screaming, "You stupid c—!"

Santee whirled on him. Grabbing him to haul him upright, she glared at him, gratified to feel him shrink away. "Don't you ever call me that," she hissed. "Clear?"

He nodded.

"Good." She gave him a little push upon release, and he staggered on the damaged knee.

"Problems?" Bobby John said as he eyed the four young men.

"Nothing I couldn't handle."

He grinned. "So I saw. How bad's his knee?"

"Nothing a little surgery won't fix."

His chuckle rumbled. "That's my girl." His glare scattered them, the injured guy lurching along calling for them to wait up.

Bobby John held three bulging bags in his hands. He held his hand up to fend off any questions. "Christmas is coming."

Santee snorted. "Yah, in about two months."

"It's never too early to start shopping."

Santee didn't know what all the secrecy was about. It wasn't like she'd be around to spill the beans to anyone before Christmas.

The sale was pretty boring. Oh, the horses were beautiful, made frisky by the weather. And the sale prices were jaw-dropping on some…especially the eye-catching ones. But it dragged. The three horses Sir Rob bid on went too high. Maybe if his training facility had been up and running and had some notoriety, he'd have taken a chance on at least one of the three. But as it was, he'd rather get two or three for the price of just one.

Santee was so restless. It kept Ruarke busy hauling her hand from the back of her neck. By the midpoint of the sale, she'd already climbed over him three times, once to go to the bathroom and twice to take Sunny out. When she went to the bathroom, she came out to find Bobby John waiting, supposedly to have her help haul snacks and drinks back. Each time she took Sunny out, Pete asked if she minded if he went along to stretch his legs. What was up with that?

A mass exodus came at the end of the first half.

The second part of the sale started. Their first choice was second into the ring. Santee watched the dark brown two-year-old mare trot confidently around the arena. She was green broke but seemed happy and unfazed by the newness around her.

Sir Rob turned around. Santee nodded, mentally crossing her fingers that she was right. Her right leg was going to be worn out from its continual nervous jouncing. Ruarke kept hold of her hand, a fact she barely noticed. He placed their interlaced fingers on her leg to quieten it down. Her hand twitched in his, desperate to be free to dig at the back of her already bloody neck.

Their second choice was a nice-looking bay gelding, but there was something... Sir Rob started the bid, but Santee laid her left hand on his shoulder. He looked around, and she gave a short shake. The gelding sold with the next bid.

A nondescript brown three-year-old mare was ridden into the ring. For some reason she garnered a lot of bidders. Finally, Sir Rob looked at Santee, and she shook her head. Reluctantly, he let her go.

They bought two more. A four-year-old gelding and a three-year-old mare.

Then came the surprise. A pale-cream-colored mare, just two years old with a very young spraddle-legged colt at her side. Santee leaned up to Sir Rob's shoulder. She didn't remember seeing her last night. Nor did she remember her in the catalog. It wasn't ideal. The colt looked only a day or so old.

Santee looked to Sir Rob just as he turned to her, almost touching nose to nose. Santee lifted her shoulders and gave a tentative nod. Sir Rob started the bid and got the pair with the opening bid. No one wanted a colt that young with winter coming on.

Seven more horses were auctioned, and the sale was over.

Only the die-hards had remained through it all.

The Sinclairs stood to go, but still Santee eyed the end of the arena where the animals entered.

Sir Rob was smiling, extremely pleased with their purchases. One look at Santee's frowning face, and he strained to see what she could possibly be staring at, but there was nothing there.

"Hey! Wait up! It ain't over yet!"

"Hey, you! Auctioneer guy!"

A guy in grubby jeans that could have stood by themselves staggered drunkenly into the arena.

"Got 'nother nag for yuh. Best of the lot!"

A squeal sounded. Part pain. Mostly pure rage.

A stallion's stifled scream.

Chapter 25

"Now see here." The auctioneer stomped across the dirt arena.

The dirty scumbag pulled a gun and held it inches from the auctioneer's nose. "You just wait. All a youse sit down 'lessen you wanna see brains splattered from here to Tuesday."

Pete made a move, but Santee laid her hand on his tense shoulder.

"Get him in here, Smitty!" Dirt Bag yelled.

A silver bag of bones was whipped into the arena. The horse was hobbled, front feet together and each back foot had a rope tying it up to his neck so the stud couldn't kick and also could barely walk. He had to hop like a rabbit, picking up his front feet and then bucking forward with his rear. Whip gashes and welts shone over the majority of his bony hide. His body was covered with sweat despite the cold temperatures. The strain of walking wobbled his delicate legs.

Santee eased forward, radiating rage. "Look at his mouth."

They had muzzled him. A strand of smooth wire had been shoved through his delicate nostril, through the apex, and out the other nostril, then down under the jaw and back up to be cinched tight so the stud couldn't bite…but he also wouldn't be able to eat. His screams of pain and hatred were muted by the ligature holding his mouth shut.

"Oh God," Sir Rob breathed.

Santee went to step over Ruarke's leg, but he captured her around the waist and tried to force her to sit down. Her eyes blazed a killing fire. "Let me go!"

Ruarke shuddered. He doubted she even recognized him at that moment. He didn't want to, but he knew she'd fight him. And if something happened to that horse, and she thought she could have prevented it, she'd never forgive him. So he released her. His heart begged her to reconsider, but she never hesitated.

"Stay." Her steely eyes flicked each person individually. "All of you."

Santee started down the stairs to the arena.

"Hey! There we go! Come on down, little lady! Take a closer look!" The gun stayed steady on the auctioneer's face while Dirt Bag waved his other hand at the suffering horse. "A real beaut, ain't he. And a stud! Think about all the colts he'll make ya!"

Santee eased over the rail and slowly lowered herself to the churned-up dirt floor. She could feel the horse eyeing her—and not as a savior but as another human that he was going to pound into the ground. Santee couldn't blame him. She'd reached that point at one time in her life too.

Santee eased closer. "Does he have any papers?"

"Papers?" He looked stymied for a moment. "'Course he gots papers. Lots and lots a papers."

Slowly, Santee moved around the horse toward the Dirt Bag. The pouch on her belt was open. Her right hand rested inside.

"Has he been semen tested?"

"Wha—?" He blinked at Smitty.

"A stud's not much use if all he throws are blanks," Santee said as she came to within arm's reach.

The auctioneer was sweating and turning gray. He had to be close to seventy and overweight. A heart attack loomed.

"Ah, well, ya got me there. But any fool can see he's ready to start humpin' them mares. Just look at them balls."

Two more steps and Santee was almost overcome by the stench, body and mouth. It was enough to make a person gag, and it took a heck of a lot to make her gag.

"Sir," Santee said to the auctioneer, "do you think you could start the bidding? I've got a hundred dollars to o—"

"A hundred bucks!" Dirt Bag bellowed. He turned to Santee, pulling the gun from the auctioneer. Santee shot her left arm up under his right. A shot boomed, the bullet exited through the roof, and the gun went sailing.

Her right hand pulled the Ruger out, thumb depressing the safety, and pointed it between Dirt Bag's rheumy eyes.

"Hey, now!" His hands came up to ward off an oncoming bullet. "You wouldn't."

"Look into my eyes and say that."

Dirt Bag's eyes widened. The stench of urine filled the air. A nasty smile curved Santee's lips. Both Dirt Bag and the auctioneer inhaled in sharply. The auctioneer was glad she was on his side.

"Sir," Santee said to the auctioneer, "I believe the bid on this poor sack of bones stands at a hundred dollars. Would you please continue the auction?"

"Y-you can't do this! It ain't legal!"

"Going once! Going twice!"

Dirt Bag made a move, but the narrowing of those damned murderous eyes nailed him and froze him in place.

"Sold to this young lady for a hundred dollars."

Santee dug into her left front pocket. For some reason she'd put a hundred-dollar bill there this morning. She hadn't known why, but she hadn't questioned the impulse. She handed it to the auctioneer. "Do you think you could get me a bill of sale before the cops get here and take Dirt Bag and Smitty away?"

"Yes, of course."

Moments later, a paper was shoved in front of Dirt Bag. Santee didn't hear Dirtbag's name. Didn't care. As long as he signed the horse over.

"This ain't right!" Dirt Bag whined. "It ain't legal. All these here people are witnesses to your forcing…stealing this fine horse from me."

Sir Rob stood up and addressed the crowd. "Anyone who saw anything illegal in this transaction, please stand and give the police your name." He sat back down.

No one rose.

"That ain't right!" Dirt Bag wailed.

Four policemen eased into the arena unnoticed. Their patrol car lights strobed through the big open arena door. "We'll take over now, miss, if you would put your gun up, please."

Santee reengaged the safety and slid the Ruger into its slot in the belt pouch.

The auctioneer grabbed her arm. "Thank you! Thank you!"

Santee put her hand over his. "Thank you for being so calm so I could do what I did. It all hinged on you."

His chest puffed out, and the grayness left his face. He wobbled just a little as, head high, he walked off to where his wife sobbed at the rail.

The stud's eyes were wild with murder. Crazed by the pain and hatred for the entire human race, he fought the ropes that rubbed his hide to bleeding. His bared teeth thrust out to bite anyone within reach. Frustrated, he squealed behind the ligature gag. He reared back to kick his hobbled forefeet out, but the rear hobbles jerked him off balance. Dust flew with the impact of his jutting bones. He squealed as he managed the impossible and lunged upright.

"Pete."

"Right here, hon."

"I'm going to need a bucket of warm water, a towel or rag, a blanket, and my pack from out in the truck. Oh, and something to cut this wire, a bolt cutter or pinchers of some kind."

"You safe for a little bit."

She nodded. "Thanks for backing me up."

"Anytime."

Santee moved to the stud's side, ignoring his warning snort. He could warn all he wanted, but he couldn't do anything about it. She put her hands on his withers. He snorted, shifting as if to kick out, but the ropes held. His flesh twitched beneath her hand as if trying to flick off a nasty horsefly. Again he turned to bite, but the wire sealed his mouth shut. He squealed and shook his majestic head in rage and frustration.

Slowly, Santee massaged the muscles of his withers, working carefully toward his ears. There was so much damaged skin it was hard to find an uninjured place to put her fingertips.

"Water's here."

"Thank you."

Santee didn't know if the stud could drink anything, but she took the bucket to him. He snorted and didn't want to, but the scent drove his cracked lips into the water to suck the best he could.

He was younger than Santee'd first thought. Maybe five at most. And on the tall side, sixteenish hands. He would be a beautiful dark silver with lighter dapples. His main and tail were dark at the roots but lightened at their tips to the silvery shine of a newly minted dime.

Santee pulled the bucket away. The horse tried to use his head's pressure to keep it, but she set it aside. The thirsty knicker cut like a knife, but she couldn't chance letting him have too much. He had so many problems to overcome; he didn't need to bloat too.

The horse tried to shake Santee's massaging fingers off his poll. He snorted a warning and turned to bite again.

"Here's the rag," Bobby John said softly.

Santee reached back for the towel. "Thanks."

"Pete'll be here in a minute. Is there anything I can do?"

"Want to start cleaning up the gashes?"

"Surely." He shrugged out of his fine leather jacket and just tossed it aside onto the dirt.

Santee pulled her jean jacket and hoodie off. She put the jacket back on and took the hoodie to the horse's head. His eyes flared white rimmed. He raised his head as high as he could, squealing a warning.

"Easy now." Santee came from the side, grabbed the frayed rope halter, and held the hoodie for the horse to see and smell. Moving slowly, she raised it toward his face.

The horse tried to back away, but the rear hobbles landed him on his butt again. He squealed in frustration and rage as he lurched upward.

Santee took the opportunity to get the hoodie over the horse's eyes. He tried to throw her off, squealing his rage. But she hung on and got the sleeves wrapped around and tied tightly.

Santee stepped back. The horse violently threw his head to throw it off. His squeals of fear and anger were hard to listen to.

A hand dropped to her shoulder and squeezed. Bobby John said softly, "You're doing real good."

Santee leaned into his strength for a moment. Her attention was drawn to the rail. She stiffened in surprise. Ruarke stood there, a scoped hunting rifle to his shoulder, aimed at the stud's head. Now that she'd moved away from danger, he lowered the muzzle. Their eyes meet. His blue eyes were clouded with worry, but he gave her a supportive nod. He might not like it, but he had her back.

Pete came with a blanket, her backpack, and another rifle. "Sir Rob's still looking for a pair of pinchers," he said. He set the blanket and pack down, then circled around to the other side of the horse with more of an angle so any rifle shot would be toward the big open doorway.

The horse had quieted. His breathing puffed the sweatshirt material that dangled over his nostrils. With every breath, he was infusing his brain with Santee's scent.

"Okay," Santee said. "When you get the cuts cleaned out, I've got some really good goop to put on them. Stinks to high heaven, but it works."

Santee stood at the horse's head—Rogue, she'd decided to call him—and lightly caressed his neck as Bobby John worked the warm water into the scabby cuts. At least it wasn't fly season so there weren't maggots to contend with.

Santee started humming as she waited for Bobby John to get a head start. The horse's, Rogue's, ears flickered at the sound, rotating like a parabolic dish. When she'd taken possession of the camper, she'd found an iPod loaded with '70s, '80s and '90s rock songs, an Apple laptop, and a small HP printer/copier. Why the previous owners left these things she had no idea, but she'd been grateful, knowing she'd never have bought them herself, but they'd provided hours of distractions when she'd needed it most. She pretty much had the lyrics to all six hundred plus songs memorized in order. So she started at the beginning.

When she opened the ointment tin, Bobby John gagged a cough. Santee chuckled. "Told you," she said as she pulled on latex gloves.

"Y'all failed to mention it'd make a runned-over skunk seem sweet as clover."

"Complain, complain, complain."

Rogue didn't like Bobby John working on his legs. He tried to pull away, but the hobbles kept his feet together. The pasterns were raw under the rope ties. Bobby John did what he could, but until the hobbles came off, there was little he could do.

The goo being worked into the horse's wounds may have stunk, but it had to be soothing. Santee could feel some of the tension in the stud's muscles easing.

The humming turned to words. The songs Bobby John knew turned into quietly sung duets.

Even the horse's underbelly hadn't been spared the lash. Santee took the rag from Bobby John, giving him a break and not wanting to ruin his nice suit pants. She crouched under Rogue's belly. Tension charged through the arena like the scream of "Fire!" on the arid prairie, as it did the through the horse. Santee continued singing while wishing Pete and Rourke would relax. The time for high anxiety was yet to come. Now the horse made no adverse moves, could make no adverse moves... The tension in the air slowly lessened, and the horse also relaxed.

It took seemingly forever to doctor the main part of the scrawny body and legs. Santee lost all sense of time.

Taking a break, Santee and Bobby John stood off to the side, letting their armed guards rest also.

"Didn't know you could sing," Bobby John commented.

Santee wrinkled her nose. "I can't, but you sure have a nice voice."

Bobby John looked at her and knew she really didn't know she had a fine range. "Four years of high school chorus and a lifetime of church choir."

"Really? Church too?"

"Yup. Every Sunday. You?"

"Nah." She shook her head. "Just singing with the radio's all. And off-key at that."

"Soooo? What's next, Kemo Sabe?"

Santee wished she really knew what she was doing rather than flying by the seat of her pants. She really didn't want to screw up this horse's chances at recovery. "I guess the fun stuff is next. We get to unhobble him."

"Oh, joy," Bobby John said.

Santee grinned at him. "Do you think you could get some clean water for him? We'll see if he wants a drink."

"Can do."

Pete stepped closer and handed Bobby John the rifle. "I'll get it. I know where to go. And Sir Rob found a bolt cutter."

"Okay," Santee said. "I think we'll leave freeing his teeth for last."

"Sounds like a good plan to me," Bobby John said.

Pete returned with the bucket and two bottles of water.

Santee, still wearing the stinky gloves, drained hers, totally unaware of how dry she'd been, or how tired. Standing around, taking a supposed break, let the stress and tension catch up. She felt as if she'd been slogging through mud for hours. And there was still a long way to go.

With a deep breath to gird her loins, so to speak, Santee got down in the dirt by Rogue's rear leg. She looked over her shoulder into Bobby John's worried face and gave him a nod.

He bent down and worked his way through the knot that released the hobble, holding the left rear leg immobile. He put a death grip on the rope. If the horse so much as twitched, he was yanking that foot out from under him.

But the horse never moved.

Santee got the rope unwound from the rear pastern and could have cried at the raw flesh. Gently she spread ointment over the skin. Rogue's muscle's quivered at the touch of the cooling ointment, but otherwise, he never moved.

Santee would have liked to take the shortcut to the other side, but she didn't think her guards would appreciate it if she scuttled under the half-wild stallion's belly. So she unkinked and stood and wobbled until Bobby John's hand caught her arm. Tiredly she gave him a smile and circled to the other back leg.

"She belongs to you?"

Rob jerked around to the man who'd snuck up on him. He recognized him as a rancher from down by the Nebraska border. From the corner of his eye, he saw Ruarke's grin. Both of them knew what Santee's reaction would have been at that description.

"Yes, she's all ours." And Rob firmly hoped that was the truth.

The man's—Ted something—sharp gaze flowed back to where Santee had freed the second back leg and was headed toward the forelegs.

"Yuh, well, if you should close down your training biz and she's looking for a new job, I'd appreciate if you'd give her my name." He held out a business card.

"I'll do that," Rob said, vowing to rip the card into itty-bitty bits and flush them down the toilet.

"And you're going to need your trailer to get that wild thing home. I've got an empty slot in mine, and I can line up some more if you'd let us haul your other horses home for you."

Rob was stunned. He hadn't given the logistics a thought of how he was going to get all the horses home. He held his hand out to Ted. "I'd really appreciate that. I can't tell you—"

Ted nodded, waving the thanks aside. He inclined his cowboy-hatted head toward the arena floor. "I never dreamed something like this was even possible. Let alone that I'd see it in person rather than just on video."

"Video?" Rob said.

"Oh, hell yes!" Ted nodded toward the stands where dozens of people still watched despite the approach of midnight. Many of those people had phones or recorders focused on the amazing event taking place.

"Hell, some of 'em are already putting it up on that YouTube thing. I'll tell the missus to send you copies."

"Thank you, Ted. I'd really appreciate that."

Ted held his hand out. "And don't you worry about those horses you bought. I'll make sure they all get to your place safe and sound. Tell your people to expect us."

"I'll do that. And…thanks."

Ted lifted his fingers to his hat brim, looked to the arena where Santee was loosening the front hobbles, and shook his head in amazement.

Ruarke stiffened, rifle focused on the stud's pea brain. No way was that damned animal going to trample his... Santee into the dirt.

Santee's legs were starting to quiver, whether from the cold or exhaustion. She eased away as the front hobbles came off in her hands.

The stallion was free, his poor legs gooed up.

Except for his head.

"Could you untie the sweatshirt?" Santee held her stinky gloved hands up.

Rogue started a little as the man's scent neared. But the soft voice and gentle hands eased his fear. He knew that neither of these humans had been the ones that hurt him, but that didn't mean he trusted them. The cover over his eyes slid away. He blinked at the brilliant light. Every breath had infused his nostrils with woman scent, but now it was gone. Yet the same scent still wafted through the fresh, rain-cleansed air to overwhelm his sensitive nostrils. He carefully watched her slow movements, human movements that before had meant pain and fear. The soft sounds she made soothed rather than enflamed.

Luckily, little damage had been rained upon his face, probably because the assholes knew that no one would buy a deformed horse. A few scrapes. A couple of cuts. His eyes seemed fine. But his mouth...

Santee rubbed goo over his lips and chin. Then she packed his nostrils so when the wire was pulled through, it took goo with it.

"Can you get the cutters?"

Santee got the bolt cutters' jaws situated between the horse's lips while Bobby John gripped the handles. She adjusted and readjusted it twice. Dang it! She was scared it would nick his tender skin, and all the gains she and Bobby John had made would vanish in an instant.

One look at Bobby John told her he was also feeling the tension. A nervous tremor traveled through the steel to her hands at the stallion's mouth.

Santee put her hands firmly around Rogue's muzzle and gave a nod.

SNIP!

The horse never twitched.

The flash of adrenaline made Santee's knees almost buckle.

"You can put the cutters down." Bobby John slowly bent down to set it aside.

"Would you straighten the short hunk of wire out?"

Bobby John's strong hands evened it out.

"Now come around to the other side and take the wire from under his jaw and straighten it out, please."

The wire was smooth, and Bobby John's hands were sweaty. His fingers were dangerously close to a very strong set of teeth. He knew Santee would hold on to the jaws to the extent of her strength, but no one's hands were any match for that horse, if he went apeshit.

The horse's whiskers were jiggled by Bobby John's big fingers. Both man and horse knew exactly where each other's parts were.

In a sing-song voice, Santee crooned, "Please be good. Please be good."

Carefully the wire was straightened perpendicular to the horse's muzzle. Breathing hard, Bobby John wiped his hands on his slacks. Then he took a two-handed grip on the wire.

They exchanged a look, both worried—Bobby John afraid he couldn't get the wire through the nose all in one smooth pull, Santee worried she couldn't control the horse.

Santee tightened her grip on the muzzle even more. She nodded.

Whoosh!

The wire slide through like an Olympic luge sled through an ice tunnel.

The stallion was totally free…whether he realized it or not.

The expected explosion of equine rage didn't happen.

Santee released Rogue's nose and eased back. The horse seemed to eye her, tiredly, as if wondering what was next.

Santee slowly lifted the bucket. The horse stuck his muzzle in deep and slurped unfetteredly. Santee patted the stallion's cheek and upper neck. His hair was so soft beneath the matted muck. And such a beautiful color. Her heart always beat faster for a gray horse. Or a black-and-white pinto. Or a black Appy with a white blanket with big black spots. Actually pretty much any horse could get her motor running. And that was a big, gigantic problem for someone who'd sworn off horses.

Santee had to pull the bucket away. The horse nickered for more, which again made her feel like a real meanie. Moving carefully, she picked up the horse blanket and slowly started unfolding it.

Rogue watched every movement and sniffed at the blanket when Santee presented it to him. He found nothing scary about it. He turned his head to follow her as she lifted it onto his back. His body had not one ounce of fat. Shivering barely created any heat. The blanket was like nothing he'd ever experienced before, so warm and given to him by the female human.

Belts tightened under his belly. He knew cinches and saddles, so he wasn't frightened by the bands.

She came back toward his head and leaned under to tighten more buckles at his chest. He put his muzzle to her back. Her delicious scent flooded through the stink in his nose. Men he knew and hated. But this female was a new experience. Her voice was soft, her touch gentle, nonthreatening.

Santee picked up the hunk of jute attached to Rogue's halter. She looked at Bobbie John but didn't find any reassurance there. Until now, she'd never turned her back on the stud. Now, she turned. Via the rope she felt Rogue's head go up.

She took a slow step away.

Then another.

At the extent of the rope, she gave it a little tug.

A soft snort sounded.

She wanted so much to see what Rogue was doing. She gave another gentle tug and went to step ahead.

A gasp seemed to reverberate throughout the arena as the rope slackened.

Rogue had taken a step!

He stopped expecting the ropes on his ankles to bring him up short. He tentatively moved again with no restriction.

He was free…except for the thin line connecting him to the female.

Human sounds from around him made him aware that it wasn't just him and the three humans in the building.

"It's all right," the female cooed deep into his soul.

Awed silence fell.

But Rogue could see them. Men lined the fence, but not the hated two. Others were scattered about. Not close. Not threatening.

The rope tugged.

He moved at its urging.

Slowly they walked, making a wide turn, and headed toward the big opening and the fresh cold air.

"Santee," Pete said softly, "I'm going to go move the trailer up closer. Be careful."

"I've got the rifle," Bobby John said.

"Okay."

Rogue had moved closer to her shoulder. From the corner of her eye, she could see his head.

Ahead truck lights flashed across the opening; the trailer streamed past.

"Bobby John? What about the other horses?"

"Don't know. Don't care. We'll get 'em tomorrow. Don't you worry about it."

Pete had the rear doors open. He stood well off to the side.

Santee stepped into the trailer and just kept walking. Rogue followed like a well-trained horse would. She guided him into a stall and attached the tie to his halter ring while taking the frayed hunk of rope off.

A net of hay hung by Rogue's head. Immediately he lifted his muzzle to it and began munching.

"I'm thinking I should stay back here with him."

"You're not riding in the trailer with a half-wild stallion," Ruarke stated, brooking no argument.

Rogue's head jerked around at the harsh male voice. Santee patted his neck and whispered sweet nothings until he went back at the flake of hay.

Santee marched to the back of the trailer and stood with hands on hips. "And who made you the Grand Poobah, Mr. Sinclair?"

"Santee." Sir Rob elbowed Ruarke aside. "The horse rode in a trailer to get here. He didn't seem scared, just walking on in like he did. I think he'll be fine."

And it would be cold and unsteady, and Santee didn't know if she had the strength to ride the next hour in the trailer. She looked at the horse contentedly tearing at the hay net. Exhaustion like she hadn't known in a very long time drooped her shoulders. Reluctantly, Santee stepped out. Mrs. Reggie stood there, Santee's hoodie over her arm, and carried Bobby John's bags in her other hand as she walked to the truck. Sir Rob held Sunny by her collar to keep her out of trouble.

"The rest of the stuff... The cutter...?"

Mrs. Reggie patted Santee's arm. "All taken care of. Everything will be back where it belongs and who it belongs to. Don't you worry. We have your bag in the truck."

"The horses—"

"All taken care of. Don't worry," Sir Rob assured her.

Sunny began whining and butting Santee's leg. Santee got down on one knee in the mud to hug her tight.

"God," Bobby John said tiredly, "what a night." He grabbed Santee's icy hand in his. "I wouldn't have missed it for the world."

The ride home was interminable. Bobby John put his head back and snored the whole way.

Santee wished she could sleep. Her eyes ached, her head throbbed, and every muscle felt as if it had been through a triathlon. She was just plain weary to the bone.

Somehow she doubted that Rogue was going to be miraculously transformed into the perfect horse. Once he started gaining some weight and getting some energy, Santee fully expected his angry studliness to rear its ugly head.

The yard was lit up for their arrival. The barn threw golden rectangles out into the glistening yard.

Sol pushed the barn door open as the truck and trailer coasted to a stop. He'd already called to let Rob know the other horses had arrived safely.

Santee didn't want to move, didn't know if she could move. Her body creaked like an old rocking chair when she slid out of after Bobby John. Her tennies skidded on the partially frozen ground, but Sir Rob grabbed her arm. She heard him grumbling something about shoes, but it didn't register in her brain.

Rogue looked as sleepy as she felt. On his best behavior, he followed her out into the late night. His nostrils flared at the new scents. He sent his stallion's cry into the night. There were some answering whickers from the barn, but no challenges, thank goodness.

Like a perfectly mannered horse, he walked past the occupied stalls to the big one in the back corner that Sol had saved for the stallion.

"I made him a nice mash," Sol said.

"Thank you," Santee murmured. She removed the halter and watched the horse find the goodies and sink his nose into it before she turned away.

Ruarke's nerves were jiving. He'd never seen anything like what happened tonight. Wouldn't have believed anyone who described it to him.

Santee seemed to weave toward him. Oh, yes, this evening was far from over! Ruarke caught her to him, his arm slid naturally around her waist. She gave him a heavy-lidded sexy smile…a real smile, not that quirky-lipped thing she usually reserved for him.

She molded her body against his side. Her intent was obvious and matched his, as stimulated by the evening's events as he was.

Ruarke turned to those following and inclined his head toward the tackroom. He mouthed the word "bathroom."

No one questioned, too exhausted to think anything but the obvious.

Some of Ruarke's best memories took place in the tackroom on the ratty couch or in the bathroom's shower. He'd lost his virginity at fourteen here to a twenty-year-old summer worker. He and Heather had made good use of the couch too, possibly even procreating there.

Ruarke angled Santee through the doorway. She stumbled, flattening herself against him. He got the door shut and spun her around, back to the cheap hollow core door.

Their bodies meshed so perfectly, his intention obvious. Her hands went fluttering up his chest as he zeroed in on her neck.

She mumbled something as she sagged against him.

"What, honey?"

The damned dog was trying to wedge herself between their legs. "Get lost, dog," Ruarke muttered.

Again Santee muttered what sounded like "bath."

Of course! She'd want to clean the horse and arena muck off.

"This way, honey!" Solicitously he led her to the bathroom and turned on the light. It was a tiny space with a toilet, a small sink, and a three-foot square shower. But it smelled clean, a sign that one of the ladies had recently been disinfecting in here. Lord knew that the men who used it were slobs.

Santee leaned against the sink, eyes shyly down while Ruarke lined her up a threadbare bath towel. If this was going to be a regular occurrence, he'd need to get some decent towels in here.

Ruarke backed out, leaving Santee and the damned pesky dog inside. It seemed a bit chilly. Couldn't have that! Ruarke nudged the thermostat up several degrees. He pulled off his coat and jacket and hung them over a saddlehorn. And he sat down to wait.

Hell with it! He stripped to his naked glory then pulled a tattered blanket across his hips. And he sat down again.

And waited.

And waited.

The excitement was beginning to wane.

He listened but couldn't hear any water running. The toilet hadn't flushed.

And waited.

And waited.

Ruarke's temper started a slow burn. He wouldn't have guessed Santee was a tease like this. Getting him all het up and letting him stew.

He shoved off the couch and limped to the door. His ear planted against it, he couldn't detect any sound: no running water, no movement, no nothing.

Of course! She was waiting for him to make the first move!

He tapped at the door.

No response.

"Santee?" he called softly. "May I come in?" He eased the door open. He didn't want to barge in and embarrass the hell out of her, but his mind pictured her sitting, naked, on the edge of the sink. Those long, long legs spread wide in invitation. The excitement that had waned flared again.

His mind was dead wrong.

The small windowless room appeared empty. But the closed shower curtain jiggled the plastic loops holding it to the rail.

Of course!

More than ready, he strode to the shower and pulled the curtain back.

On the floor, fully dressed, Santee lay curled into a fetal ball. Her body rocked slightly, back and forth as her arms curled protectively over her head.

Sunny squeezed against the wall, her muzzle across Santee's waist. Her gleaming fangs showed beneath twitching lips.

A so-soft whimper sounded. Santee tried to tighten her long body into an even tighter ball. The rocking increased.

"Son of a bitch!" Seeing that strong, spit-in-your-eye woman reduced to a whimpering puddle made Ruarke's hands ball into fists.

What the hell was she reliving in her nightmares?

Chapter 26

No one went to church. Alarms were either slept through or slammed off as the sleeper turned over.

Ruarke awoke on the tackroom couch. A ratty blanket had been tucked around him from chin to toes. Working his way out of the burrito, he discovered he was still buckass naked. His head jerked around to the bathroom, door open and light off. He'd closed the door and left the light on...the instant he'd flipped it off, a whimper had sounded, but silence returned when he'd flipped it back on.

Damn it! He hadn't intended for Santee to find him like this. God only knew what she had thought.

He went to take a shower, found the towel he'd laid out damp, and flipped over the shower rod. His mind all too readily pictured that lean body all soapy and wet. His mind's picture had the expected effect.

Hell and damnation!

Santee walked Rogue up the barn's aisle and back for the fifth time. He seemed a little perkier but still far from what he should be. The stablehands moved into the stalls to let him pass. Rogue snorted as he passed by, but the female spoke softly but kept a tight hold of the lead, which warned him that these hated men-things had better be tolerated.

The tackroom door flew open.

Rogue's head shot up. He snorted a warning and half reared.

"Easy, there. Easy." Santee crooned to him as she motioned Ruarke back. She felt her cheeks glow as she peered almost shyly at as she eased the horse past, and she could have sworn Ruarke's were ruddy, also.

Her traitorous mind didn't have to guess anymore at the big man's proportions. He was quite well-endowed.

Not that it was any of her concern. Now that the horse sale was over, she could go and find that danged elusive Texas. There wasn't going to be any hanky-panky with the boss's son.

Was that relief or regret that bottomed out her belly?

She put Rogue away, hand sliding along his scar-broken hide. What a contemptible, cowardly thing to do to a poor animal! she thought as she closed the stall door. Heading out, she rubbed each nickering nose as she passed by.

Ruarke and Sir Rob stood at the barn door waiting. Santee started to speak, but Sir Rob held up his hand. "If I may go first?"

Her eyes flitted between the two men. Something was going on…something that made her stomach flutter.

Sir Rob stepped out the door and motioned for her to follow.

Santee looked questioningly at Ruarke, but his face was as chiseled as a cigar store's wooden Indian. She stepped out into the damp twenty-degree cold. She sensed Ruarke behind her. Ahead, one of the ranch's pickups was parked. All the ranch's major players stood around, bouncing on their toes from the cold; she thought their eyes held a warying glitter.

Sir Rob motioned her closer as if to get her out of the breeze.

Nervousness tightened Santee's gut. This was it! Now was when she was going to be kicked out…right in front of everyone. Not that she hadn't been planning to leave, but it made a big difference that they wanted to get rid of her.

It kind of hurt…more than just "kind of."

Santee tried to say something, anything to salvage a shred of dignity, but Sir Rob butted in.

He seemed to have a genuine smile on his lips, just like a crocodile before it grabbed you and went unto his death spin. "Santee. First I'd like to thank you for a very successful buying trip." He chuckled. "Even the last acquisition. Unexpected as he was, he was well worth it." Applause sounded, making Santee blush.

Good thing he thought that about Rogue, Santee thought. Since he was now stuck with the horse.

312

"Second." He waved his hand to the magnetic sign on the truck's rear door, which was totally different from the Sinclair Ranch sign on every vehicle's front door.

"S & S Horse Training." Sir Rob pointed to each word as it arced across the top of the sign.

Santee nodded. She'd listened to enough of Sir Rob's hopes to know that he wanted to train horses who were as bombproof as a horse could be.

Santee looked at the grinning fools, trying to pick out who the other S was.

"Rob Sinclair," he said, pointing to the name angled in the bottom left corner.

He held his hand out to her. "May I have your hand, please?"

Past experience said that nothing good could come from putting her hand into a much larger, stronger one.

His smile didn't falter as he waited.

Santee willed her hand to be steady as she slowly put it into his warm embrace.

"Forefinger extended please."

She couldn't do it. It wouldn't come out of the relative security of her fist. Sir Rob teased his finger under it and got it extended. A little pressure pulled her closer to the pickup.

Sunny whined softly. Someone shushed her, telling her it was all right.

"S."

Sir Rob traced her finger around the capital letter in the lower right-hand corner.

"A."

Again her finger slid across the black letter.

"N."

Her lungs strained.

"T."

There was no oxygen to be had.

"E."

She fell back, yanking her hand from his.

"E," he said, without her finger to trace the letter.

Her butt landed on the cold damp ground. The impact jarred her lungs into action. She shook her head trying to shake off the cobwebs. Clapping sounded around her.

Santee scuttled back. She knew she looked like a fool, eyes gaping and mouth forming soundless words.

She launched to her feet and whirled, smack into Ruarke. His hands reached to grab her, but she twisted free.

And took off.

"Santee!"

She heard Sir Rob call, but it only goaded her on.

Rufus and Duke bounded ahead down the path she always jogged. Sunny lagged behind Santee's flat-out run.

Mrs. Reggie laid her hand on her husband's arm. "Give her a little time, Rob."

"I'm so afraid she'll vanish on me."

"I know you are, but there's only so much you can do. You can't chain her up and make her stay. She has to want to."

"But I thought—"

"I know." She patted his arm. "I know." She wanted it too. This reenergized version of Robert Sinclair was so preferable to the living-dead version she'd lived with for the last fifteen years. He'd been acting like a man twenty years younger. Reggie fanned her hand in front of her face as her cheeks heated…in a lot of very pleasurable ways. Fifty years old and you'd think they were teenagers again.

An hour crept past. The temperature outside didn't climb more than a degree or two. Inside, several pots of coffee had been consumed, as they watched and waited.

The kids were unusually subdued, sensing the adults' agitation. More than one asked where Santee was. The young ones accepted the "out for a run" answer. But the older kids were not so easily placated, especially Jamie and Deacon.

Sir Rob pushed his chair back and surged to his feet. "Enough. It's cold out. Let's go get her."

Pete, Ruarke, Bobby John, and Sir Rob piled into the pickup and headed out, all but slamming the doors in Jamie and Deacon's faces.

The frozen two-track trail rocked the truck side to side and up and down. "Damn it, Pete," Ruarke growled as he grabbed his thigh.

They'd gone a couple of miles before topping a rise and seeing her down below. She was headed toward home.

"Thank God," Sir Rob breathed.

Santee's eyes did not light up with gratitude as the pickup rolled to a stop in front of her. The forty-five-pound dog in her arms merely extended the workout that her raging hormones demanded.

Bobby John opened his door. "Bring her to me."

Santee handed Sunny in and went to march on, but Sir Rob was there blocking her way.

"Santee—"

She waved him off and went to step around him, but he side-stepped to cut her off. "Please, just listen."

She shook her head. "Don't you see? You want more from me than I have to give, and it's tearing me apart."

"Tell me. Maybe I can fix it."

Santee snorted. "Even the great Robert Sinclair can't fix this." She shook her head and groaned. "Even that."

"What?" he asked, perplexed.

"It's always 'tell me about this' or 'talk to me about that.' Wanting me to feel things. Touchy-feely things. You're killing me here."

"Okay. Just one thing then. Make me understand why you don't 'do' horses. Just that one thing."

Santee grabbed at the pain in her gut. The man just wouldn't quit. "Horses break."

Sir Rob blinked at her, trying to ferret out the hidden meaning in those two little words. "Anything can break, Santee."

She groaned and slammed her fists down on the pickup box rail. "Will you listen! Horses get their legs broken. Smashed by a steel rod because a little girl was bad. They cry and scream in pain and the little girl…all she can do is stand there. And puppies get their necks wrung and handed to the bad little girl. Kitties get drowned in a bucket of water because of the bad little girl."

"Oh God," Sir Rob moaned.

"If I go, they'll be safe with you. I know you'll take care of the dogs. And even Rogue. You'll be good to him. And you can quit worrying about me doing anything to hurt the kids…or ax murder you in your beds."

Sir Rob tried to get his arms around her, but Santee fended him off and backed away. She didn't see the tears rolling down Bobby John's face.

"I'm no good!" she cried. "You've got to let me go."

Heart caught in a wringer, Rob grabbed her by the shoulders and hung on against her, flailing to escape. "I have a few things to say before your decision is final. That little girl is not to blame—"

"She was—is! Can't you see! If she had just been good, done what He wanted."

Ice water drenched Rob. "He'd have injured them anyway."

She shook her head hard.

"He'd have done it because He enjoyed it and knew that even if the little girl did everything He wanted and did it perfectly, He could still hurt her by harming or killing the animals. Yes, you can leave your animals here." Rob walked a very fine line. He wished Sam was here with his psychological training to deal with Santee's childhood torment. "We'll do our best for them, but I can guarantee you that your Rogue will revert to his man-killer ways within a month, and I'll have to shoot him."

Santee flinched. That poor, beautiful damaged horse…he'd never had a chance.

"And the dogs. Duke will probably run off and turn into a cattle killer and get shot. Rufus may adjust since he's so easygoing. But Sunny. Within days she'll stop eating and pine herself to death. I've seen it happen."

Santee turned away. She could barely care for herself much less have the responsibility for the animals too. Unthinking, Santee caressed Rufus's head.

"You know us, Santee," Sir Rob said gently. "We're not like that man. You and I can train great horses that a parent could put a little child on and send out knowing that the horse will do its damnedest to bring that kid back safe and sound."

Santee shook her head. "I can't."

"Damn it, Santee. What do you expect to find in that god-damned Texas that you can't find here?"

She raised empty eyes to his, then stepped around him and began walking.

Sir Rob stared after her, stunned by what he'd seen…or hadn't seen in her eyes. Life.

Sunny whined the entire drive home, straining to look out the back window as Santee and the other dogs were left behind. Bobby John carried her into the house, or she'd have gone racing back out to Santee.

Mrs. Reggie met Rob at the door. "Where's Santee!"

The kids hurried up to hear the answer.

"She wanted to walk home." Heavy-footed Rob crossed to his recliner and plopped into it.

Rosarita came and put her arms around Pete, murmuring softly in Spanish.

Mrs. Reggie turned to Bobby John and saw his swollen eyes and knew it had been bad. "Ruarke?"

He shook his head and limped away.

Reggie looked at her husband who'd looked twenty years younger this morning and now looked twenty years older than his age. His slumped shoulders were those of a defeated old man. She sat down beside him and held his cold, limp hand. Her heart broke at the tears coursing down his cheeks. She scrambled into his lap and pulled his head to her breast and let the tears soak into her sweater. "We'll think of something." But he shook his head.

The kids saw Santee come home and charged out without coats and grabbed at her hands. "Come play cars with us! Please!"

For the last time, she let herself be dragged into the family room, carefully avoiding looking into the living room. She got down on the floor and chugged her truck around the playmat's imprinted roads with the boys. The house's vibes weren't the normal warm fuzzies. She'd shot her mouth off, said way more than she should have. But how many times had she told them she wasn't staying? Because of this, that, and the other thing, she'd stayed far longer than she wanted, than she should have. She'd been wishy-washy. If she'd stuck to her timeline and left regardless, it all would have been over and everyone would have adjusted by now.

"Kids, I've got to go walk the new horse," she said as she arose.

In an instant, Ruarke was there, his hand vised around her upper arm. Rufus gave a bark, and Sunny growled.

"I need to talk to you," he hissed. His handsome face was twisted by so much anger it was barely recognizable.

Deacon and Jamie were there in an instant. "Let her go!"

Santee got Ruarke's pinky and forced it backward. Surprise became pain as the pinky went beyond its natural stop.

"Ruarke was just going to ask me politely to talk with him. Weren't you?"

He nodded, teeth clenched as she released his hand.

The boys glared at Ruarke.

Santee kicked Ruarke in the ankle and tilted her head toward the boys.

Rubbing his hand, Ruarke said, "I'm sorry."

"That wasn't right!" Jamie said.

"You're not supposed to hurt girls," Deacon said. "You harp on that all the time."

The other six boys got up belligerently and stamped into place in front of Ruarke. Their hands planted on their skinny little hips as they glared at him.

"You're right," he said. "You're all right. I shouldn't have grabbed Santee like that. It was wrong, and I'm sorry."

"Group hug," Santee called and held out her arms. The little arms locked so tightly around her, and Deacon and Jamie hugged from a second ring. No one asked Ruarke to join them.

The little boys were ready to let it go and return to playing. But Deacon and Jamie remained at Santee's side.

"It's okay," Santee said. "I don't think he'll try that ever again."

Ruarke avoided looking at the three older girls who stood watching and weighing his actions. The glare in his daughters' eyes made him flush.

"Girls," Santee said, "I think it's time for Uncle Pete and Uncle Joe to teach you how to handle a situation like that." She looked at Pete and got his nod. "Starting tomorrow after homework time."

"Okay," they agreed, reluctantly turning their hot gazes away.

Santee looked to Ruarke, who made an exaggerated motion toward his suite. "I should have broken it," she whispered as she stalked past.

The dogs followed close enough to trip her up. Inside his room, Santee frowned at what were obviously two dog beds near the fireplace. Patting her leg, she got Sunny lying in the pink one with white bows and Rufus on the blue one with white paw prints on it while wondering why they were there in the first place.

Through the west windows, Santee saw movement. Duke came trotting past. His head shot up, nose twitching. He followed the scent back to the sliding glass door, sniffed noisily, then settled. Because of the one-way glass he couldn't see her, but he didn't need to.

"And I took a shower this morning," she said.

Ruarke marched up, anger oozing from him. "Can I get you something to drink?" he asked with false politeness.

"Do you have a Dr. Pepper?" she asked, knowing that he'd have no reason to have one.

But he walked over to the small refrigerator and pulled one out and a Bud Light. He looked at the beer, put it back, and pulled out a Coke instead.

"Would you care to sit down?"

He put her pop on a coaster on the couch's end table, so that was where she sat. He went to the other side and sank heavily down. With a remote he kicked the fireplace on.

He popped the top of the can and chugged at least half of it. Then he held the cold can against his pinky. "I really am sorry," he said. "I'm not that kind of guy."

"Uh-huh."

"You don't believe me?"

Santee shrugged. She opened the Dr. Pepper and took a swallow.

"Would you really have busted it?" he asked.

"Dang straight."

He nodded thoughtfully.

"And if you ever hurt me, you'd better kill me. There are no second chances in my world. No turning the other cheek. I'm a stone-cold-revenge kinda gal."

"I'll remember that."

"No need to. I'll be gone long before you have another chance to screw up."

Ruarke drained the rest of the Coke, crunched the can, and tossed it into the wastebasket. "Okay, let's get down to it."

Santee took a sip.

"How much?"

She frowned at him.

"How much is it gonna take? Spit it out!"

She took another swallow. Her brain was blank. "I have no idea…"

Ruarke snorted. He grabbed a narrow leather wallet and flipped it open, pulling a pen from the fold and clicking the nib out. "Name it."

Santee took another drink.

"A million bucks?"

The carbonation exploded in her throat. She spewed Dr. Pepper halfway across the room. Wracking coughs tortured her lungs. "W-what are you talking about?" she wheezed.

"Come on." He clicked the pen a few times. "It's obvious you're wrangling for a big payday. So how much to get you to stay here?"

Santee set the can down carefully before she could launch it at the dumbass's head. She arose slowly.

"The only stipulation is that you keep your mitts off my dad."

"My—!"

She was on him like a starving cheetah. The pen went flying from his hand. One hand landed on his shoulder while the other locked around his throat. Her eyes blazed like a million tiny shards of narsil.

Ruarke stared at her, hypnotized like an elk facing down a pack of wolves. He tried to speak, say something to discharge the deadly gleam in her eyes, but his tongue was glued to his palate. Her fingers were like talons digging in, making each breath a wheeze.

Knock! Knock!

Santee twitched, and the deadly moment passed. She inhaled as if she, too, had been held breathless. Her eyes hooded as she dismounted his legs and shifted away to sit down.

"Everything okay in there?" Bobby John called through the cracked door.

Santee arched her eyebrows, questioning him as she picked up her can of pop and took a big drink.

"Fine," Ruarke croaked.

"Nobody's killed anyone?"

Santee gave a sneery smile. "Not yet," she called. "Give us time."

A hesitant chuckle responded. "Okay then." The door clicked shut.

Santee drained the pop and felt equally as drained. She set the can carefully on the coaster. "So that's what you think of me." She pushed to her feet. "Good to know." She patted her leg for the dogs and, head high, walked out.

Goddamn! Son of a bitch!

Ruarke knew he'd blown it.

And worst of all, that wasn't what he thought about her at all.

He grabbed his head.

Where had his brain gone?

Santee walked into the family room and felt the impact of all those eyes. She didn't have the energy to smile or explain.

"I'm really tired. I'm going to check on the horse and then go take a very long nap."

"You mean a snoozy-poozy," Trey said.

"Yes, you're right. A snoozy-poozy."

Her legs felt like overcooked spaghetti noodles as she slogged to the mudroom. In a daze, she got her and the dogs' coats on before exiting.

The cold did little to revitalize her as she trudged to the barn. Her eyes traced the route to the camper, and she wondered how she was ever going to make it that far.

Maybe she could just find a hidden corner and curl up in it.

They said hypothermia was an easy way to die.

"Ruarke! What did you do?"

Ruarke flinched. He knew his dad was irate to just march into his room without so much as a knock.

"Dad."

"Don't Dad me." Rob stood beside the sofa, anger oozing from every ounce of his being. "What did you say to Santee?" Rob's eyes went to the checkbook still clutched in Ruarke's hand.

Ruarke snapped it shut but not soon enough.

"Tell me you didn't!"

Ruarke tossed the offending folder onto the coffee table.

"Oh, Ruarke." Rob dropped heavily onto the sofa. He rested his elbows on his knees and buried his face in his hands.

"You should have seen her, Ruarke, when she walked out of this room. She looked…" He searched his mind to come up with a proper description. He scraped his hands down his face. "She looked broken. That vibrant, fiery, beautiful woman looked exhausted and broken."

"I'm sorry. Okay?"

"It's not okay. Don't you see that? The thinnest of threads was all that kept her tied to us. And I think you just shattered that."

Rob pushed to his feet. Anger, a rare emotion for Rob, burned through him. "Was that your plan? I know you never really welcomed her here…didn't want her here despite the fact that I did. Has that always been your plan, to force her into a position where she'd have to leave?" He turned to go. "Because if it was, I fear that you've succeeded."

"Dad! I'll make it right!"

Rob paused but didn't turn back. "How? You called her a gold digger or worse. How do you make that right?"

Goddamn! Son of a Bitch!

Ruarke slammed his fists down on his knees. The jarring pain that shot up his leg barely registered.

Supper was subdued, with Santee a no-show. Ruarke could feel the condemnation from everyone twelve years old and older. The younger kids didn't understand but still pushed their food around and around their plates.

Finally, Ruarke couldn't stand it any longer and headed outside. Lights were on in the barn, unusual for this time of evening.

Ruarke stepped into the restless barn. Normally the animals would all be settled for the night, but there was a lot of shifting in the stalls and nervous blowing.

Sol Braun leaned against the tackroom wall, arms folded across his chest. He turned to nod at Ruarke but then faced the barn's expanse once more.

Sol had worked on the Sinclair ranch for as long as Ruarke could remember. He was "Uncle" Sol to him and the kids. To Rob, he was right-hand man, foreman, majordomo, and confidant.

"How's the stud doing?"

"Restless. And he's got everyone else worked up too."

"When was she here last?"

Sol looked sharply at Ruarke, not liking his tone one little bit. "Santee was here this afternoon and walked him. Said she was going to take a nap. Looked like she really needed one too."

A snort sounded from the far reaches of the barn, followed by a heavy thwack of hoof against wood.

"Well, she needs to get her ass down here and see to that damn horse!"

"Ruarke, don't—"

But Ruarke was already out the door and marching toward the small rectangle of light that flowed from Santee's camper. The more he tromped, the more his leg ached, the higher his temper rose.

She couldn't just get that damned uncontrollable stallion and expect Sol to take care of it! It was her responsibility! No one else's!

He cut behind the camper to the rear-facing door. A low growl accompanied the pale ghost-like shape slinking from beneath the detached trailer.

Ruarke stamped his foot at the wolf dog and waved the cane.

The wolf dog crouched lower to the ground, sounding a warning deep in his throat. He advanced carefully.

"Git, mutt!" Ruarke put a foot onto the metal stairs that angled down to the ground. Warily eyeing the canine the entire time, he eased his hand up to the door, grasped the doorlatch, and—"Thank you, God!"—it released. He hauled the door open and launched himself inside as the wolf dog sprang. The door slammed shut as the animal banged into it.

Breathing hard, jittery with adrenaline, he came nose to nose with Rufus. The dog's normally happy expression was serious, tail not wagging.

"Dammit, San—"

A mound of quilts was on the converted dinette. Only a small tuft of black hair showed. Sunny raised her head, her eyes coolly unwelcoming.

Outside, wolf howls pierced the night.

But still the form didn't so much as twitch.

Could she be dead?

The dog's panted breaths vaporized in the cool air.

Ruarke shivered. What the heck was the temperature in here? Could she have frozen to death?

He found the thermostat and shoved it higher. It kicked in and a moment later heat poured from the vents. So it wasn't that the furnace didn't work or the propane tank was empty.

A whisper of sound from the bundled shape drew the attention of both dogs. They huddled their coated bodies closer. Whimpers sounded as the body beneath the covers twitched and jerked. The dogs whined softly as if to quell the nightmares.

With nowhere else to sit other than on the toilet in the tiny bathroom, Ruarke eased down onto a corner of the dinette/bed. He crabbed backward and sat with his back to the chilly wall.

He'd barely gotten situated when a gasp sounded, startling him and the dogs. Flailing limbs fought the straitjacket formed by the quilts.

Tousle-haired, wild-eyed, and gasping, Santee shot up to a sitting position. Instantly her eyes found him and narrowed. Santee glared at the two dogs. "Some guard dogs you are."

Both dogs whined and drooped their heads as if they had understood every word.

Slightly shaking hands smoothed down her sweaty hair. She cocked her head to the cycling furnace and gave Ruarke the stink eye. "What're you doing here?" She tugged the frayed neck of the 3X sweatshirt up around her neck.

"I came to see how—"

Her eyebrow lifted, all but calling him a liar.

"That damn stud of yours is raising a ruckus in the barn."

Santee started to untangle her legs from the mess of covers. "And Mr. Braun sent you to get me?" Disbelief sounded in her voice.

"I volunteered. Besides, we need to talk."

Santee snorted as she arose, hauling the saggy sweat pants back up her hips. "The last time we 'talked,' you accused me."

"Can we just forget that conversation ever happened?"

A spark of amusement shot through those still tired-looking eyes. "Sir Rob chewed butt."

"Christ!"

Her head jerked up, and her eyes narrowed.

"Sorry." It was his turn to rub his hands over his hair. Think, dang it! Think! His eyes focused on the baggy sweats that could so easily be pushed out of the way revealing…

He swallowed hard. Don't think about that, for Pete's sake!

"I'm sorry I said those things."

Santee shrugged, the stretched neckline sliding off to uncover her shapely shoulder. "You said what you thought."

Ruarke worked his way off the bed. "That's just it." He stood before her and said what he knew was true. "I don't believe that about you."

She frowned up at him. "Then why—?"

He shrugged. Her "night sweats" scent drifted to him, making him wish her sweaty scent had another cause. He reached toward her face. The wariness in her eyes as they followed his hand tore at his gut, so he let his hand drop. "I don't know why. Jealousy because you're giving Dad something I never could…? Not that I ever wanted to. I'm no horseman, though obviously I can ride. Cattleman if need be. But horseman, no."

His eyes settled to those camouflaged breasts. Was he frustrated because she refused to get with their program…or was it frustration in other areas?

Santee's head tipped slightly sideways, eyes probing, trying to ferret out the true meaning hidden in his words.

She seemed clueless as to her effect on people…on men… Hell, on him! Ruarke carefully slid his hand behind her head and tried to draw her to him. She resisted, so he leaned closer, causing her eyes to flare. She pressed back hard against his hand as his lips moved in to her trembling ones.

Santee jerked her head aside, Ruarke's lips grazing like fire across her cheek to her ear. She brought her hands up between them, arching her body away from his.

"Sinclair, you know you don't—"

"I very much think I do." He nuzzled her ear lobe and sucked it into his warm mouth.

A zing rocketed through Santee. What the heck?

"The repercussions—"

Ruarke nibbled down her neck. "Repercussions be damned."

"You say that now."

He worked his hand up under the sweatshirt to her back's oh-so-soft skin. His hand lightly caressed, gentling her as she had that stallion last night.

Ruarke worked his lips across her jaw and nuzzled her lips. With a deft shift, he got her turned with her back to the kitchen counter and pressed in close; her hissed breath at the nudge of his arousal emboldened him.

He claimed her mouth just as her lips parted with a surprised gasp. His tongue darted into that moist warmth for a moment before withdrawing so he could look into her stunned eyes. Had she never been kissed like that before?

"Just follow my lead," he whispered huskily.

His hand slid down under her pants to grip her firm rump.

She gasped, raising up slightly, which fit her even more intimately against him. Her eyes widened, breath gasping in short bursts as she processed the sensations.

Aroooo!

Santee jerked, twisting away at the wolf dog's howl.

A fist reverberated the door.

Santee slithered around Ruarke, leaving him to grab the countertop.

Uncle Sol's voice sounded. "The stud's going wild!"

"I'll be right there," Santee called.

Santee came back to the converted dinette and sat down to pull on still damp tennies. She hauled her coat on over the sweats she'd slept in. Her cool gaze nailed Ruarke, still braced, weak-kneed against the counter. "Leave the light on, but turn down the dang heat when you leave."

She and the dogs hurriedly left.

"I wish it were that easy," Ruarke said.

Chapter 27

"I'm going to miss you." Bobby John wrapped his arms around Santee and pulled her tight. They were saying goodbye outside the terminal. Bobby John was catching a flight to Sioux Falls and then on to Chicago.

"Me too," Santee admitted. She'd never had a brother, but Bobby John felt like one...even more so than Sam.

"When I get back after the season, we need to talk you, me, and Sam."

"Bobby John..."

"Don't say it. You'll be here. I'm counting on it. Otherwise I might just as well keep on battering my brains out on the old gridiron year after year."

"You're retiring?"

"Promise you'll be here, and I will."

She frowned, her eyes sad. "I can't do that."

"I know." He squeezed her tight. Against her ear, he said, "Try. For me, try."

She sighed and nodded. She could try, but every day she had to fight against hooking up the trailer and taking off. Every single day.

"Um, Bobby John?"

He turned before entering the terminal.

"You're not going to ask me to marry you, are you?"

He snorted. "Guess I'd have to get rid of my husband first." He raised his hand to the others and was gone.

Sunny nuzzled at Santee's fingers. She patted her head. Santee had never felt this lonesome sadness before and hadn't a clue how to deal with it. Rosarita and Mrs. Reggie were dabbing at their eyes, but that emotionalism wasn't in her.

"You okay?" Ruarke asked.

Santee nodded, although she really wasn't.

"Jeez, Dad, you've gotta see this."

Ruarke stood at the front window watching Santee walk that damn stud around the yard. The horse walked quietly enough, but his Arabianish head was up, nostrils testing every molecule, just searching for a reason to explode his newfound energy on. The stud scared the crap out of Ruarke and maybe Joe also, since he seemed to hover nearby, a rifle in his arms, every time she and that damned horse were outside. It made him feel just a tad bit better.

Sensing his daughter's presence, Ruarke forced himself to look away from the window. "What is it, Shawnee?"

She brought her iPad to him. "It's Santee. She's all over the internet."

"What?"

He took the small computer. Sure enough there she was at the horse sale working with the stallion.

"Where'd this come from?"

"There's all kinds of clips of her taming that horse. It's unreal. Almost like we're living with a celebrity!"

Ruarke raised his brows at her.

Shawnee giggled and hugged his arm. "You're pretty well-known too." She grabbed her iPad and danced back to do her homework.

He was glad that his girls had a good strong female role model. God knew their mother was not, acting like an oversexed teenager still at thirty.

But for some reason, this internet notoriety bothered him. Sure, it was good advertising for his father's new horse training business. What harm could there be?

He stared at his phone's tiny screen. His search had extracted yet another short clip. Greedily he memorized her lean face, the glimpse of those pale eyes made even paler beneath such unformed raven brows. She seemed quite tall when measured against the horse. Her bulky clothing gave no hint of the body beneath, but...

"Darling."

He jerked back to the present almost guiltily. He swept his finger across the screen, and the home screen came up, a picture of his beautiful stallion.

"We must go. His Excellency awaits."

"Of course, my dear." He sighed. "Would not want to keep his Excellency waiting."

Her eyes narrowed. Something was not right with her beloved husband. He seemed so…apathetic of late.

She glanced suspiciously at the pocket, where his cell phone rested. Perhaps the answer lay in that little device.

Sunny and Rufus's ears pricked.

Aaaroooo! Duke loudly alerted. Someone was coming.

Santee shut down the laptop and dipped her hand into her pouch as she slid her legs off the dinette.

Sunny and Rufus's tails began a slow welcome as to a friend, so the Ruger remained in the pouch.

The door jerked open as "Go lay down!" was shouted and Ruarke hopped up the metal steps. The door slammed shut on the furry gray snout with the sharp white teeth only inches behind Ruarke's legs.

"Damn dog!" Ruarke turned and found Santee standing, hands on hips, glaring at him. "Sorry." Though he wasn't really sorry. That damned wolf dog was a menace…a major deterrent to his visiting any old time the mood struck, which was almost every night.

"What's wrong?" Santee knew Ruarke didn't brave the trials of Duke just for the heck of it. "The kids? Rogue?"

Ruarke held his hand out to calm her. "No. No. Everything's fine. Mind if I—?" He pointed to the thermostat.

Santee snorted and shrugged.

What a wienie!

The furnace kicked in, blowing heated air into the camper. Ruarke pulled off his coat and enjoyed the view as Santee pulled a sweatshirt off her head, the underlying tee riding up with it, exposing a lovely expanse of belly. Even a tiny glimpse of breast before Santee got it all straightened out. Alas.

She sat down, cross-legged, leaving plenty of room for Ruarke at the other end beside Rufus.

"Would you mind?" He motioned for Santee to move over. "I can't curl my legs up like that yet."

Santee studied him for a long second. He'd been here before and had never indicated he needed more room so he could stretch his leg across the cushions.

Why now?

The floor was chilly, but…

He was kicking his boots off! And he placed them neatly by the door.

What the heck?

He acted as if this was his normal routine. His expression was so innocuous that it was suspicious.

Were his blue eyes twinkling?

What the heck?

With no concrete reason not to, Santee moved the computer onto the step up to the "bedroom" and shifted her rump over, scooting Sunny tight to the outside wall.

The cushions shifted beside her, making Santee jerk around in surprise. Ruarke sat beside her, hip to hip.

Before, he always sat on the other end facing her. And he still could have, his feet could have, should have, been at her hip…not his hip pressed against hers.

And he had the gall to sit there and smile at her like everything was fine and dandy. He reached across her and took the fuzzy, warm throw from her frozen hand, pulling it across both their legs and feet.

He looked at her with lifted brows. Dang it, his cobalt eyes were definitely twinkling! Santee snapped her jaw shut and tried to shift away, but two people and a good-sized dog side by side on what was essentially a double bed left absolutely no wiggle room.

Wow, it was sure warming up fast in here. Santee could almost see steam oozing out under the throw.

And the big lummox sat there grinning at her!

If he wasn't careful, he was going to find himself flat on his ass on the floor, bum leg or no bum leg. One well-placed shove was all it would take.

"Need help stripping down another layer?"

Santee drew a huffy breath. He chuckled, dang him! She narrowed her eyes at him before turning away and primly tucked her hands into her pits...to keep them from locking around his throat and throttling the smug, arrogant, self-satisfied ass's neck.

"To what do I owe this pl—er—visit?"

A soft snort jerked Santee's head around.

Ruarke put his hand over his mouth, but the crinkles in his cheek and around his eyes showed he was still smiling...at her expense.

She sniffed and looked away. Her profile was stony, but what she wouldn't give to ditch another layer.

The furnace kicked out. Thank goodness!

"I couldn't sleep and happened to see your light was still on, so I thought I'd come for—er—a visit."

Haughtily she swiveled her head so she faced him. "First off, there is always a light on in here whether I'm awake or not. And secondly, your room is on the opposite side of the house, so you couldn't possibly have just 'happened' to see my lights." Santee shoved the throw even further off her legs, letting the blessedly cooler air flow over her.

"That's true," Ruarke admitted. "I did have to go out into the family room and look." He hadn't known that she always left a light on...like a child scared of the dark. "Are you sure you wouldn't be more comfortable without that long-sleeved T-shirt?"

She arched her brows at him. "Who says I've got anything on under it?"

Ruarke's cheeks heated. It was so easy to visualize...

Santee smiled at his discomfiture. "Are you going to tell me what this is all about, or are we going to play twenty questions?"

For a moment he seemed a whole lot less cocksure of himself. Then he smiled and shifted around to face her.

Something was wrong. She could feel it. He'd finally come to his senses and decided he'd had enough. He put his hands over her suddenly icy ones.

Her mind roiled with the logistics of dogs and horse and—

"Santee."

She blinked back to the here and now. His oh-so-blue eyes sought hers.

"I had a thought recently." Actually his mind had been a squirrel in an exercise wheel.

Santee frowned at him. "A rare occurrence?"

He finagled her left hand from under her arm. Something cold slid over her finger, but his huge hands shielded it and then covered hers.

He cleared his throat. "Santee, I feel like I—we, Mom, Dad, all of us—need some kind of peace of mind concerning you."

Her frown deepened as she looked at her warm trapped hand.

Ruarke watched her agile mind working on his oh-so-badly phrased declaration.

"Are you talking a monetary deposit? Because I don't—"

"No! No, no, no! Nothing like that." He knew better than to go there ever again.

"Then what?"

"If you were in an accident, I—we would have no legal right to even visit you in the hospital because we're not related."

She snorted. "Big effing deal. Just—"

"Santee! It would be a big deal to us! A very big deal!"

She blinked at his vehemence. She tried to ease her hand free, but his fingers were gently unyielding. Her mind was tumbling in a free fall. "So what are you propos—"

Santee's breath caught in her chest. Blood flooded her temples, pounding like jungle drums.

With a quick wrench, she yanked her hand free.

On her left ring finger was possibly the most beautiful ring she'd ever seen. Way too ostentatious for everyday wear, it had a huge purple stone in the center surrounded by a row of not-small sparkly diamonds all set in a bright shiny silvery metal.

"No," she managed to breathe. She rolled onto her knees and shoved the quaking hand at him. "Take it off!"

He held his hands up, palms out as if to fend her off. His head decisively shook side to side.

"Dang it, Ruarke!" Gorge shot hot as lava up her throat. Hand clamped tight to her mouth, she scrambled across his legs and dashed the four feet to the bathroom.

The sound of retching filled the small space.

Both dogs looked accusingly at Ruarke. He wanted to tell them that this was a good thing. For everyone.

Ruarke'd already gone round and round with Max about this. He'd had to stand firm against his friend/manager/lawyer in his stratagem of providing for his family by putting Santee's name on everything: money, investments, property, insurance…everything. Max wanted this signed and that signed to protect Ruarke from the greedy, conniving bitch Santee was going to morph into the instant she knew about her windfall, but Ruarke knew Santee. She'd run, probably to that goddamned Texas, where he'd never find her, rather than try to milk him for everything he had.

The gagging sounds had stopped.

Ruarke got up and padded to the tiny door that led to the equally tiny bathroom. He pressed his ear to it before tapping on it. "Santee?"

There was a rustling sound inside, a click from the latch, and the door opened just enough for her offensive hand to be thrust through.

"Get it off me." The words were almost a growl.

Ruarke dug out a platinum chain and draped it over her wrist. "You can take it off and wear it around your neck."

The door flew open, almost slamming him in the nose.

Santee stood in the doorway, furious eyes ablaze. "Get this… effing thing"—she shoved her fist at him so the ring would have made first contact with his nose—"off me before I flush it down the toilet!" Her teeth were clenched so tightly he feared for her molars.

He took her hand in his. "I can't."

"Wha—?"

"I won't."

"Why the—" Her eyes narrowed. "I have no intention of marrying you. Though why'd you'd ever want someone like me—" Then she nodded. "Of course!" She smacked her forehead with her other palm. "Dummy me! Give the poor, dumb bitch a pretty fake ring, let her think a guy like you'd marry her, get into her pants, use her until you get bored, and then it'll be hasta la vista, arrivederci, don't let the door hit you in the ass on your way out."

"It's not like that."

"No?" Her raven brows shot upward. "Then what's it like?"

He was on dangerous ground here. He could almost feel the tremble of an earthquake beneath his socked feet. "This is about the kids." Only a semi lie. "They need to know that their parents—you and me—are in this together and will be for the long haul."

"Until you go back to baseball and see groupies shaking their huge hooters in your face and—"

"Not happening." That was as true as it gets since his pecker only worked when Santee was around.

Santee sneered at him. Not a pretty sight...downright terrifying, in fact. "You know that movie where the guy has that affair, dumps her, and expects her to just ride off into the sunset, but instead she boils up the family bunny?"

Ruarke nodded warily.

"Well, that's me. Once you tell everyone that we're"—she made finger quotes—"'engaged,' you'd dang well better live up to it." She leaned in nose to nose. Her breath still held hints of barf that the swish of mouthwash hadn't erased. Her eyes were glacial as they nailed him. "So even though we wouldn't really be engaged, everyone would think so. And even though I have no intention of fucking you, you will abide by a no-other-sexual partners rule."

"Yes. As long as that applies to you also."

Santee snorted. "I don't believe you. You're what?" Her scathing eyes ran down and up him. "Thirty. In your sexual prime. And you think you can go celibate for the next fifteen or so years? Get real. And don't think, 'What the little twat doesn't know...' Because I'd know immediately." Those eerie eyes locked on his. "Do you believe that?"

Ruarke swallowed hard and nodded. The thought of not getting any scared him because he really liked sex, of course. But when his dick wouldn't work with anyone but Santee, it wasn't going to be too difficult to be faithful.

"Do you also believe that I would exact a vengeance upon you that would make being drawn and quartered something to wish for?"

He managed to croak, "Yes."

Santee looked at the ring, and for just a moment, she marveled at how beautiful it was and how he'd managed to choose just the perfect color of stone. Then she noted the chain dangling from her wrist.

Ruarke didn't like the sneaky look in Santee's eyes. Warily he watched as she wiggled the ring off her finger. He wouldn't have been too surprised if she'd launched it at his face, but she unclasped the chain and slid the ring onto it.

Santee turned her back to Ruarke, holding the ends of the chain around her neck. "Hook this for me, will you?"

Ruarke automatically reached out, then froze. He didn't understand why she didn't just give the ring back to him, but he knew, in his gut, if he took hold of that chain, she'd duck out under it and he'd be left with the chain and ring and no woman to go with it.

"The chain's long enough to slide over your head." He grabbed his shoes and shot out the door.

"Ruarke Sinclair! Get back here!"

He hurried sock-footed over the frozen ground.

"Don't you dare tell anyone, because this isn't a done deal!"

It was as far as he was concerned. As long as she had the ring, he could go to bed knowing she'd be here in the morning.

And the sex? He grinned confidently into the night. She wasn't as immune to him as she liked to think she was.

Santee flipped the chain so the beautiful ring landed in her palm. Then she reclasped the chain and dropped it over her head. Pulling out the collar of the sweatshirt, she felt it slither icily down her chest until the ring nestled between her breasts. Within seconds, it was toasty warm there. As if it belonged.

"Why didn't I just shove it in his pocket?" she asked the night.

She closed the door but didn't lock it. She didn't much like locked doors.

The dogs eyed her.

"Because I'm a dumbass," she told them.

She noticed his jacket lying across the edge of the dinette. Her hands reached out to the buttery leather. She picked it up and buried her nose in his scent.

"A real dumbass."

_____

Chapter 28

"Do you think that fence is high enough to keep him in once he's feeling better?"

Sol was overseeing the placement of a shelter in the corral for the restive stallion. The big box stall was not large enough. Santee was out walking him three or four times a day, but the better he felt, the less therapeutic those walks were becoming.

"I think you're right. For today it'll work. Tomorrow I'll get the guys on raising it higher."

"Thanks, Mr. Braun."

"I'd be pleased if you'd call me Uncle Sol."

"Only if you call me Santee."

He looked as if he might say it wouldn't be right but then nodded.

"And this pain in the derriere is Rogue." Santee laid her hand on the restless horse's neck. The gashes were pretty much healed. He'd put on several hundred pounds. And his coat was growing out, so he really didn't need a horse blanket any longer. He looked 100 percent better. His gray hair shone from the brushing and good food, a few lighter dapples peeking out. His dark mane flowed smooth as any woman's, the snowy tips of his tail swishing the ground.

Santee liked to walk him close to Mr. Braun—Uncle Sol— as often as possible so maybe the stallion would learn to trust the smaller nonthreatening man. There had to be someone who could handle the horse in case…

The stallion pawed at the dirt while Santee and Uncle Sol watched as the three-sided shelter was put into place and the tractor drove out.

Santee clucked at Rogue and walked him into the corral. From the corner of her eye, she saw the gate being swung shut. Together she and the horse walked the wood-fenced perimeter. Santee patted the horse's neck and talked about nothing much. The horse didn't seem too impressed.

"Santee," Sir Rob called as he turned the horse he'd been working over to one of the hands. "Dinner."

Santee released Rogue's halter. He snorted and jogged off, as if glad to be away from her and her endless babble and off-key singing.

"How'd it go today?" Sir Rob asked.

"Good. You?"

He draped his arm over her shoulders. He did it often, and it never failed to startle her. "I'm really happy with the horses we've got, but we need a few older ones, five years or older. Ones who are really ready for some intensive training and can be sold to get our name out there and really start this business."

"Where are you going to find them?"

"Oh," he chuckled and pushed the house door open for her. Construction still raged, but for the moment, the saws, compressor, and nail guns were silent. "I've got a few ideas. There are a couple of sales coming up. Thought we could take the trailer and go take a look-see."

Ruarke sat at the table, workout finished, hair slick from the shower. It had been a couple of days since the ring fiasco, but so far it didn't seem like he'd told anyone. It still hung warm and heavy between her breasts, a constant reminder of him. Maybe he was rethinking the no-sex agreement. If so, that would be fine with her. She'd gladly give him the ring back and head on out.

Ruarke, Pete, and Joe rose when she neared the table. She wanted to tell them it wasn't necessary, but it was kind of nice. Special. Something they also did when Rosarita or Mrs. Reggie came in.

"Santee," Ruarke said after dinner had been served, "I'm not happy that you're taking that horse out beyond the yard where no one can watch over you."

Santee's brows rose as her eyes iced over. "I've seen Joe and Pete hanging around with a rifle whenever I have Rogue out. And while

I appreciate the gesture, if he wanted to trample me in the dirt, he'd have me down and dead before they could get their rifles aimed."

"But—"

"No buts. He's fine. We're fine. I tell Mr. Braun every time I leave the yard so he knows where I am. And I have no intention of making endless boring circles of the yard just because you have a feather up your butt."

Pete snorted and covered it with a cough.

"And don't think about having me followed either."

"But he's a stud. Get him gelded, then fine, but now he's a walking time bomb."

Santee took a drink of water. The glass chattered a bit when she set it down. "I'm not gelding him until he proves he needs it. With me, he's fine."

"Santee—"

"Ruarke."

Their eyes battled across the table.

The others exchanged covert grins. They knew who would come out the winner in this battle.

A series of beautiful warm days hit the Black Hills, reinforcing their reputation as the "banana belt" of South Dakota. Daytime temps were in the '70s, thawing and drying out the ground.

Santee and Rogue and the dogs roamed out. Santee had started jogging, with Rogue trotting beside her. He wasn't fond of the dogs, especially Duke. They made sure to stay away from his teeth and hooves.

Santee found her eyes wandering the pine tree-covered hills. Of late she'd felt like something or someone was watching her, and not Pete or Joe. Their presence, while raising her blood pressure, wouldn't make the hair on her nape prickle. Duke was uneasy also, staring out at the surrounding forest as he trotted in front of Santee and Rogue. Could be a mountain lion. Sir Rob had lost a calf to one just last week, but that had happened nowhere near here. But the big cats roamed long distances, so it could easily be nearby.

Sooner than usual, she turned her little group around and headed for home. It was almost noon. If she wasn't back in time for dinner, they'd send out the cavalry.

"Rosarita?" Santee called from the front door.

"Sí?" she answered, coming from the kitchen.

"Do you mind if I leave Sunny and Rufus here while I take Rogue out this afternoon? They've already gone for two runs this morning, and I don't want to test Rogue by taking the stroller for Sunny yet."

"Of course!" She clapped her hands on her knees, smooching baby talk in Spanish at them.

They looked appealingly up at Santee. They loved Rosarita but didn't want to be stuck at home while Santee went off on an adventure.

"Be good, guys," Santee said as she backed out the door. They had already accepted their fates and trotted off with Rosarita in search of doggie treats. Poor, mistreated babies.

Santee was attaching the lead to Rogue's halter when the *whop-whop* of a helicopter sounded in the distance. Sir Rob hadn't said anything about having something done that required a helicopter. She supposed it could be from the Ellsworth Air Force Base. Training maneuvers or something.

"Come on, big boy." She patted his neck. The horse danced at her side. Soon even three walks weren't going to be enough exercise for him.

Ruarke was standing in the exercise room doorway when she passed. Santee eyed him warily. He hadn't voiced any concerns lately, but his stiff posture and arms folded across his chest as he glared at Rogue said it all.

"What is with the helicopter?" Pete said as he scanned the sky. "I've been hearing it, off and on, for a couple days now."

Sir Rob walked up. "I thought I could hear one also. Wonder what's going on?"

Santee and Rogue and Duke jogged along the two-track path. Rogue followed perfectly at her side, never barging past her shoulder.

It was a beautiful afternoon. Not too hot. Not too cold. The only sound was the *clop-clop* of horse's hooves and the *slap-slap* of tennies. Duke was pretty much silent…a gray ghost in motion.

Rogue's head shot up, eyes wide with wary surprise as a large white helicopter rose a mere hundred yards away.

What the heck?

All three stopped as the craft hovered, bending the pine trees with its draft and sending chaff and dirt swirling into the air.

Something stung Santee in the butt. Heat raced from the bite.

Rogue snorted in fear, reared, and spun away. The lead slipped from Santee's quickly numbing fingers as he raced off.

Twisting around, Santee saw a tiny red arrow sticking out of her butt. She staggered as she reached around to it. Her fingers barely felt the object as they pulled it out.

Ahroooo! Duke was howling at the approaching helicopter.

Santee's knees hit the dirt.

"Run, Duke!"

But the dog crouched nearby. Fangs bared.

"Ru—"

Darkness overtook her brain as a loud report blasted nearby.

"There's that dang helicopter again," Pete said. "Wish I knew what was going on."

Bang!

A rifle shot froze everyone.

"Did Santee have a rifle with her?" Joe asked.

"No," Pete said.

Clattering hoof beats proceeded the stallion's headlong race into the yard. Sol went out after the horse, the only person with a hope of capturing him.

"I'm going to shoot that damn horse," Ruarke declared as he rush-hopped to the pickup.

The helicopter's whomping seemed to rev up and then start retreating.

The truck bounded and jounced as it raced down the path. Ruarke hung on, unaware of his aching leg. His mind locked on finding a trampled woman…his woman, her blood soaking into the dirt.

Goddamn it!

Ahead there was a light-colored bump in the path where there shouldn't have been one.

The pickup slewed to a stop. Ruarke was out before it completely stopped.

Duke lay on his side in the dirt.

No sign of Santee.

Duke's feet feebly padded at the ground.

Ruarke stumbled to a stop.

Half of the dog's skull was gone. What little remained of his brain was pulsed in the concave shell. The rest was splattered in a bloody spray across the ground.

Ruarke dropped to the ground beside the dog. He put his hand into the cottony ruff, now tinged red. His eyes searched in vain for Santee, hoping against hope that she'd pop out from behind a tree or boulder, safe and sound.

Pete pointed at something on the ground. Joe pulled his phone out, punched in some numbers, and began shouting.

But Ruarke heard none of that.

The only sounds were the raspy breathing of the dog and the gurgled whines in his chest.

"Good dog, Duke," Ruarke told his one-time nemesis.

He began stroking the twitching body.

"Such a good dog."

Duke's paddling paws stopped trying to drag him to where his mistress had been.

A whimper escaped with his life.

"Don't you worry, Duke," Ruarke said. "We'll find her."

About the Author

Gayle Lynn grew up in the upper Midwest and splits her time between there and wintering in the Southwest. She resides with her family and dogs. She enjoyed a lifelong love of reading and making up stories. Until recently her stories and characters had been stored in her memory. One day she realized she was starting to forget her storylines. At that point, encouraged by her sister, she decided to write them down. Again, at the encouragement of her sister, she decided to submit her story for publication. This is the result: *Serial Killer Eyes: The Saga of Santee Smith.*